The Lodger
by Marie Belloc Lowndes

The Lodger
by Marie Belloc Lowndes

Edited by

Elyssa Warkentin

Dear Auntie Anne +
Uncle Henry,
I hope you enjoy!
Love,

Cambridge
Scholars
Publishing

The Lodger by Marie Belloc Lowndes

Edited by Elyssa Warkentin

This book first published 2015

Cambridge Scholars Publishing

Lady Stephenson Library, Newcastle upon Tyne, NE6 2PA, UK

British Library Cataloguing in Publication Data
A catalogue record for this book is available from the British Library

ISBN (10): 1-4438-7818-9
ISBN (13): 978-1-4438-7818-0

TABLE OF CONTENTS

LIST OF ILLUSTRATIONS

NOTE ON THE TEXTS

The short story "The Lodger" was first published in January 1911 in *McClure's Magazine* along with sketches by famed illustrator Henry Raleigh, which are included here. This is an original transcription of that text.

The novel version of *The Lodger* was published serially in the *Daily Telegraph* between August 2 and September 2, 1913, and then, with minor typographical edits, as a single-volume novel by Methuen later that same year. This text follows that of the Methuen volume, and is lightly annotated in order to clarify historical references which may be obscure to modern readers, particularly when they are relevant to the themes of the novel.

INTRODUCTION

In 1910, writer Marie Belloc Lowndes (1868-1947) was a guest at a fashionable literary dinner party in London. The fact of her attendance was, itself, unremarkable: her engagement book was often full to bursting and she claimed acquaintance—perhaps hyperbolically—with nearly every professional writer working in London at the time. At this dinner, however, she heard an anecdote that would inspire her most popular and enduring novel and have a profound effect upon her life.

In one of her four memoirs (published in 1941, 1942, 1946, and posthumously in 1948), Lowndes explains:

> I sat at dinner next to a man who told me that a butler and lady's maid, who had been in his parents' service, had married, and set up a humble lodging-house. They were convinced Jack the Ripper had spent the night in their house before and after he had committed the most horrible of his murders. I told myself that this might form the core of a striking short story.[1]

In this chance dinner conversation, Lowndes recognized a plot that would allow her to explore several of her greatest interests in a single book, through a unique focus on the infamous so-called "Ripper" murders: women as victims and as perpetrators of crime; women and citizenship; domesticity; the constraints of the detective-fiction genre; the interaction of gender and class; and the power and reach of mass media. The resulting novel offered a nuanced examination of the role of gender in the Ripper case itself and in the way the story circulated and evolved in the larger Victorian cultural imagination. In imagining the Ripper case as a domestic plot with a working-class, middle-aged landlady detective, Lowndes pushed the boundaries of the detective fiction genre itself.

Even in 1910, Lowndes and her dinner companions would have been conversant with many of the details of the Ripper case that had occurred more than two decades earlier. It had been the media sensation of its time, and Lowndes, who had been a bright, engaged writer of 20 years old during the months spanning the murders, would have remembered public response and near-hysteria firsthand. During the autumn of 1888, five women had been killed and mutilated in the poverty-stricken Whitechapel district of London's East End: Mary Ann Nichols, Annie Chapman, Elizabeth Stride, Catherine Eddowes, and Mary Kelly. This is virtually all that is known with any certainty about the Whitechapel killer; however, this lack of information did not stop the London press from publishing in-depth coverage of the inquests, interviews with witnesses, speculative editorials, weighty polemics, and hundreds of letters to the editors. The case was covered extensively in every London newspaper, as well as nationally and internationally. On the days following the murders, newspaper circulation spiked, and hundreds of sightseers from all over the city mobbed the crime scenes. East Enders organized themselves into vigilance committees that patrolled the streets, and the atmosphere in the East End was one of barely controlled chaos.[2] Although public interest in the case grew less intense when the killings ceased, it never waned completely, and continues to this day in pop-culture films, websites, graphic novels, and pseudo-criminological books and theories. By 1910, there had been several non-fiction books published about the murders, and short, speculative fictional accounts abounded in cheap periodicals—but there had never been a novel written about the case.

The theory espoused by Lowndes' dinner companion, that the Ripper had hidden in rented lodgings during his crime spree, was common in the years following the murders, when pundits strove to make sense of the sudden cessation in the Ripper's activities. The idea was initially proposed by at least two men directly involved in the investigation of the murders: psychiatrist Lyttleton Stewart Forbes Winslow, who believed he could identify the murderer and was consulted by police, and the painter (and sometime Ripper suspect) Walter Sickert. Each espoused the theory in the years immediately following the murders. Their stories are substantively similar, varying only slightly in their details, leading contemporary "Ripperologist" Stephen P. Ryder to argue that "the story had reached the level of urban myth within a few years of the Whitechapel murders."[3] Other theories of the Ripper's identity ranged from an escaped lunatic to a butcher to a foreign Jew to a doctor to a wealthy gentleman—even to a member of the royal family. When the murders stopped in November 1888, it was thought that perhaps the Ripper had died, that he had gone mad and been institutionalized, or that he was not from London and had now moved on to different locales: America, Europe, or Australia.[4] Because the crimes remained unsolved, the theorizing never stopped and continues vigorously to this day.

The Lodger: Publication History

In January 1911, Lowndes published a short story, "The Lodger," in the last edition of a dying American monthly magazine called *McClure's*. It is unsurprising that editors were eager to acquire Ripper-themed stories, since short fiction about the crimes was both popular and lucrative in the months and years following the murders. News of the Ripper's crimes spread quickly throughout the Western world, and writers and publishers in many different countries quickly took advantage of the case's notoriety to increase their profits. Many short, magazine-length stories appeared within months of the crimes, published as "penny dreadfuls:" cheap, sensational publications intended to be affordable and easily accessible to the lower classes. Lowndes's short story "The Lodger" draws on the tradition of these penny dreadfuls, presenting salacious "true crime" stories for the express purpose of entertainment. Lowndes's short story is the first expression of the lodger theory of the Ripper's identity in a work of fiction.

Lowndes then went on to develop the short story into a novel of the same name—the first appearance of the Ripper in a full-length novel. The novel follows the plot of the short story, each recounting the involvement of a poverty-stricken London couple with the lodger who lifts them out of financial ruin but also may be a terrifying serial killer. The novel, however, places much greater emphasis on the landlady Mrs. Bunting's character and motivations than those of her husband. It was published serially in England in the *Daily Telegraph* and then as a single volume by Methuen in 1913. The dual publication, which was not unusual for mystery, sensation, and Gothic novels, allowed Lowndes to maximize her earnings from the novel. The novel was immediately popular with the book-buying public. In her 1946 memoir, Lowndes reported that "in thirty-five years over a million copies of the novel were sold, and it has been translated into almost every language."[5] The financial success of the novel led to Lowndes's continued interest in fictionalizing crime cases; since she was often the primary financial supporter of her family, popular appeal was an important consideration in her selection of subject matter. In fact, despite her interest in a myriad of other genres such as biography, memoir, journalism, and travel writing, Lowndes remains best known as a crime novelist.

The Lodger was not a critical success until long after Lowndes's death. She recalled in the same memoir, "*The Lodger*, on publication, was hailed by the critics with universal condemnation, and when I tried to find a few lines suitable for quotation, when the novel was about to be published in America by Scribner's, I failed."[6] Decades later, the novel was lauded by writers as diverse as Ernest Hemingway and Gertrude Stein as a fine example of crime fiction. Despite Lowndes's popularity and prolific body of work, she has received surprisingly little academic attention, and her novels are now almost entirely out of print. One reason could be that Lowndes's preferred genres, true crime and detective fiction, have been slow to gain literary credibility in academic spheres. Regardless, *The Lodger* remains the novel for which Lowndes is remembered, and it is universally considered her finest work.

Lowndes's Life: Women and Writing

In many ways, Lowndes was the ideal person to undertake the task of writing the very first novelization of the Ripper's crimes: as a feminist, popular crime writer, and journalist, she had personal insight into many of the salient themes of the case. Lowndes was born in 1868 in France to a prominent family; her mother was British suffragist and writer Bessie Rayner Parkes, and her father, Louis Belloc, was a French lawyer, an invalid who died just four years after Marie's birth. Marie's only sibling, Hilaire, became a prolific writer himself. Bessie, the children, and their nurse split their time between the family home in La Celle St. Cloud, France and London, and Marie remained fluently bilingual and bicultural for the rest of her life. Her mother was a Catholic convert, and she and Hilaire remained staunchly Catholic throughout their lives. Marie's family provided her with several unconventional proto-feminist role models, and her memoirs revolve around a close-knit group of politically and artistically active women: her mother; her mother's closest friend and fellow suffragist Barbara Bodichon; her aunts and grandmothers; and her own friends. Marie's mother, Lowndes reports in her 1941 memoir, "cared ardently for literature and longed to take a place among the poets of her day."[7] She passed this love of literature on to her children, and also tried to impart her progressive political views, with varying success. In one letter to Bodichon, Bessie wrote, "I found baby Marie diligently sucking one of your pamphlets on Woman Suffrage. I let her go on doing it, as I thought some of it might in that way percolate into her infant mind."[8]

Marie's childhood was in some ways stultifying in its conventionality, despite Bessie's avowedly progressive views on childrearing. Marie was a spirited child with little interest in formal education. Bessie hired an old-fashioned English nurse for the children, a Mrs. Mew, who favoured Hilaire and disliked Marie. Emma Lowndes, Marie's great-granddaughter, writes, "It seems extraordinary that Bessie, the feminist, should have employed a woman who made her daughter unhappy, nor did this fit with her stated beliefs in freedom and initiative for her children."[9] Before the birth of her children, Bessie was stridently in favour of equal education for boys and girls, even publishing a pamphlet on the subject: *Remarks on the*

Education of Girls, with Reference to the Social, Legal, and Industrial Position of Women in the Present Day.[10] Perhaps Bessie's heavy and persistent grief at the death of her husband just two years after Hilaire's birth left her abstracted and less attentive to her daughter's upbringing and education than she might otherwise have been.

In 1888, When Marie was 20 years old, she convinced her mother to move to London with her, hoping to find writing commissions. Marie wrote, "My mother was aware I wished to be a writer, and she … made a real effort to get in touch with various men and women she had known in her youth,"[11] with the object of finding a career mentor for Marie. The two called on prominent and successful women writers such as Margaret Oliphant, Eliza Lynn Linton, and Elizabeth Charles, but Marie relates, "each and all of them … did their best to dissuade me from following in their footsteps." She adds, "Fortunately for me, I did not care what the people my mother consulted thought. What made me sad was that I saw she on the whole agreed with them."[12]

Marie's mother and the women in her circle were early proto-feminist pioneers who generally espoused increased equality between the sexes and increased freedoms for women. Their abstract views on social reform, as Marie had discovered to her detriment in the past, did not translate into action on Lowndes's behalf, and she never did find a female mentor to ease her path into professional writing. Instead, a family friend offered to introduce her to W.T. Stead, the larger-than-life newspaper reformer and editor of the *Pall Mall Gazette*. Stead was widely known for his encouragement of professional women writers, and his willingness to employ women in prominent positions at his various publications, as, indeed, he did for Lowndes, who he accepted as a contributor. He arranged for a mentor, Edmund Garrett, to teach her how to write for the press. Lowndes got on well, and was commissioned to co-author the *Pall Mall Gazette Guide to the Paris Exhibition* of 1889 which required her to travel to Paris. She quickly proved her worth as a valuable and trusted contributor. When Stead left the *Gazette* and founded the *Review of Reviews* in 1890, Lowndes followed. Their friendship was close and affectionate; a fellow *Pall Mall* staffer, E.H. Stout, even reported that "he was once so much shocked by seeing Stead kiss Marie Belloc that he remonstrated with him" (240-1).[13] For Marie, as for many women, Stead was a gatekeeper to the journalistic profession, and once she had established herself as a successful writer with the *Review of Reviews*, the path of her career became much smoother and she was able to branch out into other periodicals and long-form novels, as well.

Figure 1: Marie Belloc in 1888, twenty years old.[14]

Marie was married in 1896 to journalist Frederic Sawney Lowndes, with whom she was "always happy, though often very anxious about money."[15] The couple had three children, and Marie suffered at least one miscarriage. Frederic was on staff at the *Times*, but it was Marie who often earned the bulk of the family income through her writing both as a journalist and novelist. She was socially connected to most of the prominent literary and political figures of her day and was particularly supportive of young, unestablished, and female writers. She was also an inveterate name-dropper who kept a sharp eye on the social and political influence of her acquaintances. She often befriended the wives of prominent literary and political men, such as Constance Wilde and Margot Asquith, and praised them highly in her memoirs for the unacknowledged contributions they made to their husbands' careers. Her mother wrote of her adult daughter, "I am extremely thankful that [Marie] is radically independent, with a small income of her own and an ample power of making money."[16]

Marie shrewdly selected the subject matter for her novels in order to appeal to a broad market. She once explained this strategy to the secretary of the Society of Authors when she wrote to him suggesting an article for the society's periodical. She wrote, "at a smart restaurant in spite of the beautiful things set down on the menu, the majority of people chose sweet apple pie and cream. My object [in this article] is to draw a parallel between these people and the readers of fiction."[17] Despite this deliberate bid for popularity, however, she never compromised her own interests, be they artistic, cultural, or political. For example, although she wrote many "true crime" novels that touched on current events in order to draw in large numbers of readers, she invariably presented her characters with great subtlety and nuance, and told their stories compassionately and intelligently from a decidedly feminist perspective.

Marie earned enough money to support her family, but often worried about making ends meet. The vast body of her unpublished correspondence suggests that she struggled with financial administration: she was often scattered, constantly losing cheques and forgetting bills. Emma Lowndes speculates that she "was probably done out of large amounts of copyright fees by her agents and publishers."[18] Her inability to maintain control of her finances may have been in part due to her poor health; she suffered from various chronic conditions throughout her life and had to be careful not to overwork lest she exhaust herself and become ill. As early as 1920 she was withdrawing from social obligations due to illness and overwork; in 1932 she complained of constant weakness, saying, "I have a 'tired' heart."[19] She normally published at least one novel per year, and this grueling pace was for her, a financial necessity. She discovered that "by the end of six months, even in England, the real sale of a novel, except in extremely exceptional cases, is at an end,"[20] and she would need a new source of income. Her usual workday began in the morning: she rose with the sun or earlier and wrote in bed for several hours with her signature quill pen.[21] The afternoon was devoted to social and household tasks, and her late evenings were spent with her husband, who habitually worked an evening shift at the newspaper until his death in 1940.

Marie wrote prolifically throughout her life. By the time of her death from stomach cancer in 1947, her bibliography included some 44 novels (many of them bestsellers), many short stories, seven plays, four volumes of memoirs, several biographies, and a vast body of journalistic work. In 1971, a writer for the *Times Literary Supplement* summed up the current attitude towards the work of Lowndes and her cohort, saying, "Mrs. Belloc Lowndes was one of that monstrous regiment of writing women who flourished in Edwardian England and gave to that period something of its unique literary quality. Most of them are forgotten now.... Of their huge number of novels, only one survives: *The Lodger* remains as a minor classic of suspense, the single monument to all that labour."[22]

This is indeed damning with faint praise, and it is doubtful whether Lowndes herself would have appreciated the disparagement of a large and varied body of writers for whom she worked and campaigned tirelessly. Despite her penchant for name-dropping and social climbing, Lowndes had a great sense of affection for her fellow writers—especially young women—and believed that established writers should take some responsibility for the wellbeing of those just starting out. She had no patience for colleagues who lacked *esprit de corps* within the profession. She was a member of the Society of Authors and the League of British Dramatists, but was much more active in the Society of Women Journalists (of which she was an original member), and the Women Writers Suffrage League, of which she was for a time vice president. She gave talks and lectures at meetings, provided formal and informal mentoring to members, gave donations and subscriptions when she could, ran formal training courses, served on committees and executives, and even gave a radio lecture series.

Lowndes never forgot her difficult entry into the profession, and strove throughout her career to encourage young writers, especially women, in their aspirations. She wrote, "The memory of how I was treated ... has influenced me all my life in my treatment of would-be writers. I have always encouraged those who came to me for advice as to a literary career, and I have given, I can truly say, innumerable letters of introduction to publishers and editors."[23] Her standard advice to young women wishing to write for a living was to read widely and travel independently. A woman writer must "make up her mind to be ready to accept any kind of work given her," and not use her feminine delicacy as an excuse for shirking difficult or unconventional assignments.[24]

Still, Lowndes has a somewhat bewildering reputation for being less politically motivated than her mother and less intelligent a writer than her brother. Emma Lowndes describes Marie as a "'passive' feminist" who was "not very interested in her mother's role in 'bettering'" the position of women in British society.[25] Bessie herself wrote that her daughter "had no taste at all for intellectual pursuits, which was quite the reverse of Hilaire."[26] And yet, Marie's independence, her canny and strategic writing choices, and her tireless support for other women writers suggest the opposite.

Lowndes and Jack the Ripper

Lowndes seized upon the Jack the Ripper narrative for her short story and novel for several reasons, many of which echoed the reasons for the Victorian public's compulsive interest in the case during the Autumn of Terror in 1888. The Ripper case quickly became a nexus for pre-existing social debates about class, race, gender, and of the burgeoning power of mass media. One particularly heated aspect of this debate was the nature of women, their proper roles in society, and the causes of female deviance—all of which preoccupied Lowndes throughout her career. The figure of the prostitute, so central to Ripper narratives, seemed to embody many of these issues. The prostitute was considered by many to be the most extreme result of female sexual deviance, the "Great Social Evil" of the late-Victorian age. The categorization of women as prostitutes during the Victorian era was imprecise at best and could encompass everyone from streetwalkers to any woman appearing in public unescorted by a man. Markers of female deviance depended largely upon women's relations to men and their economic status—a clear indication of the interconnectedness of class and gender that exists at the site of the prostitute. Because the Ripper's victims were all involved with prostitution (although to varying extents), gender and sexuality are some of the most pervasive themes across most articulations of the Ripper story.

Because of the centrality of the prostitute figure, and because of the ferocity of the murderer's attacks upon the victims, critics have described the dominant cultural narrative that coalesced around the Ripper and his victims as a "mythic story of sexual danger,"[27] in which London was shown to be a dangerous place for women who transgressed the boundaries of the private sphere. In other words, the cultural narrative or "modern myth" of the Ripper's crimes presented a warning for women: if they transgressed the margins of traditional domestic femininity, they risked incurring the ferocious punishment meted out by the Ripper. The victims' public identification as prostitutes set them apart from chaste, "respectable" women, and their circulation in the public sphere only underlined this status.

Lowndes' adaptation of the Ripper case implicitly responds to this gendered story of sexual danger that emerged during the autumn of 1888 and the weeks, months, and years that followed. *The Lodger* details the experience of Mr. and Mrs. Bunting, a retired butler and maid, who take in a mysterious lodger (improbably named Mr. Sleuth) in order to avert the financial ruin that continually threatens their household. Over the course of the novel, first Mrs. Bunting and eventually Mr. Bunting begin to suspect that their strange lodger is in fact "the Avenger," an insane criminal terrorizing the streets of London, killing women with apparent abandon. Neither Mrs. Bunting nor her husband reports their suspicions to the police, fearing the financial loss his arrest would entail, despite the fact that their young friend and sole visitor, Joe Chandler, is himself a policeman. Over the course of the novel, a strange bond of sympathy develops between Mrs. Bunting and her lodger as she observes and investigates his activities. They are both outsiders to society, and Mrs. Bunting struggles with the question of her responsibility. Must she tell the police her suspicions, thus losing the lodger who is her only source of income and throwing her household back into poverty? Does her duty to society at large trump her duty to her own family and household? Does she have a duty to the women who are victimized by the Avenger? Mrs. Bunting, as the detective figure in the novel, gradually confirms her suspicions about her lodger's identity. The story ends with a dramatic dénouement in Madame Tussaud's Chamber of Horrors, when she attends an exhibit with Mr. Sleuth and he, seeing a policeman, assumes (wrongly) that she has lured him there to be captured, and flees.

As a fictionalized adaptation, *The Lodger* takes artistic liberties with the factual events of the Ripper case, although it remains true to its source material in many ways. While the general facts of the Ripper and Avenger murders are the same—a serial killer attacks women on the streets of Victorian London, causing public uproar—there are also significant differences. Motive is one. The Ripper's motivation for his crimes is often assumed to be punishment for the perceived sexual misbehaviour of London prostitutes. This theory originates with the so-called "Dear Boss" letter of September 25, 1888, the same letter that gave the Ripper his name and that was widely publicised. It contained the statement, purportedly from the killer himself, "I am down on whores and I shan't quit ripping them till I do get buckled."[28] Lowndes' Avenger says nothing about the sexual conduct of his victims, but instead targets women who appear intoxicated in public and who frequent public houses. Indeed, this is the only description we ever get of his victims. The main object of the Avenger's rage is alcoholism in women, and his obsession is driven by Biblical tracts prescribing modesty and temperance in women. There is no overt mention of any sexual motivation nor of any genital mutilation in any of the Avenger's crimes. As for the Avenger himself, his description as a mentally-unbalanced gentleman corresponds with several theories advanced about the Ripper in the London press. The press was highly and overtly politicised in its Ripper theories: upper- and middle-class mainstream publications typically characterized the Ripper as working class, perhaps a butcher, an immigrant, or Jewish. Papers with a strong working-class readership, however, such as the East End locals, tended to suggest that the killer was a gentleman, a West Ender, perhaps a doctor. Lowndes aligns herself with the latter, positing a down-at-heel gentleman for her criminal.

Lowndes also makes a significant change with regard to the settings of the murders. While all of the Ripper's murders took place in (or very close to) Whitechapel, a slum in London's East End, the Avenger's murders gradually move into the wealthier West End, which is also where the Buntings live. It seems likely that Lowndes allowed the Avenger's crimes to straddle the East and West ends of London, and changed the victim's crimes from prostitution to drinking alcohol—a habit that many 'respectable' women, after all, shared—in order to emphasize the connection between all women in the city of London. Geography is not enough to protect women from the Avenger, nor is leading a relatively respectable life, if that life includes the occasional glass of wine or beer. The threat represented by the Avenger, in other words, is not determined by class or geography, and thus should be of concern to all women. In short, Lowndes adapts the story to disallow the female reader from assuming a distance from the victims. In this way, Lowndes insists on the inherent connection and sisterhood of London women, and advocates for mutual concern and understanding between different classes of women.

Lowndes and the Female Detective

The prevailing theme in all of Lowndes's novels is women's experience with crime, either as criminals, victims, or as amateur detectives: crime was her favourite metaphor through which to explore women's struggles within a society that was often hostile to their sex. In *The Lodger*, Lowndes employs a female housekeeper as her detective. While professional female detectives are relatively rare in fiction prior to twentieth century, Mrs. Bunting is part of a rich tradition of female characters who engage in investigative activities on an amateur basis. Critics have named characters from Emily St. Aubert in Ann Radcliffe's classic Gothic novel *The Mysteries of Udolpho* (1794), to Mrs. Bucket in Dickens' *Bleak House* (1852-3), to Marian Halcombe from Wilkie Collins' *The Woman in White* (1859) as the first amateur female detective. It may in fact be fruitless to attempt to identify the originator of this character type, for the field is very broad.

Lowndes's amateur detective, Mrs. Bunting, is presented throughout the novel in highly gendered ways, and her detective skills are functions of her gender role. Further, Lowndes continually highlights the gendered nature of Mrs. Bunting's body and uses the resultantly feminine traits Mrs. Bunting exhibits to aid in her investigation. This is a common tactic for early female writers of detective fiction, who demonstrated the efficacy and appropriateness of female detectives by basing their detective skills on what society thought of as women's natural spheres of interest: domesticity and female intuition, for example. Instead of seeing traditionally female traits as handicaps, then, women writers provide their female detectives with tools that emanate from their gender.[29] Thus, *The Lodger* turns a tale of the London streets into a domestic narrative, and Mrs. Bunting uses the tools of domestic labour (cleaning implements, for example) for investigative purposes. This strategy echoes the tenets of Victorian domestic feminism, which held that women's prowess in the domestic sphere and, not coincidentally, their absence from the public sphere made them morally superior to men, who were seen as tainted with more worldly concerns.

For example, Mrs. Bunting uses her routine cleaning of Mr. Sleuth's rooms as an opportunity to conduct a "methodical search" (68) of his belongings. Lowndes writes,

> As soon as [Mr. Sleuth] had left the house, she went quickly up to the drawing-room floor. Now had come her opportunity of giving the two rooms a good dusting; but Mrs. Bunting knew well, deep in her heart, that is was not so much the dusting of Mr. Sleuth's sitting-room she wanted to do—as to engage in a vague search for—she hardly knew for what. (68)

Again and again, Mrs. Bunting's domestic responsibilities, such as cleaning, cooking, and waiting on Mr. Sleuth, provide her with opportunities for close observation and investigation. In fact, they almost lead her on in spite of herself; because she is a good housekeeper, she becomes a good detective.

Although the novel participates in many of the cultural tropes of domestic feminism, it ultimately demonstrates that women require influence beyond the domestic sphere if they are to be full and equal citizens, with rights and responsibilities to society at large. As the novel goes on, Mrs. Bunting becomes complicit with the crimes of her suspect: she confirms her suspicions through her investigation of him, but she does not turn him in—even knowing that he will go on to kill again. Domestic prowess and power within her home is not enough to motivate Mrs. Bunting to sacrifice her own financial wellbeing for the good of society at large, as a responsible citizen might be expected to do. Lowndes makes clear that there is significant danger to both the private and public spheres when they are separated so strictly along gendered lines. "Because she is subject rather than citizen," Lowndes writes, "her duty as a component part of civilized society weighs but lightly on woman's shoulders" (93). If women are excluded from standing as full equals in society—as members of the public sphere—then they cannot be expected to take an active interest in its wellbeing.

Lowndes had a colleague working in London who shared her interest in criminality and female detective characters: Agatha Christie. The two writers shared a love of the mystery genre, although Christie tended to dramatic denouements while Lowndes preferred to write slow, domestic uncoverings that explored psychological motivations. Lowndes and Christie clashed, professionally, over the character of one of Christie's most famous and successful detectives: Hercule Poirot. Christie introduced her Belgian detective in 1920 with the publication of her first novel, *The Mysterious Affair at Styles.* Remarkably, in 1920 Lowndes herself published a novel called *The Lonely House*, which introduced a character she intended to use recurrently in future work: a Frenchman named Hercules Popeau. He and Christie's Poirot are strikingly similar.

There are many possible antecedents to this composite Popeau/Poirot character, but Lowndes was convinced that Christie had somehow stolen her creation. She wrote in protest to the Secretary of the Society of Authors, "It is exactly as if someone had taken 'Sherlock Holmes' ... and called him 'Shernock Holme', using all his mannerisms and making him the central character of a murder mystery."[30] Christie's immediate and meteoric popularity rubbed salt in Lowndes's perceived wound, particularly since no publisher or theatre would accept work from Lowndes that included her Popeau after Christie's Poirot was established. Lowndes complained, "the injury done me is a very real one."[31] Whether or not Christie was unduly influenced by Lowndes' Popeau, Lowndes was unable to ever use her character again. She consulted with the legal staff of the Society of Authors, seeking financial redress, but was advised that she had no legal grounds for suit. Lowndes's letters indicate that she was quite ill and in financial distress at this time, refusing to give charity donations (which was very unusual for her) and cancelling engagements. The mysterious affair of Popeau/Poirot was never satisfactorily concluded, and it left Lowndes bitter, sick, and angry. It remains her most significant professional rivalry.

In contrast to Christie's huge and enduring success, Lowndes' literary reputation rests almost entirely upon *The Lodger*. Like many of her other novels—and indeed, like the author herself—it is somehow simultaneously entirely conventional, provocatively feminist, and commercially shrewd.

She repeatedly employed the crime fiction genre as a way of exploring the subordinate role of women in society in the late-nineteenth and early-twentieth centuries, insisting that the insider/outsider role they occupied (integral to society as wives and mothers, but locked out of institutional power and authority) was the major psychological cause of women's criminality. She returns obsessively to this theme: see, for example, *Studies in Wives* (1909), *Lilla* (1917), *The Story of Ivy* (1927), and *The Chianti Flask* (1935). Her skillful use of the crime fiction genre allowed her to combine this subtle ideological crusading with massive popularity—a canny reversal of the often anti-feminist nature of the detective genre itself.

Lowndes, the London press, and the Ripper

1888 was the first year of Lowndes's writing career proper, and although she lived in London, during the height of the Ripper crisis she was in Paris on a commission for the *Pall Mall Gazette*. She was extremely interested in both journalism and criminality, and was thus able to observe the frenzied Ripper reportage on both sides of the English Channel. Certainly, Lowndes' thematic interest in class and gender in her adaptation of the Ripper story is matched by her interest in exploring the impact of mass media on the case. She makes newspapers central to her novel, drawing both on her understanding of the Ripper case and on her personal experience as a journalist. It is difficult to overstate the importance of the London newspapers in the evolution of the Ripper narrative.

The London press in the 1880s was exceedingly diverse, due in a large part to increasing literacy rates and falling newspaper prices. By the time of the Ripper murders, there were approximately 150 daily newspapers being published in England, and nearly every segment of the population was able to both afford and read a paper. By the end of the century, newspapers had become the chief means through which the average Londoner engaged with the world outside of his or her immediate community.[32] The Victorian era thus saw the birth of the press as a vital, habitual, popular tool for engagement with the world at large, and Lowndes was eager to play a role in this exciting new world which also offered new professional opportunities for educated middle- and upper-class women.

Lowndes, the literary pragmatist, recognized that newspapers wishing to remain commercially successful must appear relevant to the day-to-day lives of their readers: people will buy, and continue to buy, news that is somehow linked to their own lives, even if the link is a tenuous one. In the autumn of 1888, middle- and upper-class women's near-hysterical fear of Jack the Ripper ensured that many newspapers sold thousands of extra copies, despite the fact that only a very small segment of the population (East End prostitutes) was likely to be at risk of actual harm from the Ripper. Newspapers managed to exploit women's fear of the Ripper, often by explicitly predicting that the Ripper would move out of the East End into more affluent sections of London and by castigating women for ostensibly inviting harm through activities as innocuous as walking unescorted in the streets. While provoking fear in women readers, the papers simultaneously targeted male readers by inviting implicit identification with both the Ripper and his pursuers. As Lowndes demonstrates satirically in *The Lodger*, these techniques allowed many London newspapers to spin the Ripper murders from a horrific tragedy into a financial windfall.

The Ripper case, however, presented the press with a problem. The absence of an identifiable criminal agent in the case created a particular problem of interpretation for the press. Without a villain or narrative closure, any story of the case was structurally incomplete. How could the narrative move forward? Since there was little factual evidence available about the Ripper himself, the London press was forced to speculate about his identity and characteristics, often relying upon preexisting, popular narrative genres such as melodrama and the Gothic. As Judith Walkowitz observes, articles about the Ripper often bear "resemblance to the literature of the fantastic: they incorporated the narrative themes and motifs of modern fantasy—social inversion, morbid psychological states, acts of violation and transgression, and descent into a social underworld."[33] Thus in the face of the unknown Ripper, the press fell back upon proven, popular generic strategies in order to construct coherent narratives for its readers.

The fact that the identity of the murderer was unknown allowed the press to speculate endlessly on who he was, what characteristics he had, how he looked, and what his motives were. Martin Fido, in *A History of British Serial Killing*, describes the killer as "gloriously mysterious,"[34] perfectly capturing the almost heroic stature the Ripper came to possess. Although his crimes, all the papers agreed, were horrific, the boldness needed to perpetrate them and the cunning required to evade the police for so long provoked the public fascination that continues to the present day. Meanwhile, coverage of the Ripper's victims tended to typecast them all simply as poverty-stricken prostitutes, degraded fallen women with few distinguishing characteristics and fewer redeeming qualities.

Other newspapers offered counter-narratives to these prevalent ways of telling the story. Progressive women's groups, Jewish organizations, and East End community associations, among other groups, took issue with the Ripper narrative constructed by the popular press. While these groups remained tremendously interested and invested in the press coverage of the Whitechapel murders, they neither ran nor influenced a large daily press, and their concerns did not routinely receive coverage in the larger-circulation dailies. Small, weekly, local papers, especially those published in the East End, took issue with the image of their area of the city that appeared in the mainstream dailies. The East End was usually portrayed in the Ripper reportage of the popular press in a less-than-positive light, as a dark, dangerous, uncivilized pocket of savagery in the heart of London. The local papers used their own coverage of the crimes to challenge this depiction. Similarly, publications by Jewish groups and progressive women's organizations responded strongly to elements of the mainstream press's Ripper reportage that they and their readerships found objectionable. The Jewish papers contested pervasive suggestions that the killer must be a foreign Jew, and women's papers raged against the living conditions of poverty-stricken prostitutes. These papers had their work cut out for them; Judith Knelman observes, "By the end of the Victorian era, gender and class bias were more evident in the press than they had been at the beginning."[35]

Cannily, Lowndes makes newspapers central to her novel. Newspapers provide the conduit through which Mr. Bunting, oblivious to his lodger's connection to the case, obtains information about the case. (In fact they are the only conduit, apart from his relationship with Joe Chandler.) One of the pleasures of the novel is the way it offers the reader a first-hand account of the thrills of the special editions and hysterical newspaper boys that accompanied this case. And Lowndes does not simply highlight the importance of the press; she actually borrows content directly from the Ripper reportage. Some headlines that the Buntings discuss include "BLOODHOUNDS TO BE SERIOUSLY CONSIDERED" (77) and "PARDON TO ACCOMPLICES" (78)—both of which were ripped from actual headlines about the Ripper case. And during the inquest scene towards the end of the novel, Lowndes calls the credibility of the press into question by showing the lengths to which journalists will go to tell the type of story they want to tell—regardless of the facts.

The Lodger is the first novelization of the Ripper case, but significantly, it is also the first known telling of the Ripper story that might allow a female reader to assume imaginative power over and control of the Ripper—to identify with a female character other than that of a victim. This figure of terror was so real to women that one 1888 newspaper reported an instance of a female reader dying of terror just reading about the case.[36] He was so real to men that hundreds immediately adopted his persona and began to harass women both physically, on the streets, and in print, in letters to the editor. The Ripper thus allowed for the expression of a potent vein of misogynist violence in late-Victorian London. Walkowitz observes that the Ripper case "established a common vocabulary and iconography for the forms of male violence that permeated the whole society."[37] But by allowing a female protagonist (and, potentially, female readers) to assume imaginative control over the Ripper/Avenger in her novel, Lowndes stages a protest against the problem of male violence against women more generally. In *The Lodger*, we have an account of the Ripper murders in which women are not solely victims, but are able to assume a measure of power and agency as detectives, and as readers.

The Afterlife of *The Lodger*

Although Lowndes was herself a playwright, she did not routinely adapt her own work for the stage. *The Lodger* was first adapted in 1916 by prolific theatre writer Horace Annesley Vachell (1861–1955), who "very freely adapted" the story as a comedy.[38] *The Lodger: Who is He?* played at the Haymarket theatre in London with Howard Ainley in the title role. It was generally well received, although the critic for the *London Times* found Vachell's comic touches to be somewhat inconsistently received by the audience.[39] Having clearly never read the novel, the critic speculates, "Probably the main story belongs to Mrs. Lowndes, because it seems to call for the quiet, easy, fireside development of the novelist and proves on the stage a little frail for the burden of four acts. We guess the love-making to be hers and the farcical trimmings Mr. Vachell's. But our attribution may be quite wrong."[40] It was, indeed, wrong. There is almost no love-making in Lowndes's novel; the emphasis on the romantic subplot and the comedic elements—the elements the critic describes as the least successful and popular with the audience—were all Vachell's. In 1917, the play debuted in New York on Broadway with Lionel Atwill as the lead, but received mixed reviews. The critic for the *New York Times* found the show to be "highly amusing" and declared Beryl Mercer as Mrs Bunting "enormously laughable as the tender-hearted but suspicious landlady." Atwill, he felt, played up the comedic elements too broadly.[41]

The New York production happened to be seen by a young aspiring filmmaker: Alfred Hitchcock. He later recalled, "I had seen a play called

Who Is He? based on Mrs. Belloc Lowndes' novel *The Lodger*. The action was set in a house that took in roomers and the landlady wondered whether her new boarder was Jack the Ripper or not. I treated it very simply, purely from her point of view."[42] Hitchcock's *The Lodger: A Story of the London Fog* was released in 1927 by Gainsborough Pictures. The very successful silent film starred matinee idol Ivor Novello and was considered by the director himself to be "the first Hitchcock picture."[43] It includes such typically Hitchcockian devices as a symbolic, transparent glass floor through which Mr. and Mrs. Bunting watch their lodger pacing and the first instance of Hitchcock's trademark cameo. Hitchcock freely adapted his source material, turning Lowndes' feminist take on the Ripper case into a narrative of false accusation and police corruption: his lodger is an innocent man hounded and threatened by a mob fuelled by prejudice and misinformation. Novello also appeared in the sound remake (or "talkie" version), *The Phantom Fiend* (1932), directed by Maurice Elvey. Over the century following the publication of the novel, film adaptations continued. In 1944, John Brahm directed *The Lodger* for Twentieth Century Fox. In 1953, Jack Palance starred in *The Man in the Attic*, directed by Hugo Fregonese for Panoramic Productions. Most recently, David Ondaatje directed a contemporary adaptation, *The Lodger* (2009), for Sony Pictures, starring Alfred Molina. Adaptations were also produced for radio and television over the course of the century. The Royal Academy of Music even commissioned Phyllis Tate to write an opera version, which was produced in 1960. The adaptations vary in quality, but their continuing appearance demonstrates the vigour of the afterlife of Lowndes's original text, which remains embedded in the popular imaginings of the Jack the Ripper murders—a touchstone for our culture's conceptualizations of murder, mystery, and violent crimes against women.

Notes

[1] Marie Belloc Lowndes, *Merry Wives of Westminster,* (London: Macmillan, 1946), 171.
[2] See Tom A. Cullen, *When London Walked in Terror,* (London: Bodley Head, 1965).
[3] See "The Lodger," *Casebook,* accessed 1 April 2015, http://www.casebook.org/suspects/lodger.html.
[4] See Donald Rumbelow, *The Complete Jack the Ripper*, (London: WH Allen, 1975), 156-61.
[5] Marie Belloc Lowndes, *Merry Wives of Westminster*, (London: Macmillan, 1946), 172.

[6] Marie Belloc Lowndes, *Merry Wives of Westminster*, (London: Macmillan, 1946), 92.

[7] Marie Belloc Lowndes, *I, Too, Have Lived in Arcadia*, (London: Macmillan, 1941), 2.

[8] Ibid.

[9] Emma Lowndes, *Turning Victorian Ladies into Women*, (Bethesda: Academica Press, 2012), 207-8.

[10] Bessie Rayner Parkes, *Remarks on the Education of Girls, with Reference to the Social, Legal, and Industrial Position of Women in the Present Day*, (London: John Chapman, 1854).

[11] Marie Belloc Lowndes, *Where Love and Friendship Dwelt*, (London: MacMillan, 1944), 145-6.

[12] Ibid.

[13] Quoted in J.W. Robertson Scott, *The Life and Death of a Newspaper*, (London: Methuen, 1952), 240-1.

[14] Photograph courtesy of the Mistress and Fellows, Girton College, Cambridge.

[15] Marie Belloc Lowndes, *Where Love and Friendship Dwelt*, (London: Dodd, Mead, 1942), 149.

[16] Emma Lowndes, *Turning Victorian Ladies into Women*, (Bethesda: Academica Press, 2012), 218.

[17] Letter to Mr. Thring, April 8, 1909. British Library archive ADD 56739.

[18] Emma Lowndes, *Turning Victorian Ladies into Women*, (Bethesda: Academica Press, 2012), 218.

[19] Letter to K. Roberts, June 17, 1932. British Library archive ADD 56740.

[20] Letter to Mr. Thring, April 3, 1928. British Library archive ADD 56739.

[21] *Oxford Dictionary of National Biography*, Matthew, Henry Colin Gray ed., Brian Harrison ed., and Lawrence Goldman ed.. 26 October 2004, http://www.oxforddnb.com.proxy1.lib.umanitoba.ca/.

[22] "View from the tea table," *TLS*, (17.9), 1971, 1180.

[23] Marie Belloc Lowndes, *Where Love and Friendship Dwelt*, (London: Dodd, Mead, 1942), 147.

[24] Marie Belloc Lowndes, "Journalism as a Profession for Women," *The Leisure Hour*, (50), December 1901, 121-127.

[25] Emma Lowndes, *Turning Victorian Ladies into Women*, (Bethesda: Academica Press, 2012), 5.

[26] Emma Lowndes, *Turning Victorian Ladies into Women*, (Bethesda: Academica Press, 2012), 208.

[27] Judith Walkowitz, *City of Dreadful Delight: Narratives of Sexual Danger in Late-Victorian London*, (Chicago: University of Chicago Press, 1992), 2.

[28] Letter transcripts and facsimiles available at "Ripper Letters," *Casebook*, accessed 1 April 2015, http://www.casebook.org/ripper_letters.

[29] See Carla T. Kungl, *Creating the Fictional Female Detective: The Sleuth Heroines of British Women Writers, 1890-1940*, (Jefferson, North Carolina: McFarland, 2006), 56.

[30] Letter to Mr. Thring, June 1, 1928. British Library archive ADD 56739.

---

[31] Ibid.

[32] Lucy Brown, *Victorian News and Newspapers,* (New York: Oxford University Press, 1985), 48.

[33] Judith Walkowitz, "Jack the Ripper and the Myth of Male Violence," *Feminist Studies* (8.3), 1982, 550.

[34] Martin Fido, *A History of British Serial Killing,* (London: Orion Publishing, 1988), 45.

[35] Judith Knelman, "Class and Gender Bias in Victorian Newspapers," *Victorian Periodicals Review* (26.1), 1993, 35.

[36] Judith Walkowitz, *City of Dreadful Delight: Narratives of Sexual Danger in Late-Victorian London,* (Chicago: University of Chicago Press, 1992), 218.

[37] Judith Walkowitz, *City of Dreadful Delight: Narratives of Sexual Danger in Late-Victorian London,* (Chicago: University of Chicago Press, 1992), 220.

[38] "Who Is He?" *London Times,* 10 December 1915, 11.

[39] Ibid.

[40] Ibid.

[41] Christopher T. George, "The Lodger, From Page to Screen," *Casebook*, accessed 1 April 2015, http://blog.casebook.org/chrisgeorge/2011/11/13/the-lodger-from-page-to-stage-to-screen.

[42] Ibid.

[43] Quoted in Peter Conrad, *The Hitchcock Murders*, (London: Faber and Faber, 2000), 34.

CHRONOLOGY OF THE RIPPER MURDERS

April 3, 1888—An East London woman named Emma Smith was sexually assaulted and robbed by a gang of young men. She died two days later as a result of her injuries. She is not now considered to have been a victim of Jack the Ripper, but hers is the first case in the London Metropolitan Police's files of the Ripper murders.

August 7, 1888—Martha Tabram was stabbed to death in George Yard. Her murder was later attributed to the Ripper by both police and the press, but she is not now usually considered a Ripper victim.

August 31, 1888—Mary Ann (Polly) Nichols, a destitute prostitute, was killed in Bucks Row. Widely considered to be the first Ripper victim, her throat was cut and her body mutilated and disemboweled.

September 8, 1888—Annie Chapman, another itinerant prostitute, was killed in Hanbury Street, her wounds matching Nichols'.

September 27, 1888—The famed "Dear Boss" letter was received at the Central News Agency, the first to use the name "Jack the Ripper." It was widely published and circulated.

September 30, 1888—The "Double Event": prostitute Elizabeth Stride was discovered at 1:00 a.m. in a yard off Berner Street, dead. Her throat had been cut, but there were no mutilations upon her body and it was supposed that her murderer had been interrupted. At 1:45 another prostitute, Catherine Eddowes, was discovered dead in Mitre Square, her throat cut, body mutilated and disemboweled, and her uterus and one kidney removed.

October 1, 1888—Queen Victoria telephoned the Home Office to expresses her shock at the murders.

October 3, 1888—The unidentified, dismembered torso of a woman was discovered in Whitehall. This has not been confirmed to be connected to the Ripper's crimes, but newspapers at the time were quick to make the association.

October 7, 1888—Whitechapel Vigilance Committee Chairman George Lusk wrote to the Home Office requesting that a pardon be granted to any of the Ripper's accomplices who could provide information to the police.

October 9, 1888—The police conducted successful trials of bloodhound tracking at Regent's Park.

October 10, 1888—The bloodhounds were tested again, this time personally by Sir Charles Warren, the head of the London Metropolitan Police. To Warren's embarrassment, this trial was not successful.

October 16, 1888—George Lusk received a package including a letter signed "From Hell" and half a human kidney purportedly taken from the body of Catharine Eddowes. The letter was widely published in the press, as were a number of other letters of uncertain provenance.

November 9, 1888—In the face of mounting criticism and public pressure, Sir Charles Warren resigned. Later that day, the fifth and likely final Ripper murder was discovered: prostitute Mary Jane Kelly was killed and mutilated in her lodging room in Dorset Street. Her throat was cut, face mutilated, flesh removed from her abdomen and thighs, breasts removed, arms, legs, and genitals slashed, intestines and other organs removed or displaced, and heart missing.

November 10, 1888—The Home Office offered a pardon to "anyone other than the murderer" coming forward with information. Despite hundreds and hundreds of letters and tips from the public, no trace was ever found of the murderer.

BIOGRAPHICAL TIMELINE

June 16, 1829—Elizabeth (Bessie) Rayner Parkes was born in Birmingham, England, to a well-connected family. Progressive and well educated, Bessie went on to publish poetry, essays, memoirs, and travel books. With Barbara Bodichon, among others, she co-founded the *English Woman's Journal*, and was one of the most prominent women's-rights campaigners in Britain.

June 20, 1830—Louis Belloc was born in France to an artistic and somewhat unconventional family; two years later the family moved to La Celle-Saint-Cloud, which was to remain the family home for several generations. He became a barrister, although due to ill health he was often unable to work.

19 September, 1867—Bessie Rayner Parkes and Louis Belloc married in London after a brief and intense courtship. It was a late marriage for both. The couple settled in Paris, but returned often to La Celle-Saint-Cloud.

August 5, 1868—Marie Adelaide Elizabeth Rayner Belloc was born to Bessie and Louis in London, in a lodging house at 11 George Street, Marylebone. Bessie had returned to London for the birth, claiming not to trust French doctors. Her labour was difficult; afterwards she wrote, "I feel like a traveler on the banks of the Amazon."[1]

July 27, 1870—Joseph Hilaire Pierre Belloc was born to Bessie and Louis at home in La Celle-Saint-Cloud, just at the start of the Franco-Prussian War. Two months later, the young family fled to London and stayed with Bessie's extended family in Great College Street for the length of the war, during which time La Celle-Saint-Cloud was ransacked. Upon their return after the war, they found that family papers, letters, and paintings were lost and destroyed.

August 19, 1872—Five years after his marriage to Bessie, Louis died, but not before he was financially ruined in a stock market crash. Subsequently, the family split their time between England and France, wintering in London and spending summers in La Celle-Saint-Cloud. Bessie wrote to supplement her family's income.

1884—Marie's first short story, "Pastel," was published in a Catholic periodical when she was 16 years old.

1888—Marie met famed newspaperman W. T. Stead, who hired her on with the *Pall Mall Gazette*. Marie spent time in Paris collaborating on a guidebook to the Paris Exhibition. She wrote for many other periodicals as well, and sent half of all her earnings to her mother.

1889—Marie's first book was published: *The Life and Letters of Charlotte Elizabeth, Princess Palatine*. It had taken her four years to write, and she was paid the small sum of £16.

1894—Marie was a founding member of the Association of Women Journalists, and remained involved in it and other organizations to promote professional women writers throughout her career, including the Women Writers' Suffrage League.

January 9, 1896—Marie married Frederick Sawney Archibald Lowndes ("Freddie"), a journalist at the *Times*, in Brompton Oratory, London. They took up residence at 11 Great College Street, Westminster. Marie documented the early years of her marriage in her memoir *The Merry Wives of Westminster* (1946). The couple was very happy together, but faced financial difficulties throughout their marriage. Marie continued to write articles, short stories, novels, memoirs, plays, and biographies.

Autumn, 1896—Marie suffered a miscarriage. Doctors feared for her life, and she was confined to her bed under the care of two nurses for several weeks.[2]

1898—Son Charles was born to Marie and Freddie. Labour and childbirth took place under anesthetic.[3]

1900—Daughter Elizabeth was born to Marie and Freddie after a labour of just two hours, and unattended by doctor or nurse.[4]

1907—Daughter Susan was born to Marie and Freddie.

1909—The Lowndes family settled at 9 Barton Street, Westminster, and remained there until 1940.

1911—Marie's short story "The Lodger" was published in the American magazine *McClure's*.

1913—Lowndes was commissioned to write a serial for London's *Daily Telegraph*. Facing some small financial hardship that necessitated borrowing money from her brother, much to her husband's displeasure, she expanded her short story to a novel-length serial which was published to great success. A slightly edited single-volume edition, *The Lodger,* was published by Methuen to poor reviews but brisk sales.

1914-1918—Marie and her family remained in London for the duration of World War I. Marie documented some of the privations and terrors they faced in her letters and memoirs.

1916—Upon turning 18, Marie's son Charles joined the war effort. He was wounded in his first battle at Flanders, and received the Military Cross. He returned to the front after his recovery, but fell ill with typhoid fever just before Armistice Day. Against regulations, Freddie and Marie joined him in Rouen to nurse him through his illness.

November 22, 1916—Marie co-signed, along with many other high-profile suffragists, a letter to the *Times* demanding that upcoming changes to the British electorate should include reforms regarding women.

March 23, 1925—Bessie died and was buried at Slindon.

1927—Alfred Hitchcock directed *The Lodger: A Story of the London Fog*, a silent film adapted from Marie's novel. It starred Marie Ault, Arthur Chesney, June Tripp, Malcolm Keen, and Ivor Novello.

1939-1945—During World War II, Marie and Freddie left central London, selling their Barton Street property and moving to a holiday home they owned near Wimbledon Common (28 Crooked Billet).

March 26, 1940—Marie's husband Freddie died from a sudden heart attack at their house in Wimbledon. Lowndes remained in mourning for the rest of her life.

1942—The widowed Marie moved back to Westminster and leased house just across the street from the one she had owned with Freddie: 1 Barton Street. She often travelled, either to visit her children or to see friends in

America and Europe. She was exceptionally well-connected within literary circles.

August 15, 1947—Plagued throughout her life with minor health complaints, on this day Marie fell ill with her last illness.

November 14, 1947—Marie died of stomach cancer at her home of her daughter Elizabeth, in Hampshire, having received Roman Catholic last rites. She was buried at La Celle-Saint-Cloud.

July 16, 1953—Hilaire died in Guildford, Surrey, after years of ill health following a stroke.

1956—Marie's last book was published posthumously: *The Young Hilaire Belloc*.

Notes

[1] Emma Lowndes, *Turning Victorian Ladies into Women*, (Bethesda: Academica Press, 2012), 184.
[2] Marie Belloc Lowndes, *Merry Wives of Westminster*, (London: Macmillan, 1946), 29-31.
[3] Marie Belloc Lowndes, *Merry Wives of Westminster*, (London: Macmillan, 1946), 52.
[4] Marie Belloc Lowndes, *Merry Wives of Westminster*, (London: Macmillan, 1946), 52.

BIBLIOGRAPHY
OF MARIE BELLOC LOWNDES'S WORK[1]

Novels and collected volumes of short fiction:
The Philosophy of the Marquise (1899)
The Heart of Penelope (1904)
Barbara Rebell (1905)
The Pulse of Life: A Story of a Passing World (1908)
The Uttermost Farthing (1908)
According to Meredith (1909)
Studies in Wives (short stories; 1909)
When No Man Pursueth (1910)
Jane Oglander (1911)
The Chink in the Armour (alternate title The House of Peril;1912)
Mary Pechell (1912)
Studies in Love and in Terror (short stories; 1913)
The Lodger (1913)
Noted Murder Mysteries (short fiction; published under pseudonym Philip
    Curtain in 1914)
The End of her Honeymoon (1914)
Not All Saints (published under pseudonym Elizabeth Rayner in 1914)
Good Old Anna (1915)
The Price of Admiralty (1915)
The Red Cross Barge (1916)
Love and Hatred (1917)
Lilla: A Part of her Life (1917)
Out of the War (alternate title Gentleman Anonymous; 1918)
The Lonely House (1920)
From Out the Vasty Deep (1920)
What Timmy Did (1922)
Why They Married (short stories; 1923)
The Philanderer (1923)
The Terriford Mystery (1924)
Some Men and Women (short stories, 1925)
Afterwards (1925)
Bread of Deceit (1925)

What Really Happened (1926)
Thou Shalt Not Kill (1927)
The Story of Ivy (1927)
Cressida: No Mystery (alternate title Love's Revenge; 1928)
One of Those Ways (1929)
Letty Lynton (1931)
Vanderlyn's Adventure (alternate title The House by the Sea; 1931)
Love is a Flame (1932)
Jenny Newstead (alternate title An Unrecorded Instance; 1932)
The Reason Why (1932)
Duchess Laura: Certain Days of her Life (alternate title The Duchess
    Intervenes; 1933)
Duchess Laura: Further Days of Her Life (1933)
Another Man's Wife (1934)
The Chianti Flask (1935)
Who Rides on a Tiger (1936)
The Second Key (alternate title The Injured Lover; 1936)
The Marriage Broker (alternate title The Fortune of Bridget Malone; 1937)
Motive (alternate title Why it Happened; 1938)
And Call it Accident (1939)
Reckless Angel (1939)
The Injured Lover (1939)
Lizzy Borden: A Study in Conjecture (1939)
The Christine Diamond (1940)
Before the Storm (1941)
What of the Night? (1942)
The Labours of Hercules (1943)
She Dwelt with Beauty (published posthumously in1949)

Memoirs:
I, Too, Have Lived in Arcadia: A Record of Love and of Childhood (1941)
Where Love and Friendship Dwelt (1943)
The Merry Wives of Westminster (1946)
A Passing World (1948)

Plays:
With All John's Love: A Play in Three Acts (1930)
The Key: A Love Drama in Three Acts (1930)
Why Be Lonely? A Comedy in Three Acts (with F.S.A. Lowndes in 1931)
What Really Happened: A Play in a Prologue, Two Acts, and an Epilogue
    (1932)

The Second Key (alternate title The Injured Lover; 1936)
The Empress Eugenie: A Three Act Play (1938)

For Children:
Told in Gallant Deeds: A Child's History of the War (1916)

Biographies:[2]
The Life and Letters of Charlotte Elizabeth, Princess Palatine (1889)
Edmond and Jules de Goncourt, with Letters, and Leaves from their
    Journals. Two volumes (1895)
His Most Gracious Majesty: King Edward the Seventh (1901)
The Prince and Princess of Wales (published anonymously in 1902)
The Empress Frederick: A Memoir (published anonymously in 1913)
The Young Hilaire Belloc (published posthumously in 1956)

Letters:
Diaries and Letters of Marie Belloc Lowndes, 1911-1947. Edited by Susan
    Lowndes Marques (1971)

Notes

[1] This bibliography does not include journalistic work or works of fiction
published exclusively in periodicals. Note that many of Lowndes's books went
through multiple printings of different editions in both England and America, not
always simultaneously. The publication dates given are the dates of the first
editions, regardless of location. Titles varied across editions; alternate titles are
provided whenever possible.
[2] According to Susan Lowndes Marques, Marie Belloc Lowndes also published
anonymous biographies on Kitchener of Khartoum, Edward Grey, and Queen
Alexandra, but if this is the case, they are now lost.

THE LODGER

1911

Figure 2: Title illustration of "The Lodger" in *McClure's Magazine*.[1]

"There he is at last, and I'm glad of it, Ellen. 'Taint a night you would wish a dog to be out in."

Mr. Bunting's voice was full of unmistakable relief. He was close to the fire, sitting back in a deep leather armchair—a clean-shaven, dapper man, still in outward appearance what he had been so long, and now no longer was—a self-respecting butler.

"You needn't feel so nervous about him; Mr. Sleuth can look out for himself, all right." Mrs. Bunting spoke in a dry, rather tart tone. She was less emotional, better balanced, than was her husband. On her the marks of past servitude were less apparent, but they were there all the same— especially in her neat black stuff dress and scrupulously clean, plain collar and cuffs. Mrs. Bunting, as a single woman, had been for long years what is known as a useful maid.

"I can't think why he wants to go out in such weather. He did it in last week's fog, too," Bunting went on complainingly.

"Well, it's none of your business—now, is it?"

"No; that's true enough. Still, 'twould be a very bad thing for us if anything happened to him. This lodger's the first bit of luck we've had for a very long time."

Mrs. Bunting made no answer to this remark. It was too obviously true to be worth answering. And she was listening—following in imagination her lodger's quick, singularly quiet—"stealthy," she called it to herself— progress through the dark, fog-filled hall and up the staircase.

"It isn't safe for decent folk to be out in such weather—not unless they have something to do that won't wait till tomorrow." Bunting had at last turned round. He was now looking straight into his wife's narrow, colorless face; he was an obstinate man, and liked to prove himself right. "I read you out the accidents in *Lloyd's* yesterday—shocking, they were, and all brought about by the fog! And then, that 'orrid monster at his work again—"

"Monster?" repeated Mrs. Bunting absently. She was trying to hear the lodger's footsteps overhead; but her husband went on as if there had been no interruption:

"It wouldn't be very pleasant to run up against such a party as that in the fog, eh?"

"What stuff you do talk!" she said sharply; and then she got up suddenly. Her husband's remark had disturbed her. She hated to think of such things as the terrible series of murders that were just then horrifying and exciting the nether world of London. Though she enjoyed pathos and sentiment,—Mrs. Bunting would listen with mild amusement to the details of a break-of-promise action,—she shrank from stories of either immorality or physical violence.

Mrs. Bunting got up from the straight-backed chair on which she had been sitting. It would soon be time for supper.

She moved about the sitting-room, flecking off an imperceptible tough of dust here, straightening a piece of furniture there.

Bunting looked around once or twice. He would have liked to ask Ellen to leave off fidgeting, but he was mild and fond of peace, so he refrained. However, she soon gave over what irritated him of her own accord.

But even then Mrs. Bunting did not at once go down to the cold kitchen, where everything was in readiness for her simple cooking. Instead, she opened the door leading into the bedroom behind, and there, closing the door quietly, stepped back into the darkness and stood motionless, listening.

At first she heard nothing, but gradually there came the sound of someone moving about in the room just overhead; try as she might, however, it was impossible for her to guess what her lodger was doing. At last she heard him open the door leading out to the landing. That meant that he would spend the rest of the evening in the rather cheerless room above the drawing-room floor—oddly enough, he liked sitting there best, though the only warmth obtainable was from a gas-stove fed by a shilling-in-the-slot arrangement.

It was indeed true that Mr. Sleuth had brought the Buntings luck, for at the time he had taken their rooms it had been touch and go with them.

After having each separately let the sheltered, impersonal, and, above all, the financially easy existence that is the compensation life offers to those men and women who deliberately take upon themselves the yoke of domestic service, these two, butler and useful maid, had suddenly, in middle age, determined to join their fortunes and savings.

Bunting was a widower; he had one pretty daughter, a girl of seventeen, who now lived, as had been the case ever since the death of her mother, with a prosperous aunt. His second wife had been reared in the Foundling Hospital, but she had gradually worked her way up into the higher ranks of the servant class, and as useful maid she had saved quite a tidy sum of money.

Unluckily, misfortune had dogged Mr. and Mrs. Bunting from the very first. The seaside place where they had begun by taking a lodging-house had become the scene of an epidemic. Then had followed a business experiment which had proved disastrous. But before going back into service, either together or separately, they had made up their minds to make one last effort, and, with the little money that remained to them, they had taken over the lease of a small house in the Marylebone Road.

Bunting, whose appearance was very good, had retained a connection with old employers and their friends, so he occasionally got a good job as a waiter. During this last month his jobs had perceptibly increased in number and in profit; Mrs. Bunting was not superstitious, but it seemed that in this matter, as in everything else, Mr. Sleuth, their new lodger, had brought them luck.

As she stood there, still listening intently in the darkness of the bedroom, she told herself, not for the first time, what Mr. Sleuth's departure would mean to her and Bunting. It would almost certainly mean ruin.

Luckily, the lodger seemed entirely pleased both with the rooms and with his landlady. There was really no reason why he should ever leave such nice lodgings. Mrs. Bunting shook off her vague sense of apprehension and unease. She turned round, took a step forward, and, feeling for the handle of the door giving into the passage, she opened it, and went down with light, firm steps into the kitchen.

She lit the gas and put a frying-pan on the stove, and then once more her mind reverted, as if in spite of herself, to her lodger, and there came back to Mrs. Bunting, very vividly, the memory of all that had happened the day Mr. Sleuth had taken her rooms.

The date of this excellent lodger's coming had been the twenty-ninth of December, and the time late-afternoon. She and Bunting had been sitting, gloomily enough, over their small banked-up fire. They had dined in the middle of the day—he on a couple of sausages, she on a little cold ham. They were utterly out of heart, each trying to pluck up courage to tell the other that it was no use trying any more. The two had also had a little tiff on that dreary afternoon. A newspaper-seller had come yelling down the Marylebone Road, shouting out, "'Orrible murder in Whitechapel!" and just because Bunting had an old uncle living in the East End he had gone out and bought a paper, and at a time, too, when every penny, nay, every halfpenny, had its full value! Mrs. Bunting remembered the circumstance because that murder in Whitechapel had been the first of these terrible crimes—there had been four since—which she would never allow Bunting to discuss in her presence, and yet which had of late begun to interest curiously, uncomfortably, even her refined mind.

But, to return to the lodger. It was then, on that dreary afternoon, that suddenly there had come to the front door a tremulous, uncertain double knock.

"'I BELIEVE—IS IT NOT A FACT THAT
YOU LET LODGINGS?'"

Figure 3: Illustration from *McClure's Magazine*.[2]

Bunting ought to have got up, but he had gone on reading the paper; and so Mrs. Bunting, with the woman's greater courage, had gone out into the passage, turned up the gas, and opened the door to see who it could be. She remembered, as if it were yesterday instead of nigh on a month ago, Mr. Sleuth's peculiar appearance. Tall, dark, lanky, an old-fashioned top hat concealing his high bald forehead, he had stood there, an odd figure of a man, blinking at her.

"I believe—is it not a fact that you let lodgings?" he had asked in a hesitating, whistling voice, a voice that she had known in a moment to be that of an educated man—of a gentleman. As he had stepped into the hall, she had noticed that in his right hand he held a narrow bag—a quite new bag of strong brown leather.

Everything had been settled in less than a quarter of an hour. Mr. Sleuth had at once "taken" to the drawing-room floor, and then, as Mrs. Bunting eagerly lit the gas in the front room above, he had looked round him and said, rubbing his hands with a nervous movement, "Capital—capital! This is just what I've been looking for!"

The sink had specially pleased him—the sink and the gas-stove. "This is quite first-rate!" he had exclaimed, "for I make all sorts of experiments. I am, you must understand, Mrs.—er—Bunting, a man of science." Then he had sat down—suddenly. "I am very tired," he had said in a low tone, "very tired indeed! I have been walking about all day."

From the very first the lodger's manner had been odd, sometimes distant and abrupt, and then, for no reason at all that she could see, confidential and plaintively confiding. But Mrs. Bunting was aware that eccentricity has always been a perquisite, as it were the special luxury, of the well born and well educated. Scholars and such-like are never quite like other people.

And then, this particular gentleman had proved himself so eminently satisfactory as to the one thing that really matters to those who let lodgings. "My name is Sleuth," he said, "S-l-e-u-t-h. Think of a hound, Mrs. Bunting, and you'll never forget my name. I could give you references," he had added, giving her, as she now remembered, a funny sidewise look, "but I prefer to dispense with them. How much did you say? Twenty-three shillings a week, with attendance? Yes, that will suit me perfectly; and I'll begin by paying my first month's rent in advance. Now, four times twenty-three shillings is"—he looked at Mrs. Bunting, and for the first time he smiled, a queer, wry smile—"ninety-two shillings."

He had taken a handful of sovereigns out of his pocket and put them down on the table. "Look here," he had said, "there's five pounds; and you can keep the change, for I shall want you to do a little shopping for me tomorrow."

After he had been in the house about an hour, the bell had rung, and the new lodger had asked Mrs. Bunting if she could oblige him with the loan of a Bible. She brought up to him her best Bible, the one that had been given to her as a wedding present by a lady with whose mother she had lived for several years. This Bible and one other book, of which the odd name was Cruden's Concordance, formed Mr. Sleuth's only reading: he spent hours each day poring over the Old Testament and over the volume which Mrs. Bunting had at last decided to be a queer kind of index to the Book.

However, to return to the lodger's first arrival. He had had no bags with him, barring the small brown bag, but very soon parcels had begun to arrive addressed to Mr. Sleuth, and it was then that Mrs. Bunting first became curious. These parcels were full of clothes; but it was quite clear to the landlady's feminine eye that none of those clothes had been made for Mr. Sleuth. They were, in fact, second-hand clothes, bought at good second-hand places, each marked, when marked at all, with a different name. And the really extraordinary thing was that occasionally a complete suit disappeared—became, as it were, obliterated from the lodger's wardrobe.

As for the bag he had brought with him, Mrs. Bunting had never caught sight of it again. And this also was certainly very strange.

Mrs. Bunting thought a great deal about that bag. She often wondered what had been in it; not a night-shirt and comb and brush, as she had at first supposed, for Mr. Sleuth had asked her to go out and buy him a brush and comb and tooth-brush the morning after his arrival. That fact was specially impressed on her memory, for at the little shop, a barber's, where she had purchased the brush and comb, the foreigner who had served her had insisted on telling her some of the horrible details of the murder that had taken place the day before in Whitechapel, and it had upset her very much.

As to where the bag was now, it was probably locked up in the lower part of a chiffonnier in the front sitting-room. Mr. Sleuth evidently always carried the key of the little cupboard on his person, for Mrs. Bunting, though she looked well for it, had never been able to find it.

And yet, never was there a more confiding or trusting gentleman. The first four days that he had been with them he had allowed his money—the considerable sum of one hundred and eighty-four pounds in gold—to lie about wrapped up in pieces of paper on his dressing-table. This was a very foolish, indeed a wrong thing to do, as she had allowed herself respectfully to point out to him; but as only answer he had laughed, a loud, discordant shout of laughter.

Mr. Sleuth had many other odd ways; but Mrs. Bunting, a true woman in spite of her prim manner and love of order, had an infinite patience with masculine vagaries.

On the first morning of Mr. Sleuth's stay in the Buntings' house, while Mrs. Bunting was out buying things for him, the new lodger had turned most of the pictures and photographs hanging in his sitting-room with their faces to the wall! But this queer action on Mr. Sleuth's part had not surprised Mrs. Bunting as much as it might have done; it recalled an incident of her long-past youth—something that had happened a matter of twenty years ago, at a time when Mrs. Bunting, then the still youthful Ellen Cottrell, had been maid to an old lady. The old lady had a favourite nephew, a bright, jolly young gentleman who had been learning to pain animals in Paris; and it was he who had had the impudence, early one summer morning, to turn to the wall six beautiful engravings of paintings done by the famous Mr. Landseer! The old lady thought the world of those pictures, but her nephew, as only excuse for the extraordinary thing he had done, had observed that "they put his eye out."

Mr. Sleuth's excuse had been much the same; for, when Mrs. Bunting had come into his sitting-room and found all her pictures, or at any rate all those of her pictures that happened to be portraits of ladies, with their faces to the wall, he had offered as only explanation, "Those women's eyes follow me about."

Mrs. Bunting had gradually become aware that Mr. Sleuth had a fear and dislike of women. When she was "doing" the staircase and landing, she often heard him reading bits of the Bible aloud to himself, and in the majority of instances the texts he chose contained uncomplimentary reference to her own sex. Only today she had stopped and listened while he uttered threateningly the awful words, "A strange woman is a narrow pit. She also lieth in wait as for a prey, and increaseth the transgressors among men." There had been a pause, and then had come, in a high singsong, "Her house is the way to hell, going down to the chambers of death." It had made Mrs. Bunting feel quite queer.

The lodger's daily habits were also peculiar. He stayed in bed all morning, and sometimes part of the afternoon, and he never went out before the street lamps were alight. Then, there was his dislike of an open fire; he generally sat in the top front room, and while there he always used the large gas-stove, not only for his experiments, which he carried on at night, but also in the daytime, for warmth.

But there! Where was the use of worrying about the lodger's funny ways? Of course, Mr. Sleuth was eccentric; if he hadn't been "just a leetle 'touched' upstairs,"—as Bunting had once described it—he wouldn't be their lodger now; he would be living in a quite different sort of way with some of his relations, or with a friend of his own class.

Mrs. Bunting, while these thoughts galloped disconnectedly through her brain, went on with her cooking, doing everything with a certain delicate and cleanly precision.

While in the middle of making the toast on which was to be poured some melted cheese, she suddenly heard a noise, or rather a series of noises. Shuffling, hesitating steps were creaking down the house above. She looked up and listened. Surely Mr. Sleuth was not going out again into the cold, foggy night? But no; for the sounds did not continue down the passage leading to the front door.

The heavy steps were coming slowly down the kitchen stairs. Nearer and nearer came the thudding sounds, and Mrs. Bunting's heart began to beat as if in response. She put out the gas-stove, unheedful of the fact that the cheese would stiffen and spoil in the cold air; and then she turned and faced the door. There was a fumbling at the handle, and a moment later the door opened and revealed, as she had known it would, her lodger.

Mr. Sleuth was clad in a plaid dressing-gown, and in his hand was a candle. When he saw the lit-up kitchen, and the woman standing in it, he looked inexplicably taken aback, almost aghast.

"Yes, sir? What can I do for you, sir? I hope you didn't ring, sir?" Mrs. Bunting did not come forward to meet her lodger; instead, she held her ground in front of the stove. Mr. Sleuth had no business to come down like this into her kitchen.

"' I CAME DOWN TO SEE IF YOU HAD A GAS-STOVE '"

Figure 4: Illustration from *McClure's Magazine*.[3]

"No, I—I didn't ring," he stammered; "I didn't know you were down here, Mrs. Bunting. Please excuse my costume. The truth is, my gas-stove has gone wrong, or, rather, that shilling-in-the-slot arrangement has done so. I came down to see if *you* had a gas-stove. I am going to ask leave to use it tonight for an experiment I want to make."

Mrs. Bunting felt troubled—oddly, unnaturally troubled. Why couldn't the lodger's experiment wait until tomorrow? "Oh, certainly, sir; but you will find it very cold down here." She looked round her dubiously.

"It seems most pleasantly warm," he observed, "warm and cozy after my cold room upstairs."

"Won't you let me make you a fire?" Mrs. Bunting's housewifely instincts were roused. "Do let me make you a fire in your bedroom, sir; I'm sure you ought to have one there these cold nights."

"By no means—I mean, I would prefer not. I do not like an open fire, Mrs. Bunting." He frowned, and still stood, a strange-looking figure, just inside the kitchen door.

"Do you want to use this stove now, sir? Is there anything I can do to help you?"

"No, not now—thank you all the same, Mrs. Bunting. I shall come down later, altogether later—probably after you and your husband have gone to bed. But I should be much obliged if you would see that the gas people come tomorrow and put my stove in order."

"Perhaps Bunting could put it right for you, sir. I'll ask him to go up."

"No, no—I don't want anything of that sort done tonight. Besides, he couldn't put it right. The cause of the trouble is quite simple. The machine is choked up with shillings; a foolish plan, so I have always felt it to be."

Mr. Sleuth spoke very pettishly, with far more heat than he was wont to speak; but Mrs. Bunting sympathized with him. She had always suspected those slot-machines to be as dishonest as if they were human. It was dreadful, the way they swallowed up the shillings!

As if he were divining her thoughts, Mr. Sleuth, walking forward, stared up at the kitchen slot-machine. "Is it nearly full?" he asked abruptly. "I expect my experiment will take some time, Mrs. Bunting."

"Oh, no, sir; there's plenty of room for shillings there still. We don't use our stove as much as you do yours, sir. I'm never in the kitchen a minute longer than I can help this cold weather."

And then, with him preceding her, Mrs. Bunting and her lodger made a slow progress to the ground floor. There Mr. Sleuth courteously bade his landlady good night, and proceeded upstairs to his own apartments.

Mrs. Bunting again went down into her kitchen, again she lit the stove, and again she cooked the toasted cheese. But she felt unnerved, afraid of she knew not what. The place seemed to her alive with alien presences, and once she caught herself listening, which was absurd, for of course she could not hope to hear what her lodger was doing two, if not three, flights upstairs. She had never been able to discover what Mr. Sleuth's experiments really were; all she knew was that they required a very high degree of heat.

The Buntings went to bed early that night. But Mrs. Bunting intended to stay awake. She wanted to know at what hour of the night her lodger would come down into the kitchen, and, above all, she was anxious as to how long he would stay there. But she had had a long day, and presently she fell asleep.

The church clock had hard by struck two in the morning, and suddenly Mrs. Bunting awoke. She felt sharply annoyed with herself. How could she have dropped off like that? Mr. Sleuth must have been down and up again hours ago!

Then, gradually, she became aware of a faint acrid odor; elusive, almost intangible, it yet seemed to encompass her and the snoring man by her side almost as a vapor might have done.

Mrs. Bunting sat up in bed and sniffed; and then, in spite of the cold, she quietly crept out of the nice, warm bedclothes and crawled along to the bottom of the bed. There Mr. Sleuth's landlady did a very curious thing; she leaned over the brass rail and put her face close to the hinge of the door. Yes, it was from there that this strange, horrible odor was coming; the smell must be very strong in the passage. Mrs. Bunting thought she knew now what became of those suits of clothes of Mrs. Sleuth's that disappeared.

As she crept back, shivering, under the bedclothes, she longed to give her sleeping husband a good shake, and in fancy she heard herself saying: "Bunting, get up! There is something strange going on downstairs that we ought to know about."

But Mr. Sleuth's landlady, as she lay by her husband's side, listening with painful intentness, knew very well that she would do nothing of the sort. The lodger had a right to destroy his clothes by burning if the fancy took him. What if he did make a certain amount of mess, a certain amount of smell, in her nice kitchen? Was he not—was he not such a good lodger! If they did anything to upset him, where could they ever hope to get another like him?

Three o'clock struck before Mrs. Bunting heard slow, heavy steps creaking up her kitchen stairs. But Mr. Sleuth did not go straight up to his own quarters, as she expected him to do. Instead, he went to the front door, and, opening it, put it on the chain. At the end of ten minutes or so he closed the front door, and by that time Mrs. Bunting had divined why the lodger had behaved in this strange fashion—it must have been to get the strong acrid smell of burning wool out of the passage. But Mrs. Bunting felt as if she herself would never get rid of the horrible odor. She felt herself to be all smell.

At last the unhappy woman fell into a deep, troubled sleep; and then she dreamed a most terrible and unnatural dream; hoarse voices seemed to be shouting in her ear, "'Orrible murder off the Edgware Road!" Then three words, indistinctly uttered, followed by "—at his work again! Awful details!"

Even in her dream Mrs. Bunting felt angered and impatient; she knew so well why she was being disturbed by this horrid nightmare. It was because of Bunting—Bunting, who insisted on talking to her of those frightful murders, in which only morbid, vulgar-minded people took any interest. Why, even now, in her dream, she could hear her husband speaking to her about it.

"Ellen,"—so she heard Bunting say in her ear,—"Ellen my dear, I am just going to get up to get a paper. It's after seven o'clock."

Mrs. Bunting sat up in bed. The shouting, nay, worse, the sound of tramping, hurrying feet smote on her ears. It had been no nightmare, then, but something infinitely worse—reality. Why couldn't Bunting have lain quietly in bed awhile longer, and let his poor wife go on dreaming? The most awful dream would have been easier to bear than this awakening.

She heard her husband go to the front door, and, as he bought the paper, exchange a few excited words with the newspaper boy. Then he came back and began silently moving about the room.

"Well!" she cried. "Why don't you tell me about it?"

"I thought you'd rather not hear."

"Of course I like to know what happens close to our own front door!" she snapped out.

And then he read out a piece of the newspaper—only a few lines, after all—telling in brief, unemotional language that the body of a woman, apparently done to death in a peculiarly atrocious fashion some hours before, had been found in a passage leading to a disused warehouse off the Marylebone Road.

"It serves that sort of hussy right!" was Mrs. Bunting's only comment.

When Mrs. Bunting went down into the kitchen, everything there looked just as she had left it, and there was no trace of the acrid smell she had expected to find there. Instead, the cavernous whitewashed room was full of fog, and she noticed that, though the shutters were bolted and barred as she had left them, the windows behind them had been widely opened to the air. She, of course, had left them shut.

She stooped and flung open the oven door of her gas-stove. Yes, it was as she had expected; a fierce heat had been generated there since she had last used the oven, and a mass of black, gluey soot had fallen through to the stone floor below.

Mrs. Bunting took the ham and eggs that she had bought the previous day for her own and Bunting's breakfast, and broiled them over the gas-ring in their sitting-room. Her husband watched her in surprised silence. She had never done such a thing before.

"I couldn't stay down there," she said, "it was so cold and foggy. I thought I'd make breakfast up here, just for today."

"Yes," he said kindly; "that's quite right, Ellen. I think you've done quite right, my dear."

But, when it came to the point, his wife could not eat any of the nice breakfast she had got ready; she only had another cup of tea.

"Are you ill?" Bunting asked solicitously.

"No," she said shortly; "of course I'm not ill. Don't be silly! The thought of that horrible thing happening so close by has upset me. Just hark to them, now!"

Through their closed windows penetrated the sound of scurrying feet and loud, ribald laughter. A crowd, nay, a mob, hastened to and from the scene of the murder.

Mrs. Bunting made her husband lock the front gate. "I don't want any of those ghouls in here!" she exclaimed angrily. And then, "What a lot of idle people there must be in the world," she said.

The coming and going went on all day. Mrs. Bunting stayed indoors; Bunting went out. After all, the ex-butler was human—it was natural that he should feel thrilled and excited. All their neighbors were the same. His wife wasn't reasonable about such things. She quarreled with him when he didn't tell her anything, and yet he was sure she would have been angry with him if he had said very much about it.

The lodger's bell rang about two o'clock, and Mrs. Bunting prepared the simple luncheon that was also his breakfast. As she rested the tray a minute on the drawing-room floor landing, she heard Mr. Sleuth's high, quavering voice reading aloud the words:

"She saith to him, Stolen waters are sweet, and bread eaten in secret is pleasant. But he knoweth not that the dead are there; and that her guests are in the depths of hell."

The landlady turned the handle of the door and walked in with the tray. Mr. Sleuth was sitting close by the window, and Mrs. Bunting's Bible lay open before him. As she came in he hastily closed the Bible and looked down at the crowd walking along the Marylebone Road.

"There seem a great man people out today," he observed, without looking round.

"Yes, sir, there do." Mrs. Bunting said nothing more, and offered no other explanation; and the lodger, as he at last turned to his landlady, smiled pleasantly. He had acquired a great linking and respect for this well-behaved, taciturn woman; she was the first person for whom he had felt any such feeling for many years past.

He took half a sovereign out of his waistcoat pocket; Mrs. Bunting noticed that it was not the same waistcoat Mr. Sleuth had been wearing the day before. "Will you please accept this half sovereign for the use of your kitchen last night?" he said. "I made as little mess as I could, but I was carrying on a rather elaborate experiment."

She held out her hand, hesitated, and then took the coin.

As she walked down the stairs, the winter sun, a yellow ball hanging in the smoky sky, glinted in on Mrs. Bunting, and lent blood-red gleams, or so it seemed to her, to the piece of gold she was holding in her hand.

II

It was a very cold night—so cold, so windy, so snow-laden the atmosphere, that everyone who could do so stayed indoors. Bunting, however, was on his way home from what had proved a very pleasant job; he had been acting as a waiter at a young lady's birthday party, and a remarkable piece of luck had come his way. The young lady had come into a fortune that day, and she had had the gracious, the surprising thought of presenting each of the hired waiters with a sovereign.

This birthday treat had put him in mind of another birthday. His daughter Daisy would be eighteen the following Saturday. Why shouldn't he send her a postal order for half a sovereign, so that she might come up and spend her birthday in London?

Having Daisy for three or four days would cheer up Ellen. Mr. Bunting, slackening his footsteps, began to think with puzzled concern of how queer his wife had seemed lately. She had become so nervous, so "jumpy," that he didn't know what to make of her sometimes.

She had never been a really good-tempered woman,—your capable, self-respecting woman seldom is,—but she had never been like what she was now. Of late she sometimes got quite hysterical; he had let fall a sharp word to her the other day, and she had sat down on a chair, thrown her black apron over her face, and burst out sobbing violently.

During the last ten days Ellen had taken to talking in her sleep. "No, no, no!" she had cried out, only the night before. "It isn't true! I would have it said! It's a lie!" And there had been a wail of horrible fear and revolt in her usually quiet, mincing voice. Yes, it would certainly be a good think for her to have Daisy's company for a bit. Phew! it *was* cold; and Bunting had stupidly forgotten his gloves. He put his hands in his pockets to keep them warm.

Suddenly he became aware that Mr. Sleuth, the lodger who seemed to have "turned their luck," as it were, was walking along on the opposite side of the solitary street.

Mr. Sleuth's tall, thin figure was rather bowed, his head bent toward the ground. His right arm was thrust into his long Inverness cape; the other occasionally sawed the air, doubtless in order to help him keep warm. He was walking rather quickly. It was clear that he had not yet become aware of the proximity of his landlord.

Bunting felt pleased to see his lodger; it increased his feeling of general satisfaction. Strange, was it not, that that odd, peculiar-looking figure should have made all the difference to his (Bunting's) and Mrs. Bunting's happiness and comfort in life?

Naturally, Bunting saw far less of the lodger than did Mrs. Bunting. Their gentleman had made it very clear that he did not like either the husband or wife to come up to his rooms without being definitely asked to do so, and Bunting had been up there only once since Mr. Sleuth's arrival five weeks before. This seemed to be a good opportunity for a little genial conversation.

Bunting, still and active man for his years, crossed the road, and, stepping briskly forward, tried to overtake Mr. Sleuth; but the more he hurried, the more the other hastened, and that without even turning to see whose steps he heard echoing behind him on the now freezing pavement.

Mr. Sleuth's own footsteps were quite inaudible—an odd circumstance, when you came to think of it, as Bunting did think of it later, lying awake by Ellen's side in the pitch-darkness. What it meant was, of course, that the lodger had rubber soles on his shoes.

The two men, the pursued and the pursuer, at last turned into the Marylebone Road. They were now within a hundred yards of him; and so, plucking up courage, Bunting called out, his voice echoing freshly on the still air:

"Mr. Sleuth, sir! Mr. Sleuth!"

The lodger stopped and turned round. He had been walking so quickly, and he was in so poor a physical condition, that the sweat was pouring down his face.

"Ah! So it's you, Mr. Bunting? I heard footsteps behind me, and I hurried on. I wish I'd known that it was only you; there are so many queer characters about at night in London."

"Not on a night like this, sir. Only honest folk who have business out of doors would be out such a night as this. It *is* cold, sir!" And then into Bunting's slow and honest mind there suddenly crept the query as to what Mr. Sleuth's own business out could be on this cold, bitter night.

"Cold?" the lodger repeated. "I can't say that I find it cold, Mr. Bunting. When the snow falls the air always becomes milder."

"Yes sir; but tonight there's such a sharp east wind. Why, it freezes the very marrow in one's bones!"

Bunting noticed that Mr. Sleuth kept his distance in a rather strange way: he walked at the edge of the pavement, leaving the rest of if, on the wall side, to his landlord.

"I lost my way," he said abruptly. "I've been over Primrose Hill to see a friend of mine, and then, coming back, I lost my way."

Bunting could well believe that, for when he had first noticed Mr. Sleuth he was coming from the east, and not, as he should have done if walking home from Primrose Hill, from the north.

They had now reached the little gate that gave on to the shabby, paved court in front of the house. Mr. Sleuth was walking up the flagged path, when, with a "By your leave, sir," the ex-butler, stepping aside, slipped in front of his lodger, in order to open the front door for him.

As he passed by Mr. Sleuth, the back of Bunting's bare left hand brushed lightly against the long Inverness cape the other man was wearing, and, to his surprise, the stretch of cloth against which his hand lay for a moment was not only damp, damp from the flakes of snow that had settled upon it, but wet—wet and gluey. Bunting thrust his left hand into his pocket; it was with the other that he placed the key in the lock of the door.

The two men passed into the hall together. The house seemed blackly dark in comparison with the lighted up road outside; and then, quite suddenly, there came over Bunting a feeling of mortal terror, an instinctive knowledge that some terrible and immediate danger was near him. A voice—the voice of his first wife, the long-dead girl to whom his mind so seldom reverted nowadays—uttered in his ear the words, "Take care!"

"I am afraid, Mr. Bunting, that you must have felt something dirty, foul, on my coat? It's too long a story to tell you now, but I brushed up against a dead animal—a dead rabbit lying across a bench on Primrose Hill."

Mr. Sleuth spoke in a very quiet voice, almost in a whisper.

"No, sir; no, I didn't notice nothing. I scarcely touched you, sir." It seemed as if a power outside himself compelled Bunting to utter those lying words. "And now, sir, I'll be saying good night to you," he added.

He waited until the lodger had gone upstairs, and then he turned into his own sitting-room. There he sat down, for he felt very queer. He did not draw his left hand out of his pocket till he heard the other man moving about in the room above. Then he lit the gas and held up his left hand; he put it close to his face. It was flecked, streaked with blood.

He took off his boots, and then, very quietly, he went into the room where his wife lay asleep. Stealthily he walked across to the toilet-table, and dipped his hand into the water jug.

The next morning Mr. Sleuth's landlord awoke with a start; he felt curiously heavy about the limbs and tired about the eyes.

Drawing his watch from under his pillow, he saw that it was nearly nine o'clock. He and Ellen had overslept. Without waking her, he got out of bed and pulled up the blind. It was snowing heavily, and, as is the way when it snows, even in London, it was strangely, curiously still.

After he had dressed he went out into the passage. A newspaper and a letter were lying on the mat. Fancy having slept through the postman's knock! He picked them both up and went into the sitting-room; then he carefully shut the door behind him, and, tossing the letter aside, spread the newspaper wide open on the table and bent over it.

As Bunting at last looked up and straightened himself, a look of inexpressible relief shone upon his stolid face. The item of news he had felt certain would be there, printed in big type on the middle sheet, was not there.

He folded the paper and laid it on a chair, and then eagerly took up his letter.

Dear Father [it ran]: I hope this finds you as well as it leaves me. Mrs. Puddle's youngest child has got scarlet fever, and aunt think I had better come away at once, just to stay with you for a few days. Please tell Ellen I won't give her no trouble.

Your loving daughter,
Daisy.

Bunting felt amazingly light-hearted; and, as we walked into the next room, he smiled broadly.

"Ellen," he cried out, "here's some news! Daisy's coming today. There's scarlet fever in their house, and Martha thinks she had better come away for a few days. She'll be here for her birthday!"

Mrs. Bunting listened in silence; she did not even open her eyes. "I can't have the girl here just now," she said shortly; "I've got just as much as I can manage to do."

But Bunting felt pugnacious, and so cheerful as to be almost light-headed. Deep down in his heart he looked back to last night with a feeling of shame and self-rebuke. Whatever had made such horrible thoughts and suspicions come into his head?

"Of course Daisy will come here," he said shortly. "If it comes to that, she'll be able to help you with the work, and she'll brisk us both up a bit."

Rather to his surprise, Mrs. Bunting said nothing in answer to this, and he changed the subject abruptly. "The lodger and me came in together last night," he observed. "He's certainly a funny kind of gentleman. It wasn't the sort of night one would choose to go for a walk over Primrose Hill, and yet that was what he had been doing—so he said."

It stopped snowing about ten o'clock, and the morning wore itself away. Just as twelve was striking, a four-wheeler drew up to the gate. It was Daisy—pink-cheeked, excited, laughing-eyed Daisy, a sight to gladden any father's heart. "Aunt said I was to have a cab if the weather was bad," she said.

There was a bit of a wrangle over the fare. King's Cross, as all the world knows, is nothing like two miles from the Marylebone Road, but the man clamored for one-and-sixpence, and hinted darkly that he had done the young lady a favor in bringing her at all.

While he and Bunting were having words, Daisy, leaving them to it, walked up the path to the door where her stepmother was awaiting her.

Suddenly there fell loud shouts on the still air. They sounded strangely eerie, breaking sharply across the muffled, snowy air.

"What's that?" said Bunting, with a look of startled fear. "Why, whatever's that?"

The cabman lowered his voice: "Them are crying out that 'orrible affair at King's Cross. He's done for two of 'em this time! That's what I meant when I said I might have got a better fare; I wouldn't say anything before Missy there, but folk 'ave been coming from all over London—like a fire; plenty of toffs, too. But there—there's nothing to see now!"

"What! Another woman murdered last night?" Bunting felt and looked convulsed with horror.

The cabman started at him, surprised. "Two of 'em, I tell yer—within a few yards of one another. He 'ave got a nerve—"

"Have they caught him?" asked Bunting perfunctorily.

"Lord, no! They'll never catch 'im! It must 'ave happened hours and hours ago—they was both stone-cold. One each end of an archway. That's why they didn't see 'em before."

The hoarse cries were coming nearer and nearer—two news vendors trying to outshout each other.

"'Orrible discovery near King's Cross!" they yelled exultantly. And as Bunting, with his daughter's bag in his hand, hurried up the path and passed through his front door, the words pursued him like a dreadful threat.

Angrily he shut out the hoarse, insistent cries. No, he had no wish to buy a paper. That kind of crime wasn't fit reading for a young girl, such a girl as was his Daisy, brought up as carefully as if she had been a young lady by her strict Methody aunt.

As he stood in his little hall, trying to feel "all right" again, he could hear Daisy's voice—high, voluble, excited—giving her stepmother a long account of the scarlet-ever case to which she owed her presence in London. But, as Bunting pushed open the door of the sitting-room, there came a note of sharp alarm in his daughter's voice, and he heard her say: "Why, Ellen! Whatever is the matter? You do look bad!" and his wife's muffled answer: "Open the window—do."

Rushing across the room, Bunting pushed up the sash. The newspaper-sellers were now just outside the house. "Horrible discovery near King's Cross—a clue to the murderer!" they yelled. And then, helplessly, Mrs. Bunting began to laugh. She laughed and laughed and laughed, rocking herself to and fro as if in an ecstasy of mirth.

"Why, father, whatever's the matter with her?" Daisy looked quite scared.

"She's in 'sterics—that's what it is," he said shortly. "I'll just get the water-jug. Wait a minute."

Bunting felt very put out, and yet glad, too, for this queer seizure of Ellen's almost made him forget the sick terror with which he had been possessed a moment before. That he and his wife should be obsessed by the same fear, the same terror, never crossed his simple, slow-working mind.

The lodger's bell rang. That, or the threat of the water-jug, had a magical effect on Mrs. Bunting. She rose to her feet, still trembling, but composed.

As Mrs. Bunting went upstairs she felt her legs trembling under her, and put out a shaking hand to clutch at the bannister for support. She waited a few minutes on the landing, and then knocked at the door of her lodger's parlor.

But Mr. Sleuth's voice answered from the bedroom. "I'm not well," he called out querulously; "I think I caught a chill going out to see a friend last night. I'll be obliged if you'll bring me up a cup of tea and put it outside my door, Mrs. Bunting."

"Very well, sir."

Mrs. Bunting went downstairs and made her lodger a cup of tea over the gas-ring, Bunting watching her the while in heavy silence.

During their midday dinner the husband and wife had a little discussion as to where Daisy should sleep. It had already been settled that a bed should be made up for her in the sitting-room, but Bunting saw reason to change this plan. As the two women were clearing away the dishes, he looked up and said shortly: "I think 'twould be better if Daisy were to sleep with you, Ellen, and I were to sleep in the sitting-room."

Ellen acquiesced quietly.

Daisy was a good-natured girl; she liked London, and wanted to make herself useful to her stepmother. "I'll wash up; don't you bother to come downstairs," she said.

Bunting began to walk up and down the room. His wife gave him a furtive glance; she wondered what he was thinking about.

"Didn't you get a paper?" she said at last.

"There's the paper," he said crossly, "the paper we always do take in, the *Telegraph*." His look challenged her to a further question.

"I thought they was shouting something in the street—I mean just before I was took bad."

But he made no answer; instead, he went to the top of the staircase and called out sharply: "Daisy! Daisy, child, are you there?"

"Yes, father," she answered from below.

"Better come upstairs out of that cold kitchen."

He came back into the sitting room again.

"Ellen, is the lodger in? I haven't heard him moving about. I don't want Daisy to be mixed up with him."

"Mr. Sleuth is not well today," his wife answered; "he is remaining in bed a bit. Daisy needn't have anything to do with him. She'll have her work cut out looking after things down here. That's where I want her to help me."

"Agreed," he said.

When it grew dark, Bunting went out and bought and evening paper. He read it out of doors in the biting cold, standing beneath a street lamp. He wanted to see what was the clue to the murderer.

The clue proved to be a very slender one—merely the imprint in the snowy slush of a half-worn rubber sole; and it was, of course, by no means certain that the sole belonged to the boot or shoe of the murderer of the two doomed women who had met so swift and awful a death in the arch near King's Cross station. The paper's special investigator pointed out that there were thousands of such soles being worn in London. Bunting found comfort in that obvious fact. He felt grateful to the special investigator for having stated it so clearly.

As he approached his house, he heard curious sounds coming from the inner side of the low wall that shut off the courtyard from the pavement. Under ordinary circumstances Bunting would have gone at once to drive whoever was there out into the roadway. Now he stayed outside, sick with suspense and anxiety. Was it possible that their place was being watched—already?

But it was only Mr. Sleuth. To Bunting's astonishment, the lodger suddenly stepped forward from behind the wall on to the flagged path. He was carrying a brown-paper parcel, and, as he walked along, the new boots he was wearing creaked and the tap-tap of wooden heels rang out on the stones.

"WAS IT POSSIBLE THAT THEIR PLACE WAS BEING WATCHED—ALREADY?"

Figure 5: Illustration from *McClure's Magazine*.[4]

Bunting, still hidden outside the gate, suddenly understood what his lodger had been doing the other side of the wall. Mr. Sleuth had been out to buy himself a pair of boots, and had gone inside the gate to put them on, placing his old footgear in the paper in which the new boots had been wrapped.

Bunting waited until Mr. Sleuth had let himself into the house; then he also walked up the flagged pathway, and put his latch-key in the door.

In the next three days each of Bunting's waking hours held its meed of aching fear and suspense. From his point of view, almost any alternative would be preferable to that which to most people would have seemed the only one open to him. He told himself that it would be ruin for him and for his Ellen to be mixed up publicly in such a terrible affair. It would track them to their dying day.

Bunting was also always debating within himself as to whether he should tell Ellen of this frightful suspicion. He could not believe that what had become so plain to himself could long be concealed from all the world, and yet he did not credit his wife with the same intelligence. He did not even notice that, although she waited on Mr. Sleuth as assiduously as ever, Mrs. Bunting never mentioned the lodger.

Mr. Sleuth, meanwhile, kept upstairs; he had given up going out altogether. He still felt, so he assured his landlady, far from well.

Daisy was another complication, the more so that the girl, whom her father longed to send away and whom he would hardly let out of his sight, showed herself inconveniently inquisitive concerning the lodger.

"Whatever does he do with himself all day?" she asked her stepmother.

"Well, just now he's reading the Bible," Mrs. Bunting had answered, very shortly and dryly.

"Well, I never! That's a funny thing for a gentleman to do!" Such had been Daisy's pert remark, and her stepmother had snubbed her well for it.

III

Daisy's eighteenth birthday dawned uneventfully. Her father gave her what he had always promised she should have on her eighteenth birthday—a watch. It was a pretty little silver watch, which Bunting had bought second-hand on the last day he had been happy; it seemed a long time ago now.

Mrs. Bunting thought a silver watch a very extravagant present, but she had always had the good sense not to interfere between her husband and his child. Besides, her mind was now full of other things. She was beginning to fear that Bunting suspected something, and she was filled with watchful anxiety and unease. What if he were to do anything silly—mix them up with the police, for instance? It certainly would be ruination to them both. But there—one never knew, with men! Her husband, however, kept his own counsel absolutely.

Daisy's birthday was on Saturday. In the middle of the morning Ellen and Daisy went down into the kitchen. Bunting didn't like the feeling that there was only one flight of stairs between Mr. Sleuth and himself, so he quietly slipped out of the house and went to buy himself an ounce of tobacco.

In the last four days Bunting had avoided his usual haunts. But today the unfortunate man had a curious longing for human companionship—companionship, that is, other than that of Ellen and Daisy. This feeling led him into a small, populous thoroughfare hard by the Edgware Road. There were more people there than usual, for the housewives of the neighborhood were doing their marketing for Sunday.

Bunting passed the time of day with the tobacconist, and the two fell into desultory talk. To the ex-butler's surprise, the man said nothing at all to him on the subject of which all the neighborhood must still be talking.

And then, quite suddenly, while still standing by the counter, and before he had paid for the packet of tobacco he held in his hand, Bunting, through the open door, saw, with horrified surprise, that his wife was standing outside a green-grocer's shop just opposite. Muttering a word of apology, he rushed out of the shop and across the road.

"Ellen!" he gasped hoarsely. "You've never gone and left my little girl alone in the house?"

Mrs. Bunting's face went chalky white. "I thought you were indoors," she said. "You *were* indoors. Whatever made you come out for, without first making sure I was there?"

Bunting made no answer; but, as they stared at each other in exasperated silence, *each knew that the other knew.*

They turned and scurried down the street.

"Don't run," he said suddenly; "we shall get there just as quickly if we walk fast. People are noticing you, Ellen. Don't run."

He spoke breathlessly, but it was breathlessness induced by fear and excitement, not by the quick pace at which they were walking.

At last they reached their own gate. Bunting pushed past in front of his wife. After all, Daisy was his child—Ellen couldn't know how he was feeling. He made the path almost in one leap, and fumbled for a moment with his latch-key. The door opened.

"Daisy!" he called out in a wailing voice. "Daisy, my dear, where are you?"

"Here I am, father; what is it?"

"She's all right!" Bunting turned his gray face to his wife. "She's all right, Ellen!" Then he waited a moment, leaning against the wall of the passage. "It did give me a turn," he said; and then, warningly, "Don't frighten the girl, Ellen."

Daisy was standing before the fire in the sitting-room, admiring herself in the glass. "Oh, father," she said, without turning round, "I've seen the lodger! He's quite a nice gentleman—though, to be sure, he does look a cure! He came down to ask Ellen for something, and we had quite a nice little chat. I told him it was my birthday, and he asked me to go to Madame Tussaud's with him this afternoon." She laughed a little self-consciously. "Of course I could see he was 'centric, and then at first he spoke so funnily. 'And who be you?' he says, threatening-like. And I says to him, 'I'm Mr. Bunting's daughter, sir.' 'Then you're a very fortunate girl'—that's what he said, Ellen—'to 'ave such a nice stepmother as you've got. That's why,' he says, 'you look such a good, innocent girl.' And then he quoted a bit of the prayer-book at me. 'Keep innocency,' he says, wagging his head at me. Lor'! It made me feel as if I was with aunt again."

"KEEP INNOCENCY," HE SAYS, WAGGING HIS HEAD AT ME."

Figure 6: Illustration from *McClure's Magazine*.[5]

"I won't have you going out with the lodger—that's flat." Bunting spoke in a muffled, angry tone. He was wiping his forehead with one hand, while with the other he mechanically squeezed the little packet of tobacco, for which, as he now remembered, he had forgotten to pay.

Daisy pouted. "Oh, father, I think you might let me have a treat on my birthday! I told him Saturday wasn't a very good day—at least, so I'd heard—for Madame Tussaud's. Then he said we could go early, while the fine folk are still having their dinners. He wants you to come, too." She turned to her stepmother, then giggled happily. "The lodger has a wonderful fancy for you, Ellen; if I was father, I'd feel quite jealous!"

Her last words were cut across by a loud knock on the door. Bunting and his wife looked at each other apprehensively.

Both felt a curious thrill of relief when they saw that it was only Mr. Sleuth—Mr. Sleuth dressed to go out: the tall hat he had worn when he first came to them was in his hand, and he was wearing a heavy overcoat.

"I saw you had come in,"—he addressed Mrs. Bunting in his high, whistling, hesitating voice,—"and so I've come down to ask if you and Miss Bunting will come to Madame Tussaud's now. I have never seen these famous waxworks, though I've heard of the place all my life."

As Bunting forced himself to look fixedly at his lodger, a sudden doubt, bringing with it a sense of immeasurable relief, came to him. Surely it was inconceivable that this gentle, mild-mannered gentleman could be the monster of cruelty and cunning that Bunting had but a moment ago believed him to be!

"You're very kind, sir, I'm sure." He tried to catch his wife's eye, but Mrs. Bunting was looking away, staring into vacancy. She still, of course, wore the bonnet and cloak in which she had just been out to do her marketing. Daisy was already putting on her hat and coat.

Madame Tussaud's had hitherto held pleasant memories for Mrs. Bunting. In the days when she and Bunting were courting they often spent part of their "afternoon out" there. The butler had an acquaintance, a man named Hopkins, who was one of the waxworks' staff, and this man had sometimes given him passes for "self and lady." But this was the first time Mrs. Bunting had been inside the place since she had come to live almost next door, as it were, to the big building.

The ill-sorted trio walked up the great staircase and into the first gallery; and there Mr. Sleuth suddenly stopped short. The presence of those curious, still figures, suggesting death in life, seemed to surprise and affright him.

Daisy took quick advantage of the lodger's hesitation and unease.

"Oh, Ellen," she cried, "do let us begin by going into the Chamber of Horrors! I've never been in there. Aunt made father promise he wouldn't take me, the only time I've ever been here. But now that I'm eighteen, I can do just as I like; besides, aunt will never know!"

Mr. Sleuth looked down at her.

"Yes," he said, "let us go into the Chamber of Horrors; that's a good idea, Miss Bunting."

They turned into the great room in which the Napoleonic relics are kept, and which leads into the curious, vault-like chamber where waxen effigies of dead criminals stand grouped in wooden docks. Mrs. Bunting was at once disturbed and relieved to see her husband's old acquaintance, Mr. Hopkins, in charge of the turnstile admitting the public to the Chamber of Horrors.

"Well, you *are* a stranger," the man observed genially. "I do believe this is the very first time I've seen you in here, Mrs. Bunting, since you married!"

"Yes," she said; "that is so. And this is my husband's daughter, Daisy; I expect you've heard of her, Mr. Hopkins. And this"—she hesitated a moment—"is our lodger, Mr. Sleuth."

But Mr. Sleuth frowned and shuffled away. Daisy, leaving her stepmother's side, joined him.

Mrs. Bunting pit down three sixpences.

"Wait a minute," said Hopkins; "you can't go into the Chamber of Horrors just yet. But you won't have to wait more than four or five minutes, Mrs. Bunting. It's this way, you see; our boss is in there, showing a party round." He lowered his voice. "It's Sir John Burney—I suppose you know who Sir John Burney is?"

"No," she answered indifferently; "I don't know that I ever heard of him." She felt slightly—oh, very slightly—uneasy about Daisy. She would like her stepdaughter to keep well within sight and sound. Mr. Sleuth was taking the girl to the other end of the room.

"Well, I hope you never *will* know him—not in any personal sense, Mrs. Bunting." The man chuckled. "He's the Head Commissioner of Police—that's what Sir John Burney is. One of the gentlemen he's showing round our place is the Paris Prefect of Police, whose job is on all fours, so to speak, with Sir John's. The Frenchy has brought his daughter with him, and there are several other ladies. Ladies always like 'orrors, Mrs. Bunting; that's our experience here. 'Oh, take me to the Chamber of 'Orrors!'—that's what they say the minute they gets into the building."

A group of people, all talking and laughing together, were advancing from within toward the turnstile.

Mrs. Bunting stared at them nervously. She wondered which of them was the gentleman with whom Mr. Hopkins had hoped she would never be brought into personal contact. She quickly picked him out. He was a tall, powerful, nice-looking gentleman with a commanding manner. Just now he was smiling down into the face of a young lady. "Monsieur Barberoux us quite right," he was saying; "the English law is too kind to the criminal, especially to the murderer. If we conducted our trials in the French fashion, the place we have just left would be very much fuller than it is today! A man of whose guilt we are absolutely assured is oftener than not acquitted, and then the public taunt us with 'another undiscovered crime'!"

"D'you mean, Sir John, that murderers sometimes escape scot-free? Take the man who has been committing all those awful murders this last month. Of course, I don't know much about it, for father won't let me read about it, but I can't help being interested!" Her girlish voice rang out, and Mrs. Bunting heard every word distinctly.

The party gathered round, listening eagerly to hear what the Head Commissioner would say next.

"Yes." He spoke very deliberately. "I think we may say—now, don't give me away to a newspaper fellow, Miss Rose—that we do know perfectly well who the murderer in question is—"

Several of those standing near by uttered expressions of surprise and incredulity.

"Then why don't you catch him?" cried the girl indignantly.

"I didn't say we know *where* he is; I only said we know *who* he is; or, rather, perhaps I ought to say that we have a very strong suspicion of his identity."

Sir John's French colleague looked up quickly. "The Hamburg and Liverpool man?" he said interrogatively.

The other nodded. "Yes; I suppose you've had the case turned up?"

Then, speaking very quickly, as if he wished to dismiss the subject from his own mind and from that of his auditors, he went on:

"Two murders of the kind were committed eight years ago—one in Hamburg, the other just afterward in Liverpool, and there were certain peculiarities connected with the crimes which made it clear they were committed by the same hand. The perpetrator was caught, fortunately for us red-handed, just as he was leaving the house of his victim, for in Liverpool the murder was committed in a house. I myself say the unhappy man—I say unhappy, for there is no doubt at all that he was mad,"—he hesitated, and added in a lower tone,—"suffering from an acute form of religious mania. I myself saw him at some length. But now comes the really interesting point. Just a month ago this criminal lunatic, as we must regard him, made his escape from the asylum where he was confined. He arranged the whole thing with extraordinary cunning and intelligence, and we should probably have caught him long ago were it not that he managed, when on his way out of the place, to annex a considerable sum of money in gold with which the wages of the staff were about to be paid."

The Frenchman again spoke. "Why have you not circulated a description?" he asked.

"We did that at once,"—Sir John Burney smiled a little grimly,—"but only among our own people. We dare not circulated the man's description among the general public. You see, we may be mistaken, after all."

"That is not very probable!" The Frenchman smiled a satirical little smile.

A moment later the party were walking in Indian file through the turnstile, Sir John Burney leading the way.

Mrs. Bunting looked straight before her. Even had she wished to do so, she had neither time nor power to warn her lodger of his danger.

Daisy and her companion were now coming down the room, bearing straight for the Head Commissioner of Police. In another moment Mr. Sleuth and Sir John Burney would be face to face.

Suddenly Mr. Sleuth swerved to one side. A terrible change came over his pale, narrow face; it became discomposed, livid with rage and terror.

But, to Mrs. Bunting's relief,—yes, to her inexpressible relief,—Sir John Burney and his friends swept on. They passed by Mr. Sleuth unconcernedly, unaware, or so it seemed to her, that there was any one else in the room but themselves.

"Hurry up, Mrs. Bunting," said the turnstile keeper; "you and your friends will have the place all to yourselves." From and official he had become a man, and it was the man in Mr. Hopkins that gallantly addressed pretty Daisy Bunting. "It seems strange that a young lady like you should want to go in and see all those 'orrible frights," he said jestingly.

"Mrs. Bunting, may I trouble you to come over here for a moment?" The words were hissed rather than spoken by Mr. Sleuth's lips.

His landlady took a doubtful step forward.

"A last word with you, Mrs. Bunting." The lodger's face was still distorted with fear and passion. "Do not think to escape the consequences of your hideous treachery. I trusted you, Mrs. Bunting, and you betrayed me! But I am protected by a higher power, for I still have work to do. Your end will be bitter as wormwood and sharp as a two-edged sword. Your feet shall go down to death, and your steps take hold on hell." Even while Mr. Sleuth was uttering these strange, dreadful words, he was looking around, his eyes glancing this way and that, seeking a way of escape.

"SUDDENLY MR. SLEUTH SWERVED TO ONE SIDE"

Figure 7: Illustration from *McClure's Magazine*.[6]

At last his eyes became fixed on a small placard placed about a curtain. "Emergency Exit" was written there. Leaving his landlady's side, he walked over to the turnstile. He fumbled in his pocket for a moment, and then touched the man on the arm. "I feel ill," he said, speaking very rapidly; "very ill indeed! It's the atmosphere of this place. I want you to let me out by the quickest way. It would be a pity for me to faint here—especially with ladies about." His left hand shot out and placed what he had been fumbling for in his pocket on the other's bare palm. "I see there's an emergency exit over there. Would it be possible for me to get out that way?"

"Well, yes, sir; I think so." The man hesitated; he felt a slight, a very slight, feeling of misgiving. He looked at Daisy, flushed and smiling, happy and unconcerned, and then at Mrs. Bunting. She was very pale; but surely her lodger's sudden seizure was enough to make her feel worried.

Hopkins felt the half sovereign pleasantly tickling his palm. The Prefect of Police had given him only half a crown—mean, shabby foreigner!

"Yes, I can let you out that way," he said at last, "and perhaps when you're standing out in the air on the iron balcony you'll feel better. But then, you know, sir, you'll have to come round to the front if you want to come in again, for those emergency doors only open outward."

"Yes, yes," said Mr. Sleuth hurriedly; "I quite understand! If I feel better I'll come in by the front way, and pay another shilling—that's only fair."

"You needn't do that if you'll just explain what happened here."

The man went and pulled the curtain aside, and put his shoulder against the door. It burst open, and the light for a moment blinded Mr. Sleuth. He passed his hand over his eyes.

"Thank you," he said; "thank you. I shall get all right here."

Five days later Bunting identified the body of a man found drowned in the Regent's Canal as that of his late lodger; and, the morning following, a gardener working in the Regent's Park found a newspaper in which were wrapped, together with a half-worn pair of rubber-soled shoes, two surgical knives. This fact was not chronicled in any newspaper; but a very pretty and picturesque paragraph went the round of the press, about the same time, concerning a small box filled with sovereigns which had been forwarded anonymously to the Governor of the Foundling Hospital.

Mr. and Mrs. Bunting are now in the service of an old lady, by whom they are feared as well as respected, and whom they make very comfortable.

Notes

[1] *McClure's Magazine,* January 1911, 262.
[2] *McClure's Magazine,* January 1911, 264.
[3] *McClure's Magazine,* January 1911, 265.
[4] *McClure's Magazine,* January 1911, 269.
[5] *McClure's Magazine,* January 1911, 273.
[6] *McClure's Magazine,* January 1911, 275.

THE LODGER

1913

CHAPTER ONE

Robert Bunting and Ellen his wife sat before their dully burning, carefully-banked-up fire.

The room, especially when it be known that it was part of a house standing in a grimy, if not exactly sordid, London thoroughfare, was exceptionally clean and well-cared-for. A casual stranger, more particularly one of a superior class to their own, on suddenly opening the door of that sitting-room, would have thought that Mr. and Mrs. Bunting presented a very pleasant, cosy picture of comfortable married life. Bunting, who was leaning back in a deep leather arm-chair, was clean-shaven and dapper, still in appearance what he had been for many years of his life—a self-respecting man-servant.

On his wife, now sitting up in an uncomfortable straight-backed chair, the marks of past servitude were less apparent; but they were there all the same—in her neat black stuff dress, and in her scrupulously clean, plain collar and cuffs. Mrs. Bunting, as a single woman, had been what is known as a useful maid.

But peculiarly true of average English life is the time-worn English proverb as to appearances being deceitful. Mr. and Mrs. Bunting were sitting in a very nice room and in their time—how long ago it now seemed!—both husband and wife had been proud of their carefully chosen belongings. Everything in the room was strong and substantial, and each article of furniture had been bought at a well-conducted auction held in a private house.

Thus the red damask curtains which now shut out the fog-laden, drizzling atmosphere of the Marylebone Road, had cost a mere song, and yet they might have been warranted to last another thirty years. A great bargain also had been the excellent Axminster carpet which covered the floor; as, again, the arm-chair in which Bunting now sat forward, staring into the dull, small fire. In fact, that arm-chair had been an extravagance of Mrs. Bunting. She had wanted her husband to be comfortable after the day's work was done, and she had paid thirty-seven shillings for the chair. Only yesterday Bunting had tried to find a purchaser for it, but the man who had come to look at it, guessing their cruel necessities, had only offered them twelve shillings and sixpence for it; so for the present they were keeping their arm-chair.

But man and woman want something more than mere material comfort, much as that is valued by the Buntings of this world. So, on the walls of the sitting-room, hung neatly framed if now rather faded photographs—photographs of Mr. and Mrs. Bunting's various former employers, and of the pretty country houses in which they had separately lived during the long years they had spent in a not unhappy servitude.

But appearances were not only deceitful, they were more than usually deceitful with regard to these unfortunate people. In spite of their good furniture—that substantial outward sign of respectability which is the last thing which wise folk who fall into trouble try to dispose of—they were almost at the end of their tether. Already they had learnt to go hungry, and they were beginning to learn to go cold. Tobacco, the last thing the sober man foregoes among his comforts, had been given up some time ago by Bunting. And even Mrs. Bunting—prim, prudent, careful woman as she was in her way—had realised what this must mean to him. So well, indeed, had she understood that some days back she had crept out and bought him a packet of Virginia.

Bunting had been touched—touched as he had not been for years by any woman's thought and love for him. Painful tears had forced themselves into his eyes, and husband and wife had both felt in their odd, unemotional way, moved to the heart.

Fortunately he never guessed—how could he have guessed, with his slow, normal, rather dull mind?—that his poor Ellen had since more than once bitterly regretted that fourpence-ha'penny, for they were now very near the soundless depths which divide those who dwell on the safe tableland of security—those, that is, who are sure of making a respectable, if not a happy, living—and the submerged multitude who, through some lack in themselves, or owing to the conditions under which our strange civilisation has become organised, struggle rudderless till they die in workhouse, hospital, or prison.

Had the Buntings been in a class lower than their own, had they belonged to the great company of human beings technically known to so many of us as the poor, there would have been friendly neighbours ready to help them, and the same would have been the case had they belonged to the class of smug, well-meaning, if unimaginative, folk whom they had spent so much of their lives in serving.

There was only one person in the world who might possibly be brought to help them. That was an aunt of Bunting's first wife. With this woman, the widow of a man who had been well-to-do, lived Daisy, Bunting's only child by his first wife, and during the last long two days he had been trying to make up his mind to write to the old lady, and that though he suspected that she would almost certainly retort with a cruel, sharp rebuff.

As to their few acquaintances, former fellow-servants, and so on, they had gradually fallen out of touch with them. There was but one friend who often came to see them in their deep trouble. This was a young fellow named Chandler, under whose grandfather Bunting had been footman years and years ago. Joe Chandler had never gone into service; he was attached to the police; in fact not to put too fine a point upon it, young Chandler was a detective.[1]

When they had first taken the house which had brought them, so they both thought, such bad luck, Bunting had encouraged the young chap to come often, for his tales were well worth listening to—quite exciting at times. But now poor Bunting didn't want to hear that sort of stories— stories of people being cleverly "nabbed," or stupidly allowed to escape the fate they always, from Chandler's point of view, richly deserved.

But Joe still came very faithfully once or twice a week, so timing his calls that neither host nor hostess need press food upon him —nay, more, he had done that which showed him to have a good and feeling heart. He had offered his father's old acquaintance a loan, and Bunting, at last, had taken 30s.[2] Very little of that money now remained: Bunting still could jingle a few coppers in his pocket; and Mrs. Bunting had 2s. 9d.; that and the rent they would have to pay in five weeks, was all they had left. Everything of the light, portable sort that would fetch money had been sold. Mrs. Bunting had a fierce horror of the pawnshop. She had never put her feet in such a place, and she declared she never would—she would rather starve first.

But she had said nothing when there had occurred the gradual disappearance of various little possessions she knew that Bunting valued, notably of the old-fashioned gold watch-chain which had been given to him after the death of his first master, a master he had nursed faithfully and kindly through a long and terrible illness. There had also vanished a twisted gold tie-pin, and a large mourning ring, both gifts of former employers.

When people are living near that deep pit which divides the secure from the insecure—when they see themselves creeping closer and closer to its dread edge—they are apt, however loquacious by nature, to fall into long silences. Bunting had always been a talker, but now he talked no more. Neither did Mrs. Bunting, but then she had always been a silent woman, and that was perhaps one reason why Bunting had felt drawn to her from the very first moment he had seen her.

It had fallen out in this way. A lady had just engaged him as butler, and he had been shown, by the man whose place he was to take, into the dining-room. There, to use his own expression, he had discovered Ellen Green, carefully pouring out the glass of port wine which her then mistress always drank at 11.30 every morning. And as he, the new butler, had seen her engaged in this task, as he had watched her carefully stopper the decanter and put it back into the old wine-cooler, he had said to himself, "That is the woman for me!"

But now her stillness, her—her dumbness, had got on the unfortunate man's nerves. He no longer felt like going into the various little shops, close by, patronised by him in more prosperous days, and Mrs. Bunting also went afield to make the slender purchases which still had to be made every day or two, if they were to be saved from actually starving to death.

Suddenly, across the stillness of the dark November evening there came the muffled sounds of hurrying feet and of loud, shrill shouting outside—boys crying the late afternoon editions of the evening papers.

Bunting turned uneasily in his chair. The giving up of a daily paper had been, after his tobacco, his bitterest deprivation. And the paper was an older habit than the tobacco, for servants are great readers of newspapers.

As the shouts came through the closed windows and the thick damask curtains, Bunting felt a sudden sense of mind hunger fall upon him.

It was a shame—a damned shame—that he shouldn't know what was happening in the world outside! Only criminals are kept from hearing news of what is going on beyond their prison walls. And those shouts, those hoarse, sharp cries must portend that something really exciting had happened, something warranted to make a man forget for the moment his own intimate, gnawing troubles.

He got up, and going towards the nearest window strained his ears to listen. There fell on them, emerging now and again from the confused babel of hoarse shouts, the one clear word "Murder!"

Slowly Bunting's brain pieced the loud, indistinct cries into some sort of connected order. Yes, that was it—"Horrible Murder! Murder at St. Pancras!" Bunting remembered vaguely another murder which had been committed near St. Pancras—that of an old lady by her servant-maid. It had happened a great many years ago, but was still vividly remembered, as of special and natural interest, among the class to which he had belonged.

The newsboys—for there were more than one of them, a rather unusual thing in the Marylebone Road—were coming nearer and nearer; now they had adopted another cry, but he could not quite catch what they were crying. They were still shouting hoarsely, excitedly, but he could only hear a word or two now and then. Suddenly "The Avenger! The Avenger at his work again!" broke on his ear.

During the last fortnight four very curious and brutal murders had been committed in London and within a comparatively small area.

The first had aroused no special interest—even the second had only been awarded, in the paper Bunting was still then taking in, quite a small paragraph.

Then had come the third—and with that a wave of keen excitement, for pinned to the dress of the victim—a drunken woman—had been found a three-cornered piece of paper, on which was written, in red ink, and in printed characters, the words,

THE AVENGER

It was then realised, not only by those whose business it is to investigate such terrible happenings, but also by the vast world of men and women who take an intelligent interest in such sinister mysteries, that the same miscreant had committed all three crimes; and before that extraordinary fact had had time to soak well into the public mind there took place yet another murder, and again the murderer had been to special pains to make it clear that some obscure and terrible lust for vengeance possessed him.

Now everyone was talking of The Avenger and his crimes! Even the man who left their ha'porth of milk at the door each morning had spoken to Bunting about them that very day.

Bunting came back to the fire and looked down at his wife with mild excitement. Then, seeing her pale, apathetic face, her look of weary, mournful absorption, a wave of irritation swept through him. He felt he could have shaken her!

Ellen had hardly taken the trouble to listen when he, Bunting, had come back to bed that morning, and told her what the milkman had said. In fact, she had been quite nasty about it, intimating that she didn't like hearing about such horrid things.

It was a curious fact that though Mrs. Bunting enjoyed tales of pathos and sentiment, and would listen with frigid amusement to the details of a breach of promise action, she shrank from stories of immorality or of physical violence. In the old, happy days, when they could afford to buy a paper, aye, and more than one paper daily, Bunting had often had to choke down his interest in some exciting "case" or "mystery" which was affording him pleasant mental relaxation, because any allusion to it sharply angered Ellen.

But now he was at once too dull and too miserable to care how she felt.

Walking away from the window he took a slow, uncertain step towards the door; when there he turned half round, and there came over his close-shaven, round face the rather sly, pleading look with which a child about to do something naughty glances at its parent.

But Mrs. Bunting remained quite still; her thin, narrow shoulders just showed above the back of the chair on which she was sitting, bolt upright, staring before her as if into vacancy.

Bunting turned round, opened the door, and quickly he went out into the dark hall—they had given up lighting the gas there some time ago—and opened the front door.

Walking down the small flagged path outside, he flung open the iron gate which gave on to the damp pavement. But there he hesitated. The coppers in his pocket seemed to have shrunk in number, and he remembered ruefully how far Ellen could make even four pennies go.

Then a boy ran up to him with a sheaf of evening papers, and Bunting, being sorely tempted—fell. "Give me a *Sun*," he said roughly, "*Sun* or *Echo!*"

But the boy, scarcely stopping to take breath, shook his head. "Only penny papers left," he gasped. "What'll yer 'ave, sir?"

With an eagerness which was mingled with shame, Bunting drew a penny out of his pocket and took a paper—it was the *Evening Standard*—from the boy's hand.

Then, very slowly, he shut the gate and walked back through the raw, cold air, up the flagged path, shivering yet full of eager, joyful anticipation.

Thanks to that penny he had just spent so recklessly he would pass a happy hour, taken, for once, out of his anxious, despondent, miserable self. It irritated him shrewdly to know that these moments of respite from carking care would not be shared with his poor wife, with careworn, troubled Ellen.

A hot wave of unease, almost of remorse, swept over Bunting. Ellen would never have spent that penny on herself—he knew that well enough—and if it hadn't been so cold, so foggy, so—so drizzly, he would have gone out again through the gate and stood under the street lamp to take his pleasure. He dreaded with a nervous dread the glance of Ellen's cold, reproving light-blue eye. That glance would tell him that he had had no business to waste a penny on a paper, and that well he knew it!

Suddenly the door in front of him opened, and he beard a familiar voice saying crossly, yet anxiously, "What on earth are you doing out there, Bunting? Come in—do! You'll catch your death of cold! I don't want to have you ill on my hands as well as everything else!" Mrs. Bunting rarely uttered so many words at once nowadays.

He walked in through the front door of his cheerless house. "I went out to get a paper," he said sullenly.

After all, he was master. He had as much right to spend the money as she had; for the matter of that the money on which they were now both living had been lent, nay, pressed on him—not on Ellen—by that decent young chap, Joe Chandler. And he, Bunting, had done all he could; he had pawned everything he could pawn, while Ellen, so he resentfully noticed, still wore her wedding ring.

He stepped past her heavily, and though she said nothing, he knew she grudged him his coming joy. Then, full of rage with her and contempt for himself, and giving himself the luxury of a mild, a very mild, oath—Ellen had very early made it clear she would have no swearing in her presence—he lit the hall gas full-flare.

"How can we hope to get lodgers if they can't even see the card?" he shouted angrily.

And there was truth in what he said, for now that he had lit the gas, the oblong card, though not the word "Apartments" printed on it, could be plainly seen out-lined against the old-fashioned fanlight above the front door.

Bunting went into the sitting-room, silently followed by his wife, and then, sitting down in his nice arm-chair, he poked the little banked-up fire. It was the first time Bunting had poked the fire for many a long day, and this exertion of marital authority made him feel better. A man has to assert himself sometimes, and he, Bunting, had not asserted himself enough lately.

A little colour came into Mrs. Bunting's pale face. She was not used to be flouted in this way. For Bunting, when not thoroughly upset, was the mildest of men.

She began moving about the room, flicking off an imperceptible touch of dust here, straightening a piece of furniture there.

But her hands trembled—they trembled with excitement, with self-pity, with anger. A penny? It was dreadful—dreadful to have to worry about a penny! But they had come to the point when one has to worry about pennies. Strange that her husband didn't realise that.

Bunting looked round once or twice; he would have liked to ask Ellen to leave off fidgeting, but he was fond of peace, and perhaps, by now, a little bit ashamed of himself, so he refrained from remark, and she soon gave over what irritated him of her own accord.

But Mrs. Bunting did not come and sit down as her husband would have liked her to do. The sight of him, absorbed in his paper as he was, irritated her, and made her long to get away from him. Opening the door which separated the sitting-room from the bedroom behind, and—shutting out the aggravating vision of Bunting sitting comfortably by the now brightly burning fire, with the Evening Standard spread out before him— she sat down in the cold darkness, and pressed her hands against her temples.

Never, never had she felt so hopeless, so—so broken as now. Where was the good of having been an upright, conscientious, self-respecting woman all her life long, if it only led to this utter, degrading poverty and wretchedness? She and Bunting were just past the age which gentlefolk think proper in a married couple seeking to enter service together, unless, that is, the wife happens to be a professed cook. A cook and a butler can always get a nice situation. But Mrs. Bunting was no cook. She could do all right the simple things any lodger she might get would require, but that was all.

Lodgers? How foolish she had been to think of taking lodgers! For it had been her doing. Bunting had been like butter in her hands.

Yet they had begun well, with a lodging-house in a seaside place. There they had prospered, not as they had hoped to do, but still pretty well; and then had come an epidemic of scarlet fever, and that had meant ruin for them, and for dozens, nay, hundreds, of other luckless people. Then had followed a business experiment which had proved even more disastrous, and which had left them in debt—in debt to an extent they could never hope to repay, to a good-natured former employer.

After that, instead of going back to service, as they might have done, perhaps, either together or separately, they had made up their minds to make one last effort, and they had taken over, with the trifle of money that remained to them, the lease of this house in the Marylebone Road.

In former days, when they had each been leading the sheltered, impersonal, and, above all, financially easy existence which is the compensation life offers to those men and women who deliberately take upon themselves the yoke of domestic service, they had both lived in houses overlooking Regent's Park. It had seemed a wise plan to settle in the same neighbourhood, the more so that Bunting, who had a good appearance, had retained the kind of connection which enables a man to get a job now and again as waiter at private parties.

But life moves quickly, jaggedly, for people like the Buntings. Two of his former masters had moved to another part of London, and a caterer in Baker Street whom he had known went bankrupt.

And now? Well, just now Bunting could not have taken a job had one been offered him, for he had pawned his dress clothes. He had not asked his wife's permission to do this, as so good a husband ought to have done. He had just gone out and done it. And she had not had the heart to say anything; nay, it was with part of the money that he had handed her silently the evening he did it that she had bought that last packet of tobacco.

And then, as Mrs. Bunting sat there thinking these painful thoughts, there suddenly came to the front door the sound of a loud, tremulous, uncertain double knock.

CHAPTER TWO

Mrs. Bunting jumped nervously to her feet. She stood for a moment listening in the darkness, a darkness made the blacker by the line of light under the door behind which sat Bunting reading his paper.

And then it came again, that loud, tremulous, uncertain double knock; not a knock, so the listener told herself, that boded any good. Would-be lodgers gave sharp, quick, bold, confident raps. No; this must be some kind of beggar. The queerest people came at all hours, and asked—whining or threatening—for money.

Mrs. Bunting had had some sinister experiences with men and women—especially women—drawn from that nameless, mysterious class made up of the human flotsam and jetsam which drifts about every great city. But since she had taken to leaving the gas in the passage unlit at night she had been very little troubled with that kind of visitors, those human bats which are attracted by any kind of light but leave alone those who live in darkness.

She opened the door of the sitting-room. It was Bunting's place to go to the front door, but she knew far better than he did how to deal with difficult or obtrusive callers. Still, somehow, she would have liked him to go to-night. But Bunting sat on, absorbed in his newspaper; all he did at the sound of the bedroom door opening was to look up and say, "Didn't you hear a knock?"

Without answering his question she went out into the hall.

Slowly she opened the front door.

On the top of the three steps which led up to the door, there stood the long, lanky figure of a man, clad in an Inverness cape and an old-fashioned top hat. He waited for a few seconds blinking at her, perhaps dazzled by the light of the gas in the passage. Mrs. Bunting's trained perception told her at once that this man, odd as he looked, was a gentleman, belonging by birth to the class with whom her former employment had brought her in contact.

"Is it not a fact that you let lodgings?" he asked, and there was something shrill, unbalanced, hesitating, in his voice.

"Yes, sir," she said uncertainly—it was a long, long time since anyone had come after their lodgings, anyone, that is, that they could think of taking into their respectable house.

Instinctively she stepped a little to one side, and the stranger walked past her, and so into the hall.

And then, for the first time, Mrs. Bunting noticed that he held a narrow bag in his left hand. It was quite a new bag, made of strong brown leather.

"I am looking for some quiet rooms," he said; then he repeated the words, "quiet rooms," in a dreamy, absent way, and as he uttered them he looked nervously round him.

Then his sallow face brightened, for the hall had been carefully furnished, and was very clean.

There was a neat hat-and-umbrella stand, and the stranger's weary feet fell soft on a good, serviceable dark-red drugget, which matched in colour the flock-paper on the walls.

A very superior lodging-house this, and evidently a superior lodging-house keeper.

"You'd find my rooms quite quiet, sir," she said gently. "And just now I have four to let. The house is empty, save for my husband and me, sir."

Mrs. Bunting spoke in a civil, passionless voice. It seemed too good to be true, this sudden coming of a possible lodger, and of a lodger who spoke in the pleasant, courteous way and voice which recalled to the poor woman her happy, far-off days of youth and of security. "That sounds very suitable," he said. "Four rooms? Well, perhaps I ought only to take two rooms, but, still, I should like to see all four before I make my choice."

How fortunate, how very fortunate it was that Bunting had lit the gas! But for that circumstance this gentleman would have passed them by.

She turned towards the staircase, quite forgetting in her agitation that the front door was still open; and it was the stranger whom she already in her mind described as "the lodger," who turned and rather quickly walked down the passage and shut it.

"Oh, thank you, sir!" she exclaimed. "I'm sorry you should have had the trouble."

For a moment their eyes met. "It's not safe to leave a front door open in London," he said, rather sharply. "I hope you do not often do that. It would be so easy for anyone to slip in."

Mrs. Bunting felt rather upset. The stranger had still spoken courteously, but he was evidently very much put out.

"I assure you, sir, I never leave my front door open," she answered hastily. "You needn't be at all afraid of that!"

And then, through the closed door of the sitting-room, came the sound of Bunting coughing—it was just a little, hard cough, but Mrs. Bunting's future lodger started violently.

"Who's that?" he said, putting out a hand and clutching her arm. "Whatever was that?"

"Only my husband, sir. He went out to buy a paper a few minutes ago, and the cold just caught him, I suppose."

"Your husband—?" he looked at her intently, suspiciously. "What — what, may I ask, is your husband's occupation?"

Mrs. Bunting drew herself up. The question as to Bunting's occupation was no one's business but theirs. Still, it wouldn't do for her to show offence. "He goes out waiting," she said stiffly. "He was a gentleman's servant, sir. He could, of course, valet you should you require him to do so."

And then she turned and led the way up the steep, narrow staircase.

At the top of the first flight of stairs was what Mrs. Bunting, to herself, called the drawing-room floor. It consisted of a sitting-room in front, and a bedroom behind. She opened the door of the sitting-room and quickly lit the chandelier.

This front room was pleasant enough, though perhaps a little over-encumbered with furniture. Covering the floor was a green carpet simulating moss; four chairs were placed round the table which occupied the exact middle of the apartment, and in the corner, opposite the door giving on to the landing, was a roomy, old-fashioned chiffonnier.

On the dark-green walls hung a series of eight engravings, portraits of early Victorian belles, clad in lace and tarlatan ball dresses, clipped from an old *Book of Beauty*. Mrs. Bunting was very fond of these pictures; she thought they gave the drawing-room a note of elegance and refinement.[3]

As she hurriedly turned up the gas she was glad, glad indeed, that she had summoned up sufficient energy, two days ago, to give the room a thorough turn-out.

It had remained for a long time in the state in which it had been left by its last dishonest, dirty occupants when they had been scared into going away by Bunting's rough threats of the police. But now it was in apple-pie order, with one paramount exception, of which Mrs. Bunting was painfully aware. There were no white curtains to the windows, but that omission could soon be remedied if this gentleman really took the lodgings.

But what was this—? The stranger was looking round him rather dubiously. "This is rather—rather too grand for me," he said at last "I should like to see your other rooms, Mrs. er—"

"—Bunting," she said softly. "Bunting, sir."

And as she spoke the dark, heavy load of care again came down and settled on her sad, burdened heart. Perhaps she had been mistaken, after all—or rather, she had not been mistaken in one sense, but perhaps this gentleman was a poor gentleman—too poor, that is, to afford the rent of more than one room, say eight or ten shillings a week; eight or ten shillings a week would be very little use to her and Bunting, though better than nothing at all.

"Will you just look at the bedroom, sir?"

"No," he said, "no. I think I should like to see what you have farther up the house, Mrs.——," and then, as if making a prodigious mental effort, he brought out her name, "Bunting," with a kind of gasp.

The two top rooms were, of course, immediately above the drawing-room floor. But they looked poor and mean, owing to the fact that they were bare of any kind of ornament. Very little trouble had been taken over their arrangement; in fact, they had been left in much the same condition as that in which the Buntings had found them.

For the matter of that, it is difficult to make a nice, genteel sitting-room out of an apartment of which the principal features are a sink and a big gas stove. The gas stove, of an obsolete pattern, was fed by a tiresome, shilling-in-the-slot arrangement.[4] It had been the property of the people from whom the Buntings had taken over the lease of the house, who, knowing it to be of no monetary value, had thrown it in among the humble fittings they had left behind.

What furniture there was in the room was substantial and clean, as everything belonging to Mrs. Bunting was bound to be, but it was a bare, uncomfortable-looking place, and the landlady now felt sorry that she had done nothing to make it appear more attractive.

To her surprise, however, her companion's dark, sensitive, hatchet-shaped face became irradiated with satisfaction. "Capital! Capital!" he exclaimed, for the first time putting down the bag he held at his feet, and rubbing his long, thin hands together with a quick, nervous movement.

"This is just what I have been looking for." He walked with long, eager strides towards the gas stove. "First-rate—quite first-rate! Exactly what I wanted to find! You must understand, Mrs.—er— Bunting, that I am a man of science. I make, that is, all sorts of experiments, and I often require the—ah, well, the presence of great heat."

He shot out a hand, which she noticed shook a little, towards the stove. "This, too, will be useful—exceedingly useful, to me," and he touched the edge of the stone sink with a lingering, caressing touch.

He threw his head back and passed his hand over his high, bare forehead; then, moving towards a chair, he sat down—wearily. "I'm tired," he muttered in a low voice, "tired—tired! I've been walking about all day, Mrs. Bunting, and I could find nothing to sit down upon. They do not put benches for tired men in the London streets. They do so on the

Continent. In some ways they are far more humane on the Continent than
they are in England, Mrs. Bunting."

"Indeed, sir," she said civilly; and then, after a nervous glance, she
asked the question of which the answer would mean so much to her, "Then
you mean to take my rooms, sir?"

"This room, certainly," he said, looking round. "This room is exactly
what I have been looking for, and longing for, the last few days;" and then
hastily he added, "I mean this kind of place is what I have always wanted
to possess, Mrs. Bunting. You would be surprised if you knew how
difficult it is to get anything of the sort. But now my weary search has
ended, and that is a relief—a very, very great relief to me!"

He stood up and looked round him with a dreamy, abstracted air. And
then, "Where's my bag?" he asked suddenly, and there came a note of
sharp, angry fear in his voice. He glared at the quiet woman standing
before him, and for a moment Mrs. Bunting felt a tremor of fright shoot
through her. It seemed a pity that Bunting was so far away, right down the
house.

But Mrs. Bunting was aware that eccentricity has always been a
perquisite, as it were the special luxury, of the well-born and of the well-
educated. Scholars, as she well knew, are never quite like other people,
and her new lodger was undoubtedly a scholar. "Surely I had a bag when I
came in?" he said in a scared, troubled voice.

"Here it is, sir," she said soothingly, and, stooping, picked it up and
handed it to him. And as she did so she noticed that the bag was not at all
heavy; it was evidently by no means full.

He took it eagerly from her. "I beg your pardon," he muttered. "But
there is something in that bag which is very precious to me—something I
procured with infinite difficulty, and which I could never get again without
running into great danger, Mrs. Bunting. That must be the excuse for my
late agitation."

"About terms, sir?" she said a little timidly, returning to the subject
which meant so much, so very much to her.

"About terms?" he echoed. And then there came a pause. "My name is
Sleuth," he said suddenly,—"S-l-e-u-t-h. Think of a hound, Mrs. Bunting,
and you'll never forget my name. I could provide you with a reference—"
(he gave her what she described to herself as a funny, sideways look), "but
I should prefer you to dispense with that, if you don't mind. I am quite
willing to pay you—well, shall we say a month in advance?"

A spot of red shot into Mrs. Bunting's cheeks. She felt sick with
relief—nay, with a joy which was almost pain. She had not known till that

moment how hungry she was—how eager for—a good meal. "That would be all right, sir," she murmured.

"And what are you going to charge me?" There had come a kindly, almost a friendly note into his voice. "With attendance, mind! I shall expect you to give me attendance, and I need hardly ask if you can cook, Mrs. Bunting?"

"Oh, yes, sir," she said. "I am a plain cook. What would you say to twenty-five shillings a week, sir?" She looked at him deprecatingly, and as he did not answer she went on falteringly, "You see, sir, it may seem a good deal, but you would have the best of attendance and careful cooking—and my husband, sir—he would be pleased to valet you."

"I shouldn't want anything of that sort done for me," said Mr. Sleuth hastily. "I prefer looking after my own clothes. I am used to waiting on myself. But, Mrs. Bunting, I have a great dislike to sharing lodgings—"

She interrupted eagerly, "I could let you have the use of the two floors for the same price—that is, until we get another lodger. I shouldn't like you to sleep in the back room up here, sir. It's such a poor little room. You could do as you say, sir—do your work and your experiments up here, and then have your meals in the drawing-room."

"Yes," he said hesitatingly, "that sounds a good plan. And if I offered you two pounds, or two guineas? Might I then rely on your not taking another lodger?"[5]

"Yes," she said quietly. "I'd be very glad only to have you to wait on, sir."

"I suppose you have a key to the door of this room, Mrs. Bunting? I don't like to be disturbed while I'm working."

He waited a moment, and then said again, rather urgently, "I suppose you have a key to this door, Mrs. Bunting?"

"Oh, yes, sir, there's a key—a very nice little key. The people who lived here before had a new kind of lock put on to the door." She went over, and throwing the door open, showed him that a round disk had been fitted above the old keyhole.

He nodded his head, and then, after standing silent a little, as if absorbed in thought, "Forty-two shillings a week? Yes, that will suit me perfectly. And I'll begin now by paying my first month's rent in advance. Now, four times forty-two shillings is"—he jerked his head back and stared at his new landlady; for the first time he smiled, a queer, wry smile—"why, just eight pounds eight shillings, Mrs. Bunting!"

He thrust his hand through into an inner pocket of his long cape-like coat and took out a handful of sovereigns. Then he began putting these down in a row on the bare wooden table which stood in the centre of the room. "Here's five—six—seven—eight—nine—ten pounds. You'd better keep the odd change, Mrs. Bunting, for I shall want you to do some shopping for me to-morrow morning. I met with a misfortune to-day." But the new lodger did not speak as if his misfortune, whatever it was, weighed on his spirits.

"Indeed, sir. I'm sorry to hear that." Mrs. Bunting's heart was going thump—thump—thump. She felt extraordinarily moved, dizzy with relief and joy.

"Yes, a very great misfortune! I lost my luggage, the few things I managed to bring away with me." His voice dropped suddenly. "I shouldn't have said that," he muttered. "I was a fool to say that!" Then, more loudly, "Someone said to me, 'You can't go into a lodging-house without any luggage. They wouldn't take you in.' But you have taken me in, Mrs. Bunting, and I'm grateful for—for the kind way you have met me—" He looked at her feelingly, appealingly, and Mrs. Bunting was touched. She was beginning to feel very kindly towards her new lodger.

"I hope I know a gentleman when I see one," she said, with a break in her staid voice.

"I shall have to see about getting some clothes to-morrow, Mrs. Bunting."
Again he looked at her appealingly.

"I expect you'd like to wash your hands now, sir. And would you tell me what you'd like for supper? We haven't much in the house."

"Oh, anything'll do," he said hastily. "I don't want you to go out for me. It's a cold, foggy, wet night, Mrs. Bunting. If you have a little bread-and-butter and a cup of milk I shall be quite satisfied."

"I have a nice sausage," she said hesitatingly.

It was a very nice sausage, and she had bought it that same morning for Bunting's supper; as to herself, she had been going to content herself with a little bread and cheese. But now—wonderful, almost, intoxicating thought—she could send Bunting out to get anything they both liked. The ten sovereigns lay in her hand full of comfort and good cheer.

"A sausage? No, I fear that will hardly do. I never touch flesh meat," he said; "it is a long, long time since I tasted a sausage, Mrs. Bunting."

"Is it indeed, sir?" She hesitated a moment, then asked stiffly,

"And will you be requiring any beer, or wine, sir?"

A strange, wild look of lowering wrath suddenly filled Mr. Sleuth's pale face.

"Certainly not. I thought I had made that quite clear, Mrs. Bunting. I had hoped to hear that you were an abstainer—"

"So I am, sir, lifelong. And so's Bunting been since we married." She might have said, had she been a woman given to make such confidences, that she had made Bunting abstain very early in their acquaintance. That he had given in about that had been the thing that first made her believe that he was sincere in all the nonsense that he talked to her, in those far-away days of his courting. Glad she was now that he had taken the pledge as a younger man; but for that nothing would have kept him from the drink during the bad times they had gone through.

And then, going downstairs, she showed Mr. Sleuth the nice bedroom which opened out of the drawing-room. It was a replica of Mrs. Bunting's own room just underneath, excepting that everything up here had cost just a little more, and was therefore rather better in quality.

The new lodger looked round him with such a strange expression of content and peace stealing over his worn face. "A haven of rest," he muttered; and then, "'He bringeth them to their desired haven.' Beautiful words, Mrs. Bunting."[6]

"Yes, sir."

Mrs. Bunting felt a little startled. It was the first time anyone had quoted the Bible to her for many a long day. But it seemed to set the seal, as it were, on Mr. Sleuth's respectability.

What a comfort it was, too, that she had to deal with only one lodger, and that a gentleman, instead of with a married couple! Very peculiar married couples had drifted in and out of Mr. and Mrs. Bunting's lodgings, not only here, in London, but at the seaside.

How unlucky they had been, to be sure! Since they had come to London not a single pair of lodgers had been even moderately respectable and kindly. The last lot had belonged to that horrible underworld of men and women who, having, as the phrase goes, seen better days, now only keep their heads above water with the help of petty fraud.

"I'll bring you up some hot water in a minute, sir, and some clean towels," she said, going to the door.

And then Mr. Sleuth turned quickly round. "Mrs. Bunting"—and as he spoke he stammered a little—"I—I don't want you to interpret the word attendance too liberally. You need not run yourself off your feet for me. I'm accustomed to look after myself."

And, queerly, uncomfortably, she felt herself dismissed—even a little snubbed. "All right, sir," she said. "I'll only just let you know when I've your supper ready."

CHAPTER THREE

But what was a little snub compared with the intense relief and joy of going down and telling Bunting of the great piece of good fortune which had fallen their way?

Staid Mrs. Bunting seemed to make but one leap down the steep stairs. In the hall, however, she pulled herself together, and tried to still her agitation. She had always disliked and despised any show of emotion; she called such betrayal of feeling "making a fuss."

Opening the door of their sitting-room, she stood for a moment looking at her husband's bent back, and she realised, with a pang of pain, how the last few weeks had aged him.

Bunting suddenly looked round, and, seeing his wife, stood up. He put the paper he had been holding down on to the table: "Well," he said, "well, who was it, then?"

He felt rather ashamed of himself; it was he who ought to have answered the door and done all that parleying of which he had heard murmurs.

And then in a moment his wife's hand shot out, and the ten sovereigns fell in a little clinking heap on the table.

"Look there!" she whispered, with an excited, tearful quiver in her voice. "Look there, Bunting!"

And Bunting did look there, but with a troubled, frowning gaze.

He was not quick-witted, but at once he jumped to the conclusion that his wife had just had in a furniture dealer, and that this ten pounds represented all their nice furniture upstairs. If that were so, then it was the beginning of the end. That furniture in the first-floor front had cost—Ellen had reminded him of the fact bitterly only yesterday—seventeen pounds nine shillings, and every single item had been a bargain. It was too bad that she had only got ten pounds for it.

Yet he hadn't the heart to reproach her.

He did not speak as he looked across at her, and meeting that troubled, rebuking glance, she guessed what it was that he thought had happened.

"We've a new lodger!" she cried. "And—and, Bunting? He's quite the gentleman! He actually offered to pay four weeks in advance, at two guineas a week."

"No, never!"

Bunting moved quickly round the table, and together they stood there, fascinated by the little heap of gold. "But there's ten sovereigns here," he said suddenly.

"Yes, the gentleman said I'd have to buy some things for him to-morrow. And, oh, Bunting, he's so well spoken, I really felt that—I really felt that—" and then Mrs. Bunting, taking a step or two sideways, sat down, and throwing her little black apron over her face burst into gasping sobs.

Bunting patted her back timidly. "Ellen?" he said, much moved by her agitation, "Ellen? Don't take on so, my dear—"

"I won't," she sobbed, "I—I won't! I'm a fool—I know I am! But, oh, I didn't think we was ever going to have any luck again!"

And then she told him—or rather tried to tell him—what the lodger was like. Mrs. Bunting was no hand at talking, but one thing she did impress on her husband's mind, namely, that Mr. Sleuth was eccentric, as so many clever people are eccentric—that is, in a harmless way—and that he must be humoured.

"He says he doesn't want to be waited on much," she said at last wiping her eyes, "but I can see he will want a good bit of looking after, all the same, poor gentleman."

And just as the words left her mouth there came the unfamiliar sound of a loud ring. It was that of the drawing-room bell being pulled again and again.

Bunting looked at his wife eagerly. "I think I'd better go up, eh, Ellen?" he said. He felt quite anxious to see their new lodger. For the matter of that, it would be a relief to be doing something again.

"Yes," she answered, "you go up! Don't keep him waiting! I wonder what it is he wants? I said I'd let him know when his supper was ready."

A moment later Bunting came down again. There was an odd smile on his face. "Whatever d'you think he wanted?" he whispered mysteriously. And as she said nothing, he went on, "He's asked me for the loan of a Bible!"

"Well, I don't see anything so out of the way in that," she said hastily, "'specially if he don't feel well. I'll take it up to him."

And then going to a small table which stood between the two windows, Mrs. Bunting took off it a large Bible, which had been given to her as a wedding present by a married lady with whose mother she had lived for several years.

"He said it would do quite well when you take up his supper," said Bunting; and, then, "Ellen? He's a queer-looking cove—not like any gentleman *I* ever had to do with."

"He *is* a gentleman," said Mrs. Bunting rather fiercely.

"Oh, yes, that's all right." But still he looked at her doubtfully. "I asked him if he'd like me to just put away his clothes. But, Ellen, he said he hadn't got any clothes!"

"No more he hasn't;" she spoke quickly, defensively. "He had the misfortune to lose his luggage. He's one dishonest folk 'ud take advantage of."

"Yes, one can see that with half an eye," Bunting agreed.

And then there was silence for a few moments, while Mrs. Bunting put down on a little bit of paper the things she wanted her husband to go out and buy for her. She handed him the list, together with a sovereign. "Be as quick as you can," she said, "for I feel a bit hungry. I'll be going down now to see about Mr. Sleuth's supper. He only wants a glass of milk and two eggs. I'm glad I've never fallen to bad eggs!"

"Sleuth," echoed Bunting, staring at her. "What a queer name! How d'you spell it—S-l-u-t-h?"

"No," she shot out, "S-l-e-u-t-h."

"Oh," he said doubtfully.

"He said, 'Think of a hound and you'll never forget my name,'" and Mrs. Bunting smiled.

When he got to the door, Bunting turned round: "We'll now be able to pay young Chandler back some o' that thirty shillings. I am glad." She nodded; her heart, as the saying is, too full for words.

And then each went about his and her business—Bunting out into the drenching fog, his wife down to her cold kitchen.

The lodger's tray was soon ready; everything upon it nicely and daintily arranged. Mrs. Bunting knew how to wait upon a gentleman.

Just as the landlady was going up the kitchen stair, she suddenly remembered Mr. Sleuth's request for a Bible. Putting the tray down in the hall, she went into her sitting-room and took up the Book; but when back in the hall she hesitated a moment as to whether it was worth while to make two journeys. But, no, she thought she could manage; clasping the large, heavy volume under her arm, and taking up the tray, she walked slowly up the staircase.

But a great surprise awaited her; in fact, when Mr. Sleuth's landlady opened the door of the drawing-room she very nearly dropped the tray. She actually did drop the Bible, and it fell with a heavy thud to the ground.

The new lodger had turned all those nice framed engravings of the early Victorian beauties, of which Mrs. Bunting had been so proud, with their faces to the wall!

For a moment she was really too surprised to speak. Putting the tray down on the table, she stooped and picked up the Book. It troubled her that the Book should have fallen to the ground; but really she hadn't been able to help it—it was mercy that the tray hadn't fallen, too.

Mr. Sleuth got up. "I—I have taken the liberty to arrange the room as I should wish it to be," he said awkwardly. "You see, Mrs.—er—Bunting, I felt as I sat here that these women's eyes followed me about. It was a most unpleasant sensation, and gave me quite an eerie feeling."

The landlady was now laying a small tablecloth over half of the table. She made no answer to her lodger's remark, for the good reason that she did not know what to say.

Her silence seemed to distress Mr. Sleuth. After what seemed a long pause, he spoke again.

"I prefer bare walls, Mrs. Bunting," he spoke with some agitation. "As a matter of fact, I have been used to seeing bare walls about me for a long time." And then, at last his landlady answered him, in a composed, soothing voice, which somehow did him good to hear. "I quite understand, sir. And when Bunting comes in he shall take the pictures all down. We have plenty of space in our own rooms for them."

"Thank you—thank you very much."

Mr. Sleuth appeared greatly relieved.

"And I have brought you up my Bible, sir. I understood you wanted the loan of it?"

Mr. Sleuth stared at her as if dazed for a moment; and then, rousing himself, he said, "Yes, yes, I do. There is no reading like the Book. There is something there which suits every state of mind, aye, and of body too—"

"Very true, sir." And then Mrs. Bunting, having laid out what really looked a very appetising little meal, turned round and quietly shut the door.

She went down straight into her sitting-room and waited there for Bunting, instead of going to the kitchen to clear up. And as she did so there came to her a comfortable recollection, an incident of her long-past youth, in the days when she, then Ellen Green, had maided a dear old lady.

The old lady had a favourite nephew—a bright, jolly young gentleman, who was learning to paint animals in Paris. And one morning Mr. Algernon—that was his rather peculiar Christian name—had had the impudence to turn to the wall six beautiful engravings of paintings done by the famous Mr. Landseer![7]

Mrs. Bunting remembered all the circumstances as if they had only occurred yesterday, and yet she had not thought of them for years.

It was quite early; she had come down—for in those days maids weren't thought so much of as they are now, and she slept with the upper housemaid, and it was the upper housemaid's duty to be down very early—and, there, in the dining-room, she had found Mr. Algernon engaged in turning each engraving to the wall! Now, his aunt thought all the world of those pictures, and Ellen had felt quite concerned, for it doesn't do for a young gentleman to put himself wrong with a kind aunt.

"Oh, sir," she had exclaimed in dismay, "whatever are you doing?" And even now she could almost hear his merry voice, as he had answered, "I am doing my duty, fair Helen"—he had always called her "fair Helen" when no one was listening. "How can I draw ordinary animals when I see these half-human monsters staring at me all the time I am having my breakfast, my lunch, and my dinner?" That was what Mr. Algernon had said in his own saucy way, and that was what he repeated in a more serious, respectful manner to his aunt, when that dear old lady had come downstairs. In fact he had declared, quite soberly, that the beautiful animals painted by Mr. Landseer put his eye out!

But his aunt had been very much annoyed—in fact, she had made him turn the pictures all back again; and as long as he stayed there he just had to put up with what he called "those half-human monsters." Mrs. Bunting, sitting there, thinking the matter of Mr. Sleuth's odd behaviour over, was glad to recall that funny incident of her long-gone youth. It seemed to prove that her new lodger was not so strange as he appeared to be. Still, when Bunting came in, she did not tell him the queer thing which had happened. She told herself that she would be quite able to manage the taking down of the pictures in the drawing-room herself.

But before getting ready their own supper, Mr. Sleuth's landlady went upstairs to clear away, and when on the staircase she heard the sound of— was it talking, in the drawing-room? Startled, she waited a moment on the landing outside the drawing-room door, then she realised that it was only the lodger reading aloud to himself. There was something very awful in the words which rose and fell on her listening ears:

"A strange woman is a narrow gate. She also lieth in wait as for a prey, and increaseth the transgressors among men."

She remained where she was, her hand on the handle of the door, and again there broke on her shrinking ears that curious, high, sing-song voice, "Her house is the way to hell, going down to the chambers of death."[8]

It made the listener feel quite queer. But at last she summoned up courage, knocked, and walked in.

"I'd better clear away, sir, had I not?" she said. And Mr. Sleuth nodded.

Then he got up and closed the Book. "I think I'll go to bed now," he said. "I am very, very tired. I've had a long and a very weary day, Mrs. Bunting."

After he had disappeared into the back room, Mrs. Bunting climbed up on a chair and unhooked the pictures which had so offended Mr. Sleuth. Each left an unsightly mark on the wall—but that, after all, could not be helped.

Treading softly, so that Bunting should not hear her, she carried them down, two by two, and stood them behind her bed.

CHAPTER FOUR

Mrs. Bunting woke up the next morning feeling happier than she had felt for a very, very long time.

For just one moment she could not think why she felt so different—and then she suddenly remembered.

How comfortable it was to know that upstairs, just over her head, lay, in the well-found bed she had bought with such satisfaction at an auction held in a Baker Street house, a lodger who was paying two guineas a week! Something seemed to tell her that Mr. Sleuth would be "a permanency." In any case, it wouldn't be her fault if he wasn't. As to his—his queerness, well, there's always something funny in everybody. But after she had got up, and as the morning wore itself away, Mrs. Bunting grew a little anxious, for there came no sound at all from the new lodger's rooms. At twelve, however, the drawing-room bell rang. Mrs. Bunting hurried upstairs. She was painfully anxious to please and satisfy Mr. Sleuth. His coming had only been in the nick of time to save them from terrible disaster.

She found her lodger up, and fully dressed. He was sitting at the round table which occupied the middle of the sitting-room, and his landlady's large Bible lay open before him.

As Mrs. Bunting came in, he looked up, and she was troubled to see how tired and worn he seemed.

"You did not happen," he asked, "to have a Concordance, Mrs. Bunting?"

She shook her head; she had no idea what a Concordance could be, but she was quite sure that she had nothing of the sort about.

And then her new lodger proceeded to tell her what it was he desired her to buy for him. She had supposed the bag he had brought with him to contain certain little necessaries of civilised life—such articles, for instance, as a comb and brush, a set of razors, a toothbrush, to say nothing of a couple of nightshirts—but no, that was evidently not so, for Mr. Sleuth required all these things to be bought now.

After having cooked him a nice breakfast Mrs. Bunting hurried out to purchase the things of which he was in urgent need.

How pleasant it was to feel that there was money in her purse again—not only someone else's money, but money she was now in the very act of earning so agreeably.

Mrs. Bunting first made her way to a little barber's shop close by. It was there she purchased the brush and comb and the razors. It was a funny, rather smelly little place, and she hurried as much as she could, the more so that the foreigner who served her insisted on telling her some of the strange, peculiar details of this Avenger murder which had taken place forty-eight hours before, and in which Bunting took such a morbid interest.

The conversation upset Mrs. Bunting. She didn't want to think of anything painful or disagreeable on such a day as this.

Then she came back and showed the lodger her various purchases. Mr. Sleuth was pleased with everything, and thanked her most courteously. But when she suggested doing his bedroom he frowned, and looked quite put out.

"Please wait till this evening," he said hastily. "It is my custom to stay at home all day. I only care to walk about the streets when the lights are lit. You must bear with me, Mrs. Bunting, if I seem a little, just a little, unlike the lodgers you have been accustomed to. And I must ask you to understand that I must not be disturbed when thinking out my problems—" He broke off short, sighed, then added solemnly, "for mine are the great problems of life and death."

And Mrs. Bunting willingly fell in with his wishes. In spite of her prim manner and love of order, Mr. Sleuth's landlady was a true woman—she had, that is, an infinite patience with masculine vagaries and oddities.

When she was downstairs again, Mr. Sleuth's landlady met with a surprise; but it was quite a pleasant surprise. While she had been upstairs, talking to the lodger, Bunting's young friend, Joe Chandler, the detective, had come in, and as she walked into the sitting-room she saw that her husband was pushing half a sovereign across the table towards Joe.

Joe Chandler's fair, good-natured face was full of satisfaction: not at seeing his money again, mark you, but at the news Bunting had evidently been telling him—that news of the sudden wonderful change in their fortunes, the coming of an ideal lodger.

"Mr. Sleuth don't want me to do his bedroom till he's gone out!" she exclaimed. And then she sat down for a bit of a rest.

It was a comfort to know that the lodger was eating his good breakfast, and there was no need to think of him for the present. In a few minutes she would be going down to make her own and Bunting's dinner, and she told Joe Chandler that he might as well stop and have a bite with them.

Her heart warmed to the young man, for Mrs. Bunting was in a mood which seldom surprised her—a mood to be pleased with anything and everything. Nay, more. When Bunting began to ask Joe Chandler about the last of those awful Avenger murders, she even listened with a certain languid interest to all he had to say.

In the morning paper which Bunting had begun taking again that very day three columns were devoted to the extraordinary mystery which was now beginning to be the one topic of talk all over London, West and East, North and South. Bunting had read out little bits about it while they ate their breakfast, and in spite of herself Mrs. Bunting had felt thrilled and excited.

"They do say," observed Bunting cautiously, "They do say, Joe, that the police have a clue they won't say nothing about?" He looked expectantly at his visitor. To Bunting the fact that Chandler was attached to the detective section of the Metropolitan Police invested the young man with a kind of sinister glory—especially just now, when these awful and mysterious crimes were amazing and terrifying the town.

"Them who says that says wrong," answered Chandler slowly, and a look of unease, of resentment came over his fair, stolid face. "'Twould make a good bit of difference to me if the Yard had a clue."

And then Mrs. Bunting interposed. "Why that, Joe?" she said, smiling indulgently; the young man's keenness about his work pleased her. And in his slow, sure way Joe Chandler was very keen, and took his job very seriously. He put his whole heart and mind into it.

"Well, 'tis this way," he explained. "From to-day I'm on this business myself. You see, Mrs. Bunting, the Yard's nettled—that's what it is, and we're all on our mettle—that we are. I was right down sorry for the poor chap who was on point duty in the street where the last one happened—"

"No!" said Bunting incredulously. "You don't mean there was a policeman there, within a few yards?"

That fact hadn't been recorded in his newspaper.

Chandler nodded. "That's exactly what I do mean, Mr. Bunting! The man is near off his head, so I'm told. He did hear a yell, so he says, but he took no notice—there are a good few yells in that part o' London, as you can guess. People always quarrelling and rowing at one another in such low parts."

"Have you seen the bits of grey paper on which the monster writes his name?" inquired Bunting eagerly.

Public imagination had been much stirred by the account of those three-cornered pieces of grey paper, pinned to the victims' skirts, on which was roughly written in red ink and in printed characters the words "The Avenger."

His round, fat face was full of questioning eagerness. He put his elbows on the table, and stared across expectantly at the young man.

"Yes, I have," said Joe briefly.

"A funny kind of visiting card, eh!" Bunting laughed; the notion struck him as downright comic.

But Mrs. Bunting coloured. "It isn't a thing to make a joke about," she said reprovingly.

And Chandler backed her up. "No, indeed," he said feelingly. "I'll never forget what I've been made to see over this job. And as for that grey bit of paper, Mr. Bunting—or, rather, those grey bits of paper"—he corrected himself hastily—"you know they've three of them now at the Yard—well, they gives me the horrors!"

And then he jumped up. "That reminds me that I oughtn't to be wasting my time in pleasant company—"

"Won't you stay and have a bit of dinner?" said Mrs. Bunting solicitously.

But the detective shook his head. "No," he said, "I had a bite before I came out. Our job's a queer kind of job, as you know. A lot's left to our discretion, so to speak, but it don't leave us much time for lazing about, I can tell you."

When he reached the door he turned round, and with elaborate carelessness he inquired, "Any chance of Miss Daisy coming to London again soon?"

Bunting shook his head, but his face brightened. He was very, very fond of his only child; the pity was he saw her so seldom. "No," he said, "I'm afraid not Joe. Old Aunt, as we calls the old lady, keeps Daisy pretty tightly tied to her apron-string. She was quite put about that week the child was up with us last June."

"Indeed? Well, so long!"

After his wife had let their friend out, Bunting said cheerfully, "Joe seems to like our Daisy, eh, Ellen?"

But Mrs. Bunting shook her head scornfully. She did not exactly dislike the girl, though she did not hold with the way Bunting's daughter was being managed by that old aunt of hers—an idle, good-for-nothing way, very different from the fashion in which she herself had been trained at the Foundling, for Mrs. Bunting as a little child had known no other home, no other family than those provided by good Captain Coram.[9]

"Joe Chandler's too sensible a young chap to be thinking of girls yet awhile," she said tartly.

"No doubt you're right," Bunting agreed. "Times be changed. In my young days chaps always had time for that. 'Twas just a notion that came into my head, hearing him asking, anxious-like, after her."

About five o'clock, after the street lamps were well alight, Mr. Sleuth went out, and that same evening there came two parcels addressed to his landlady. These parcels contained clothes. But it was quite clear to Mrs. Bunting's eyes that they were not new clothes. In fact, they had evidently been bought in some good second-hand clothes-shop. A funny thing for a real gentleman like Mr. Sleuth to do! It proved that he had given up all hope of getting back his lost luggage.

When the lodger had gone out he had not taken his bag with him, of that Mrs. Bunting was positive. And yet, though she searched high and low for it, she could not find the place where Mr. Sleuth kept it. And at last, had it not been that she was a very clear-headed woman, with a good memory, she would have been disposed to think that the bag had never existed, save in her imagination.

But no, she could not tell herself that! She remembered exactly how it had looked when Mr. Sleuth had first stood, a strange, queer-looking figure of a man, on her doorstep.

She further remembered how he had put the bag down on the floor of the top front room, and then, forgetting what he had done, how he had asked her eagerly, in a tone of angry fear, where the bag was—only to find it safely lodged at his feet!

As time went on Mrs. Bunting thought a great deal about that bag, for, strange and amazing fact, she never saw Mr. Sleuth's bag again. But, of course, she soon formed a theory as to its whereabouts. The brown leather bag which had formed Mr. Sleuth's only luggage the afternoon of his arrival was almost certainly locked up in the lower part of the drawing-room chiffonnier. Mr. Sleuth evidently always carried the key of the little corner cupboard about his person; Mrs. Bunting had also had a good hunt for that key, but, as was the case with the bag, the key disappeared, and she never saw either the one or the other again.

CHAPTER FIVE

How quietly, how uneventfully, how pleasantly, sped the next few days. Already life was settling down into a groove. Waiting on Mr. Sleuth was just what Mrs. Bunting could manage to do easily, and without tiring herself.

It had at once become clear that the lodger preferred to be waited on only by one person, and that person his landlady. He gave her very little trouble. Indeed, it did her good having to wait on the lodger; it even did her good that he was not like other gentlemen; for the fact occupied her mind, and in a way it amused her. The more so that whatever his oddities Mr. Sleuth had none of those tiresome, disagreeable ways with which landladies are only too familiar, and which seem peculiar only to those human beings who also happen to be lodgers. To take but one point: Mr. Sleuth did not ask to be called unduly early. Bunting and his Ellen had fallen into the way of lying rather late in the morning, and it was a great comfort not to have to turn out to make the lodger a cup of tea at seven, or even half-past seven. Mr. Sleuth seldom required anything before eleven.

But odd he certainly was.

The second evening he had been with them Mr. Sleuth had brought in a book of which the queer name was Cruden's Concordance. That and the Bible—Mrs. Bunting had soon discovered that there was a relation between the two books—seemed to be the lodger's only reading. He spent hours each day, generally after he had eaten the breakfast which also served for luncheon, poring over the Old Testament and over that strange kind of index to the Book.

As for the delicate and yet the all-important question of money, Mr. Sleuth was everything—everything that the most exacting landlady could have wished. Never had there been a more confiding or trusting gentleman. On the very first day he had been with them he had allowed his money—the considerable sum of one hundred and eighty-four sovereigns—to lie about wrapped up in little pieces of rather dirty newspaper on his dressing-table. That had quite upset Mrs. Bunting. She had allowed herself respectfully to point out to him that what he was doing was foolish, indeed wrong. But as only answer he had laughed, and she had been startled when the loud, unusual and discordant sound had issued from his thin lips.

"I know those I can trust," he had answered, stuttering rather, as was his way when moved. "And—and I assure you, Mrs. Bunting, that I hardly have to speak to a human being—especially to a woman" (and he had drawn in his breath with a hissing sound) "before I know exactly what manner of person is before me."

It hadn't taken the landlady very long to find out that her lodger had a queer kind of fear and dislike of women. When she was doing the staircase and landings she would often hear Mr. Sleuth reading aloud to himself passages in the Bible that were very uncomplimentary to her sex. But Mrs. Bunting had no very great opinion of her sister woman, so that didn't put her out. Besides, where one's lodger is concerned, a dislike of women is better than—well, than the other thing.

In any case, where would have been the good of worrying about the lodger's funny ways? Of course, Mr. Sleuth was eccentric. If he hadn't been, as Bunting funnily styled it, "just a leetle touched upstairs," he wouldn't be here, living this strange, solitary life in lodgings. He would be living in quite a different sort of way with some of his relatives, or with a friend of his own class.

There came a time when Mrs. Bunting, looking back—as even the least imaginative of us are apt to look back to any part of our own past lives which becomes for any reason poignantly memorable—wondered how soon it was that she had discovered that her lodger was given to creeping out of the house at a time when almost all living things prefer to sleep.

She brought herself to believe—but I am inclined to doubt whether she was right in so believing—that the first time she became aware of this strange nocturnal habit of Mr. Sleuth's happened to be during the night which preceded the day on which she had observed a very curious circumstance. This very curious circumstance was the complete disappearance of one of Mr. Sleuth's three suits of clothes.

It always passes my comprehension how people can remember, over any length of time, not every moment of certain happenings, for that is natural enough, but the day, the hour, the minute when these happenings took place! Much as she thought about it afterwards, even Mrs. Bunting never quite made up her mind whether it was during the fifth or the sixth night of Mr. Sleuth's stay under her roof that she became aware that he had gone out at two in the morning and had only come in at five.

But that there did come such a night is certain—as certain as is the fact that her discovery coincided with various occurrences which were destined to remain retrospectively memorable.

It was intensely dark, intensely quiet—the darkest quietest hour of the night, when suddenly Mrs. Bunting was awakened from a deep, dreamless sleep by sounds at once unexpected and familiar. She knew at once what those sounds were. They were those made by Mr. Sleuth, first coming down the stairs, and walking on tiptoe—she was sure it was on tiptoe— past her door, and finally softly shutting the front door behind him.

Try as she would, Mrs. Bunting found it quite impossible to go to sleep again. There she lay wide awake, afraid to move lest Bunting should waken up too, till she heard Mr. Sleuth, three hours later, creep back into the house and so up to bed.

Then, and not till then, she slept again. But in the morning she felt very tired, so tired indeed, that she had been very glad when Bunting good-naturedly suggested that he should go out and do their little bit of marketing.

The worthy couple had very soon discovered that in the matter of catering it was not altogether an easy matter to satisfy Mr. Sleuth, and that though he always tried to appear pleased. This perfect lodger had one serious fault from the point of view of those who keep lodgings. Strange to say, he was a vegetarian.[10] He would not eat meat in any form. He sometimes, however, condescended to a chicken, and when he did so condescend he generously intimated that Mr. and Mrs. Bunting were welcome to a share in it.

Now to-day—this day of which the happenings were to linger in Mrs. Bunting's mind so very long, and to remain so very vivid, it had been arranged that Mr. Sleuth was to have some fish for his lunch, while what he left was to be "done up" to serve for his simple supper.

Knowing that Bunting would be out for at least an hour, for he was a gregarious soul, and liked to have a gossip in the shops he frequented, Mrs. Bunting rose and dressed in a leisurely manner; then she went and "did" her front sitting-room.

She felt languid and dull, as one is apt to feel after a broken night, and it was a comfort to her to know that Mr. Sleuth was not likely to ring before twelve.

But long before twelve a loud ring suddenly clanged through the quiet house. She knew it for the front door bell.

Mrs. Bunting frowned. No doubt the ring betokened one of those tiresome people who come round for old bottles and such-like fal-lals.

She went slowly, reluctantly to the door. And then her face cleared, for it was that good young chap, Joe Chandler, who stood waiting outside.

He was breathing a little hard, as if he had walked over-quickly through the moist, foggy air.

"Why, Joe?" said Mrs. Bunting wonderingly. "Come in—do! Bunting's out, but he won't be very long now. You've been quite a stranger these last few days."

"Well, you know why, Mrs. Bunting—"

She stared at him for a moment, wondering what he could mean. Then, suddenly she remembered. Why, of course, Joe was on a big job just now—the job of trying to catch The Avenger! Her husband had alluded to the fact again and again when reading out to her little bits from the halfpenny evening paper he was taking again.

She led the way to the sitting-room. It was a good thing Bunting had insisted on lighting the fire before he went out, for now the room was nice and warm—and it was just horrible outside. She had felt a chill go right through her as she had stood, even for that second, at the front door.

And she hadn't been alone to feel it, for, "I say, it is jolly to be in here, out of that awful cold!" exclaimed Chandler, sitting down heavily in Bunting's easy chair.

And then Mrs. Bunting bethought herself that the young man was tired, as well as cold. He was pale, almost pallid under his usual healthy, tanned complexion—the complexion of the man who lives much out of doors.

"Wouldn't you like me just to make you a cup of tea?" she said solicitously.

"Well, to tell truth, I should be right down thankful for one, Mrs. Bunting!" Then he looked round, and again he said her name, "Mrs. Bunting—?"

He spoke in so odd, so thick a tone that she turned quickly. "Yes, what is it, Joe?" she asked. And then, in sudden terror, "You've never come to tell me that anything's happened to Bunting? He's not had an accident?"

"Goodness, no! Whatever made you think that? But—but, Mrs. Bunting, there's been another of them!"

His voice dropped almost to a whisper. He was staring at her with unhappy, it seemed to her terror-filled, eyes.

"Another of them?" She looked at him, bewildered—at a loss. And then what he meant flashed across her—"another of them" meant another of these strange, mysterious, awful murders.

But her relief for the moment was so great—for she really had thought for a second that he had come to give her ill news of Bunting—that the feeling that she did experience on hearing this piece of news was actually pleasurable, though she would have been much shocked had that fact been brought to her notice.

Almost in spite of herself, Mrs. Bunting had become keenly interested in the amazing series of crimes which was occupying the imagination of the whole of London's nether-world. Even her refined mind had busied itself for the last two or three days with the strange problem so frequently presented to it by Bunting—for Bunting, now that they were no longer worried, took an open, unashamed, intense interest in "The Avenger" and his doings.

She took the kettle off the gas-ring. "It's a pity Bunting isn't here," she said, drawing in her breath. "He'd a-liked so much to hear you tell all about it, Joe."

As she spoke she was pouring boiling water into a little teapot.

But Chandler said nothing, and she turned and glanced at him. "Why, you do look bad!" she exclaimed.

And, indeed, the young fellow did look bad—very bad indeed.

"I can't help it," he said, with a kind of gasp. "It was your saying that about my telling you all about it that made me turn queer. You see, this time I was one of the first there, and it fairly turned me sick—that it did. Oh, it was too awful, Mrs. Bunting! Don't talk of it."

He began gulping down the hot tea before it was well made.

She looked at him with sympathetic interest. "Why, Joe," she said, "I never would have thought, with all the horrible sights you see, that anything could upset you like that."

"This isn't like anything there's ever been before," he said. "And then—then—oh, Mrs. Bunting, 'twas I that discovered the piece of paper this time."

"Then it is true," she cried eagerly. "It is The Avenger's bit of paper! Bunting always said it was. He never believed in that practical joker."

"I did," said Chandler reluctantly. "You see, there are some queer fellows even—even—" (he lowered his voice, and looked round him as if the walls had ears)—"even in the Force, Mrs. Bunting, and these murders have fair got on our nerves."

"No, never!" she said. "D'you think that a Bobby might do a thing like that?"[11]

He nodded impatiently, as if the question wasn't worth answering. Then, "It was all along of that bit of paper and my finding it while the poor soul was still warm,"—he shuddered—"that brought me out West this morning. One of our bosses lives close by, in Prince Albert Terrace, and I had to go and tell him all about it. They never offered me a bit or a sup—I think they might have done that, don't you, Mrs. Bunting?"

"Yes," she said absently. "Yes, I do think so."

"But, there, I don't know that I ought to say that," went on Chandler. "He had me up in his dressing-room, and was very considerate-like to me while I was telling him."

"Have a bit of something now?" she said suddenly.

"Oh, no, I couldn't eat anything," he said hastily. "I don't feel as if I could ever eat anything any more."

"That'll only make you ill." Mrs. Bunting spoke rather crossly, for she was a sensible woman. And to please her he took a bite out of the slice of bread-and-butter she had cut for him.

"I expect you're right," he said. "And I've a goodish heavy day in front of me. Been up since four, too—"

"Four?" she said. "Was it then they found—" she hesitated a moment, and then said, "it?"

He nodded. "It was just a chance I was near by. If I'd been half a minute sooner either I or the officer who found her must have knocked up against that—that monster. But two or three people do think they saw him slinking away."

"What was he like?" she asked curiously.

"Well, that's hard to answer. You see, there was such an awful fog. But there's one thing they all agree about. He was carrying a bag—"

"A bag?" repeated Mrs. Bunting, in a low voice. "Whatever sort of bag might it have been, Joe?"

There had come across her—just right in her middle, like—such a strange sensation, a curious kind of tremor, or fluttering.

She was at a loss to account for it.

"Just a hand-bag," said Joe Chandler vaguely. "A woman I spoke to— cross-examining her, like—who was positive she had seen him, said, 'Just a tall, thin shadow—that's what he was, a tall, thin shadow of a man— with a bag.'"

"With a bag?" repeated Mrs. Bunting absently. "How very strange and peculiar—"

"Why, no, not strange at all. He has to carry the thing he does the deed with in something, Mrs. Bunting. We've always wondered how he hid it. They generally throws the knife or fire-arms away, you know."

"Do they, indeed?" Mrs. Bunting still spoke in that absent, wondering way. She was thinking that she really must try and see what the lodger had done with his bag. It was possible—in fact, when one came to think of it, it was very probable—that he had just lost it, being so forgetful a gentleman, on one of the days he had gone out, as she knew he was fond of doing, into the Regent's Park.

"There'll be a description circulated in an hour or two," went on Chandler. "Perhaps that'll help catch him. There isn't a London man or woman, I don't suppose, who wouldn't give a good bit to lay that chap by the heels. Well, I suppose I must be going now."

"Won't you wait a bit longer for Bunting?" she said hesitatingly.

"No, I can't do that. But I'll come in, maybe, either this evening or to-morrow, and tell you any more that's happened. Thanks kindly for the tea. It's made a man of me, Mrs. Bunting."

"Well, you've had enough to unman you, Joe."

"Aye, that I have," he said heavily.

A few minutes later Bunting did come in, and he and his wife had quite a little tiff—the first tiff they had had since Mr. Sleuth became their lodger.

It fell out this way. When he heard who had been there, Bunting was angry that Mrs. Bunting hadn't got more details of the horrible occurrence which had taken place that morning, out of Chandler.

"You don't mean to say, Ellen, that you can't even tell me where it happened?" he said indignantly. "I suppose you put Chandler off—that's what you did! Why, whatever did he come here for, excepting to tell us all about it?"

"He came to have something to eat and drink," snapped out Mrs. Bunting. "That's what the poor lad came for, if you wants to know. He could hardly speak of it at all—he felt so bad. In fact, he didn't say a word about it until he'd come right into the room and sat down. He told me quite enough!"

"Didn't he tell you if the piece of paper on which the murderer had written his name was square or three-cornered?" demanded Bunting.

"No; he did not. And that isn't the sort of thing I should have cared to ask him."

"The more fool you!" And then he stopped abruptly. The newsboys were coming down the Marylebone Road, shouting out the awful discovery which had been made that morning—that of The Avenger's fifth murder. Bunting went out to buy a paper, and his wife took the things he had brought in down to the kitchen.

The noise the newspaper-sellers made outside had evidently wakened Mr. Sleuth, for his landlady hadn't been in the kitchen ten minutes before his bell rang.

CHAPTER SIX

Mr. Sleuth's bell rang again.

Mr. Sleuth's breakfast was quite ready, but for the first time since he had been her lodger Mrs. Bunting did not answer the summons at once. But when there came the second imperative tinkle—for electric bells had not been fitted into that old-fashioned house—she made up her mind to go upstairs.

As she emerged into the hall from the kitchen stairway, Bunting, sitting comfortably in their parlour, heard his wife stepping heavily under the load of the well-laden tray.

"Wait a minute!" he called out. "I'll help you, Ellen," and he came out and took the tray from her.

She said nothing, and together they proceeded up to the drawing-room floor landing.

There she stopped him. "Here," she whispered quickly, "you give me that, Bunting. The lodger won't like your going in to him." And then, as he obeyed her, and was about to turn downstairs again, she added in a rather acid tone, "You might open the door for me, at any rate! How can I manage to do it with this here heavy tray on my hands?"

She spoke in a queer, jerky way, and Bunting felt surprised—rather put out. Ellen wasn't exactly what you'd call a lively, jolly woman, but when things were going well—as now—she was generally equable enough. He supposed she was still resentful of the way he had spoken to her about young Chandler and the new Avenger murder.

However, he was always for peace, so he opened the drawing-room door, and as soon as he had started going downstairs Mrs. Bunting walked into the room.

And then at once there came over her the queerest feeling of relief, of lightness of heart.

As usual, the lodger was sitting at his old place, reading the Bible.

Somehow—she could not have told you why, she would not willingly have told herself—she had expected to see Mr. Sleuth looking different. But no, he appeared to be exactly the same—in fact, as he glanced up at her a pleasanter smile than usual lighted up his thin, pallid face.

"Well, Mrs. Bunting," he said genially, "I overslept myself this morning, but I feel all the better for the rest."

"I'm glad of that, sir," she answered, in a low voice. "One of the ladies I once lived with used to say, 'Rest is an old-fashioned remedy, but it's the best remedy of all.'"

Mr. Sleuth himself removed the Bible and Cruden's Concordance off the table out of her way, and then he stood watching his landlady laying the cloth.

Suddenly he spoke again. He was not often so talkative in the morning. "I think, Mrs. Bunting, that there was someone with you outside the door just now?"

"Yes, sir. Bunting helped me up with the tray."

"I'm afraid I give you a good deal of trouble," he said hesitatingly.

But she answered quickly, "Oh, no, sir! Not at all, sir! I was only saying yesterday that we've never had a lodger that gave us as little trouble as you do, sir."

"I'm glad of that. I am aware that my habits are somewhat peculiar."

He looked at her fixedly, as if expecting her to give some sort of denial to this observation. But Mrs. Bunting was an honest and truthful woman. It never occurred to her to question his statement. Mr. Sleuth's habits were somewhat peculiar. Take that going out at night, or rather in the early morning, for instance? So she remained silent.

After she had laid the lodger's breakfast on the table she prepared to leave the room. "I suppose I'm not to do your room till you goes out, sir?"

And Mr. Sleuth looked up sharply. "No, no!" he said. "I never want my room done when I am engaged in studying the Scriptures, Mrs. Bunting. But I am not going out to-day. I shall be carrying out a somewhat elaborate experiment—upstairs. If I go out at all" he waited a moment, and again he looked at her fixedly "—I shall wait till night-time to do so." And then, coming back to the matter in hand, he added hastily, "Perhaps you could do my room when I go upstairs, about five o'clock—if that time is convenient to you, that is?"

"Oh, yes, sir! That'll do nicely!"

Mrs. Bunting went downstairs, and as she did so she took herself wordlessly, ruthlessly to task, but she did not face—even in her inmost heart—the strange tenors and tremors which had so shaken her. She only repeated to herself again and again, "I've got upset—that's what I've done," and then she spoke aloud, "I must get myself a dose at the chemist's next time I'm out. That's what I must do."[12]

And just as she murmured the word "do," there came a loud double knock on the front door.

It was only the postman's knock, but the postman was an unfamiliar visitor in that house, and Mrs. Bunting started violently. She was nervous,

that's what was the matter with her,—so she told herself angrily. No doubt
this was a letter for Mr. Sleuth; the lodger must have relations and
acquaintances somewhere in the world. All gentlefolk have. But when she
picked the small envelope off the hall floor, she saw it was a letter from
Daisy, her husband's daughter.

"Bunting!" she called out sharply. "Here's a letter for you."

She opened the door of their sitting-room and looked in. Yes, there was
her husband, sitting back comfortably in his easy chair, reading a paper.
And as she saw his broad, rather rounded back, Mrs. Bunting felt a sudden
thrill of sharp irritation. There he was, doing nothing—in fact, doing worse
than nothing—wasting his time reading all about those horrid crimes.

She sighed—a long, unconscious sigh. Bunting was getting into idle
ways, bad ways for a man of his years. But how could she prevent it? He
had been such an active, conscientious sort of man when they had first
made acquaintance...

She also could remember, even more clearly than Bunting did himself,
that first meeting of theirs in the dining-room of No. 90 Cumberland
Terrace. As she had stood there, pouring out her mistress's glass of port
wine, she had not been too much absorbed in her task to have a good out-
of-her-eye look at the spruce, nice, respectable-looking fellow who was
standing over by the window. How superior he had appeared even then to
the man she already hoped he would succeed as butler!

To-day, perhaps because she was not feeling quite herself, the past rose
before her very vividly, and a lump came into her throat.

Putting the letter addressed to her husband on the table, she closed the
door softly, and went down into the kitchen; there were various little
things to put away and clean up, as well as their dinner to cook. And all
the time she was down there she fixed her mind obstinately, determinedly
on Bunting and on the problem of Bunting. She wondered what she'd
better do to get him into good ways again.

Thanks to Mr. Sleuth, their outlook was now moderately bright. A
week ago everything had seemed utterly hopeless. It seemed as if nothing
could save them from disaster. But everything was now changed!

Perhaps it would be well for her to go and see the new proprietor of
that registry office, in Baker Street, which had lately changed hands. It
would be a good thing for Bunting to get even an occasional job—for the
matter of that he could now take up a fairly regular thing in the way of
waiting. Mrs. Bunting knew that it isn't easy to get a man out of idle ways
once he has acquired those ways.

When, at last, she went upstairs again she felt a little ashamed of what she had been thinking, for Bunting had laid the cloth, and laid it very nicely, too, and brought up the two chairs to the table.

"Ellen?" he cried eagerly, "here's news! Daisy's coming to-morrow! There's scarlet fever in their house.[13] Old Aunt thinks she'd better come away for a few days. So, you see, she'll be here for her birthday. Eighteen, that's what she be on the nineteenth! It do make me feel old—that it do!"

Mrs. Bunting put down the tray. "I can't have the girl here just now," she said shortly. "I've just as much to do as I can manage. The lodger gives me more trouble than you seem to think for."

"Rubbish!" he said sharply. "I'll help you with the lodger. It's your own fault you haven't had help with him before. Of course, Daisy must come here. Whatever other place could the girl go to?"

Bunting felt pugnacious—so cheerful as to be almost light-hearted. But as he looked across at his wife his feeling of satisfaction vanished. Ellen's face was pinched and drawn to-day; she looked ill—ill and horribly tired. It was very aggravating of her to go and behave like this—just when they were beginning to get on nicely again.

"For the matter of that," he said suddenly, "Daisy'll be able to help you with the work, Ellen, and she'll brisk us both up a bit."

Mrs. Bunting made no answer. She sat down heavily at the table. And then she said languidly, "You might as well show me the girl's letter."

He handed it across to her, and she read it slowly to herself.

> DEAR FATHER (it ran)—I hope this finds you as well at it leaves me. Mrs. Puddle's youngest has got scarlet fever, and Aunt thinks I had better come away at once, just to stay with you for a few days. Please tell Ellen I won't give her no trouble. I'll start at ten if I don't hear nothing.—Your loving daughter,
>
> Daisy.

"Yes, I suppose Daisy will have to come here," Mrs. Bunting slowly. "It'll do her good to have a bit of work to do for once in her life."

And with that ungraciously worded permission Bunting had to content himself.

Quietly the rest of that eventful day sped by. When dusk fell Mr. Sleuth's landlady heard him go upstairs to the top floor. She remembered that this was the signal for her to go and do his room.

He was a tidy man, was the lodger; he did not throw his things about as so many gentlemen do, leaving them all over the place. No, he kept everything scrupulously tidy. His clothes, and the various articles Mrs. Bunting had bought for him during the first two days he had been there, were carefully arranged in the chest of drawers. He had lately purchased a pair of boots. Those he had arrived in were peculiar-looking footgear, buff leather shoes with rubber soles, and he had told his landlady on that very first day that he never wished them to go down to be cleaned.

A funny idea—a funny habit that, of going out for a walk after midnight in weather so cold and foggy that all other folk were glad to be at home, snug in bed. But then Mr. Sleuth himself admitted that he was a funny sort of gentleman.

After she had done his bedroom the landlady went into the sitting-room and gave it a good dusting. This room was not kept quite as nice as she would have liked it to be. Mrs. Bunting longed to give the drawing-room something of a good turn out; but Mr. Sleuth disliked her to be moving about in it when he himself was in his bedroom; and when up he sat there almost all the time. Delighted as he had seemed to be with the top room, he only used it when making his mysterious experiments, and never during the day-time.

And now, this afternoon, she looked at the rosewood chiffonnier with longing eyes—she even gave that pretty little piece of furniture a slight shake. If only the doors would fly open, as the locked doors of old cupboards sometimes do, even after they have been securely fastened, how pleased she would be, how much more comfortable somehow she would feel!

But the chiffonnier refused to give up its secret.

About eight o'clock on that same evening Joe Chandler came in, just for a few minutes' chat. He had recovered from his agitation of the morning, but he was full of eager excitement, and Mrs. Bunting listened in silence, intensely interested in spite of herself, while he and Bunting talked.

"Yes," he said, "I'm as right as a trivet now! I've had a good rest—laid down all this afternoon. You see, the Yard thinks there's going to be something on to-night. He's always done them in pairs."

"So he has," exclaimed Bunting wonderingly. "So he has! Now, I never thought o' that. Then you think, Joe, that the monster'll be on the job again to-night?"

Chandler nodded. "Yes. And I think there's a very good chance of his being caught too—"

"I suppose there'll be a lot on the watch to-night, eh?"

"I should think there will be! How many of our men d'you think there'll be on night duty to-night, Mr. Bunting?"

Bunting shook his head. "I don't know," he said helplessly.

"I mean extra," suggested Chandler, in an encouraging voice.

"A thousand?" ventured Bunting.

"Five thousand, Mr. Bunting."

"Never!" exclaimed Bunting, amazed.

And even Mrs. Bunting echoed "Never!" incredulously.

"Yes, that there will. You see, the Boss has got his monkey up!" Chandler drew a folded-up newspaper out of his coat pocket. "Just listen to this:

> The police have reluctantly to admit that they have no clue to the perpetrators of these horrible crimes, and we cannot feel any surprise at the information that a popular attack has been organised on the Chief Commissioner of the Metropolitan Police. There is even talk of an indignation mass meeting.

"What d'you think of that? That's not a pleasant thing for a gentleman as is doing his best to read, eh?"

"Well, it does seem queer that the police can't catch him, now doesn't it?" said Bunting argumentatively.

"I don't think it's queer at all," said young Chandler crossly. "Now you just listen again! Here's a bit of the truth for once— in a newspaper." And slowly he read out:

> The detection of crime in London now resembles a game of blind man's buff, in which the detective has his hands tied and his eyes bandaged. Thus is he turned loose to hunt the murderer through the slums of a great city.

"Whatever does that mean?" said Bunting. "Your hands aren't tied, and your eyes aren't bandaged, Joe?"

"It's metaphorical-like that it's intended, Mr. Bunting. We haven't got the same facilities—no, not a quarter of them—that the French 'tecs have."

And then, for the first time, Mrs. Bunting spoke: "What was that word, Joe—'perpetrators'? I mean that first bit you read out."

"Yes," he said, turning to her eagerly.

"Then do they think there's more than one of them?" she said, and a look of relief came over her thin face.

"There's some of our chaps thinks it's a gang," said Chandler. "They say it can't be the work of one man."

"What do you think, Joe?"

"Well, Mrs. Bunting, I don't know what to think. I'm fair puzzled."

He got up. "Don't you come to the door. I'll shut it all right. So long! See you to-morrow, perhaps." As he had done the other evening, Mr. and Mrs. Bunting's visitor stopped at the door. "Any news of Miss Daisy?" he asked casually.

"Yes; she's coming to-morrow," said her father. "They've got scarlet fever at her place. So Old Aunt thinks she'd better clear out."

The husband and wife went to bed early that night, but Mrs. Bunting found she could not sleep. She lay wide awake, hearing the hours, the half-hours, the quarters chime out from the belfry of the old church close by.

And then, just as she was dozing off—it must have been about one o'clock—she heard the sound she had half unconsciously been expecting to hear, that of the lodger's stealthy footsteps coming down the stairs just outside her room.

He crept along the passage and let himself out very, very quietly.

But though she tried to keep awake, Mrs. Bunting did not hear him come in again, for she soon fell into a heavy sleep.

Oddly enough, she was the first to wake the next morning; odder still, it was she, not Bunting, who jumped out of bed, and going out into the passage, picked up the newspaper which had just been pushed through the letter-box.

But having picked it up, Mrs. Bunting did not go back at once into her bedroom. Instead she lit the gas in the passage, and leaning up against the wall to steady herself, for she was trembling with cold and fatigue, she opened the paper.

Yes, there was the heading she sought:

The AVENGER Murders

But, oh, how glad she was to see the words that followed:

Up to the time of going to press there is little new to report concerning the extraordinary series of crimes which are amazing, and, indeed, staggering not only London, but the whole civilised world, and which would seem to be the work of some woman-hating teetotal fanatic. Since yesterday morning, when the last of these dastardly murders was committed, no reliable clue to the perpetrator, or perpetrators, has been obtained, though several arrests were made in the course of the day. In every case, however, those arrested were able to prove a satisfactory alibi.

And then, a little lower down:

The excitement grows and grows. It is not too much to say that even a stranger to London would know that something very unusual was in the air. As for the place where the murder was committed last night—

"Last night!" thought Mrs. Bunting, startled; and then she realised that "last night," in this connection, meant the night before last.

She began the sentence again:

As for the place where the murder was committed last night, all approaches to it were still blocked up to a late hour by hundreds of onlookers, though, of course, nothing now remains in the way of traces of the tragedy.

Slowly and carefully Mrs. Bunting folded the paper up again in its original creases, and then she stooped and put it back down on the mat where she had found it. She then turned out the gas, and going back into bed she lay down by her still sleeping husband.

"Anything the matter?" Bunting murmured, and stirred uneasily. "Anything the matter, Ellen?"

She answered in a whisper, a whisper thrilling with a strange gladness, "No, nothing, Bunting—nothing the matter! Go to sleep again, my dear."

They got up an hour later, both in a happy, cheerful mood. Bunting rejoiced at the thought of his daughter's coming, and even Daisy's stepmother told herself that it would be pleasant having the girl about the house to help her a bit.

About ten o'clock Bunting went out to do some shopping. He brought back with him a nice little bit of pork for Daisy's dinner, and three mince-pies. He even remembered to get some apples for the sauce.

CHAPTER SEVEN

Just as twelve was striking a four-wheeler drew up to the gate.

It brought Daisy—pink-cheeked, excited, laughing-eyed Daisy—a sight to gladden any father's heart.

"Old Aunt said I was to have a cab if the weather was bad," she cried out joyously.

There was a bit of a wrangle over the fare. King's Cross, as all the world knows, is nothing like two miles from the Marylebone Road, but the man clamoured for one and sixpence, and hinted darkly that he had done the young lady a favour in bringing her at all.

While he and Bunting were having words, Daisy, leaving them to it, walked up the flagged path to the door where her stepmother was awaiting her.

As they were exchanging a rather frigid kiss, indeed, 'twas a mere peck on Mrs. Bunting's part, there fell, with startling suddenness, loud cries on the still, cold air. Long-drawn and wailing, they sounded strangely sad as they rose and fell across the distant roar of traffic in the Edgware Road.

"What's that?" exclaimed Bunting wonderingly. "Why, whatever's that?"

The cabman lowered his voice. "Them's 'a-crying out that 'orrible affair at King's Cross. He's done for two of 'em this time! That's what I meant when I said I might 'a got a better fare. I wouldn't say nothink before little missy there, but folk 'ave been coming from all over London the last five or six hours; plenty of toffs, too—but there, there's nothing to see now!"

"What? Another woman murdered last night?"

Bunting felt tremendously thrilled. What had the five thousand constables been about to let such a dreadful thing happen?

The cabman stared at him, surprised. "Two of 'em, I tell yer—within a few yards of one another. He 'ave—got a nerve—But, of course, they was drunk. He 'ave got a down on the drink!"

"Have they caught him?" asked Bunting perfunctorily.

"Lord, no! They'll never catch 'im! It must 'ave happened hours and hours ago—they was both stone cold. One each end of a little passage what ain't used no more. That's why they didn't find 'em before."

The hoarse cries were coming nearer and nearer—two news vendors trying to outshout each other.

"'Orrible discovery near King's Cross!" they yelled exultingly. "The Avenger again!"

And Bunting, with his daughter's large straw hold-all in his hand, ran forward into the roadway and recklessly gave a boy a penny for a halfpenny paper.

He felt very much moved and excited. Somehow his acquaintance with young Joe Chandler made these murders seem a personal affair. He hoped that Chandler would come in soon and tell them all about it, as he had done yesterday morning when he, Bunting, had unluckily been out.

As he walked back into the little hall, he heard Daisy's voice—high, voluble, excited—giving her stepmother a long account of the scarlet fever case, and how at first Old Aunt's neighbours had thought it was not scarlet fever at all, but just nettlerash.

But as Bunting pushed open the door of the sitting-room, there came a note of sharp alarm in his daughter's voice, and he heard her cry, "Why, Ellen, whatever is the matter? You do look bad!" and his wife's muffled answer, "Open the window—do."

"'Orrible discovery near King's Cross—a clue at last!" yelled the newspaper-boys triumphantly.

And then, helplessly, Mrs. Bunting began to laugh. She laughed, and laughed, and laughed, rocking herself to and fro as if in an ecstasy of mirth.

"Why, father, whatever's the matter with her?"

Daisy looked quite scared.

"She's in 'sterics—that's what it is," he said shortly. "I'll just get the water-jug. Wait a minute!"

Bunting felt very put out. Ellen was ridiculous—that's what she was, to be so easily upset.

The lodger's bell suddenly pealed through the quiet house. Either that sound, or maybe the threat of the water-jug, had a magical effect on Mrs. Bunting. She rose to her feet, still shaking all over, but mentally composed.

"I'll go up," she said a little chokingly. "As for you, child, just run down into the kitchen. You'll find a piece of pork roasting in the oven. You might start paring the apples for the sauce."

As Mrs. Bunting went upstairs her legs felt as if they were made of cotton wool. She put out a trembling hand, and clutched at the banister for support. But soon, making a great effort over herself, she began to feel more steady; and after waiting for a few moments on the landing, she knocked at the door of the drawing-room.

Mr. Sleuth's voice answered her from the bedroom. "I'm not well," he called out querulously; "I think I've caught a chill. I should be obliged if you would kindly bring me up a cup of tea, and put it outside my door, Mrs. Bunting."

"Very well, sir."

Mrs. Bunting turned and went downstairs. She still felt queer and giddy, so instead of going into the kitchen, she made the lodger his cup of tea over her sitting-room gas-ring.

During their midday dinner the husband and wife had a little discussion as to where Daisy should sleep. It had been settled that a bed should be made up for her in the top back room, but Mrs. Bunting saw reason to change this plan. "I think 'twould be better if Daisy were to sleep with me, Bunting, and you was to sleep upstairs."

Bunting felt and looked rather surprised, but he acquiesced. Ellen was probably right; the girl would be rather lonely up there, and, after all, they didn't know much about the lodger, though he seemed a respectable gentleman enough.

Daisy was a good-natured girl; she liked London, and wanted to make herself useful to her stepmother. "I'll wash up; don't you bother to come downstairs," she said cheerfully.

Bunting began to walk up and down the room. His wife gave him a furtive glance; she wondered what he was thinking about.

"Didn't you get a paper?" she said at last.

"Yes, of course I did," he answered hastily. "But I've put it away. I thought you'd rather not look at it, as you're that nervous."

Again she glanced at him quickly, furtively, but he seemed just as usual—he evidently meant just what he said and no more.

"I thought they was shouting something in the street—I mean just before I was took bad."

It was now Bunting's turn to stare at his wife quickly and rather furtively. He had felt sure that her sudden attack of queerness, of hysterics—call it what you might—had been due to the shouting outside. She was not the only woman in London who had got the Avenger murders on her nerves. His morning paper said quite a lot of women were afraid to go out alone. Was it possible that the curious way she had been taken just now had had nothing to do with the shouts and excitement outside?

"Don't you know what it was they were calling out?" he asked slowly.

Mrs. Bunting looked across at him. She would have given a very great deal to be able to lie, to pretend that she did not know what those dreadful cries had portended. But when it came to the point she found she could not do so.

"Yes," she said dully. "I heard a word here and there. There's been another murder, hasn't there?"

"Two other murders," he said soberly.[14]

"Two? That's worse news!" She turned so pale—a sallow greenish-white—that Bunting thought she was again going queer.

"Ellen?" he said warningly, "Ellen, now do have a care! I can't think what's come over you about these murders. Turn your mind away from them, do! We needn't talk about them—not so much, that is—"

"But I wants to talk about them," cried Mrs. Bunting hysterically.

The husband and wife were standing, one each side of the table, the man with his back to the fire, the woman with her back to the door.

Bunting, staring across at his wife, felt sadly perplexed and disturbed. She really did seem ill; even her slight, spare figure looked shrunk. For the first time, so he told himself ruefully, Ellen was beginning to look her full age. Her slender hands—she had kept the pretty, soft white hands of the woman who has never done rough work—grasped the edge of the table with a convulsive movement.

Bunting didn't at all like the look of her. "Oh, dear," he said to himself, "I do hope Ellen isn't going to be ill! That would be a to-do just now."

"Tell me about it," she commanded, in a low voice. "Can't you see I'm waiting to hear? Be quick now, Bunting!"

"There isn't very much to tell," he said reluctantly. "There's precious little in this paper, anyway. But the cabman what brought Daisy told me—"

"Well?"

"What I said just now. There's two of 'em this time, and they'd both been drinking heavily, poor creatures."

"Was it where the others was done?" she asked looking at her husband fearfully.

"No," he said awkwardly. "No, it wasn't, Ellen. It was a good bit farther West—in fact, not so very far from here.[15] Near King's Cross—that's how the cabman knew about it, you see. They seems to have been done in a passage which isn't used no more." And then, as he thought his wife's eyes were beginning to look rather funny, he added hastily. "There, that's enough for the present! We shall soon be hearing a lot more about it from Joe Chandler. He's pretty sure to come in some time to-day."

"Then the five thousand constables weren't no use?" said Mrs. Bunting slowly.

She had relaxed her grip of the table, and was standing more upright.

"No use at all," said Bunting briefly. "He is artful and no mistake about it. But wait a minute—" he turned and took up the paper which he had laid aside, on a chair. "Yes they says here that they has a clue."

"A clue, Bunting?" Mrs. Bunting spoke in a soft, weak, die-away voice, and again, stooping somewhat, she grasped the edge of the table.

But her husband was not noticing her now. He was holding the paper close up to his eyes, and he read from it, in a tone of considerable satisfaction:

> It is gratifying to be able to state that the police at last believe they are in possession of a clue which will lead to the arrest of the—

and then Bunting dropped the paper and rushed round the table.

His wife, with a curious sighing moan, had slipped down on to the floor, taking with her the tablecloth as she went. She lay there in what appeared to be a dead faint. And Bunting, scared out of his wits, opened the door and screamed out, "Daisy! Daisy! Come up, child. Ellen's took bad again."

And Daisy, hurrying in, showed an amount of sense and resource which even at this anxious moment roused her fond father's admiration.

"Get a wet sponge, Dad—quick!" she cried, "a sponge,—and, if you've got such a thing, a drop o' brandy. I'll see after her!" And then, after he had got the little medicine flask, "I can't think what's wrong with Ellen," said Daisy wonderingly. "She seemed quite all right when I first came in. She was listening, interested-like, to what I was telling her, and then, suddenly—well, you saw how she was took, father? 'Tain't like Ellen this, is it now?"

"No," he whispered. "No, 'tain't. But you see, child, we've been going through a pretty bad time—worse nor I should ever have let you know of, my dear. Ellen's just feeling it now—that's what it is. She didn't say nothing, for Ellen's a good plucked one, but it's told on her—it's told on her!"

And then Mrs. Bunting, sitting up, slowly opened her eyes, and instinctively put her hand up to her head to see if her hair was all right.

She hadn't really been quite "off." It would have been better for her if she had. She had simply had an awful feeling that she couldn't stand up—more, that she must fall down. Bunting's words touched a most unwonted chord in the poor woman's heart, and the eyes which she opened were full of tears. She had not thought her husband knew how she had suffered during those weeks of starving and waiting.

But she had a morbid dislike of any betrayal of sentiment. To her such betrayal betokened "foolishness," and so all she said was, "There's no need to make a fuss! I only turned over a little queer. I never was right off, Daisy."

Pettishly she pushed away the glass in which Bunting had hurriedly poured a little brandy. "I wouldn't touch such stuff—no, not if I was dying!" she exclaimed.

Putting out a languid hand, she pulled herself up, with the help of the table, on to her feet. "Go down again to the kitchen, child"; but there was a sob, a kind of tremor in her voice.

"You haven't been eating properly, Ellen—that's what's the matter with you," said Bunting suddenly. "Now I come to think of it, you haven't eat half enough these last two days. I always did say—in old days many a time I telled you—that a woman couldn't live on air. But there, you never believed me!"

Daisy stood looking from one to the other, a shadow over her bright, pretty face. "I'd no idea you'd had such a bad time, father," she said feelingly. "Why didn't you let me know about it? I might have got something out of Old Aunt."

"We didn't want anything of that sort," said her stepmother hastily. "But of course—well, I expect I'm still feeling the worry now. I don't seem able to forget it. Those days of waiting, of—of—" she restrained herself; another moment and the word "starving" would have left her lips.

"But everything's all right now," said Bunting eagerly, "all right, thanks to Mr. Sleuth, that is."

"Yes," repeated his wife, in a low, strange tone of voice. "Yes, we're all right now, and as you say, Bunting, it's all along of Mr. Sleuth." She walked across to a chair and sat down on it. "I'm just a little tottery still," she muttered.

And Daisy, looking at her, turned to her father and said in a whisper, but not so low but that Mrs. Bunting heard her, "Don't you think Ellen ought to see a doctor, father? He might give her something that would pull her round."

"I won't see no doctor!" said Mrs. Bunting with sudden emphasis. "I saw enough of doctors in my last place. Thirty-eight doctors in ten months did my poor missis have. Just determined on having 'em she was! Did they save her? No! She died just the same! Maybe a bit sooner."

"She was a freak, was your last mistress, Ellen," began Bunting aggressively.

Ellen had insisted on staying on in that place till her poor mistress died. They might have been married some months before they were married but for that fact. Bunting had always resented it.

His wife smile wanly. "We won't have no words about that," she said, and again she spoke in a softer, kindlier tone than usual. "Daisy? If you won't go down to the kitchen again, then I must"—she turned to her stepdaughter, and the girl flew out of the room.

"I think the child grows prettier every minute," said Bunting fondly.

"Folks are too apt to forget that beauty is but skin deep," said his wife. She was beginning to feel better. "But still, I do agree, Bunting, that Daisy's well enough. And she seems more willing, too."

"I say, we mustn't forget the lodger's dinner," Bunting spoke uneasily. "It's a bit of fish to-day, isn't it? Hadn't I better just tell Daisy to see to it, and then I can take it up to him, as you're not feeling quite the thing, Ellen?"

"I'm quite well enough to take up Mr. Sleuth's luncheon," she said quickly. It irritated her to hear her husband speak of the lodger's dinner. They had dinner in the middle of the day, but Mr. Sleuth had luncheon. However odd he might be, Mrs. Bunting never forgot her lodger was a gentleman.

"After all, he likes me to wait on him, doesn't he? I can manage all right. Don't you worry," she added after a long pause.

CHAPTER EIGHT

Perhaps because his luncheon was served to him a good deal later than usual, Mr. Sleuth ate his nice piece of steamed sole upstairs with far heartier an appetite than his landlady had eaten her nice slice of roast pork downstairs.

"I hope you're feeling a little better, sir," Mrs. Bunting had forced herself to say when she first took in his tray.

And he had answered plaintively, querulously, "No, I can't say I feel well to-day, Mrs. Bunting. I am tired—very tired. And as I lay in bed I seemed to hear so many sounds—so much crying and shouting. I trust the Marylebone Road is not going to become a noisy thoroughfare, Mrs. Bunting?"

"Oh, no, sir, I don't think that. We're generally reckoned very quiet indeed, sir."

She waited a moment—try as she would, she could not allude to what those unwonted shouts and noises had betokened. "I expect you've got a chill, sir," she said suddenly. "If I was you, I shouldn't go out this afternoon; I'd just stay quietly indoors. There's a lot of rough people about—" Perhaps there was an undercurrent of warning, of painful pleading, in her toneless voice which penetrated in some way to the brain of the lodger, for Mr. Sleuth looked up, and an uneasy, watchful look came into his luminous grey eyes.

"I'm sorry to hear that, Mrs. Bunting. But I think I'll take your advice. That is, I will stay quietly at home, I am never at a loss to know what to do with myself so long as I can study the Book of Books."

"Then you're not afraid about your eyes, sir?" said Mrs. Bunting curiously. Somehow she was beginning to feel better. It comforted her to be up here, talking to Mr. Sleuth, instead of thinking about him downstairs. It seemed to banish the terror which filled her soul—aye, and her body, too—at other times. When she was with him Mr. Sleuth was so gentle, so reasonable, so—so grateful.

Poor kindly, solitary Mr. Sleuth! This kind of gentleman surely wouldn't hurt a fly, let alone a human being. Eccentric—so much must be admitted. But Mrs. Bunting had seen a good deal of eccentric folk, eccentric women rather than eccentric men, in her long career as useful maid.

Being at ordinary times an exceptionally sensible, well-balanced
woman, she had never, in old days, allowed her mind to dwell on certain
things she had learnt as to the aberrations of which human nature is
capable—even well-born, well-nurtured, gentle human nature—as
exemplified in some of the households where she had served. It would,
indeed, be unfortunate if she now became morbid or—or hysterical.

So it was in a sharp, cheerful voice, almost the voice in which she had
talked during the first few days of Mr. Sleuth's stay in her house, that she
exclaimed, "Well, sir, I'll be up again to clear away in about half an hour.
And if you'll forgive me for saying so, I hope you will stay in and have a
rest to-day. Nasty, muggy weather—that's what it is! If there's any little
thing you want, me or Bunting can go out and get it."

It must have been about four o'clock when there came a ring at the front
door.

The three were sitting chatting together, for Daisy had washed up—she
really was saving her stepmother a good bit of trouble—and the girl was
now amusing her elders by a funny account of Old Aunt's pernickety
ways.

"Whoever can that be?" said Bunting, looking up. "It's too early for
Joe Chandler, surely."

"I'll go," said his wife, hurriedly jumping up from her chair. "I'll go!
We don't want no strangers in here."

And as she stepped down the short bit of passage she said to herself,
"A clue? What clue?"

But when she opened the front door a glad sigh of relief broke from
her. "Why, Joe? We never thought 'twas you! But you're very welcome,
I'm sure. Come in."

And Chandler came in, a rather sheepish look on his good-looking, fair
young face.

"I thought maybe that Mr. Bunting would like to know—" he began, in
a loud, cheerful voice, and Mrs. Bunting hurriedly checked him. She
didn't want the lodger upstairs to hear what young Chandler might be
going to say.

"Don't talk so loud," she said a little sharply. "The lodger is not very
well to-day. He's had a cold," she added hastily, "and during the last two
or three days he hasn't been able to go out."

She wondered at her temerity, her—her hypocrisy, and that moment,
those few words, marked an epoch in Ellen Bunting's life. It was the first
time she had told a bold and deliberate lie. She was one of those women—

there are many, many such—to whom there is a whole world of difference between the suppression of the truth and the utterance of an untruth.

But Chandler paid no heed to her remarks. "Has Miss Daisy arrived?" he asked, in a lower voice.

She nodded. And then he went through into the room where the father and daughter were sitting.

"Well?" said Bunting, starting up. "Well, Joe? Now you can tell us all about that mysterious clue. I suppose it'd be too good news to expect you to tell us they've caught him?"

"No fear of such good news as that yet awhile. If they'd caught him," said Joe ruefully, "well, I don't suppose I should be here, Mr. Bunting. But the Yard are circulating a description at last. And—well, they've found his weapon!"

"No?" cried Bunting excitedly. "You don't say so! Whatever sort of a thing is it? And are they sure 'tis his?"

"Well, 'tain't sure, but it seems to be likely."

Mrs. Bunting had slipped into the room and shut the door behind her. But she was still standing with her back against the door, looking at the group in front of her. None of them were thinking of her—she thanked God for that! She could hear everything that was said without joining in the talk and excitement.

"Listen to this!" cried Joe Chandler exultantly. "'Tain't given out yet—not for the public, that is—but we was all given it by eight o'clock this morning. Quick work that, eh?" He read out:

WANTED

A man, of age approximately 28, slight in figure, height approximately 5 ft. 8 in. Complexion dark. No beard or whiskers. Wearing a black diagonal coat, hard felt hat, high white collar, and tie. Carried a newspaper parcel. Very respectable appearance.

Mrs. Bunting walked forward. She gave a long, fluttering sigh of unutterable relief.

"There's the chap!" said Joe Chandler triumphantly. "And now, Miss Daisy"—he turned to her jokingly, but there was a funny little tremor in his frank, cheerful-sounding voice—"if you knows of any nice, likely young fellow that answers to that description—well, you've only got to walk in and earn your reward of five hundred pounds."

"Five hundred pounds!" cried Daisy and her father simultaneously.

"Yes. That's what the Lord Mayor offered yesterday. Some private bloke—nothing official about it. But we of the Yard is barred from taking that reward, worse luck. And it's too bad, for we has all the trouble, after all."

"Just hand that bit of paper over, will you?" said Bunting. "I'd like to con it over to myself."

Chandler threw over the bit of flimsy.

A moment later Bunting looked up and handed it back. "Well, it's clear enough, isn't it?"

"Yes. And there's hundreds—nay, thousands—of young fellows that might be a description of," said Chandler sarcastically. "As a pal of mine said this morning, 'There isn't a chap will like to carry a newspaper parcel after this.' And it won't do to have a respectable appearance—eh?"

Daisy's voice rang out in merry, pealing laughter. She greatly appreciated Mr. Chandler's witticism.

"Why on earth didn't the people who saw him try and catch him?" asked Bunting suddenly.

And Mrs. Bunting broke in, in a lower voice, "Yes, Joe—that seems odd, don't it?"

Joe Chandler coughed. "Well, it's this way," he said. "No one person did see all that. The man who's described here is just made up from the description of two different folk who think they saw him. You see, the murders must have taken place—well, now, let me see—perhaps at two o'clock this last time. Two o'clock—that's the idea. Well, at such a time as that not many people are about, especially on a foggy night. Yes, one woman declares she saw a young chap walking away from the spot where 'twas done; and another one—but that was a good bit later—says The Avenger passed by her. It's mostly her they're following in this 'ere description. And then the boss who has charge of that sort of thing looked up what other people had said—I mean when the other crimes was committed. That's how he made up this 'Wanted.'"

"Then The Avenger may be quite a different sort of man?" said Bunting slowly, disappointedly.

"Well, of course he may be. But, no; I think that description fits him all right," said Chandler; but he also spoke in a hesitating voice.

"You was saying, Joe, that they found a weapon?" observed Bunting insinuatingly.

He was glad that Ellen allowed the discussion to go on—in fact, that she even seemed to take an intelligent interest in it. She had come up close to them, and now looked quite her old self again.

"Yes. They believe they've found the weapon what he does his awful deeds with," said Chandler. "At any rate, within a hundred yards of that little dark passage where they found the bodies—one at each end, that

was—there was discovered this morning a very peculiar kind o' knife—
'keen as a razor, pointed as a dagger'— that's the exact words the boss
used when he was describing it to a lot of us. He seemed to think a lot
more of that clue than of the other—I mean than of the description people
gave of the chap who walked quickly by with a newspaper parcel. But now
there's a pretty job in front of us. Every shop where they sell or might a'
sold, such a thing as that knife, including every eating-house in the East
End, has got to be called at!"

"Whatever for?" asked Daisy.

"Why, with an idea of finding out if anyone saw such a knife fooling
about there any time, and, if so, in whose possession it was at the time.
But, Mr. Bunting"—Chandler's voice changed; it became businesslike,
official—"they're not going to say anything about that—not in
newspapers—till to-morrow, so don't you go and tell anybody. You see,
we don't want to frighten the fellow off. If he knew they'd got his knife—
well, he might just make himself scarce, and they don't want that! If it's
discovered that any knife of that kind was sold, say a month ago, to some
customer whose ways are known, then—then—"

"What'll happen then?" said Mrs. Bunting, coming nearer.

"Well, then, nothing'll be put about it in the papers at all," said
Chandler deliberately. "The only objec' of letting the public know about it
would be if nothink was found—I mean if the search of the shops, and so
on, was no good. Then, of course, we must try and find out someone—
some private person-like, who's watched that knife in the criminal's
possession. It's there the reward—the five hundred pounds will come in."

"Oh, I'd give anything to see that knife!" exclaimed Daisy, clasping
her hands together.

"You cruel, bloodthirsty, girl!" cried her stepmother passionately.

They all looked round at her, surprised.

"Come, come, Ellen!" said Bunting reprovingly.

"Well, it is a horrible idea!" said his wife sullenly. "To go and sell a
fellow-being for five hundred pounds."

But Daisy was offended. "Of course I'd like to see it!" she cried
defiantly. "I never said nothing about the reward. That was Mr. Chandler
said that! I only said I'd like to see the knife."

Chandler looked at her soothingly. "Well, the day may come when you
will see it," he said slowly.

A great idea had come into his mind.

"No! What makes you think that?"

"If they catches him, and if you comes along with me to see our Black
Museum at the Yard,[16] you'll certainly see the knife, Miss Daisy. They

keeps all them kind of things there. So if, as I say, this weapon should lead to the conviction of The Avenger—well, then, that knife 'ull be there, and you'll see it!"

"The Black Museum? Why, whatever do they have a museum in your place for?" asked Daisy wonderingly. "I thought there was only the British Museum—"

And then even Mrs. Bunting, as well as Bunting and Chandler, laughed aloud.

"You are a goosey girl!" said her father fondly. "Why, there's a lot of museums in London; the town's thick with 'em. Ask Ellen there. She and me used to go to them kind of places when we was courting—if the weather was bad."

"But our museum's the one that would interest Miss Daisy," broke in Chandler eagerly. "It's a regular Chamber of 'Orrors!"

"Why, Joe, you never told us about that place before," said Bunting excitedly. "D'you really mean that there's a museum where they keeps all sorts of things connected with crimes? Things like knives murders have been committed with?"

"Knives?" cried Joe, pleased at having become the centre of attention, for Daisy had also fixed her blue eyes on him, and even Mrs. Bunting looked at him expectantly. "Much more than knives, Mr. Bunting! Why, they've got there, in little bottles, the real poison what people have been done away with."

"And can you go there whenever you like?" asked Daisy wonderingly. She had not realised before what extraordinary and agreeable privileges are attached to the position of a detective member of the London Police Force.

"Well, I suppose I could—" Joe smiled. "Anyway I can certainly get leave to take a friend there." He looked meaningly at Daisy, and Daisy looked eagerly at him.

But would Ellen ever let her go out by herself with Mr. Chandler? Ellen was so prim, so—so irritatingly proper. But what was this father was saying? "D'you really mean that, Joe?"

"Yes, of course I do!"

"Well, then, look here! If it isn't asking too much of a favour, I should like to go along there with you very much one day. I don't want to wait till The Avenger's caught"—Bunting smiled broadly. "I'd be quite content as it is with what there is in that museum o' yours. Ellen, there,"—he looked across at his wife—"don't agree with me about such things. Yet I don't think I'm a bloodthirsty man! But I'm just terribly interested in all that sort of thing—always have been. I used to positively envy the butler in that Balham Mystery!"[17]

Again a look passed between Daisy and the young man—it was a look which contained and carried a great many things backwards and forwards, such as—"Now, isn't it funny that your father should want to go to such a place? But still, I can't help it if he does want to go, so we must put up with his company, though it would have been much nicer for us to go just by our two selves." And then Daisy's look answered quite as plainly, though perhaps Joe didn't read her glance quite as clearly as she had read his: "Yes, it is tiresome. But father means well; and 'twill be very pleasant going there, even if he does come too."

"Well, what d'you say to the day after to-morrow, Mr. Bunting? I'd call for you here about—shall we say half-past two?—and just take you and Miss Daisy down to the Yard. 'Twouldn't take very long; we could go all the way by bus, right down to Westminster Bridge." He looked round at his hostess: "Wouldn't you join us, Mrs. Bunting? 'Tis truly a wonderful interesting place."

But his hostess shook her head decidedly. "'Twould turn me sick," she exclaimed, "to see the bottle of poison what had done away with the life of some poor creature! And as for knives—!" a look of real horror, of startled fear, crept over her pale face.

"There, there!" said Bunting hastily. "Live and let live—that's what I always say. Ellen ain't on in this turn. She can just stay at home and mind the cat—I beg his pardon, I mean the lodger!"

"I won't have Mr. Sleuth laughed at," said Mrs. Bunting darkly. "But there! I'm sure it's very kind of you, Joe, to think of giving Bunting and Daisy such a rare treat"—she spoke sarcastically, but none of the three who heard her understood that.

CHAPTER NINE

The moment she passed though the great arched door which admits the stranger to that portion of New Scotland Yard where throbs the heart of that great organism which fights the forces of civilised crime, Daisy Bunting felt that she had indeed become free of the Kingdom of Romance. Even the lift in which the three of them were whirled up to one of the upper floors of the huge building was to the girl a new and delightful experience. Daisy had always lived a simple, quiet life in the little country town where dwelt Old Aunt and this was the first time a lift had come her way.

With a touch of personal pride in the vast building, Joe Chandler marched his friends down a wide, airy corridor.

Daisy clung to her father's arm, a little bewildered, a little oppressed by her good fortune. Her happy young voice was stilled by the awe she felt at the wonderful place where she found herself, and by the glimpses she caught of great rooms full of busy, silent men engaged in unravelling—or so she supposed—the mysteries of crime.

They were passing a half-open door when Chandler suddenly stopped short. "Look in there," he said, in a low voice, addressing the father rather than the daughter, "that's the Finger-Print Room.[18] We've records here of over two hundred thousand men's and women's finger-tips! I expect you know, Mr. Bunting, as how, once we've got the print of a man's five finger-tips, well, he's done for—if he ever does anything else, that is. Once we've got that bit of him registered he can't never escape us—no, not if he tries ever so. But though there's nigh on a quarter of a million records in there, yet it don't take—well, not half an hour, for them to tell whether any particular man has ever been convicted before! Wonderful thought, ain't it?"

"Wonderful!" said Bunting, drawing a deep breath. And then a troubled look came over his stolid face. "Wonderful, but also a very fearful thought for the poor wretches as has got their finger-prints in, Joe."

Joe laughed. "Agreed!" he said. "And the cleverer ones knows that only too well. Why, not long ago, one man who knew his record was here safe, managed to slash about his fingers something awful, just so as to make a blurred impression—you takes my meaning? But there, at the end of six weeks the skin grew all right again, and in exactly the same little creases as before!"

"Poor devil!" said Bunting under his breath, and a cloud even came over Daisy's bright eager face.

They were now going along a narrower passage, and then again they came to a half-open door, leading into a room far smaller than that of the Finger-Print Identification Room.

"If you'll glance in there," said Joe briefly, "you'll see how we finds out all about any man whose finger-tips has given him away, so to speak. It's here we keeps an account of what he's done, his previous convictions, and so on. His finger-tips are where I told you, and his record in there— just connected by a number."

"Wonderful!" said Bunting, drawing in his breath. But Daisy was longing to get on—to get to the Black Museum. All this that Joe and her father were saying was quite unreal to her, and, for the matter of that not worth taking the trouble to understand. However, she had not long to wait.

A broad-shouldered, pleasant-looking young fellow, who seemed on very friendly terms with Joe Chandler, came forward suddenly, and, unlocking a common-place-looking door, ushered the little party of three through into the Black Museum.

For a moment there came across Daisy a feeling of keen disappointment and surprise. This big, light room simply reminded her of what they called the Science Room in the public library of the town where she lived with Old Aunt. Here, as there, the centre was taken up with plain glass cases fixed at a height from the floor which enabled their contents to be looked at closely.

She walked forward and peered into the case nearest the door. The exhibits shown there were mostly small, shabby-looking little things, the sort of things one might turn out of an old rubbish cupboard in an untidy house—old medicine bottles, a soiled neckerchief, what looked like a child's broken lantern, even a box of pills…

As for the walls, they were covered with the queerest-looking objects; bits of old iron, odd-looking things made of wood and leather, and so on.

It was really rather disappointing.

Then Daisy Bunting gradually became aware that standing on a shelf just below the first of the broad, spacious windows which made the great room look so light and shadowless, was a row of life-size white plaster heads, each head slightly inclined to the right. There were about a dozen of these, not more—and they had such odd, staring, helpless, real-looking faces.

"Whatever's those?" asked Bunting in a low voice.

Daisy clung a thought closer to her father's arm. Even she guessed that these strange, pathetic, staring faces were the death-masks of those men and women who had fulfilled the awful law which ordains that the murderer shall be, in his turn, done to death.

"All hanged!" said the guardian of the Black Museum briefly. "Casts taken after death."

Bunting smiled nervously. "They don't look dead somehow. They looks more as if they were listening," he said.

"That's the fault of Jack Ketch," said the man facetiously.[19] "It's his idea—that of knotting his patient's necktie under the left ear! That's what he does to each of the gentlemen to whom he has to act valet on just one occasion only. It makes them lean just a bit to one side. You look here—?"

Daisy and her father came a little closer, and the speaker pointed with his finger to a little dent imprinted on the left side of each neck; running from this indentation was a curious little furrow, well ridged above, showing how tightly Jack Ketch's necktie had been drawn when its wearer was hurried through the gates of eternity.

"They looks foolish-like, rather than terrified, or—or hurt," said Bunting wonderingly.

He was extraordinarily moved and fascinated by those dumb, staring faces.

But young Chandler exclaimed in a cheerful, matter-of-fact voice, "Well, a man would look foolish at such a time as that, with all his plans brought to naught—and knowing he's only got a second to live—now wouldn't he?"

"Yes, I suppose he would," said Bunting slowly.

Daisy had gone a little pale. The sinister, breathless atmosphere of the place was beginning to tell on her. She now began to understand that the shabby little objects lying there in the glass case close to her were each and all links in the chain of evidence which, in almost every case, had brought some guilty man or woman to the gallows.

"We had a yellow gentleman here the other day," observed the guardian suddenly; "one of those Brahmins—so they calls themselves. Well, you'd a been quite surprised to see how that heathen took on! He declared—what was the word he used?"—he turned to Chandler.

"He said that each of these things, with the exception of the casts, mind you—queer to say, he left them out—exuded evil, that was the word he used! Exuded—squeezed out it means. He said that being here made him feel very bad. And twasn't all nonsense either. He turned quite green under his yellow skin, and we had to shove him out quick. He didn't feel better till he'd got right to the other end of the passage!"

"There now! Who'd ever think of that?" said Bunting. "I should say that man 'ud got something on his conscience, wouldn't you?"

"Well, I needn't stay now," said Joe's good-natured friend. "You show your friends round, Chandler. You knows the place nearly as well as I do, don't you?"

He smiled at Joe's visitors, as if to say good-bye, but it seemed that he could not tear himself away after all.

"Look here," he said to Bunting. "In this here little case are the tools of Charles Peace.[20] I expect you've heard of him."

"I should think I have!" cried Bunting eagerly.

"Many gents as comes here thinks this case the most interesting of all. Peace was such a wonderful man! A great inventor they say he would have been, had he been put in the way of it. Here's his ladder; you see it folds up quite compactly, and makes a nice little bundle—just like a bundle of old sticks any man might have been seen carrying about London in those days without attracting any attention. Why, it probably helped him to look like an honest working man time and time again, for on being arrested he declared most solemnly he'd always carried that ladder openly under his arm."

"The daring of that!" cried Bunting.

"Yes, and when the ladder was opened out it could reach from the ground to the second storey of any old house. And, oh! how clever he was! Just open one section, and you see the other sections open automatically; so Peace could stand on the ground and force the thing quietly up to any window he wished to reach. Then he'd go away again, having done his job, with a mere bundle of old wood under his arm! My word, he was artful! I wonder if you've heard the tale of how Peace once lost a finger. Well, he guessed the constables were instructed to look out for a man missing a finger; so what did he do?"

"Put on a false finger," suggested Bunting.

"No, indeed! Peace made up his mind just to do without a hand altogether. Here's his false stump: you see, it's made of wood—wood and black felt? Well, that just held his hand nicely. Why, we considers that one of the most ingenious contrivances in the whole museum."

Meanwhile, Daisy had let go her hold of her father. With Chandler in delighted attendance, she had moved away to the farther end of the great room, and now she was bending over yet another glass case. "Whatever are those little bottles for?" she asked wonderingly.

There were five small phials, filled with varying quantities of cloudy liquids.

"They're full of poison, Miss Daisy, that's what they are. There's enough arsenic in that little whack o' brandy to do for you and me—aye, and for your father as well, I should say."

"Then chemists shouldn't sell such stuff," said Daisy, smiling. Poison was so remote from herself, that the sight of these little bottles only brought a pleasant thrill.

"No more they don't. That was sneaked out of a flypaper, that was. Lady said she wanted a cosmetic for her complexion, but what she was really going for was flypapers for to do away with her husband. She'd got a bit tired of him, I suspect."

"Perhaps he was a horrid man, and deserved to be done away with," said Daisy. The idea struck them both as so very comic that they began to laugh aloud in unison.

"Did you ever hear what a certain Mrs. Pearce did?"[21] asked Chandler, becoming suddenly serious.

"Oh, yes," said Daisy, and she shuddered a little. "That was the wicked, wicked woman what killed a pretty little baby and its mother. They've got her in Madame Tussaud's.[22] But Ellen, she won't let me go to the Chamber of Horrors. She wouldn't let father take me there last time I was in London. Cruel of her, I called it. But somehow I don't feel as if I wanted to go there now, after having been here!"

"Well," said Chandler slowly, "we've a case full of relics of Mrs. Pearce. But the pram the bodies were found in, that's at Madame Tussaud's—at least so they claim, I can't say. Now here's something just as curious, and not near so dreadful. See that man's jacket there?"

"Yes," said Daisy falteringly. She was beginning to feel oppressed, frightened. She no longer wondered that the Indian gentleman had been taken queer.

"A burglar shot a man dead who'd disturbed him, and by mistake he went and left that jacket behind him. Our people noticed that one of the buttons was broken in two. Well, that don't seem much of a clue, does it, Miss Daisy? Will you believe me when I tells you that that other bit of button was discovered, and that it hanged the fellow? And 'twas the more wonderful because all three buttons was different!"

Daisy stared wonderingly, down at the little broken button which had hung a man. "And whatever's that!" she asked, pointing to a piece of dirty-looking stuff.

"Well," said Chandler reluctantly, "that's rather a horrible thing—that is. That's a bit o' shirt that was buried with a woman—buried in the ground, I mean—after her husband had cut her up and tried, to burn her. 'Twas that bit o' shirt that brought him to the gallows."

"I considers your museum's a very horrid place!" said Daisy pettishly, turning away.

She longed to be out in the passage again, away from this brightly lighted, cheerful-looking, sinister room.

But her father was now absorbed in the case containing various types of infernal machines. "Beautiful little works of art some of them are," said his guide eagerly, and Bunting could not but agree.

"Come along—do, father!" said Daisy quickly. "I've seen about enough now. If I was to stay in here much longer it 'ud give me the horrors. I don't want to have no nightmares to-night. It's dreadful to think there are so many wicked people in the world. Why, we might knock up against some murderer any minute without knowing it, mightn't we?"

"Not you, Miss Daisy," said Chandler smilingly. "I don't suppose you'll ever come across even a common swindler, let alone anyone who's committed a murder—not one in a million does that. Why, even I have never had anything to do with a proper murder case!"

But Bunting was in no hurry. He was thoroughly enjoying every moment of the time. Just now he was studying intently the various photographs which hung on the walls of the Black Museum; especially was he pleased to see those connected with a famous and still mysterious case which had taken place not long before in Scotland, and in which the servant of the man who died had played a considerable part—not in elucidating, but in obscuring, the mystery.

"I suppose a good many murderers get off?" he said musingly.

And Joe Chandler's friend nodded. "I should think they did!" he exclaimed. "There's no such thing as justice here in England. 'Tis odds on the murderer every time. 'Tisn't one in ten that come to the end he should do—to the gallows, that is."

"And what d'you think about what's going on now—I mean about those Avenger murders?"

Bunting lowered his voice, but Daisy and Chandler were already moving towards the door.

"I don't believe he'll ever be caught," said the other confidentially. "In some ways 'tis a lot more of a job to catch a madman than 'tis to run down just an ordinary criminal. And, of course—leastways to my thinking—The Avenger is a madman—one of the cunning, quiet sort. Have you heard about the letter?" his voice dropped lower.[23]

"No," said Bunting, staring eagerly at him. "What letter d'you mean?"

"Well, there's a letter—it'll be in this museum some day—which came just before that last double event. 'Twas signed 'The Avenger,' in just the same printed characters as on that bit of paper he always leaves behind him. Mind you, it don't follow that it actually was The Avenger what sent that letter here, but it looks uncommonly like it, and I know that the Boss attaches quite a lot of importance to it."

"And where was it posted?" asked Bunting. "That might be a bit of a clue, you know."

"Oh, no," said the other. "They always goes a very long way to post anything—criminals do. It stands to reason they would. But this particular one was put in the Edgware Road Post Office."

"What? Close to us?" said Bunting. "Goodness! dreadful!"

"Any of us might knock up against him any minute. I don't suppose The Avenger's in any way peculiar-looking—in fact we know he ain't."

"Then you think that woman as says she saw him did see him?" asked Bunting hesitatingly.

"Our description was made up from what she said," answered the other cautiously. "But, there, you can't tell! In a case like that it's groping—groping in the dark all the time—and it's just a lucky accident if it comes out right in the end. Of course, it's upsetting us all very much here. You can't wonder at that!"

"No, indeed," said Bunting quickly. "I give you my word, I've hardly thought of anything else for the last month."

Daisy had disappeared, and when her father joined her in the passage she was listening, with downcast eyes, to what Joe Chandler was saying.

He was telling her about his real home, of the place where his mother lived, at Richmond—that it was a nice little house, close to the park. He was asking her whether she could manage to come out there one afternoon, explaining that his mother would give them tea, and how nice it would be.

"I don't see why Ellen shouldn't let me," the girl said rebelliously. "But she's that old-fashioned and pernickety is Ellen—a regular old maid! And, you see, Mr. Chandler, when I'm staying with them, father don't like for me to do anything that Ellen don't approve of. But she's got quite fond of you, so perhaps if you ask her—?" She looked at him, and he nodded sagely.

"Don't you be afraid," he said confidently. "I'll get round Mrs. Bunting. But, Miss Daisy"—he grew very red—"I'd just like to ask you a question—no offence meant—"

"Yes?" said Daisy a little breathlessly. "There's father close to us, Mr. Chandler. Tell me quick; what is it?"

"Well, I take it, by what you said just now, that you've never walked out with any young fellow?"

Daisy hesitated a moment; then a very pretty dimple came into her cheek. "No," she said sadly. "No, Mr. Chandler, that I have not." In a burst of candour she added, "You see, I never had the chance!"

And Joe Chandler smiled, well pleased.

CHAPTER TEN

By what she regarded as a fortunate chance, Mrs. Bunting found herself for close on an hour quite alone in the house during her husband's and Daisy's jaunt with young Chandler.

Mr. Sleuth did not often go out in the daytime, but on this particular afternoon, after he had finished his tea, when dusk was falling, he suddenly observed that he wanted a new suit of clothes, and his landlady eagerly acquiesced in his going out to purchase it.

As soon as he had left the house, she went quickly up to the drawing-room floor. Now had come her opportunity of giving the two rooms a good dusting; but Mrs. Bunting knew well, deep in her heart, that it was not so much the dusting of Mr. Sleuth's sitting-room she wanted to do—as to engage in a vague search for—she hardly knew for what.

During the years she had been in service Mrs. Bunting had always had a deep, wordless contempt for those of her fellow-servants who read their employers' private letters, and who furtively peeped into desks and cupboards in the hope, more vague than positive, of discovering family skeletons.

But now, with regard to Mr. Sleuth, she was ready, aye, eager, to do herself what she had once so scorned others for doing.

Beginning with the bedroom, she started on a methodical search. He was a very tidy gentleman was the lodger, and his few things, under-garments, and so on, were in apple-pie order. She had early undertaken, much to his satisfaction, to do the very little bit of washing he required done, with her own and Bunting's. Luckily he wore soft shirts.

At one time Mrs. Bunting had always had a woman in to help her with this tiresome weekly job, but lately she had grown quite clever at it herself. The only things she had to send out were Bunting's shirts. Everything else she managed to do herself.

From the chest of drawers she now turned her attention to the dressing-table.

Mr. Sleuth did not take his money with him when he went out, he generally left it in one of the drawers below the old-fashioned looking-glass. And now, in a perfunctory way, his landlady pulled out the little drawer, but she did not touch what was lying there; she only glanced at the heap of sovereigns and a few bits of silver. The lodger had taken just enough money with him to buy the clothes he required. He had consulted her as to how much they would cost, making no secret of why he was going out, and the fact had vaguely comforted Mrs. Bunting.

Now she lifted the toilet-cover, and even rolled up the carpet a little way, but no, there was nothing there, not so much as a scrap of paper. And at last, when more or less giving up the search, as she came and went between the two rooms, leaving the connecting door wide open, her mind became full of uneasy speculation and wonder as to the lodger's past life.

Odd Mr. Sleuth must surely always have been, but odd in a sensible sort of way, having on the whole the same moral ideals of conduct as have other people of his class. He was queer about the drink—one might say almost crazy on the subject—but there, as to that, he wasn't the only one! She, Ellen Bunting, had once lived with a lady who was just like that, who was quite crazed, that is, on the question of drink and drunkards—She looked round the neat drawing-room with vague dissatisfaction. There was only one place where anything could be kept concealed—that place was the substantial if small mahogany chiffonnier. And then an idea suddenly came to Mrs. Bunting, one she had never thought of before.

After listening intently for a moment, lest something should suddenly bring Mr. Sleuth home earlier than she expected, she went to the corner where the chiffonnier stood, and, exerting the whole of her not very great physical strength, she tipped forward the heavy piece of furniture.

As she did so, she heard a queer rumbling sound,—something rolling about on the second shelf, something which had not been there before Mr. Sleuth's arrival. Slowly, laboriously, she tipped the chiffonnier backwards and forwards—once, twice, thrice—satisfied, yet strangely troubled in her mind, for she now felt sure that the bag of which the disappearance had so surprised her was there, safely locked away by its owner.

Suddenly a very uncomfortable thought came to Mrs. Bunting's mind. She hoped Mr. Sleuth would not notice that his bag had shifted inside the cupboard. A moment later, with sharp dismay, Mr. Sleuth's landlady realised that the fact that she had moved the chiffonnier must become known to her lodger, for a thin trickle of some dark-coloured liquid was oozing out though the bottom of the little cupboard door.

She stooped down and touched the stuff. It showed red, bright red, on her finger.

Mrs. Bunting grew chalky white, then recovered herself quickly. In fact the colour rushed into her face, and she grew hot all over.

It was only a bottle of red ink she had upset—that was all! How could she have thought it was anything else?

It was the more silly of her—so she told herself in scornful condemnation—because she knew that the lodger used red ink.[24] Certain pages of Cruden's Concordance were covered with notes written in Mr. Sleuth's peculiar upright handwriting. In fact in some places you couldn't see the margin, so closely covered was it with remarks and notes of interrogation.

Mr. Sleuth had foolishly placed his bottle of red ink in the chiffonnier—that was what her poor, foolish gentleman had done; and it was owing to her inquisitiveness, her restless wish to know things she would be none the better, none the happier, for knowing, that this accident had taken place.

She mopped up with her duster the few drops of ink which had fallen on the green carpet and then, still feeling, as she angrily told herself, foolishly upset she went once more into the back room.

It was curious that Mr. Sleuth possessed no notepaper. She would have expected him to have made that one of his first purchases—the more so that paper is so very cheap, especially that rather dirty-looking grey Silurian paper. Mrs. Bunting had once lived with a lady who always used two kinds of notepaper, white for her friends and equals, grey for those whom she called "common people." She, Ellen Green, as she then was, had always resented the fact. Strange she should remember it now, stranger in a way because that employer of her's had not been a real lady, and Mr. Sleuth, whatever his peculiarities, was, in every sense of the word, a real gentleman. Somehow Mrs. Bunting felt sure that if he had bought any notepaper it would have been white—white and probably cream-laid—not grey and cheap.

Again she opened the drawer of the old-fashioned wardrobe and lifted up the few pieces of underclothing Mr. Sleuth now possessed.

But there was nothing there—nothing, that is, hidden away. When one came to think of it there seemed something strange in the notion of leaving all one's money where anyone could take it, and in locking up such a valueless thing as a cheap sham leather bag, to say nothing of a bottle of ink.

Mrs. Bunting once more opened out each of the tiny drawers below the looking-glass, each delicately fashioned of fine old mahogany. Mr. Sleuth kept his money in the centre drawer.

The glass had only cost seven-and-sixpence, and, after the auction a dealer had come and offered her first fifteen shillings, and then a guinea for it. Not long ago, in Baker Street, she had seen a looking-glass which was the very spit of this one, labeled "Chippendale, Antique. £21 5s 0d."

There lay Mr. Sleuth's money—the sovereigns, as the landlady well knew, would each and all gradually pass into her's and Bunting's possession, honestly earned by them no doubt but unattainable—in act unearnable—excepting in connection with the present owner of those dully shining gold sovereigns.

At last she went downstairs to await Mr. Sleuth's return.

When she heard the key turn in the door, she came out into the passage.

"I'm sorry to say I've had an accident, sir," she said a little breathlessly. "Taking advantage of your being out I went up to dust the drawing-room, and while I was trying to get behind the chiffonnier it tilted. I'm afraid, sir, that a bottle of ink that was inside may have got broken, for just a few drops oozed out, sir. But I hope there's no harm done. I wiped it up as well as I could, seeing that the doors of the chiffonnier are locked."

Mr. Sleuth stared at her with a wild, almost a terrified glance. But Mrs. Bunting stood her ground. She felt far less afraid now than she had felt before he came in. Then she had been so frightened that she had nearly gone out of the house, on to the pavement, for company.

"Of course I had no idea, sir, that you kept any ink in there."

She spoke as if she were on the defensive, and the lodger's brow cleared.

"I was aware you used ink, sir," Mrs. Bunting went on, "for I have seen you marking that book of yours—I mean the book you read together with the Bible. Would you like me to go out and get you another bottle, sir?"

"No," said Mr. Sleuth. "No, I thank you. I will at once proceed upstairs and see what damage has been done. When I require you I shall ring."

He shuffled past her, and five minutes later the drawing-room bell did ring.

At once, from the door, Mrs. Bunting saw that the chiffonnier was wide open, and that the shelves were empty save for the bottle of red ink which had turned over and now lay in a red pool of its own making on the lower shelf.

"I'm afraid it will have stained the wood, Mrs. Bunting. Perhaps I was ill-advised to keep my ink in there."

"Oh, no, sir! That doesn't matter at all. Only a drop or two fell out on to the carpet, and they don't show, as you see, sir, for it's a dark corner. Shall I take the bottle away? I may as well."

Mr. Sleuth hesitated. "No," he said, after a long pause, "I think not, Mrs. Bunting. For the very little I require it the ink remaining in the bottle will do quite well, especially if I add a little water, or better still, a little tea, to what already remains in the bottle. I only require it to mark up passages which happen to be of peculiar interest in my Concordance—a work, Mrs. Bunting, which I should have taken great pleasure in compiling myself had not this—ah—this gentleman called Cruden, been before."

Not only Bunting, but Daisy also, thought Ellen far pleasanter in her manner than usual that evening. She listened to all they had to say about their interesting visit to the Black Museum, and did not snub either of them—no, not even when Bunting told of the dreadful, haunting, silly-looking death-masks taken from the hanged.

But a few minutes after that, when her husband suddenly asked her a question, Mrs. Bunting answered at random. It was clear she had not heard the last few words he had been saying.

"A penny for your thoughts!" he said jocularly. But she shook her head.

Daisy slipped out of the room, and, five minutes later, came back dressed up in a blue-and-white check silk gown.

"My!" said her father. "You do look fine, Daisy. I've never seen you wearing that before."

"And a rare figure of fun she looks in it!" observed Mrs. Bunting sarcastically. And then, "I suppose this dressing up means that you're expecting someone. I should have thought both of you must have seen enough of young Chandler for one day. I wonder when that young chap does his work—that I do! He never seems too busy to come and waste an hour or two here."

But that was the only nasty thing Ellen said all that evening. And even Daisy noticed that her stepmother seemed dazed and unlike herself. She went about her cooking and the various little things she had to do even more silently than was her wont.

Yet under that still, almost sullen, manner, how fierce was the storm of dread, of sombre anguish, and, yes, of sick suspense, which shook her soul, and which so far affected her poor, ailing body that often she felt as if she could not force herself to accomplish her simple round of daily work.

After they had finished supper Bunting went out and bought a penny evening paper, but as he came in he announced, with a rather rueful smile, that he had read so much of that nasty little print this last week or two that his eyes hurt him.

"Let me read aloud a bit to you, father," said Daisy eagerly, and he handed her the paper.

Scarcely had Daisy opened her lips when a loud ring and a knock echoed through the house.

CHAPTER ELEVEN

It was only Joe. Somehow, even Bunting called him "Joe" now, and no longer "Chandler," as he had mostly used to do.

Mrs. Bunting had opened the front door only a very little way. She wasn't going to have any strangers pushing in past her.

To her sharpened, suffering senses her house had become a citadel which must be defended; aye, even if the besiegers were a mighty horde with right on their side. And she was always expecting that first single spy who would herald the battalion against whom her only weapon would be her woman's wit and cunning.

But when she saw who stood there smiling at her, the muscles of her face relaxed, and it lost the tense, anxious, almost agonised look it assumed the moment she turned her back on her husband and stepdaughter.

"Why, Joe," she whispered, for she had left the door open behind her, and Daisy had already begun to read aloud, as her father had bidden her. "Come in, do! It's fairly cold to-night."

A glance at his face had shown her that there was no fresh news.

Joe Chandler walked in, past her, into the little hall. Cold? Well, he didn't feel cold, for he had walked quickly to be the sooner where he was now.

Nine days had gone by since that last terrible occurrence, the double murder which had been committed early in the morning of the day Daisy had arrived in London. And though the thousands of men belonging to the Metropolitan Police—to say nothing of the smaller, more alert body of detectives attached to the Force—were keenly on the alert, not one but had begun to feel that there was nothing to be alert about. Familiarity, even with horror, breeds contempt.

But with the public it was far otherwise. Each day something happened to revive and keep alive the mingled horror and interest this strange, enigmatic series of crimes had evoked. Even the more sober organs of the Press went on attacking, with gathering severity and indignation, the Commissioner of Police; and at the huge demonstration held in Victoria Park two days before violent speeches had also been made against the Home Secretary.[25]

But just now Joe Chandler wanted to forget all that. The little house in the Marylebone Road had become to him an enchanted isle of dreams, to which his thoughts were ever turning when he had a moment to spare from what had grown to be a wearisome, because an unsatisfactory, job. He secretly agreed with one of his pals who had exclaimed, and that within twenty-four hours of the last double crime, "Why, 'twould be easier to find a needle in a rick o' hay than this—bloke!"

And if that had been true then, how much truer it was now—after nine long, empty days had gone by?

Quickly he divested himself of his great-coat, muffler, and low hat. Then he put his finger on his lip, and motioned smilingly to Mrs. Bunting to wait a moment. From where he stood in the hall the father and daughter made a pleasant little picture of contented domesticity. Joe Chandler's honest heart swelled at the sight.

Daisy, wearing the blue-and-white check silk dress about which her stepmother and she had had words, sat on a low stool on the left side of the fire, while Bunting, leaning back in his own comfortable arm-chair, was listening, his hand to his ear, in an attitude—as it was the first time she had caught him doing it, the fact brought a pang to Mrs. Bunting—which showed that age was beginning to creep over the listener.

One of Daisy's duties as companion to her great-aunt was that of reading the newspaper aloud, and she prided herself on her accomplishment.

Just as Joe had put his finger on his lip Daisy had been asking, "Shall I read this, father?"

And Bunting had answered quickly, "Aye, do, my dear."

He was absorbed in what he was hearing, and, on seeing Joe at the door, he had only just nodded his head. The young man was becoming so frequent a visitor as to be almost one of themselves.

Daisy read out: "The Avenger: A—" And then she stopped short, for the next word puzzled her greatly. Bravely, however, she went on. "A the-o-ry."

"Go in—do!" whispered Mrs. Bunting to her visitor. "Why should we stay out here in the cold? It's ridiculous."

"I don't want to interrupt Miss Daisy," whispered Chandler back, rather hoarsely.

"Well, you'll hear it all the better in the room. Don't think she'll stop because of you, bless you! There's nothing shy about our Daisy!"

The young man resented the tart, short tone. "Poor little girl!" he said to himself tenderly. "That's what it is having a stepmother, instead of a proper mother." But he obeyed Mrs. Bunting, and then he was pleased he had done so, for Daisy looked up, and a bright blush came over her pretty face.

"Joe begs you won't stop yet awhile. Go on with your reading," commanded Mrs. Bunting quickly. "Now, Joe, you can go and sit over there, close to Daisy, and then you won't miss a word."

There was a sarcastic inflection in her voice, even Chandler noticed that, but he obeyed her with alacrity, and crossing the room he went and sat on a chair just behind Daisy. From there he could note with reverent delight the charming way her fair hair grew upwards from the nape of her slender neck.

The AVENGER: A THE-O-RY

began Daisy again, clearing her throat.

> DEAR Sir—I have a suggestion to put forward for which I think there is a great deal to be said. It seems to me very probable that The Avenger—to give him the name by which he apparently wishes to be known—comprises in his own person the peculiarities of Jekyll and Hyde, Mr. Louis Stevenson's now famous hero.
>
> The culprit, according to my point of view, is a quiet, pleasant-looking gentleman who lives somewhere in the West End of London. He has, however, a tragedy in his past life. He is the husband of a dipsomaniac wife. She is, of course, under care, and is never mentioned in the house where he lives, maybe with his widowed mother and perhaps a maiden sister. They notice that he has become gloomy and brooding of late, but he lives his usual life, occupying himself each day with some harmless hobby. On foggy nights, once the quiet household is plunged in sleep, he creeps out of the house, maybe between one and two o'clock, and swiftly makes his way straight to what has become The Avenger's murder area. Picking out a likely victim, he approaches her with Judas-like gentleness, and having committed his awful crime, goes quietly home again. After a good bath and breakfast, he turns up happy, once more the quiet individual who is an excellent son, a kind brother, esteemed and even beloved by a large circle of friends and acquaintances. Meantime, the police are searching about the scene of the tragedy for what they regard as the usual type of criminal lunatic.

I give this theory, Sir, for what it is worth, but I confess that I am
amazed the police have so wholly confined their inquiries to the
part of London where these murders have been actually
committed. I am quite sure from all that has come out—and we
must remember that full information is never given to the
newspapers—The Avenger should be sought for in the West and
not in the East End of London —Believe me to remain, Sir, yours
very truly—

Again Daisy hesitated, and then with an effort she brought out the word
"Gab-o-ri-you," said she.

"What a funny name!" said Bunting wonderingly.

And then Joe broke in: "That's the name of a French chap what wrote
detective stories," he said. "Pretty good, some of them are, too!"[26]

"Then this Gaboriyou has come over to study these Avenger murders, I
take it?" said Bunting.

"Oh, no," Joe spoke with confidence. "Whoever's written that silly
letter just signed that name for fun."

"It is a silly letter," Mrs. Bunting had broken in resentfully. "I wonder
a respectable paper prints such rubbish."

"Fancy if The Avenger did turn out to be a gentleman!" cried Daisy, in
an awe-struck voice. "There'd be a how-to-do!"

"There may be something in the notion," said her father thoughtfully.
"After all, the monster must be somewhere. This very minute he must be
somewhere a-hiding of himself."

"Of course he's somewhere," said Mrs. Bunting scornfully.

She had just heard Mr. Sleuth moving overhead. 'Twould soon be time
for the lodger's supper.

She hurried on: "But what I do say is that—that—he has nothing to do
with the West End. Why, they say it's a sailor from the Docks —that's a
good bit more likely, I take it. But there, I'm fair sick of the whole subject!
We talk of nothing else in this house. The Avenger this—The Avenger
that—"

"I expect Joe has something to tell us new to-night," said Bunting
cheerfully. "Well, Joe, is there anything new?"

"I say, father, just listen to this!" Daisy broke in excitedly. She read
out:

BLOODHOUNDS TO BE SERIOUSLY CONSIDERED[27]

"Bloodhounds?" repeated Mrs. Bunting, and there was terror in her tone. "Why bloodhounds? That do seem to me a most horrible idea!"

Bunting looked across at her, mildly astonished. "Why, 'twould be a very good idea, if 'twas possible to have bloodhounds in a town. But, there, how can that be done in London, full of butchers' shops, to say nothing of slaughter-yards and other places o' that sort?"

But Daisy went on, and to her stepmother's shrinking ear there seemed a horrible thrill of delight; of gloating pleasure, in her fresh young voice.

"Hark to this," she said:

> A man who had committed a murder in a lonely wood near Blackburn was traced by the help of a bloodhound, and thanks to the sagacious instincts of the animal, the miscreant was finally convicted and hanged.

"La, now! Who'd ever have thought of such a thing?" Bunting exclaimed, in admiration. "The newspapers do have some useful hints in sometimes, Joe."

But young Chandler shook his head. "Bloodhounds ain't no use," he said; "no use at all! If the Yard was to listen to all the suggestions that the last few days have brought in—well, all I can say is our work would be cut out for us—not but what it's cut out for us now, if it comes to that!" He sighed ruefully. He was beginning to feel very tired; if only he could stay in this pleasant, cosy room listening to Daisy Bunting reading on and on forever, instead of having to go out, as he would presently have to do, into the cold and foggy night!

Joe Chandler was fast becoming very sick of his new job. There was a lot of unpleasantness attached to the business, too. Why, even in the house where he lived, and in the little cook-shop where he habitually took his meals, the people round him had taken to taunt him with the remissness of the police. More than that one of his pals, a man he'd always looked up to, because the young fellow had the gift of the gab, had actually been among those who had spoken at the big demonstration in Victoria Park, making a violent speech, not only against the Commissioner of the Metropolitan Police, but also against the Home Secretary.

But Daisy, like most people who believe themselves blessed with the possession of an accomplishment, had no mind to leave off reading just yet.

"Here's another notion!" she exclaimed. "Another letter, father!"

PARDON TO ACCOMPLICES

DEAR Sir—During the last day or two several of the more Intelligent of my acquaintances have suggested that The Avenger, whoever he may be, must be known to a certain number of persons. It is impossible that the perpetrator of such deeds, however nomad he may be in his habits—

"Now I wonder what 'nomad' can be?" Daisy interrupted herself, and looked round at her little audience.

"I've always declared the fellow had all his senses about him," observed Bunting confidently.

Daisy went on, quite satisfied:

—however nomad he may be in his habit; must have some habitat where his ways are known to at least one person. Now the person who knows the terrible secret is evidently withholding information in expectation of a reward, or maybe because, being an accessory after the fact, he or she is now afraid of the consequences. My suggestion, Sir, is that the Home Secretary promise a free pardon. The more so that only thus can this miscreant be brought to justice. Unless he was caught red-handed in the act, it will be exceedingly difficult to trace the crime committed to any individual, for English law looks very askance at circumstantial evidence.

"There's something worth listening to in that letter," said Joe, leaning forward.

Now he was almost touching Daisy, and he smiled involuntarily as she turned her gay, pretty little face the better to hear what he was saying.

"Yes, Mr. Chandler?" she said interrogatively.

"Well, d'you remember that fellow what killed an old gentleman in a railway carriage? He took refuge with someone—a woman his mother had known, and she kept him hidden for quite a long time. But at last she gave him up, and she got a big reward, too!"

"I don't think I'd like to give anybody up for a reward," said Bunting, in his slow, dogmatic way.

"Oh, yes, you would, Mr. Bunting," said Chandler confidently. "You'd only be doing what it's the plain duty of everyone—everyone, that is, who's a good citizen. And you'd be getting something for doing it, which is more than most people gets as does their duty."

"A man as gives up someone for a reward is no better than a common informer," went on Bunting obstinately. "And no man 'ud care to be called that! It's different for you, Joe," he added hastily. "It's your job to catch those who've done anything wrong. And a man'd be a fool who'd take refuge—like with you. He'd be walking into the lion's mouth—" Bunting laughed.

And then Daisy broke in coquettishly: "If I'd done anything I wouldn't mind going for help to Mr. Chandler," she said.

And Joe, with eyes kindling, cried, "No. And if you did you needn't be afraid I'd give you up, Miss Daisy!"

And then, to their amazement, there suddenly broke from Mrs. Bunting, sitting with bowed head over the table, an exclamation of impatience and anger, and, it seemed to those listening, of pain.

"Why, Ellen, don't you feel well?" asked Bunting quickly.

"Just a spasm, a sharp stitch in my side, like," answered the poor woman heavily. "It's over now. Don't mind me."

"But I don't believe—no, that I don't—that there's anybody in the world who knows who The Avenger is," went on Chandler quickly. "It stands to reason that anybody'd give him up—in their own interest, if not in anyone else's. Who'd shelter such a creature? Why, 'twould be dangerous to have him in the house along with one!"

"Then it's your idea that he's not responsible for the wicked things he does?" Mrs. Bunting raised her head, and looked over at Chandler with eager, anxious eyes.

"I'd be sorry to think he wasn't responsible enough to hang!" said Chandler deliberately. "After all the trouble he's been giving us, too!"

"Hanging'd be too good for that chap," said Bunting.

"Not if he's not responsible," said his wife sharply. "I never heard of anything so cruel—that I never did! If the man's a madman, he ought to be in an asylum—that's where he ought to be."

"Hark to her now!" Bunting looked at his Ellen with amusement. "Contrary isn't the word for her! But there, I've noticed the last few days that she seemed to be taking that monster's part. That's what comes of being a born total abstainer."

Mrs. Bunting had got up from her chair. "What nonsense you do talk!" she said angrily. "Not but what it's a good thing if these murders have emptied the public-houses of women for a bit. England's drink is England's shame—I'll never depart from that! Now, Daisy, child, get up, do! Put down that paper. We've heard quite enough. You can be laying the cloth while I goes down the kitchen."

"Yes, you mustn't be forgetting the lodger's supper," called out Bunting. "Mr. Sleuth don't always ring—" he turned to Chandler.

"For one thing, he's often out about this time."

"Not often—just now and again, when he wants to buy something," snapped out Mrs. Bunting. "But I hadn't forgot his supper. He never do want it before eight o'clock."

"Let me take up the lodger's supper, Ellen," Daisy's eager voice broke in. She had got up in obedience to her stepmother, and was now laying the cloth.

"Certainly not! I told you he only wanted me to wait on him. You have your work cut out looking after things down here—that's where I wants you to help me."

Chandler also got up. Somehow he didn't like to be doing nothing while Daisy was so busy. "Yes," he said, looking across at Mrs. Bunting, "I'd forgotten about your lodger. Going on all right, eh?"

"Never knew so quiet and well-behaved a gentleman," said Bunting. "He turned our luck, did Mr. Sleuth."

His wife left the room, and after she had gone Daisy laughed. "You'll hardly believe it, Mr. Chandler, but I've never seen this wonderful lodger. Ellen keeps him to herself, that she does! If I was father I'd be jealous!"

Both men laughed. Ellen? No, the idea was too funny.

CHAPTER TWELVE

"All I can say is, I think Daisy ought to go. One can't always do just what one wants to do—not in this world, at any rate!"

Mrs. Bunting did not seem to be addressing anyone in particular, though both her husband and her stepdaughter were in the room. She was standing by the table, staring straight before her, and as she spoke she avoided looking at either Bunting or Daisy. There was in her voice a tone of cross decision, of thin finality, with which they were both acquainted, and to which each listener knew the other would have to bow.

There was silence for a moment, then Daisy broke out passionately, "I don't see why I should go if I don't want to!" she cried. "You'll allow I've been useful to you, Ellen? 'Tisn't even as if you was quite well."

"I am quite well—perfectly well!" snapped out Mrs. Bunting, and she turned her pale, drawn face, and looked angrily at her stepdaughter.

"'Tain't often I has a chance of being with you and father." There were tears in Daisy's voice, and Bunting glanced deprecatingly at his wife.

An invitation had come to Daisy—an invitation from her own dead mother's sister, who was housekeeper in a big house in Belgrave Square. "The family" had gone away for the Christmas holidays, and Aunt Margaret—Daisy was her godchild—had begged that her niece might come and spend two or three days with her.

But the girl had already had more than one taste of what life was like in the great gloomy basement of 100 Belgrave Square. Aunt Margaret was one of those old-fashioned servants for whom the modern employer is always sighing. While "the family" were away it was her joy—she regarded it as a privilege—to wash sixty-seven pieces of very valuable china contained in two cabinets in the drawing-room; she also slept in every bed by turns, to keep them all well aired. These were the two duties with which she intended her young niece to assist her, and Daisy's soul sickened at the prospect.

But the matter had to be settled at once. The letter had come an hour ago, containing a stamped telegraph form, and Aunt Margaret was not one to be trifled with.

Since breakfast the three had talked of nothing else, and from the very first Mrs. Bunting had said that Daisy ought to go—that there was no doubt about it, that it did not admit of discussion. But discuss it they all did, and for once Bunting stood up to his wife. But that, as was natural, only made his Ellen harder and more set on her own view.

"What the child says is true," he observed. "It isn't as if you was quite well. You've been took bad twice in the last few days—you can't deny of it, Ellen. Why shouldn't I just take a bus and go over and see Margaret? I'd tell her just how it is. She'd understand, bless you!"

"I won't have you doing nothing of the sort!" cried Mrs. Bunting, speaking almost as passionately as her stepdaughter had done. "Haven't I a right to be ill, haven't I a right to be took bad, aye, and to feel all right again—same as other people?"

Daisy turned round and clasped her hands. "Oh, Ellen!" she cried; "do say that you can't spare me! I don't want to go across to that horrid old dungeon of a place."

"Do as you like," said Mrs. Bunting sullenly. "I'm fair tired of you both! There'll come a day, Daisy, when you'll know, like me, that money is the main thing that matters in this world; and when your Aunt Margaret's left her savings to somebody else just because you wouldn't spend a few days with her this Christmas, then you'll know what it's like to go without—you'll know what a fool you were, and that nothing can't alter it anymore!"

And then, with victory actually in her grasp, poor Daisy saw it snatched from her.

"Ellen is right," Bunting said heavily. "Money does matter—a terrible deal—though I never thought to hear Ellen say 'twas the only thing that mattered. But 'twould be foolish—very, very foolish, my girl, to offend your Aunt Margaret. It'll only be two days after all—two days isn't a very long time."

But Daisy did not hear her father's last words. She had already rushed from the room, and gone down to the kitchen to hide her childish tears of disappointment—the childish tears which came because she was beginning to be a woman, with a woman's natural instinct for building her own human nest.

Aunt Margaret was not one to tolerate the comings of any strange young man, and she had a peculiar dislike to the police.

"Who'd ever have thought she'd have minded as much as that!" Bunting looked across at Ellen deprecatingly; already his heart was misgiving him.

"It's plain enough why she's become so fond of us all of a sudden," said Mrs. Bunting sarcastically. And as her husband stared at her uncomprehendingly, she added, in a tantalising tone, "as plain as the nose on your face, my man."

"What d'you mean?" he said. "I daresay I'm a bit slow, Ellen, but I really don't know what you'd be at?"

"Don't you remember telling me before Daisy came here that Joe Chandler had become sweet on her last summer? I thought it only foolishness then, but I've come round to your view—that's all."

Bunting nodded his head slowly. Yes, Joe had got into the way of coming very often, and there had been the expedition to that gruesome Scotland Yard museum, but somehow he, Bunting, had been so interested in the Avenger murders that he hadn't thought of Joe in any other connection—not this time, at any rate.

"And do you think Daisy likes him?" There was an unwonted tone of excitement, of tenderness, in Bunting's voice.

His wife looked over at him; and a thin smile, not an unkindly smile by any means, lit up her pale face. "I've never been one to prophesy," she answered deliberately. "But this I don't mind telling you, Bunting— Daisy'll have plenty o' time to get tired of Joe Chandler before they two are dead. Mark my words!"

"Well, she might do worse," said Bunting ruminatingly. "He's as steady as God makes them, and he's already earning thirty-two shillings a week. But I wonder how Old Aunt'd like the notion? I don't see her parting with Daisy before she must."

"I wouldn't let no old aunt interfere with me about such a thing as that!" cried Mrs. Bunting. "No, not for millions of gold!" And Bunting looked at her in silent wonder. Ellen was singing a very different tune now to what she'd sung a few minutes ago, when she was so keen about the girl going to Belgrave Square.

"If she still seems upset while she's having her dinner," said his wife suddenly, "well, you just wait till I've gone out for something, and then you just say to her, 'Absence makes the heart grow fonder'—just that, and nothing more! She'll take it from you. And I shouldn't be surprised if it comforted her quite a lot."

"For the matter of that, there's no reason why Joe Chandler shouldn't go over and see her there," said Bunting hesitatingly.

"Oh, yes, there is," said Mrs. Bunting, smiling shrewdly. "Plenty of reason. Daisy'll be a very foolish girl if she allows her aunt to know any of her secrets. I've only seen that woman once, but I know exactly the sort Margaret is. She's just waiting for Old Aunt to drop off and then she'll want to have Daisy herself—to wait on her, like. She'd turn quite nasty if she thought there was a young fellow what stood in her way."

She glanced at the dock, the pretty little eight-day clock which had been a wedding present from a kind friend of her last mistress. It had mysteriously disappeared during their time of trouble, and had as mysteriously reappeared three or four days after Mr. Sleuth's arrival.

"I've time to go out with that telegram," she said briskly—somehow she felt better, different to what she had done the last few days—"and then it'll be done. It's no good having more words about it, and I expect we should have plenty more words if I wait till the child comes upstairs again."

She did not speak unkindly, and Bunting looked at her rather wonderingly. Ellen very seldom spoke of Daisy as "the child"—in fact, he could only remember her having done so once before, and that was a long time ago. They had been talking over their future life together, and she had said, very solemnly, "Bunting, I promise I will do my duty—as much as lies in my power, that is—by the child."

But Ellen had not had much opportunity of doing her duty by Daisy. As not infrequently happens with the duties that we are willing to do, that particular duty had been taken over by someone else who had no mind to let it go.

"What shall I do if Mr. Sleuth rings?" asked Bunting, rather nervously. It was the first time since the lodger had come to them that Ellen had offered to go out in the morning.

She hesitated. In her anxiety to have the matter of Daisy settled, she had forgotten Mr. Sleuth. Strange that she should have done so—strange, and, to herself, very comfortable and pleasant.

"Oh, well, you can just go up and knock at the door and say I'll be back in a few minutes—that I had to go out with a message. He's quite a reasonable gentleman." She went into the back room to put on her bonnet and thick jacket for it was very cold—getting colder every minute.

As she stood, buttoning her gloves—she wouldn't have gone out untidy for the world—Bunting suddenly came across to her. "Give us a kiss, old girl," he said. And his wife turned up her face.

"One 'ud think it was catching!" she said, but there was a lilt in her voice.

"So it is," Bunting briefly answered. "Didn't that old cook get married just after us? She'd never 'a thought of it if it hadn't been for you!"

But once she was out, walking along the damp, uneven pavement, Mr. Sleuth revenged himself for his landlady's temporary forgetfulness.

During the last two days the lodger had been queer, odder than usual, unlike himself, or, rather, very much as he had been some ten days ago, just before that double murder had taken place.

The night before, while Daisy was telling all about the dreadful place to which Joe Chandler had taken her and her father, Mrs. Bunting had heard Mr. Sleuth moving about overhead, restlessly walking up and down his sitting-room. And later, when she took up his supper, she had listened a moment outside the door, while he read aloud some of the texts his soul delighted in—terrible texts telling of the grim joys attendant on revenge.

Mrs. Bunting was so absorbed in her thoughts, so possessed with the curious personality of her lodger, that she did not look where she was going, and suddenly a young woman bumped up against her.

She started violently and looked round, dazed, as the young person muttered a word of apology;—then she again fell into deep thought.

It was a good thing Daisy was going away for a few days; it made the problem of Mr. Sleuth and his queer ways less disturbing. She, Ellen, was sorry she had spoken so sharp-like to the girl, but after all it wasn't wonderful that she had been snappy. This last night she had hardly slept at all. Instead, she had lain awake listening—and there is nothing so tiring as to lie awake listening for a sound that never comes.

The house had remained so still you could have heard a pin drop. Mr. Sleuth, lying snug in his nice warm bed upstairs, had not stirred. Had he stirred his landlady was bound to have heard him, for his bed was, as we know, just above hers. No, during those long hours of darkness Daisy's light, regular breathing was all that had fallen on Mrs. Bunting's ears.

And then her mind switched off Mr. Sleuth. She made a determined effort to expel him, to toss him, as it were, out of her thoughts.

It seemed strange that The Avenger had stayed his hand, for, as Joe had said only last evening, it was full time that he should again turn that awful, mysterious searchlight of his on himself. Mrs. Bunting always visioned The Avenger as a black shadow in the centre a bright blinding light—but the shadow had no form or definite substance. Sometimes he looked like one thing, sometimes like another...

Mrs. Bunting had now come to the corner which led up the street where there was a Post Office. But instead of turning sharp to the left she stopped short for a minute.

There had suddenly come over her a feeling of horrible self-rebuke and even self-loathing. It was dreadful that she, of all women, should have longed to hear that another murder had been committed last night!

Yet such was the shameful fact. She had listened all through breakfast hoping to hear the dread news being shouted outside; yes, and more or less during the long discussion which had followed on the receipt of Margaret's letter she had been hoping—hoping against hope—that those dreadful triumphant shouts of the newspaper-sellers still might come echoing down the Marylebone Road. And yet hypocrite that she was, she had reproved Bunting when he had expressed, not disappointment exactly—but, well, surprise, that nothing had happened last night.

Now her mind switched off to Joe Chandler. Strange to think how afraid she had been of that young man! She was no longer afraid of him, or hardly at all. He was dotty—that's what was the matter with him, dotty with love for rosy-cheeked, blue-eyed little Daisy. Anything might now go on, right under Joe Chandler's very nose—but, bless you, he'd never see it! Last summer, when this affair, this nonsense of young Chandler and Daisy had begun, she had had very little patience with it all. In fact, the memory of the way Joe had gone on then, the tiresome way he would be always dropping in, had been one reason (though not the most important reason of all) why she had felt so terribly put about at the idea of the girl coming again. But now? Well, now she had become quite tolerant, quite kindly—at any rate as far as Joe Chandler was concerned.

She wondered why.

Still, 'twouldn't do Joe a bit of harm not to see the girl for a couple of days. In fact 'twould be a very good thing, for then he'd think of Daisy— think of her to the exclusion of all else. Absence does make the heart grow fonder—at first, at any rate. Mrs. Bunting was well aware of that. During the long course of hers and Bunting's mild courting, they'd been separated for about three months, and it was that three months which had made up her mind for her. She had got so used to Bunting that she couldn't do without him, and she had felt—oddest fact of all—acutely, miserably jealous. But she hadn't let him know that—no fear!

Of course, Joe mustn't neglect his job—that would never do. But what a good thing it was, after all, that he wasn't like some of those detective chaps that are written about in stories—the sort of chaps that know everything, see everything, guess everything—even where there isn't anything to see, or know, or guess!

Why, to take only one little fact—Joe Chandler had never shown the slightest curiosity about their lodger...

Mrs. Bunting pulled herself together with a start, and hurried quickly on. Bunting would begin to wonder what had happened to her.

She went into the Post Office and handed the form to the young woman without a word. Margaret, a sensible woman, who was accustomed to manage other people's affairs, had even written out the words: "Will be with you to tea.—DAISY."

It was a comfort to have the thing settled once for all. If anything horrible was going to happen in the next two or three days—it was just as well Daisy shouldn't be at home. Not that there was any real danger that anything would happen,—Mrs. Bunting felt sure of that.

By this time she was out in the street again, and she began mentally counting up the number of murders The Avenger had committed. Nine, or was it ten? Surely by now The Avenger must be avenged? Surely by now, if—as that writer in the newspaper had suggested—he was a quiet, blameless gentleman living in the West End, whatever vengeance he had to wreak, must be satisfied?

She began hurrying homewards; it wouldn't do for the lodger to ring before she had got back. Bunting would never know how to manage Mr. Sleuth, especially if Mr. Sleuth was in one of his queer moods.

Mrs. Bunting put the key into the front door lock and passed into the house. Then her heart stood still with fear and terror. There came the sound of voices—of voices she thought she did not know—in the sitting-room.

She opened the door, and then drew a long breath. It was only Joe Chandler—Joe, Daisy, and Bunting, talking together. They stopped rather guiltily as she came in, but not before she had heard Chandler utter the words: "That don't mean nothing! I'll just run out and send another saying you won't come, Miss Daisy."

And then the strangest smile came over Mrs. Bunting's face. There had fallen on her ear the still distant, but unmistakable, shouts which betokened that something had happened last night—something which made it worthwhile for the newspaper-sellers to come crying down the Marylebone Road.

"Well?" she said a little breathlessly. "Well, Joe? I suppose you've brought us news? I suppose there's been another?"

He looked at her, surprised. "No, that there hasn't, Mrs. Bunting—not as far as I know, that is. Oh, you're thinking of those newspaper chaps? They've got to cry out something," he grinned. "You wouldn't 'a thought folk was so bloodthirsty. They're just shouting out that there's been an arrest; but we don't take no stock of that. It's a Scotchman what gave himself up last night at Dorking. He'd been drinking, and was a-pitying of himself. Why, since this business began, there's been about twenty arrests, but they've all come to nothing."

"Why, Ellen, you looks quite sad, quite disappointed," said Bunting jokingly. "Come to think of it, it's high time The Avenger was at work again." He laughed as he made his grim joke. Then turned to young Chandler: "Well, you'll be glad when it's all over, my lad."

"Glad in a way," said Chandler unwillingly. "But one 'ud have liked to have caught him. One doesn't like to know such a creature's at large, now, does one?"

Mrs. Bunting had taken off her bonnet and jacket. "I must just go and see about Mr. Sleuth's breakfast," she said in a weary, dispirited voice, and left them there.

She felt disappointed, and very, very depressed. As to the plot which had been hatching when she came in, that had no chance of success; Bunting would never dare let Daisy send out another telegram contradicting the first. Besides, Daisy's stepmother shrewdly suspected that by now the girl herself wouldn't care to do such a thing. Daisy had plenty of sense tucked away somewhere in her pretty little head. If it ever became her fate to live as a married woman in London, it would be best to stay on the right side of Aunt Margaret.

And when she came into her kitchen the stepmother's heart became very soft, for Daisy had got everything beautifully ready. In fact, there was nothing to do but to boil Mr. Sleuth's two eggs. Feeling suddenly more cheerful than she had felt of late, Mrs. Bunting took the tray upstairs.

"As it was rather late, I didn't wait for you to ring, sir," she said.

And the lodger looked up from the table where, as usual, he was studying with painful, almost agonising intentness, the Book. "Quite right, Mrs. Bunting—quite right! I have been pondering over the command, 'Work while it is yet light.'"

"Yes, sir?" she said, and a queer, cold feeling stole over her heart. "Yes, sir?"

"'The spirit is willing, but the flesh—the flesh is weak,'" said Mr. Sleuth, with a heavy sigh.

"You studies too hard, and too long—that's what's ailing you, sir," said Mr. Sleuth's landlady suddenly.

When Mrs. Bunting went down again she found that a great deal had been settled in her absence; among other things, that Joe Chandler was going to escort Miss Daisy across to Belgrave Square. He could carry Daisy's modest bag, and if they wanted to ride instead of walk, why, they could take the bus from Baker Street Station to Victoria—that would land them very near Belgrave Square.

But Daisy seemed quite willing to walk; she hadn't had a walk, she declared, for a long, long time—and then she blushed rosy red, and even her stepmother had to admit to herself that Daisy was very nice looking, not at all the sort of girl who ought to be allowed to go about the London streets by herself.

CHAPTER THIRTEEN

Daisy's father and stepmother stood side by side at the front door, watching the girl and young Chandler walk off into the darkness.

A yellow pall of fog had suddenly descended on London, and Joe had come a full half-hour before they expected him, explaining, rather lamely, that it was the fog which had brought him so soon.

"If we was to have waited much longer, perhaps, 'twouldn't have been possible to walk a yard," he explained, and they had accepted, silently, his explanation.

"I hope it's quite safe sending her off like that?" Bunting looked deprecatingly at his wife. She had already told him more than once that he was too fussy about Daisy, that about his daughter he was like an old hen with her last chicken.

"She's safer than she would be, with you or me. She couldn't have a smarter young fellow to look after her."

"It'll be awful thick at Hyde Park Corner," said Bunting. "It's always worse there than anywhere else. If I was Joe I'd 'a taken her by the Underground Railway to Victoria—that 'ud been the best way, considering the weather 'tis."

"They don't think anything of the weather, bless you!" said his wife. "They'll walk and walk as long as there's a glimmer left for 'em to steer by. Daisy's just been pining to have a walk with that young chap. I wonder you didn't notice how disappointed they both were when you was so set on going along with them to that horrid place."

"D'you really mean that, Ellen?" Bunting looked upset. "I understood Joe to say he liked my company."

"Oh, did you?" said Mrs. Bunting dryly. "I expect he liked it just about as much as we liked the company of that old cook who would go out with us when we was courting. It always was a wonder to me how the woman could force herself upon two people who didn't want her."

"But I'm Daisy's father; and an old friend of Chandler," said Bunting remonstratingly. "I'm quite different from that cook. She was nothing to us, and we was nothing to her."

"She'd have liked to be something to you, I make no doubt," observed his Ellen, shaking her head, and her husband smiled, a little foolishly.

By this time they were back in their nice, cosy sitting-room, and a feeling of not altogether unpleasant lassitude stole over Mrs. Bunting. It was a comfort to have Daisy out of her way for a bit. The girl, in some ways, was very wide awake and inquisitive, and she had early betrayed what her stepmother thought to be a very unseemly and silly curiosity concerning the lodger. "You might just let me have one peep at him, Ellen?" she had pleaded, only that morning. But Ellen had shaken her head. "No, that I won't! He's a very quiet gentleman; but he knows exactly what he likes, and he don't like anyone but me waiting on him. Why, even your father's hardly seen him."

But that, naturally, had only increased Daisy's desire to view Mr. Sleuth.

There was another reason why Mrs. Bunting was glad that her stepdaughter had gone away for two days. During her absence young Chandler was far less likely to haunt them in the way he had taken to doing lately, the more so that, in spite of what she had said to her husband, Mrs. Bunting felt sure that Daisy would ask Joe Chandler to call at Belgrave Square. 'Twouldn't be human nature—at any rate, not girlish human nature—not to do so, even if Joe's coming did anger Aunt Margaret.

Yes, it was pretty safe that with Daisy away they, the Buntings, would be rid of that young chap for a bit, and that would be a good thing.

When Daisy wasn't there to occupy the whole of his attention, Mrs. Bunting felt queerly afraid of Chandler. After all, he was a detective—it was his job to be always nosing about, trying to find out things. And, though she couldn't fairly say to herself that he had done much of that sort of thing in her house, he might start doing it any minute. And then—then—where would she, and—and Mr. Sleuth, be?

She thought of the bottle of red ink—of the leather bag which must be hidden somewhere—and her heart almost stopped beating. Those were the sort of things which, in the stories Bunting was so fond of reading, always led to the detection of famous criminals...

Mr. Sleuth's bell for tea rang that afternoon far earlier than usual. The fog had probably misled him, and made him think it later than it was.

When she went up, "I would like a cup of tea now, and just one piece of bread-and-butter," the lodger said wearily. "I don't feel like having anything else this afternoon."

"It's a horrible day," Mrs. Bunting observed, in a cheerier voice than usual. "No wonder you don't feel hungry, sir. And then it isn't so very long since you had your dinner, is it?"

"No," he said absently. "No, it isn't, Mrs. Bunting."

She went down, made the tea, and brought it up again. And then, as she came into the room, she uttered an exclamation of sharp dismay.

Mr. Sleuth was dressed for going out. He was wearing his long Inverness cloak, and his queer old high hat lay on the table, ready for him to put on.

"You're never going out this afternoon, sir?" she asked falteringly. "Why, the fog's awful; you can't see a yard ahead of you!"

Unknown to herself, Mrs. Bunting's voice had risen almost to a scream. She moved back, still holding the tray, and stood between the door and her lodger, as if she meant to bar his way—to erect between Mr. Sleuth and the dark, foggy world outside a living barrier.

"The weather never affects me at all," he said sullenly; and he looked at her with so wild and pleading a look in his eyes that, slowly, reluctantly, she moved aside. As she did so she noticed for the first time that Mr. Sleuth held something in his right hand. It was the key of the chiffonnier cupboard. He had been on his way there when her coming in had disturbed him.

"It's very kind of you to be so concerned about me," he stammered, "but—but, Mrs. Bunting, you must excuse me if I say that I do not welcome such solicitude. I prefer to be left alone. I—I cannot stay in your house if I feel that my comings and goings are watched—spied upon."

She pulled herself together. "No one spies upon you, sir," she said, with considerable dignity. "I've done my best to satisfy you—"

"You have—you have!" he spoke in a distressed, apologetic tone. "But you spoke just now as if you were trying to prevent my doing what I wish to do—indeed, what I have to do. For years I have been misunderstood—persecuted"—he waited a moment, then in a hollow voice added the one word, "tortured! Do not tell me that you are going to add yourself to the number of my tormentors, Mrs. Bunting?"

She stared at him helplessly. "Don't you be afraid I'll ever be that, sir. I only spoke as I did because—well, sir, because I thought it really wasn't safe for a gentleman to go out this afternoon. Why, there's hardly anyone about, though we're so near Christmas."

He walked across to the window and looked out. "The fog is clearing somewhat; Mrs. Bunting," but there was no relief in his voice, rather was there disappointment and dread.

Plucking up courage, she followed him. Yes, Mr. Sleuth was right. The fog was lifting—rolling off in that sudden, mysterious way in which local fogs sometimes do lift in London.

He turned sharply from the window. "Our conversation has made me forget an important thing, Mrs. Bunting. I should be glad if you would just leave out a glass of milk and some bread-and-butter for me this evening. I shall not require supper when I come in, for after my walk I shall probably go straight upstairs to carry through a very difficult experiment."

"Very good, sir." And then Mrs. Bunting left the lodger.

But when she found herself downstairs in the fog-laden hall, for it had drifted in as she and her husband had stood at the door seeing Daisy off, instead of going in to Bunting she did a very odd thing—a thing she had never thought of doing in her life before. She pressed her hot forehead against the cool bit of looking-glass let into the hat-and-umbrella stand. "I don't know what to do!" she moaned to herself, and then, "I can't bear it! I can't bear it!"

But though she felt that her secret suspense and trouble was becoming intolerable, the one way in which she could have ended her misery never occurred to Mrs. Bunting.

In the long history of crime it has very, very seldom happened that a woman has betrayed one who has taken refuge with her. The timorous and cautious woman has not infrequently hunted a human being fleeing from his pursuer from her door, but she has not revealed the fact that he was ever there. In fact, it may almost be said that such betrayal has never taken place unless the betrayer has been actuated by love of gain, or by a longing for revenge. So far, perhaps because she is subject rather than citizen, her duty as a component part of civilised society weighs but lightly on woman's shoulders.

And then—and then, in a sort of way, Mrs. Bunting had become attached to Mr. Sleuth. A wan smile would sometimes light up his sad face when he saw her come in with one of his meals, and when this happened Mrs. Bunting felt pleased—pleased and vaguely touched. In between those—those dreadful events outside, which filled her with such suspicion, such anguish and such suspense, she never felt any fear, only pity, for Mr. Sleuth.

Often and often, when lying wide awake at night, she turned over the strange problem in her mind. After all, the lodger must have lived somewhere during his forty-odd years of life. She did not even know if Mr. Sleuth had any brothers or sisters; friends she knew he had none. But, however odd and eccentric he was, he had evidently, or so she supposed, led a quiet, undistinguished kind of life, till—till now.

What had made him alter all of a sudden—if, that is, he had altered? That was what Mrs. Bunting was always debating fitfully with herself; and, what was more, and very terribly, to the point, having altered, why should he not in time go back to what he evidently had been—that is, a blameless, quiet gentleman?

If only he would! If only he would!

As she stood in the hall, cooling her hot forehead, all these thoughts, these hopes and fears, jostled at lightning speed through her brain.

She remembered what young Chandler had said the other day—that there had never been, in the history of the world, so strange a murderer as The Avenger had proved himself to be.

She and Bunting, aye, and little Daisy too, had hung, fascinated, on Joe's words, as he had told them of other famous series of murders which had taken place in the past, not only in England but abroad—especially abroad.

One woman, whom all the people round her believed to be a kind, respectable soul, had poisoned no fewer than fifteen people in order to get their insurance money. Then there had been the terrible tale of an apparently respectable, contented innkeeper and his wife, who, living at the entrance to a wood, killed all those humble travellers who took shelter under their roof, simply for their clothes, and any valuables they possessed. But in all those stories the murderer or murderers always had a very strong motive, the motive being, in almost every case, a wicked lust for gold.

At last, after having passed her handkerchief over her forehead, she went into the room where Bunting was sitting smoking his pipe.

"The fog's lifting a bit," she said in an ill-assured voice. "I hope that by this time Daisy and that Joe Chandler are right out of it."

But the other shook his head silently. "No such luck!" he said briefly. "You don't know what it's like in Hyde Park, Ellen. I expect 'twill soon be just as heavy here as 'twas half an hour ago!"

She wandered over to the window, and pulled the curtain back. "Quite a lot of people have come out, anyway," she observed.

"There's a fine Christmas show in the Edgware Road. I was thinking of asking if you wouldn't like to go along there with me."

"No," she said dully. "I'm quite content to stay at home."

She was listening—listening for the sounds which would betoken that the lodger was coming downstairs.

At last she heard the cautious, stuffless tread of his rubber-soled shoes shuffling along the hall. But Bunting only woke to the fact when the front door shut to.

"That's never Mr. Sleuth going out?" He turned on his wife, startled. "Why, the poor gentleman'll come to harm—that he will! One has to be wide awake on an evening like this. I hope he hasn't taken any of his money out with him."

"'Tisn't the first time Mr. Sleuth's been out in a fog," said Mrs. Bunting somberly.

Somehow she couldn't help uttering these over-true words. And then she turned, eager and half frightened, to see how Bunting had taken what she said.

But he looked quite placid, as if he had hardly heard her. "We don't get the good old fogs we used to get—not what people used to call 'London particulars.' I expect the lodger feels like Mrs. Crowley—I've often told you about her, Ellen?"

Mrs. Bunting nodded.

Mrs. Crowley had been one of Bunting's ladies, one of those he had liked best—a cheerful, jolly lady, who used often to give her servants what she called a treat. It was seldom the kind of treat they would have chosen for themselves, but still they appreciated her kind thought.

"Mrs. Crowley used to say," went on Bunting, in his slow, dogmatic way, "that she never minded how bad the weather was in London, so long as it was London and not the country. Mr. Crowley, he liked the country best, but Mrs. Crowley always felt dull-like there. Fog never kept her from going out—no, that it didn't. She wasn't a bit afraid. But—" he turned round and looked at his wife—"I am a bit surprised at Mr. Sleuth. I should have thought him a timid kind of gentleman—"

He waited a moment, and she felt forced to answer him.

"I wouldn't exactly call him timid," she said, in a low voice, "but he is very quiet, certainly. That's why he dislikes going out when there are a lot of people bustling about the streets. I don't suppose he'll be out long."

She hoped with all her soul that Mr. Sleuth would be in very soon— that he would be daunted by the now increasing gloom.

Somehow she did not feel she could sit still for very long. She got up, and went over to the farthest window.

The fog had lifted, certainly. She could see the lamp-lights on the other side of the Marylebone Road, glimmering redly; and shadowy figures were hurrying past, mostly making their way towards the Edgware Road, to see the Christmas shops.

At last to his wife's relief, Bunting got up too. He went over to the cupboard where he kept his little store of books, and took one out.

"I think I'll read a bit," he said. "Seems a long time since I've looked at a book. The papers was so jolly interesting for a bit, but now there's nothing in 'em."

His wife remained silent. She knew what he meant. A good many days had gone by since the last two Avenger murders, and the papers had very little to say about them that they hadn't said in different language a dozen times before.

She went into her bedroom and came back with a bit of plain sewing.

Mrs. Bunting was fond of sewing, and Bunting liked to see her so engaged. Since Mr. Sleuth had come to be their lodger she had not had much time for that sort of work.

It was funny how quiet the house was without either Daisy, or—or the lodger, in it.

At last she let her needle remain idle, and the bit of cambric slipped down on her knee, while she listened, longingly, for Mr. Sleuth's return home.

And as the minutes sped by she fell to wondering with a painful wonder if she would ever see her lodger again, for, from what she knew of Mr. Sleuth, Mrs. Bunting felt sure that if he got into any kind of—well, trouble outside, he would never betray where he had lived during the last few weeks.

No, in such a case the lodger would disappear in as sudden a way as he had come. And Bunting would never suspect, would never know, until, perhaps—God, what a horrible thought—a picture published in some newspaper might bring a certain dreadful fact to Bunting's knowledge.

But if that happened—if that unthinkably awful thing came to pass, she made up her mind, here and now, never to say anything. She also would pretend to be amazed, shocked, unutterably horrified at the astounding revelation.

CHAPTER FOURTEEN

"There he is at last, and I'm glad of it, Ellen. 'Tain't a night you would wish a dog to be out in."

Bunting's voice was full of relief, but he did not turn round and look at his wife as he spoke; instead, he continued to read the evening paper he held in his hand.

He was still close to the fire, sitting back comfortably in his nice arm-chair. He looked very well—well and ruddy. Mrs. Bunting stared across at him with a touch of sharp envy, nay, more, of resentment. And this was very curious, for she was, in her own dry way, very fond of Bunting.

"You needn't feel so nervous about him; Mr. Sleuth can look out for himself all right."

Bunting laid the paper he had been reading down on his knee. "I can't think why he wanted to go out in such weather," he said impatiently.

"Well, it's none of your business, Bunting, now, is it?"

"No, that's true enough. Still, 'twould be a very bad thing for us if anything happened to him. This lodger's the first bit of luck we've had for a terrible long time, Ellen."

Mrs. Bunting moved a little impatiently in her high chair. She remained silent for a moment. What Bunting had said was too obvious to be worth answering. Also she was listening, following in imagination her lodger's quick, singularly quiet progress—"stealthy" she called it to herself—through the fog-filled, lamp-lit hall. Yes, now he was going up the staircase. What was that Bunting was saying?

"It isn't safe for decent folk to be out in such weather—no, that it ain't, not unless they have something to do that won't wait till to-morrow." The speaker was looking straight into his wife's narrow, colourless face. Bunting was an obstinate man, and liked to prove himself right. "I've a good mind to speak to him about it, that I have! He ought to be told that it isn't safe—not for the sort of man he is—to be wandering about the streets at night. I read you out the accidents in Lloyd's—shocking, they were, and all brought about by the fog! And then, that horrid monster 'ull soon be at his work again—"

"Monster?" repeated Mrs. Bunting absently.

She was trying to hear the lodger's footsteps overhead. She was very curious to know whether he had gone into his nice sitting-room, or straight upstairs, to that cold experiment-room, as he now always called it.

But her husband went on as if he had not heard her, and she gave up trying to listen to what was going on above.

"It wouldn't be very pleasant to run up against such a party as that in the fog, eh, Ellen?" He spoke as if the notion had a certain pleasant thrill in it after all.

"What stuff you do talk!" said Mrs. Bunting sharply. And then she got up. Her husband's remarks had disturbed her. Why couldn't they talk of something pleasant when they did have a quiet bit of time together?

Bunting looked down again at his paper, and she moved quietly about the room. Very soon it would be time for supper, and to-night she was going to cook her husband a nice piece of toasted cheese. That fortunate man, as she was fond of telling him, with mingled contempt and envy, had the digestion of an ostrich, and yet he was rather fanciful, as gentlemen's servants who have lived in good places often are.

Yes, Bunting was very lucky in the matter of his digestion. Mrs. Bunting prided herself on having a nice mind, and she would never have allowed an unrefined word—such a word as "stomach," for instance, to say nothing of an even plainer term—to pass her lips, except, of course, to a doctor in a sick-room.

Mr. Sleuth's landlady did not go down at once into her cold kitchen; instead, with a sudden furtive movement, she opened the door leading into her bedroom, and then, closing the door quietly, stepped back into the darkness, and stood motionless, listening.

At first she heard nothing, but gradually there stole on her listening ears the sound of someone moving softly about in the room just overhead, that is, in Mr. Sleuth's bedroom. But, try as she might, it was impossible for her to guess what the lodger was doing.

At last she heard him open the door leading out on the little landing. She could hear the stairs creaking. That meant, no doubt, that Mr. Sleuth would pass the rest of the evening in the cheerless room above. He hadn't spent any time up there for quite a long while—in fact, not for nearly ten days. 'Twas odd he chose to-night, when it was so foggy, to carry out an experiment.

She groped her way to a chair and sat down. She felt very tired—strangely tired, as if she had gone through some great physical exertion.

Yes, it was true that Mr. Sleuth had brought her and Bunting luck, and it was wrong, very wrong, of her ever to forget that.

As she sat there she also reminded herself, and not for the first time, what the lodger's departure would mean. It would almost certainly mean ruin; just as his staying meant all sorts of good things, of which physical comfort was the least. If Mr. Sleuth stayed on with them, as he showed every intention of doing, it meant respectability, and, above all, security.

Mrs. Bunting thought of Mr. Sleuth's money. He never received a letter, and yet he must have some kind of income—so much was clear. She supposed he went and drew his money, in sovereigns, out of a bank as he required it.

Her mind swung round, consciously, deliberately, away from Mr. Sleuth.

The Avenger? What a strange name! Again she assured herself that there would come a time when The Avenger, whoever he was, must feel satiated; when he would feel himself to be, so to speak, avenged.

To go back to Mr. Sleuth; it was lucky that the lodger seemed so pleased, not only with the rooms, but with his landlord and landlady—indeed, there was no real reason why Mr. Sleuth should ever wish to leave such nice lodgings.

Mrs. Bunting suddenly stood up. She made a strong effort, and shook off her awful sense of apprehension and unease. Feeling for the handle of the door giving into the passage she turned it, and then, with light, firm steps, she went down into the kitchen.

When they had first taken the house, the basement had been made by her care, if not into a pleasant, then, at any rate, into a very clean place. She had had it whitewashed, and against the still white walls the gas stove loomed up, a great square of black iron and bright steel. It was a large gas-stove, the kind for which one pays four shillings a quarter rent to the gas company, and here, in the kitchen, there was no foolish shilling-in-the-slot arrangement. Mrs. Bunting was too shrewd a woman to have anything to do with that kind of business. There was a proper gas-meter, and she paid for what she consumed after she had consumed it.

Putting her candle down on the well-scrubbed wooden table, she turned up the gas-jet, and blew out the candle.

Then, lighting one of the gas-rings, she put a frying-pan on the stove, and once more her mind reverted, as if in spite of herself, to Mr. Sleuth. Never had there been a more confiding or trusting gentleman than the lodger, and yet in some ways he was so secret, so—so peculiar.

She thought of the bag—that bag which had rumbled about so queerly in the chiffonnier. Something seemed to tell her that tonight the lodger had taken that bag out with him.

And then she thrust away the thought of the bag almost violently from her mind, and went back to the more agreeable thought of Mr. Sleuth's income, and of how little trouble he gave. Of course, the lodger was eccentric, otherwise he wouldn't be their lodger at all—he would be living in quite a different sort of way with some of his relations, or with a friend in his own class.

While these thoughts galloped disconnectedly through her mind, Mrs. Bunting went on with her cooking, preparing the cheese, cutting it up into little shreds, carefully measuring out the butter, doing everything, as was always her way, with a certain delicate and cleanly precision.

And then, while in the middle of toasting the bread on which was to be poured the melted cheese, she suddenly heard sounds which startled her, made her feel uncomfortable.

Shuffling, hesitating steps were creaking down the house.

She looked up and listened.

Surely the lodger was not going out again into the cold and foggy night—going out, as he had done the other evening, for a second time? But no; the sounds she heard, the sounds of now familiar footsteps, did not continue down the passage leading to the front door.

Instead—Why, what was this she heard now? She began to listen so intently that the bread she was holding at the end of the toasting-fork grew quite black. With a start she became aware that this was so, and she frowned, vexed with herself. That came of not attending to one's work.

Mr. Sleuth was evidently about to do what he had never yet done. He was coming down into the kitchen.

Nearer and nearer came the thudding sounds, treading heavily on the kitchen stairs, and Mrs. Bunting's heart began to beat as if in response. She put out the flame of the gas-ring, unheedful of the fact that the cheese would stiffen and spoil in the cold air.

Then she turned and faced the door.

There came a fumbling at the handle, and a moment later the door opened, and revealed, as she had at once known and feared it would do, the lodger.

Mr. Sleuth looked even odder than usual. He was clad in a plaid dressing-gown, which she had never seen him wear before, though she knew that he had purchased it not long after his arrival. In his hand was a lighted candle.

When he saw the kitchen all lighted up, and the woman standing in it, the lodger looked inexplicably taken aback, almost aghast.

"Yes, sir? What can I do for you, sir? I hope you didn't ring, sir?"

Mrs. Bunting held her ground in front of the stove. Mr. Sleuth had no business to come like this into her kitchen, and she intended to let him know that such was her view.

"No, I—I didn't ring," he stammered awkwardly. "The truth is, I didn't know you were here, Mrs. Bunting. Please excuse my costume. My gas-stove has gone wrong, or, rather, that shilling-in-the-slot arrangement has done so. So I came down to see if you had a gas-stove. I am going to ask you to allow me to use it to-night for an important experiment I wish to make."

Mrs. Bunting's heart was beating quickly—quickly. She felt horribly troubled, unnaturally so. Why couldn't Mr. Sleuth's experiment wait till the morning? She stared at him dubiously, but there was that in his face that made her at once afraid and pitiful. It was a wild, eager, imploring look.

"Oh, certainly, sir; but you will find it very cold down here."

"It seems most pleasantly warm," he observed, his voice full of relief, "warm and cosy, after my cold room upstairs."

Warm and cosy? Mrs. Bunting stared at him in amazement. Nay, even that cheerless room at the top of the house must be far warmer and more cosy than this cold underground kitchen could possibly be.

"I'll make you a fire, sir. We never use the grate, but it's in perfect order, for the first thing I did after I came into the house was to have the chimney swept. It was terribly dirty. It might have set the house on fire." Mrs. Bunting's housewifely instincts were roused. "For the matter of that, you ought to have a fire in your bedroom this cold night."

"By no means—I would prefer not. I certainly do not want a fire there. I dislike an open fire, Mrs. Bunting. I thought I had told you as much."

Mr. Sleuth frowned. He stood there, a strange-looking figure, his candle still alight, just inside the kitchen door.

"I shan't be very long, sir. Just about a quarter of an hour. You could come down then. I'll have everything quite tidy for you. Is there anything I can do to help you?"

"I do not require the use of your kitchen yet—thank you all the same, Mrs. Bunting. I shall come down later—altogether later—after you and your husband have gone to bed. But I should be much obliged if you would see that the gas people come to-morrow and put my stove in order. It might be done while I am out. That the shilling-in-the-slot machine should go wrong is very unpleasant. It has upset me greatly."

"Perhaps Bunting could put it right for you, sir. For the matter of that, I could ask him to go up now."

"No, no, I don't want anything of that sort done to-night. Besides, he couldn't put it right. I am something of an expert, Mrs. Bunting, and I have done all I could. The cause of the trouble is quite simple. The machine is choked up with shillings; a very foolish plan, so I always felt it to be."

Mr. Sleuth spoke pettishly, with far more heat than he was wont to speak, but Mrs. Bunting sympathised with him in this matter. She had always suspected that those slot machines were as dishonest as if they were human. It was dreadful, the way they swallowed up the shillings! She had had one once, so she knew.

And as if he were divining her thoughts, Mr. Sleuth walked forward and stared at the stove. "Then you haven't got a slot machine?" he said wonderingly. "I'm very glad of that, for I expect my experiment will take some time. But, of course, I shall pay you something for the use of the stove, Mrs. Bunting."

"Oh, no, sir, I wouldn't think of charging you anything for that. We don't use our stove very much, you know, sir. I'm never in the kitchen a minute longer than I can help this cold weather."

Mrs. Bunting was beginning to feel better. When she was actually in Mr. Sleuth's presence her morbid fears would be lulled, perhaps because his manner almost invariably was gentle and very quiet. But still there came over her an eerie feeling, as, with him preceding her, they made a slow progress to the ground floor.

Once there, the lodger courteously bade his landlady good-night, and proceeded upstairs to his own apartments.

Mrs. Bunting returned to the kitchen. Again she lighted the stove; but she felt unnerved, afraid of she knew not what. As she was cooking the cheese, she tried to concentrate her mind on what she was doing, and on the whole she succeeded. But another part of her mind seemed to be working independently, asking her insistent questions.

The place seemed to her alive with alien presences, and once she caught herself listening—which was absurd, for, of course, she could not hope to hear what Mr. Sleuth was doing two, if not three, flights upstairs. She wondered in what the lodger's experiments consisted. It was odd that she had never been able to discover what it was he really did with that big gas-stove. All she knew was that he used a very high degree of heat.

CHAPTER FIFTEEN

The Buntings went to bed early that night. But Mrs. Bunting made up her mind to keep awake. She was set upon knowing at what hour of the night the lodger would come down into her kitchen to carry through his experiment, and, above all, she was anxious to know how long he would stay there.

But she had had a long and a very anxious day, and presently she fell asleep.

The church clock hard by struck two, and, suddenly Mrs. Bunting awoke. She felt put out, sharply annoyed with herself. How could she have dropped off like that? Mr. Sleuth must have been down and up again hours ago!

Then, gradually, she became aware that there was a faint acrid odour in the room. Elusive, intangible, it yet seemed to encompass her and the snoring man by her side, almost as a vapour might have done.

Mrs. Bunting sat up in bed and sniffed; and then, in spite of the cold, she quietly crept out of her nice, warm bedclothes, and crawled along to the bottom of the bed. When there, Mr. Sleuth's landlady did a very curious thing; she leaned over the brass rail and put her face close to the hinge of the door giving into the hall. Yes, it was from here that this strange, horrible odor was coming; the smell must be very strong in the passage.

As, shivering, she crept back under the bedclothes, she longed to give her sleeping husband a good shake, and in fancy she heard herself saying, "Bunting, get up! There's something strange and dreadful going on downstairs which we ought to know about."

But as she lay there, by her husband's side, listening with painful intentness for the slightest sound, she knew very well that she would do nothing of the sort.

What if the lodger did make a certain amount of mess—a certain amount of smell—in her nice clean kitchen? Was he not—was he not an almost perfect lodger? If they did anything to upset him, where could they ever hope to get another like him?

Three o'clock struck before Mrs. Bunting heard slow, heavy steps creaking up the kitchen stairs. But Mr. Sleuth did not go straight up to his own quarters, as she had expected him to do. Instead, he went to the front door, and, opening it, put on the chain. Then he came past her door, and she thought—but could not be sure—that he sat down on the stairs.

At the end of ten minutes or so she heard him go down the passage again. Very softly he closed the front door. By then she had divined why the lodger had behaved in this funny fashion. He wanted to get the strong, acrid smell of burning—was it of burning wool?—out of the house.

But Mrs. Bunting, lying there in the darkness, listening to the lodger creeping upstairs, felt as if she herself would never get rid of the horrible odour.

Mrs. Bunting felt herself to be all smell.

At last the unhappy woman fell into a deep, troubled sleep; and then she dreamed a most terrible and unnatural dream. Hoarse voices seemed to be shouting in her ear: "The Avenger close here! The Avenger close here!" "'Orrible murder off the Edgware Road!" "The Avenger at his work again!"

And even in her dream Mrs. Bunting felt angered—angered and impatient. She knew so well why she was being disturbed by this horrid nightmare! It was because of Bunting—Bunting, who could think and talk of nothing else than those frightful murders, in which only morbid and vulgar-minded people took any interest.

Why, even now, in her dream, she could hear her husband speaking to her about it:

"Ellen"—so she heard Bunting murmur in her ear—"Ellen, my dear, I'm just going to get up to get a paper. It's after seven o'clock."

The shouting—nay, worse, the sound of tramping, hurrying feet smote on her shrinking ears. Pushing back her hair off her forehead with both hands, she sat up and listened.

It had been no nightmare, then, but something infinitely worse—reality.

Why couldn't Bunting have lain quiet abed for awhile longer, and let his poor wife go on dreaming? The most awful dream would have been easier to bear than this awakening.

She heard her husband go to the front door, and, as he bought the paper, exchange a few excited words with the newspaper-seller. Then he came back. There was a pause, and she heard him lighting the gas-ring in the sitting-room.

Bunting always made his wife a cup of tea in the morning. He had promised to do this when they first married, and he had never yet broken his word. It was a very little thing and a very usual thing, no doubt, for a kind husband to do, but this morning the knowledge that he was doing it brought tears to Mrs. Bunting's pale blue eyes. This morning he seemed to be rather longer than usual over the job.

When, at last, he came in with the little tray, Bunting found his wife lying with her face to the wall.

"Here's your tea, Ellen," he said, and there was a thrill of eager, nay happy, excitement in his voice.

She turned herself round and sat up. "Well?" she asked. "Well? Why don't you tell me about it?"

"I thought you was asleep," he stammered out. "I thought, Ellen, you never heard nothing."

"How could I have slept through all that din? Of course I heard. Why don't you tell me?"

"I've hardly had time to glance at the paper myself," he said slowly.

"You was reading it just now," she said severely, "for I heard the rustling. You begun reading it before you lit the gas-ring. Don't tell me! What was that they was shouting about the Edgware Road?"

"Well," said Bunting, "as you do know, I may as well tell you. The Avenger's moving West—that's what he's doing.[28] Last time 'twas King's Cross—now 'tis the Edgware Road. I said he'd come our way, and he has come our way!"

"You just go and get me that paper," she commanded. "I wants to see for myself."

Bunting went into the next room; then he came back and handed her silently the odd-looking, thin little sheet.

"Why, whatever's this?" she asked. "This ain't our paper!"

"'Course not," he answered, a trifle crossly. "It's a special early edition of the *Sun*, just because of The Avenger. Here's the bit about it"—he showed her the exact spot. But she would have found it, even by the comparatively bad light of the gas-jet now flaring over the dressing-table, for the news was printed in large, clear characters:—

> Once more the murder fiend who chooses to call himself The Avenger has escaped detection. While the whole attention of the police, and of the great army of amateur detectives who are taking an interest in this strange series of atrocious crimes, were concentrating their attention round the East End and King's Cross, he moved swiftly and silently Westward. And, choosing a time when the Edgware Road is at its busiest and most thronged, did another human being to death with lightning-like quickness and savagery.

Within fifty yards of the deserted warehouse yard where he had lured his victim to destruction were passing up and down scores of happy, busy people, intent on their Christmas shopping. Into that cheerful throng he must have plunged within a moment of committing his atrocious crime. And it was only owing to the merest accident that the body was discovered as soon as it was—that is, just after midnight.

Dr. Dowtray, who was called to the spot at once, is of opinion that the woman had been dead at least three hours, if not four. It was at first thought—we were going to say, hoped—that this murder had nothing to do with the series which is now puzzling and horrifying the whole of the civilised world. But no—pinned on the edge of the dead woman's dress was the usual now familiar triangular piece of grey paper—the grimmest visiting card ever designed by the wit of man! And this time The Avenger has surpassed himself as regards his audacity and daring—so cold in its maniacal fanaticism and abhorrent wickedness.

All the time that Mrs. Bunting was reading with slow, painful intentness, her husband was looking at her, longing, yet afraid, to burst out with a new idea which he was burning to confide even to his Ellen's unsympathetic ears.

At last, when she had quite finished, she looked up defiantly.

"Haven't you anything better to do than to stare at me like that?" she said irritably. "Murder or no murder, I've got to get up! Go away—do!"

And Bunting went off into the next room.

After he had gone, his wife lay back and closed her eyes. She tried to think of nothing. Nay, more—so strong, so determined was her will that for a few moments she actually did think of nothing. She felt terribly tired and weak, brain and body both quiescent, as does a person who is recovering from a long, wearing illness.

Presently detached, puerile thoughts drifted across the surface of her mind like little clouds across a summer sky. She wondered if those horrid newspaper men were allowed to shout in Belgrave Square; she wondered if, in that case, Margaret, who was so unlike her brother-in-law, would get up and buy a paper. But no. Margaret was not one to leave her nice warm bed for such a silly reason as that.

Was it to-morrow Daisy was coming back? Yes—to-morrow, not to-day. Well, that was a comfort, at any rate. What amusing things Daisy would be able to tell about her visit to Margaret! The girl had an excellent gift of mimicry. And Margaret, with her precise, funny ways, her perpetual talk about "the family," lent herself to the cruel gift.

And then Mrs. Bunting's mind—her poor, weak, tired mind—wandered off to young Chandler. A funny thing love was, when you came to think of it—which she, Ellen Bunting, didn't often do. There was Joe, a likely young fellow, seeing a lot of young women, and pretty young women, too,—quite as pretty as Daisy, and ten times more artful—and yet there! He passed them all by, had done so ever since last summer, though you might be sure that they, artful minxes, by no manner of means passed him by,—without giving them a thought! As Daisy wasn't here, he would probably keep away to-day. There was comfort in that thought, too.

And then Mrs. Bunting sat up, and memory returned in a dreadful turgid flood. If Joe did come in, she must nerve herself to hear all that—that talk there'd be about The Avenger between him and Bunting.

Slowly she dragged herself out of bed, feeling exactly as if she had just recovered from an illness which had left her very weak, very, very tired in body and soul.

She stood for a moment listening—listening, and shivering, for it was very cold. Considering how early it still was, there seemed a lot of coming and going in the Marylebone Road. She could hear the unaccustomed sounds through her closed door and the tightly fastened windows of the sitting-room. There must be a regular crowd of men and women, on foot and in cabs, hurrying to the scene of The Avenger's last extraordinary crime.

She heard the sudden thud made by their usual morning paper falling from the letter-box on to the floor of the hall, and a moment later came the sound of Bunting quickly, quietly going out and getting it. She visualised him coming back, and sitting down with a sigh of satisfaction by the newly-lit fire.

Languidly she began dressing herself to the accompaniment of distant tramping and of noise of passing traffic, which increased in volume and in sound as the moments slipped by.

When Mrs. Bunting went down into her kitchen everything looked just as she had left it, and there was no trace of the acrid smell she had expected to find there. Instead, the cavernous, whitewashed room was full of fog, but she noticed that, though the shutters were bolted and barred as she had left them, the windows behind them had been widely opened to the air. She had left them shut.

Making a "spill" out of a twist of newspaper—she had been taught the art as a girl by one of her old mistresses—she stooped and flung open the oven-door of her gas-stove. Yes, it was as she had expected, a fierce heat had been generated there since she had last used the oven, and through to the stone floor below had fallen a mass of black, gluey soot.

Mrs. Bunting took the ham and eggs that she had bought the previous day for her own and Bunting's breakfast upstairs, and broiled them over the gas-ring in their sitting-room. Her husband watched her in surprised silence. She had never done such a thing before.

"I couldn't stay down there," she said; "it was so cold and foggy. I thought I'd make breakfast up here, just for to-day."

"Yes," he said kindly; "that's quite right, Ellen. I think you've done quite right, my dear."

But, when it came to the point, his wife could not eat any of the nice breakfast she had got ready; she only had another cup of tea.

"I'm afraid you're ill, Ellen?" Bunting asked solicitously.

"No," she said shortly; "I'm not ill at all. Don't be silly! The thought of that horrible thing happening so close by has upset me, and put me off my food. Just hark to them now!"

Through their closed windows penetrated the sound of scurrying feet and loud, ribald laughter. What a crowd; nay, what a mob, must be hastening busily to and from the spot where there was now nothing to be seen!

Mrs. Bunting made her husband lock the front gate. "I don't want any of those ghouls in here!" she exclaimed angrily. And then, "What a lot of idle people there are in the world!" she said.

CHAPTER SIXTEEN

Bunting began moving about the room restlessly. He would go to the window; stand there awhile staring out at the people hurrying past; then, coming back to the fireplace, sit down.

But he could not stay long quiet. After a glance at his paper, up he would rise from his chair, and go to the window again.

"I wish you'd stay still," his wife said at last. And then, a few minutes later, "Hadn't you better put your hat and coat on and go out?" she exclaimed.

And Bunting, with a rather shamed expression, did put on his hat and coat and go out.

As he did so he told himself that, after all, he was but human; it was natural that he should be thrilled and excited by the dreadful, extraordinary thing which had just happened close by. Ellen wasn't reasonable about such things. How queer and disagreeable she had been that very morning—angry with him because he had gone out to hear what all the row was about, and even more angry when he had come back and said nothing, because he thought it would annoy her to hear about it!

Meanwhile, Mrs. Bunting forced herself to go down again into the kitchen, and as she went through into the low, whitewashed place, a tremor of fear, of quick terror, came over her. She turned and did what she had never in her life done before, and what she had never heard of anyone else doing in a kitchen. She bolted the door.

But, having done this, finding herself at last alone, shut off from everybody, she was still beset by a strange, uncanny dread. She felt as if she were locked in with an invisible presence, which mocked and jeered, reproached and threatened her, by turns.

Why had she allowed, nay encouraged, Daisy to go away for two days? Daisy, at any rate, was company—kind, young, unsuspecting company. With Daisy she could be her old sharp self. It was such a comfort to be with someone to whom she not only need, but ought to, say nothing. When with Bunting she was pursued by a sick feeling of guilt, of shame. She was the man's wedded wife—in his stolid way he was very kind to her, and yet she was keeping from him something he certainly had a right to know.

Not for worlds, however, would she have told Bunting of her dreadful suspicion—nay, of her almost certainty.

At last she went across to the door and unlocked it. Then she went upstairs and turned out her bedroom. That made her feel a little better.

She longed for Bunting to return, and yet in a way she was relieved by his absence. She would have liked to feel him near by, and yet she welcomed anything that took her husband out of the house.

And as Mrs. Bunting swept and dusted, trying to put her whole mind into what she was doing, she was asking herself all the time what was going on upstairs.

What a good rest the lodger was having! But there, that was only natural. Mr. Sleuth, as she well knew, had been up a long time last night, or rather this morning.

Suddenly, the drawing-room bell rang. But Mr. Sleuth's landlady did not go up, as she generally did, before getting ready the simple meal which was the lodger's luncheon and breakfast combined. Instead, she went downstairs again and hurriedly prepared the lodger's food.

Then, very slowly, with her heart beating queerly, she walked up, and just outside the sitting-room—for she felt sure that Mr. Sleuth had got up, that he was there already, waiting for her—she rested the tray on the top of the banisters and listened. For a few moments she heard nothing; then through the door came the high, quavering voice with which she had become so familiar: "'She saith to him, stolen waters are sweet, and bread eaten in secret is pleasant. But he knoweth not that the dead are there, and that her guests are in the depths of hell.'"[29]

There was a long pause. Mrs. Bunting could hear the leaves of her Bible being turned over, eagerly, busily; and then again Mr. Sleuth broke out, this time in a softer voice:

"'She hath cast down many wounded from her; yea, many strong men have been slain by her.'" And in a softer, lower, plaintive tone came the words: "'I applied my heart to know, and to search, and to seek out wisdom and the reason of things; and to know the wickedness of folly, even of foolishness and madness.'"[30]

And as she stood there listening, a feeling of keen distress, of spiritual oppression, came over Mrs. Bunting. For the first time in her life she visioned the infinite mystery, the sadness and strangeness, of human life.

Poor Mr. Sleuth—poor unhappy, distraught Mr. Sleuth! An overwhelming pity blotted out for a moment the fear, aye, and the loathing, she had been feeling for her lodger.

She knocked at the door, and then she took up her tray.

"Come in, Mrs. Bunting." Mr. Sleuth's voice sounded feebler, more toneless than usual.

She turned the handle of the door and walked in. The lodger was not sitting in his usual place; he had taken the little round table on which his candle generally rested when he read in bed, out of his bedroom, and placed it over by the drawing-room window. On it were placed, open, the Bible and the Concordance. But as his landlady came in, Mr. Sleuth hastily closed the Bible, and began staring dreamily out of the window, down at the sordid, hurrying crowd of men and women which now swept along the Marylebone Road.

"There seem a great many people out today," he observed, without looking round.

"Yes, sir, there do."

Mrs. Bunting began busying herself with laying the cloth and putting out the breakfast-lunch, and as she did so she was seized with a mortal, instinctive terror of the man sitting there.

At last Mr. Sleuth got up and turned round. She forced herself to look at him. How tired, how worn, he looked, and—how strange!

Walking towards the table on which lay his meal, he rubbed his hands together with a nervous gesture—it was a gesture he only made when something had pleased, nay, satisfied him. Mrs. Bunting, looking at him, remembered that he had rubbed his hands together thus when he had first seen the room upstairs, and realised that it contained a large gas-stove and a convenient sink.

What Mr. Sleuth was doing now also reminded her in an odd way of a play she had once seen—a play to which a young man had taken her when she was a girl, unnumbered years ago, and which had thrilled and fascinated her. "Out, out, damned spot!"[31] that was what the tall, fierce, beautiful lady who had played the part of a queen had said, twisting her hands together just as the lodger was doing now.

"It's a fine day," said Mr. Sleuth, sitting down and unfolding his napkin. "The fog has cleared. I do not know if you will agree with me, Mrs. Bunting, but I always feel brighter when the sun is shining, as it is now, at any rate, trying to shine." He looked at her inquiringly, but Mrs. Bunting could not speak. She only nodded. However, that did not affect Mr. Sleuth adversely.

He had acquired a great liking and respect for this well-balanced, taciturn woman. She was the first woman for whom he had experienced any such feeling for many years past.

He looked down at the still covered dish, and shook his head. "I don't feel as if I could eat very much to-day," he said plaintively. And then he suddenly took a half-sovereign out of his waistcoat pocket.

Already Mrs. Bunting had noticed that it was not the same waistcoat Mr. Sleuth had been wearing the day before.

"Mrs. Bunting, may I ask you to come here?"

And after a moment of hesitation his landlady obeyed him.

"Will you please accept this little gift for the use you kindly allowed me to make of your kitchen last night?" he said quietly. "I tried to make as little mess as I could, Mrs. Bunting, but—well, the truth is I was carrying out a very elaborate experiment."

Mrs. Bunting held out her hand, she hesitated, and then she took the coin. The fingers which for a moment brushed lightly against her palm were icy cold—cold and clammy. Mr. Sleuth was evidently not well.

As she walked down the stairs, the winter sun, a scarlet ball hanging in the smoky sky, glinted in on Mr. Sleuth's landlady, and threw blood-red gleams, or so it seemed to her, on to the piece of gold she was holding in her hand.

The day went by, as other days had gone by in that quiet household, but, of course, there was far greater animation outside the little house than was usually the case.

Perhaps because the sun was shining for the first time for some days, the whole of London seemed to be making holiday in that part of the town.

When Bunting at last came back, his wife listened silently while he told her of the extraordinary excitement reigning everywhere. And then, after he had been talking a long while, she suddenly shot a strange look at him.

"I suppose you went to see the place?" she said.

And guiltily he acknowledged that he had done so.

"Well?"

"Well, there wasn't anything much to see—not now. But, oh, Ellen, the daring of him! Why, Ellen, if the poor soul had had time to cry out— which they don't believe she had—it's impossible someone wouldn't 'a heard her. They say that if he goes on doing it like that—in the afternoon, like—he never will be caught. He must have just got mixed up with all the other people within ten seconds of what he'd done!"

During the afternoon Bunting bought papers recklessly—in fact, he must have spent the best part of six-pence. But in spite of all the supposed and suggested clues, there was nothing—nothing at all new to read, less, in fact than ever before.

The police, it was clear, were quite at a loss, and Mrs. Bunting began to feel curiously better, less tired, less ill, less—less terrified than she had felt through the morning.

And then something happened which broke with dramatic suddenness the quietude of the day.

They had had their tea, and Bunting was reading the last of the papers he had run out to buy, when suddenly there came a loud, thundering, double knock at the door.

Mrs. Bunting looked up, startled. "Why, whoever can that be?" she said.

But as Bunting got up she added quickly, "You just sit down again. I'll go myself. Sounds like someone after lodgings. I'll soon send them to the right-about!"

And then she left the room, but not before there had come another loud double knock.

Mrs. Bunting opened the front door. In a moment she saw that the person who stood there was a stranger to her. He was a big, dark man, with fierce, black moustaches. And somehow—she could not have told you why—he suggested a policeman to Mrs. Bunting's mind.

This notion of hers was confirmed by the very first words he uttered. For, "I'm here to execute a warrant!" he exclaimed in a theatrical, hollow tone.

With a weak cry of protest Mrs. Bunting suddenly threw out her arms as if to bar the way; she turned deadly white—but then, in an instant the supposed stranger's laugh rang out, with loud, jovial, familiar sound!

"There now, Mrs. Bunting! I never thought I'd take you in as well as all that!"

It was Joe Chandler—Joe Chandler dressed up, as she knew he sometimes, not very often, did dress up in the course of his work.

Mrs. Bunting began laughing—laughing helplessly, hysterically, just as she had done on the morning of Daisy's arrival, when the newspaper-sellers had come shouting down the Marylebone Road.

"What's all this about?" Bunting came out

Young Chandler ruefully shut the front door. "I didn't mean to upset her like this," he said, looking foolish; "'twas just my silly nonsense, Mr. Bunting." And together they helped her into the sitting-room.

But, once there, poor Mrs. Bunting went on worse than ever; she threw her black apron over her face, and began to sob hysterically.

"I made sure she'd know who I was when I spoke," went on the young fellow apologetically. "But, there now, I have upset her. I am sorry!"

"It don't matter!" she exclaimed, throwing the apron off her face, but the tears were still streaming from her eyes as she sobbed and laughed by turns. "Don't matter one little bit, Joe! 'Twas stupid of me to be so taken aback. But, there, that murder that's happened close by, it's just upset me—upset me altogether to-day."

"Enough to upset anyone—that was," acknowledged the young man ruefully. "I've only come in for a minute, like. I haven't no right to come when I'm on duty like this—"

Joe Chandler was looking longingly at what remains of the meal were still on the table.

"You can take a minute just to have a bite and a sup," said Bunting hospitably; "and then you can tell us any news there is, Joe. We're right in the middle of everything now, ain't we?" He spoke with evident enjoyment, almost pride, in the gruesome fact.

Joe nodded. Already his mouth was full of bread-and-butter. He waited a moment, and then: "Well I have got one piece of news—not that I suppose it'll interest you very much."

They both looked at him—Mrs. Bunting suddenly calm, though her breast still heaved from time to time.

"Our Boss has resigned!" said Joe Chandler slowly, impressively.[32]

"No! Not the Commissioner o' Police?" exclaimed Bunting.

"Yes, he has. He just can't bear what's said about us any longer—and I don't wonder! He done his best, and so's we all. The public have just gone daft—in the West End, that is, to-day. As for the papers, well, they're something cruel—that's what they are. And the ridiculous ideas they print! You'd never believe the things they asks us to do—and quite serious-like."

"What d'you mean?" questioned Mrs. Bunting. She really wanted to know.

"Well, the Courier declares that there ought to be a house-to-house investigation—all over London. Just think of it! Everybody to let the police go all over their house, from garret to kitchen, just to see if The Avenger isn't concealed there. Dotty, I calls it! Why, 'twould take us months and months just to do that one job in a town like London."

"I'd like to see them dare come into my house!" said Mrs. Bunting angrily.

"It's all along of them blarsted papers that The Avenger went to work a different way this time," said Chandler slowly.

Bunting had pushed a tin of sardines towards his guest, and was eagerly listening. "How d'you mean?" he asked. "I don't take your meaning, Joe."

"Well, you see, it's this way. The newspapers was always saying how extraordinary it was that The Avenger chose such a peculiar time to do his deeds—I mean, the time when no one's about the streets. Now, doesn't it stand to reason that the fellow, reading all that, and seeing the sense of it, said to himself, 'I'll go on another tack this time'? Just listen to this!" He pulled a strip of paper, part of a column cut from a newspaper, out of his pocket:

AN EX-LORD MAYOR OF LONDON ON THE AVENGER

'Will the murderer be caught? Yes,' replied Sir John, 'he will certainly be caught—probably when he commits his next crime. A whole army of bloodhounds, metaphorical and literal, will be on his track the moment he draws blood again. With the whole community against him, he cannot escape, especially when it be remembered that he chooses the quietest hour in the twenty-four to commit his crimes.

'Londoners are now in such a state of nerves—if I may use the expression, in such a state of funk—that every passer-by, however innocent, is looked at with suspicion by his neighbour if his avocation happens to take him abroad between the hours of one and three in the morning.'

"I'd like to gag that ex-Lord Mayor!" concluded Joe Chandler wrathfully.

Just then the lodger's bell rang.

"Let me go up, my dear," said Bunting.

His wife still looked pale and shaken by the fright she had had.

"No, no," she said hastily. "You stop down here, and talk to Joe. I'll look after Mr. Sleuth. He may be wanting his supper just a bit earlier than usual to-day."

Slowly, painfully, again feeling as if her legs were made of cotton wool, she dragged herself up to the first floor, knocked at the door, and then went in.

"You did ring, sir?" she said, in her quiet, respectful way.

And Mr. Sleuth looked up.

She thought—but, as she reminded herself afterwards, it might have been just her idea, and nothing else—that for the first time the lodger looked frightened—frightened and cowed.

"I heard a noise downstairs," he said fretfully, "and I wanted to know what it was all about. As I told you, Mrs. Bunting, when I first took these rooms, quiet is essential to me."

"It was just a friend of ours, sir. I'm sorry you were disturbed. Would you like the knocker taken off to-morrow? Bunting'll be pleased to do it if you don't like to hear the sound of the knocks."

"Oh, no, I wouldn't put you to such trouble as that." Mr. Sleuth looked quite relieved. "Just a friend of yours, was it, Mrs. Bunting? He made a great deal of noise."

"Just a young fellow," she said apologetically. "The son of one of Bunting's old friends. He often comes here, sir; but he never did give such a great big double knock as that before. I'll speak to him about it."

"Oh, no, Mrs. Bunting. I would really prefer you did nothing of the kind. It was just a passing annoyance—nothing more!"

She waited a moment. How strange that Mr. Sleuth said nothing of the hoarse cries which had made of the road outside a perfect Bedlam every hour or two throughout that day. But no, Mr. Sleuth made no allusion to what might well have disturbed any quiet gentleman at his reading.

"I thought maybe you'd like to have supper a little earlier to-night, sir?"

"Just when you like, Mrs. Bunting—just when it's convenient. I do not wish to put you out in any way."

She felt herself dismissed, and going out quietly, closed the door.

As she did so, she heard the front door banging to. She sighed—Joe Chandler was really a very noisy young fellow.

CHAPTER SEVENTEEN

Mrs. Bunting slept well the night following that during which the lodger had been engaged in making his mysterious experiments in her kitchen. She was so tired, so utterly exhausted, that sleep came to her the moment she laid her head upon her pillow.

Perhaps that was why she rose so early the next morning. Hardly giving herself time to swallow the tea Bunting had made and brought her, she got up and dressed.

She had suddenly come to the conclusion that the hall and staircase required a thorough "doing down," and she did not even wait till they had eaten their breakfast before beginning her labours. It made Bunting feel quite uncomfortable. As he sat by the fire reading his morning paper—the paper which was again of such absorbing interest—he called out, "There's no need for so much hurry, Ellen. Daisy'll be back to-day. Why don't you wait till she's come home to help you?"

But from the hall where she was busy dusting, sweeping, polishing, his wife's voice came back: "Girl's ain't no good at this sort of work. Don't you worry about me. I feel as if I'd enjoy doing an extra bit of cleaning to-day. I don't like to feel as anyone could come in and see my place dirty."

"No fear of that!" Bunting chuckled. And then a new thought struck him. "Ain't you afraid of waking the lodger?" he called out.

"Mr. Sleuth slept most of yesterday, and all last night," she answered quickly. "As it is, I study him over-much; it's a long, long time since I've done this staircase down."

All the time she was engaged in doing the hall, Mrs. Bunting left the sitting-room door wide open.

That was a queer thing of her to do, but Bunting didn't like to get up and shut her out, as it were. Still, try as he would, he couldn't read with any comfort while all that noise was going on. He had never known Ellen make such a lot of noise before. Once or twice he looked up and frowned rather crossly.

There came a sudden silence, and he was startled to see that. Ellen was standing in the doorway, staring at him, doing nothing.

"Come in," he said, "do! Ain't you finished yet?"

"I was only resting a minute," she said. "You don't tell me nothing. I'd like to know if there's anything—I mean anything new—in the paper this morning."

She spoke in a muffled voice, almost as if she were ashamed of her unusual curiosity; and her look of fatigue, of pallor, made Bunting suddenly uneasy. "Come in—do!" he repeated sharply. "You've done quite enough—and before breakfast, too. 'Tain't necessary. Come in and shut that door."

He spoke authoritatively, and his wife, for a wonder, obeyed him.

She came in, and did what she had never done before—brought the broom with her, and put it up against the wall in the corner.

Then she sat down.

"I think I'll make breakfast up here," she said. "I—I feel cold, Bunting." And her husband stared at her surprised, for drops of perspiration were glistening on her forehead.

He got up. "All right. I'll go down and bring the eggs up. Don't you worry. For the matter of that, I can cook them downstairs if you like."

"No," she said obstinately. "I'd rather do my own work. You just bring them up here—that'll be all right. To-morrow morning we'll have Daisy to help see to things."

"Come over here and sit down comfortable in my chair," he suggested kindly. "You never do take any bit of rest, Ellen. I never see'd such a woman!"

And again she got up and meekly obeyed him, walking across the room with languid steps.

He watched her, anxiously, uncomfortably.

She took up the newspaper he had just laid down, and Bunting took two steps towards her.

"I'll show you the most interesting bit" he said eagerly. "It's the piece headed, 'Our Special Investigator.' You see, they've started a special investigator of their own, and he's got hold of a lot of little facts the police seem to have overlooked. The man who writes all that—I mean the Special Investigator—was a famous 'tec in his time, and he's just come back out of his retirement o' purpose to do this bit of work for the paper. You read what he says—I shouldn't be a bit surprised if he ends by getting that reward! One can see he just loves the work of tracking people down."

"There's nothing to be proud of in such a job," said his wife listlessly.

"He'll have something to be proud of if he catches The Avenger!" cried Bunting. He was too keen about this affair to be put off by Ellen's contradictory remarks. "You just notice that bit about the rubber soles.

Now, no one's thought o' that. I'll just tell Chandler—he don't seem to me to be half awake, that young man don't."

"He's quite wide awake enough without you saying things to him! How about those eggs, Bunting? I feel quite ready for my breakfast even if you don't—"

Mrs. Bunting now spoke in what her husband sometimes secretly described to himself as "Ellen's snarling voice."

He turned away and left the room, feeling oddly troubled. There was something queer about her, and he couldn't make it out. He didn't mind it when she spoke sharply and nastily to him. He was used to that. But now she was so up and down; so different from what she used to be! In old days she had always been the same, but now a man never knew where to have her.

And as he went downstairs he pondered uneasily over his wife's changed ways and manner.

Take the question of his easy chair. A very small matter, no doubt, but he had never known Ellen sit in that chair—no, not even once, for a minute, since it had been purchased by her as a present for him.

They had been so happy, so happy, and so—so restful, during that first week after Mr. Sleuth had come to them. Perhaps it was the sudden, dramatic change from agonising anxiety to peace and security which had been too much for Ellen—yes, that was what was the matter with her, that and the universal excitement about these Avenger murders, which were shaking the nerves of all London. Even Bunting, unobservant as he was, had come to realise that his wife took a morbid interest in these terrible happenings. And it was the more queer of her to do so that at first she refused to discuss them, and said openly that she was utterly uninterested in murder or crime of any sort.

He, Bunting, had always had a mild pleasure in such things. In his time he had been a great reader of detective tales, and even now he thought there was no pleasanter reading. It was that which had first drawn him to Joe Chandler, and made him welcome the young chap as cordially as he had done when they first came to London.

But though Ellen had tolerated, she had never encouraged, that sort of talk between the two men. More than once she had exclaimed reproachfully: "To hear you two, one would think there was no nice, respectable, quiet people left in the world!"

But now all that was changed. She was as keen as anyone could be to hear the latest details of an Avenger crime. True, she took her own view of any theory suggested. But there! Ellen always had had her own notions about everything under the sun. Ellen was a woman who thought for herself—a clever woman, not an everyday woman by any manner of means.

While these thoughts were going disconnectedly through his mind, Bunting was breaking four eggs into a basin. He was going to give Ellen a nice little surprise—to cook an omelette as a French chef had once taught him to do, years and years ago. He didn't know how she would take his doing such a thing after what she had said; but never mind, she would enjoy the omelette when done. Ellen hadn't been eating her food properly of late.

And when he went up again, his wife, to his relief, and, it must be admitted, to his surprise, took it very well. She had not even noticed how long he had been downstairs, for she had been reading with intense, painful care the column that the great daily paper they took in had allotted to the one-time famous detective.

According to this Special Investigator's own account he had discovered all sorts of things that had escaped the eye of the police and of the official detectives. For instance, owing, he admitted, to a fortunate chance, he had been at the place where the two last murders had been committed very soon after the double crime had been discovered—in fact within half an hour, and he had found, or so he felt sure, on the slippery, wet pavement imprints of the murderer's right foot.

The paper reproduced the impression of a half-worn rubber sole. At the same time, he also admitted—for the Special Investigator was very honest, and he had a good bit of space to fill in the enterprising paper which had engaged him to probe the awful mystery—that there were thousands of rubber soles being worn in London...

And when she came to that statement Mrs. Bunting looked up, and there came a wan smile over her thin, closely-shut lips. It was quite true—that about rubber soles; there were thousands of rubber soles being worn just now. She felt grateful to the Special Investigator for having stated the fact so clearly.

The column ended up with the words:

> And to-day will take place the inquest on the double crime of ten days ago. To my mind it would be well if a preliminary public inquiry could be held at once. Say, on the very day the discovery of a fresh murder is made. In that way alone would it be possible to weigh and sift the evidence offered by members of the general public. For when a week or more has elapsed, and these same people have been examined and cross-examined in private by the police, their impressions have had time to become blurred and

hopelessly confused. On that last occasion but one there seems no doubt that several people, at any rate two women and one man, actually saw the murderer hurrying from the scene of his atrocious double crime—this being so, to-day's investigation may be of the highest value and importance. To-morrow I hope to give an account of the impression made on me by the inquest, and by any statements made during its course.

Even when her husband had come in with the tray Mrs. Bunting had gone on reading, only lifting up her eyes for a moment. At last he said rather crossly, "Put down that paper, Ellen, this minute! The omelette I've cooked for you will be just like leather if you don't eat it."

But once his wife had eaten her breakfast—and, to Bunting's mortification, she left more than half the nice omelette untouched—she took the paper up again. She turned over the big sheets, until she found, at the foot of one of the ten columns devoted to The Avenger and his crimes, the information she wanted, and then uttered an exclamation under her breath.

What Mrs. Bunting had been looking for—what at last she had found—was the time and place of the inquest which was to be held that day. The hour named was a rather odd time—two o'clock in the afternoon, but, from Mrs. Bunting's point of view, it was most convenient.

By two o'clock, nay, by half-past one, the lodger would have had his lunch; by hurrying matters a little she and Bunting would have had their dinner, and—and Daisy wasn't coming home till tea-time.

She got up out of her husband's chair. "I think you're right," she said, in a quick, hoarse tone. "I mean about me seeing a doctor, Bunting. I think I will go and see a doctor this very afternoon."

"Wouldn't you like me to go with you?" he asked.

"No, that I wouldn't. In fact I wouldn't go at all you was to go with me."

"All right," he said vexedly. "Please yourself, my dear; you know best."

"I should think I did know best where my own health is concerned."

Even Bunting was incensed by this lack of gratitude. "'Twas I said, long ago, you ought to go and see the doctor; 'twas you said you wouldn't!" he exclaimed pugnaciously.

"Well, I've never said you was never right, have I? At any rate, I'm going."

"Have you a pain anywhere?" He stared at her with a look of real solicitude on his fat, phlegmatic face.

Somehow Ellen didn't look right, standing there opposite him. Her shoulders seemed to have shrunk; even her cheeks had fallen in a little. She had never looked so bad—not even when they had been half starving, and dreadfully, dreadfully worked.

"Yes," she said briefly, "I've a pain in my head, at the back of my neck. It doesn't often leave me; it gets worse when anything upsets me, like I was upset last night by Joe Chandler."

"He was a silly ass to come and do a thing like that!" said Bunting crossly. "I'd a good mind to tell him so, too. But I must say, Ellen, I wonder he took you in—he didn't me!"

"Well, you had no chance he should—you knew who it was," she said slowly.

And Bunting remained silent, for Ellen was right. Joe Chandler had already spoken when he, Bunting, came out into the hall, and saw their cleverly disguised visitor.

"Those big black moustaches," he went on complainingly, "and that black wig—why, 'twas too ridic'lous—that's what I call it!"

"Not to anyone who didn't know Joe," she said sharply.

"Well, I don't know. He didn't look like a real man—nohow. If he's a wise lad, he won't let our Daisy ever see him looking like that!" and Bunting laughed, a comfortable laugh.

He had thought a good deal about Daisy and young Chandler the last two days, and, on the whole, he was well pleased. It was a dull, unnatural life the girl was leading with Old Aunt. And Joe was earning good money. They wouldn't have long to wait, these two young people, as a beau and his girl often have to wait, as he, Bunting, and Daisy's mother had had to do, for ever so long before they could be married. No, there was no reason why they shouldn't be spliced quite soon—if so the fancy took them. And Bunting had very little doubt that so the fancy would take Joe, at any rate.

But there was plenty of time. Daisy wouldn't be eighteen till the week after next. They might wait till she was twenty. By that time Old Aunt might be dead, and Daisy might have come into quite a tidy little bit of money.

"What are you smiling at?" said his wife sharply.

And he shook himself. "I—smiling? At nothing that I knows of." Then he waited a moment. "Well, if you will know, Ellen, I was just thinking of Daisy and that young chap Joe Chandler. He is gone on her, ain't he?"

"Gone?" And then Mrs. Bunting laughed, a queer, odd, not unkindly laugh. "Gone, Bunting?" she repeated. "Why, he's out o' sight—right, out of sight!"

Then hesitatingly, and looking narrowly at her husband, she went on, twisting a bit of her black apron with her fingers as she spoke:—"I suppose he'll be going over this afternoon to fetch her? Or—or d'you think he'll have to be at that inquest, Bunting?"

"Inquest? What inquest?" He looked at her puzzled.

"Why, the inquest on them bodies found in the passage near by King's Cross."

"Oh, no; he'd have no call to be at the inquest. For the matter o' that, I know he's going over to fetch Daisy. He said so last night—just when you went up to the lodger."

"That's just as well." Mrs. Bunting spoke with considerable satisfaction. "Otherwise I suppose you'd ha' had to go. I wouldn't like the house left—not with us out of it. Mr. Sleuth would be upset if there came a ring at the door."

"Oh, I won't leave the house, don't you be afraid, Ellen—not while you're out."

"Not even if I'm out a good while, Bunting."

"No fear. Of course, you'll be a long time if it's your idea to see that doctor at Ealing?"

He looked at her questioningly, and Mrs. Bunting nodded. Somehow nodding didn't seem as bad as speaking a lie.

CHAPTER EIGHTEEN

Any ordeal is far less terrifying, far easier to meet with courage, when it is repeated, than is even a milder experience which is entirely novel.

Mrs. Bunting had already attended an inquest, in the character of a witness, and it was one of the few happenings of her life which was sharply etched against the somewhat blurred screen of her memory.[33]

In a country house where the then Ellen Green had been staying for a fortnight with her elderly mistress, there had occurred one of those sudden, pitiful tragedies which occasionally destroy the serenity, the apparent decorum, of a large, respectable household.

The under-housemaid, a pretty, happy-natured girl, had drowned herself for love of the footman, who had given his sweetheart cause for bitter jealousy. The girl had chosen to speak of her troubles to the strange lady's maid rather than to her own fellow-servants, and it was during the conversation the two women had had together that the girl had threatened to take her own life.

As Mrs. Bunting put on her outdoor clothes, preparatory to going out, she recalled very clearly all the details of that dreadful affair, and of the part she herself had unwillingly played in it.

She visualised the country inn where the inquest on that poor, unfortunate creature had been held.

The butler had escorted her from the Hall, for he also was to give evidence, and as they came up there had been a look of cheerful animation about the inn yard; people coming and going, many women as well as men, village folk, among whom the dead girl's fate had aroused a great deal of interest, and the kind of horror which those who live on a dull countryside welcome rather than avoid.

Everyone there had been particularly nice and polite to her, to Ellen Green; there had been a time of waiting in a room upstairs in the old inn, and the witnesses had been accommodated, not only with chairs, but with cake and wine.

She remembered how she had dreaded being a witness, how she had felt as if she would like to run away from her nice, easy place, rather than have to get up and tell the little that she knew of the sad business.

But it had not been so very dreadful after all. The coroner had been a kindly-spoken gentleman; in fact he had complimented her on the clear, sensible way she had given her evidence concerning the exact words the unhappy girl had used.

One thing Ellen Green had said, in answer to a question put by an inquisitive juryman, had raised a laugh in the crowded, low-ceilinged room. "Ought not Miss Ellen Green," so the man had asked, "to have told someone of the girl's threat? If she had done so, might not the girl have been prevented from throwing herself into the lake?" And she, the witness, had answered, with some asperity—for by that time the coroner's kind manner had put her at her ease—that she had not attached any importance to what the girl had threatened to do, never believing that any young woman could be so silly as to drown herself for love!

Vaguely Mrs. Bunting supposed that the inquest at which she was going to be present this afternoon would be like that country inquest of long ago.

It had been no mere perfunctory inquiry; she remembered very well how little by little that pleasant-spoken gentleman, the coroner, had got the whole truth out—the story, that is, of how that horrid footman, whom she, Ellen Green, had disliked from the first minute she had set eyes on him, had taken up with another young woman. It had been supposed that this fact would not be elicited by the coroner; but it had been, quietly, remorselessly; more, the dead girl's letters had been read out—piteous, queerly expressed letters, full of wild love and bitter, threatening jealousy. And the jury had censured the young man most severely; she remembered the look on his face when the people, shrinking back, had made a passage for him to slink out of the crowded room.

Come to think of it now, it was strange she had never told Bunting that long-ago tale. It had occurred years before she knew him, and somehow nothing had ever happened to make her tell him about it.

She wondered whether Bunting had ever been to an inquest. She longed to ask him. But if she asked him now, this minute, he might guess where she was thinking of going.

And then, while still moving about her bedroom, she shook her head— no, no, Bunting would never guess such a thing; he would never, never suspect her of telling him a lie.

Stop—had she told a lie? She did mean to go to the doctor after the inquest was finished—if there was time, that is. She wondered uneasily how long such an inquiry was likely to last. In this case, as so very little had been discovered, the proceedings would surely be very formal— formal and therefore short.

She herself had one quite definite object—that of hearing the evidence of those who believed they had seen the murderer leaving the spot where his victims lay weltering in their still flowing blood. She was filled with a painful, secret, and, yes, eager curiosity to hear how those who were so positive about the matter would describe the appearance of The Avenger. After all, a lot of people must have seen him, for, as Bunting had said only the day before to young Chandler, The Avenger was not a ghost; he was a living man with some kind of hiding-place where he was known, and where he spent his time between his awful crimes.

As she came back to the sitting-room, her extreme pallor struck her husband.

"Why, Ellen," he said, "it is time you went to the doctor. You looks just as if you was going to a funeral. I'll come along with you as far as the station. You're going by train, ain't you? Not by bus, eh? It's a very long way to Ealing, you know."

"There you go! Breaking your solemn promise to me the very first minute!" But somehow she did not speak unkindly, only fretfully and sadly.

And Bunting hung his head. "Why, to be sure I'd gone and clean forgot the lodger! But will you be all right, Ellen? Why not wait till to-morrow, and take Daisy with you?"

"I like doing my own business in my own way, and not in someone else's way!" she snapped out; and then more gently, for Bunting really looked concerned, and she did feel very far from well, "I'll be all right, old man. Don't you worry about me!"

As she turned to go across to the door, she drew the black shawl she had put over her long jacket more closely round her.

She felt ashamed, deeply ashamed, of deceiving so kind a husband. And yet, what could she do? How could she share her dreadful burden with poor Bunting? Why, 'twould be enough to make a man go daft. Even she often felt as if she could stand it no longer—as if she would give the world to tell someone—anyone—what it was that she suspected, what deep in her heart she so feared to be the truth.

But, unknown to herself, the fresh outside air, fog-laden though it was, soon began to do her good. She had gone out far too little the last few days, for she had had a nervous terror of leaving the house unprotected, as also a great unwillingness to allow Bunting to come into contact with the lodger.

When she reached the Underground station she stopped short. There were two ways of getting to St. Pancras—she could go by bus, or she could go by train. She decided on the latter. But before turning into the station her eyes strayed over the bills of the early afternoon papers lying on the ground.

Two words,

THE AVENGER

stared up at her in varying type.

Drawing her black shawl yet a little closer about her shoulders, Mrs. Bunting looked down at the placards. She did not feel inclined to buy a paper, as many of the people round her were doing. Her eyes were smarting, even now, from their unaccustomed following of the close print in the paper Bunting took in.

Slowly she turned, at last, into the Underground station.

And now a piece of extraordinary good fortune befell Mrs. Bunting.

The third-class carriage in which she took her place happened to be empty, save for the presence of a police inspector. And once they were well away she summoned up courage, and asked him the question she knew she would have to ask of someone within the next few minutes.

"Can you tell me," she said, in a low voice, "where death inquests are held"—she moistened her lips, waited a moment, and then concluded—"in the neighbourhood of King's Cross?"

The man turned and, looked at her attentively. She did not look at all the sort of Londoner who goes to an inquest—there are many such—just for the fun of the thing. Approvingly, for he was a widower, he noted her neat black coat and skirt; and the plain Princess bonnet which framed her pale, refined face.

"I'm going to the Coroner's Court myself." he said good-naturedly. "So you can come along of me. You see there's that big Avenger inquest going on to-day, so I think they'll have had to make other arrangements for—hum, hum—ordinary cases." And as she looked at him dumbly, he went on, "There'll be a mighty crowd of people at The Avenger inquest— a lot of ticket folk to be accommodated, to say nothing of the public."

"That's the inquest I'm going to," faltered Mrs. Bunting. She could scarcely get the words out. She realised with acute discomfort, yes, and shame, how strange, how untoward, was that which she was going to do. Fancy a respectable woman wanting to attend a murder inquest!

During the last few days all her perceptions had become sharpened by suspense and fear. She realised now, as she looked into the stolid face of her unknown friend, how she herself would have regarded any woman who wanted to attend such an inquiry from a simple, morbid feeling of curiosity. And yet—and yet that was just what she was about to do herself.

"I've got a reason for wanting to go there," she murmured. It was a comfort to unburden herself this little way even to a stranger.

"Ah!" he said reflectively. "A—a relative connected with one of the two victims' husbands, I presume?"

And Mrs. Bunting bent her head.

"Going to give evidence?" he asked casually, and then he turned and looked at Mrs. Bunting with far more attention than he had yet done.

"Oh, no!" There was a world of horror, of fear in the speaker's voice.

And the inspector felt concerned and sorry. "Hadn't seen her for quite a long time, I suppose?"

"Never had, seen her. I'm from the country." Something impelled Mrs. Bunting to say these words. But she hastily corrected herself, "At least, I was."

"Will he be there?"

She looked at him dumbly; not in the least knowing to whom he was alluding.

"I mean the husband," went on the inspector hastily. "I felt sorry for the last poor chap—I mean the husband of the last one—he seemed so awfully miserable. You see, she'd been a good wife and a good mother till she took to the drink."

"It always is so," breathed out Mrs. Bunting.

"Aye." He waited a moment. "D'you know anyone about the court?" he asked.

She shook her head.

"Well, don't you worry. I'll take you in along o' me. You'd never get in by yourself."

They got out; and oh, the comfort of being in some one's charge, of having a determined man in uniform to look after one! And yet even now there was to Mrs. Bunting something dream-like, unsubstantial about the whole business.

"If he knew—if he only knew what I know!" she kept saying over and over again to herself as she walked lightly by the big, burly form of the police inspector.

"'Tisn't far—not three minutes," he said suddenly. "Am I walking too quick for you, ma'am?"'

"No, not at all. I'm a quick walker."

And then suddenly they turned a corner and came on a mass of people, a densely packed crowd of men and women, staring at a mean-looking little door sunk into a high wall.

"Better take my arm," the inspector suggested. "Make way there! Make way!" he cried authoritatively; and he swept her through the serried ranks which parted at the sound of his voice, at the sight of his uniform.

"Lucky you met me," he said, smiling. "You'd never have got through alone. And 'tain't a nice crowd, not by any manner of means."

The small door opened just a little way, and they found themselves on a narrow stone-flagged path, leading into a square yard. A few men were out there, smoking.

Before preceding her into the building which rose at the back of the yard, Mrs. Bunting's kind new friend took out his watch. "There's another twenty minutes before they'll begin," he said. "There's the mortuary"—he pointed with his thumb to a low room built out to the right of the court. "Would you like to go in and see them?" he whispered.

"Oh, no!" she cried, in a tone of extreme horror. And he looked down at her with sympathy, and with increased respect. She was a nice, respectable woman, she was. She had not come here imbued with any morbid, horrible curiosity, but because she thought it her duty to do so. He suspected her of being sister-in-law to one of The Avenger's victims.

They walked through into a big room or hall, now full of men talking in subdued yet eager, animated tones.

"I think you'd better sit down here," he said considerately, and, leading her to one of the benches that stood out from the whitewashed walls— "unless you'd rather be with the witnesses, that is."

But again she said, "Oh, no!" And then, with an effort, "Oughtn't I to go into the court now, if it's likely to be so full?"

"Don't you worry," he said kindly. "I'll see you get a proper place. I must leave you now for a minute, but I'll come back in good time and look after you."

She raised the thick veil she had pulled down over her face while they were going through that sinister, wolfish-looking crowd outside, and looked about her.

Many of the gentlemen—they mostly wore tall hats and good overcoats—standing round and about her looked vaguely familiar. She picked out one at once. He was a famous journalist, whose shrewd, animated face was familiar to her owing to the fact that it was widely advertised in connection with a preparation for the hair—the preparation which in happier, more prosperous days Bunting had had great faith in, and used, or so he always said, with great benefit to himself. This gentleman was the centre of an eager circle; half a dozen men were talking to him, listening deferentially when he spoke, and each of these men, so Mrs. Bunting realised, was a Somebody.

How strange, how amazing, to reflect that from all parts of London, from their doubtless important avocations, one unseen, mysterious beckoner had brought all these men here together, to this sordid place, on this bitterly cold, dreary day. Here they were, all thinking of, talking of, evoking one unknown, mysterious personality —that of the shadowy and yet terribly real human being who chose to call himself The Avenger. And somewhere, not so very far away from them all The Avenger was keeping these clever, astute, highly trained minds—aye, and bodies, too—at bay.

Even Mrs. Bunting, sitting here unnoticed, realised the irony of her presence among them.

CHAPTER NINETEEN

It seemed to Mrs. Bunting that she had been sitting there a long time—it was really about a quarter of an hour—when her official friend came back.

"Better come along now," he whispered; "it'll begin soon."

She followed him out into a passage, up a row of steep stone steps, and so into the Coroner's Court.

The court was big, well-lighted room, in some ways not unlike a chapel, the more so that a kind of gallery ran half-way round, a gallery evidently set aside for the general public, for it was now crammed to its utmost capacity.

Mrs. Bunting glanced timidly towards the serried row of faces. Had it not been for her good fortune in meeting the man she was now following, it was there that she would have had to try and make her way. And she would have failed. Those people had rushed in the moment the doors were opened, pushing, fighting their way in a way she could never have pushed or fought.

There were just a few women among them, set, determined-looking women, belonging to every class, but made one by their love of sensation and their power of forcing their way in where they wanted to be. But the women were few; the great majority of those standing there were men—men who were also representative of every class of Londoner.

The centre of the court was like an arena; it was sunk two or three steps below the surrounding gallery. Just now it was comparatively clear of people, save for the benches on which sat the men who were to compose the jury. Some way from these men, huddled together in a kind of big pew, stood seven people—three women and four men.

"D'you see the witnesses?" whispered the inspector, pointing these out to her. He supposed her to know one of them with familiar knowledge, but, if that were so, she made no sign.

Between the windows, facing the whole room, was a kind of little platform, on which stood a desk and an arm-chair. Mrs. Bunting guessed rightly that it was there the coroner would sit. And to the left of the platform was the witness-stand, also raised considerably above the jury.

Amazingly different, and far, far more grim and awe-inspiring than the scene of the inquest which had taken place so long ago, on that bright April day, in the village inn. There the coroner had sat on the same level as the jury, and the witnesses had simply stepped forward one by one, and taken their place before him.

Looking round her fearfully, Mrs. Bunting thought she would surely die if ever she were exposed to the ordeal of standing in that curious box-like stand, and she stared across at the bench where sat the seven witnesses with a feeling of sincere pity in her heart.

But even she soon realised that her pity was wasted. Each woman witness looked eager, excited, and animated; well pleased to be the centre of attention and attraction to the general public. It was plain each was enjoying her part of important, if humble, actress in the thrilling drama which was now absorbing the attention of all London—it might almost be said of the whole world.

Looking at these women, Mrs. Bunting wondered vaguely which was which. Was it that rather draggle-tailed-looking young person who had certainly, or almost certainly, seen The Avenger within ten seconds of the double crime being committed? The woman who, aroused by one of his victims' cry of terror, had rushed to her window and seen the murderer's shadowy form pass swiftly by in the fog?

Yet another woman, so Mrs. Bunting now remembered, had given a most circumstantial account of what The Avenger looked like, for he, it was supposed, had actually brushed by her as he passed.

Those two women now before her had been interrogated and cross-examined again and again, not only by the police, but by representatives of every newspaper in London. It was from what they had both said—unluckily their accounts materially differed—that that official description of The Avenger had been worked up—that which described him as being a good-looking, respectable young fellow of twenty-eight, carrying a newspaper parcel.

As for the third woman, she was doubtless an acquaintance, a boon companion of the dead.

Mrs. Bunting looked away from the witnesses, and focused her gaze on another unfamiliar sight. Specially prominent, running indeed through the whole length of the shut-in space, that is, from the coroner's high dais right across to the opening in the wooden barrier, was an ink-splashed table at which, when she had first taken her place, there had been sitting three men busily sketching; but now every seat at the table was occupied by tired, intelligent-looking men, each with a notebook, or with some loose sheets of paper, before him.

"Them's the reporters," whispered her friend. "They don't like coming till the last minute, for they has to be the last to go. At an ordinary inquest there are only two—maybe three—attending, but now every paper in the kingdom has pretty well applied for a pass to that reporters' table."

He looked consideringly down into the well of the court. "Now let me see what I can do for you—"

Then he beckoned to the coroner's officer: "Perhaps you could put this lady just over there, in a corner by herself? Related to a relation of the deceased, but doesn't want to be—" He whispered a word or two, and the other nodded sympathetically, and looked at Mrs. Bunting with interest. "I'll put her just here," he muttered. "There's no one coming there to-day. You see, there are only seven witnesses—sometimes we have a lot more than that."

And he kindly put her on a now empty bench opposite to where the seven witnesses stood and sat with their eager, set faces, ready—aye, more than ready—to play their part.

For a moment every eye in the court was focused on Mrs. Bunting, but soon those who had stared so hungrily, so intently, at her, realised that she had nothing to do with the case. She was evidently there as a spectator, and, more fortunate than most, she had a "friend at court," and so was able to sit comfortably, instead of having to stand in the crowd.

But she was not long left in isolation. Very soon some of the important-looking gentlemen she had seen downstairs came into the court, and were ushered over to her seat while two or three among them, including the famous writer whose face was so familiar that it almost seemed to Mrs. Bunting like that of a kindly acquaintance, were accommodated at the reporters' table.

"Gentlemen, the Coroner."

The jury stood up, shuffling their feet, and then sat down again; over the spectators there fell a sudden silence.

And then what immediately followed recalled to Mrs. Bunting, for the first time, that informal little country inquest of long ago.

First came the "Oyez! Oyez!" the old Norman-French summons to all whose business it is to attend a solemn inquiry into the death—sudden, unexplained, terrible—of a fellow-being.

The jury—there were fourteen of them—all stood up again. They raised their hands and solemnly chanted together the curious words of their oath. Then came a quick, informal exchange of sentences 'twixt the coroner and his officer.

Yes, everything was in order. The jury had viewed the bodies—he quickly corrected himself—the body, for, technically speaking, the inquest just about to be held only concerned one body.

And then, amid a silence so absolute that the slightest rustle could be heard through the court, the coroner—a clever-looking gentleman, though not so old as Mrs. Bunting thought he ought to have been to occupy so important a position on so important a day—gave a little history, as it were, of the terrible and mysterious Avenger crimes.

He spoke very clearly, warming to his work as he went on.

He told them that he had been present at the inquest held on one of The Avenger's former victims. "I only went through professional curiosity," he threw in by way of parenthesis, "little thinking, gentlemen, that the inquest on one of these unhappy creatures would ever be held in my court."

On and on, he went, though he had, in truth, but little to say, and though that little was known to every one of his listeners.

Mrs. Bunting heard one of the older gentlemen sitting near her whisper to another: "Drawing it out all he can; that's what he's doing. Having the time of his life, evidently!" And then the other whispered back, so low that she could only just catch the words, "Aye, aye. But he's a good chap—I knew his father; we were at school together. Takes his job very seriously, you know—he does to-day, at any rate."

She was listening intently, waiting for a word, a sentence, which would relieve her hidden terrors, or, on the other hand, confirm them. But the word, the sentence, was never uttered.

And yet, at the very end of his long peroration, the coroner did throw out a hint which might mean anything—or nothing.

"I am glad to say that we hope to obtain such evidence to-day as will in time lead to the apprehension of the miscreant who has committed, and is still committing, these terrible crimes."

Mrs. Bunting stared uneasily up into the coroner's firm, determined-looking face. What did he mean by that? Was there any new evidence—evidence of which Joe Chandler, for instance, was ignorant? And, as if in answer to the unspoken question, her heart gave a sudden leap, for a big, burly man had taken his place in the witness-box—a policeman who had not been sitting with the other witnesses.

But soon her uneasy terror became stilled. This witness was simply the constable who had found the first body. In quick, business-like tones he described exactly what had happened to him on that cold, foggy morning ten days ago. He was shown a plan, and he marked it slowly, carefully, with a thick finger. That was the exact place—no, he was making a mistake—that was the place where the other body had lain. He explained apologetically that he had got rather mixed up between the two bodies—that of Johanna Cobbett and Sophy Hurtle.

And then the coroner intervened authoritatively: "For the purpose of this inquiry," he said, "we must, I think, for a moment consider the two murders together."

After that, the witness went on far more comfortably; and as he proceeded, in a quick monotone, the full and deadly horror of The Avenger's acts came over Mrs. Bunting in a great seething flood of sick fear and—and, yes, remorse.

Up to now she had given very little thought—if, indeed, any thought—to the drink-sodden victims of The Avenger. It was he who had filled her thoughts,—he and those who were trying to track him down. But now? Now she felt sick and sorry she had come here to-day. She wondered if she would ever be able to get the vision the policeman's words had conjured up out of her mind—out of her memory.

And then there came an eager stir of excitement and of attention throughout the whole court, for the policeman had stepped down out of the witness-box, and one of the women witnesses was being conducted to his place.

Mrs. Bunting looked with interest and sympathy at the woman, remembering how she herself had trembled with fear, trembled as that poor, bedraggled, common-looking person was trembling now. The woman had looked so cheerful, so—so well pleased with herself till a minute ago, but now she had become very pale, and she looked round her as a hunted animal might have done.

But the coroner was very kind, very soothing and gentle in his manner, just as that other coroner had been when dealing with Ellen Green at the inquest on that poor drowned girl.

After the witness had repeated in a toneless voice the solemn words of the oath, she began to be taken, step by step, though her story. At once Mrs. Bunting realised that this was the woman who claimed to have seen The Avenger from her bedroom window. Gaining confidence, as she went on, the witness described how she had heard a long-drawn, stifled screech, and, aroused from deep sleep, had instinctively jumped out of bed and rushed to her window.

The coroner looked down at something lying on his desk. "Let me see! Here is the plan. Yes—I think I understand that the house in which you are lodging exactly faces the alley where the two crimes were committed?"

And there arose a quick, futile discussion. The house did not face the alley, but the window of the witness's bedroom faced the alley.

"A distinction without a difference," said the coroner testily. "And now tell us as clearly and quickly as you can what you saw when you looked out."

There fell a dead silence on the crowded court. And then the woman broke out, speaking more volubly and firmly than she had yet done. "I saw 'im!" she cried. "I shall never forget it—no, not till my dying day!" And she looked round defiantly.

Mrs. Bunting suddenly remembered a chat one of the newspaper men had had with a person who slept under this woman's room. That person had unkindly said she felt sure that Lizzie Cole had not got up that night— that she had made up the whole story. She, the speaker, slept lightly, and that night had been tending a sick child. Accordingly, she would have heard if there had been either the scream described by Lizzie Cole, or the sound of Lizzie Cole jumping out of bed.

"We quite understand that you think you saw the"—the coroner hesitated—"the individual who had just perpetrated these terrible crimes. But what we want to have from you is a description of him. In spite of the foggy atmosphere about which all are agreed, you say you saw him distinctly, walking along for some yards below your window. Now, please, try and tell us what he was like."

The woman began twisting and untwisting the corner of a coloured handkerchief she held in her hand.

"Let us begin at the beginning," said the coroner patiently. "What sort of a hat was this man wearing when you saw him hurrying from the passage?"

"It was just a black 'at" said the witness at last, in a husky, rather anxious tone.

"Yes—just a black hat. And a coat—were you able to see what sort of a coat he was wearing?"

"'E 'adn't got no coat" she said decidedly. "No coat at all! I remembers that very perticulerly. I thought it queer, as it was so cold— everybody as can wears some sort o' coat this weather!"

A juryman who had been looking at a strip of newspaper, and apparently not attending at all to what the witness was saying, here jumped up and put out his hand.

"Yes?" the coroner turned to him.

"I just want to say that this 'ere witness—if her name is Lizzie Cole, began by saying The Avenger was wearing a coat—a big, heavy coat. I've got it here, in this bit of paper."

"I never said so!" cried the woman passionately. "I was made to say all those things by the young man what came to me from the *Evening Sun*. Just put in what 'e liked in 'is paper, 'e did—not what I said at all!"

At this there was some laughter, quickly suppressed.

"In future," said the coroner severely, addressing the juryman, who had now sat down again, "you must ask any question you wish to ask through your foreman, and please wait till I have concluded my examination of the witness."

But this interruption, this—this accusation, had utterly upset the witness. She began contradicting herself hopelessly. The man she had seen hurrying by in the semi-darkness below was tall—no, he was short. He was thin—no, he was a stoutish young man. And as to whether he was carrying anything, there was quite an acrimonious discussion.

Most positively, most confidently, the witness declared that she had seen a newspaper parcel under his arm; it had bulged out at the back—so she declared. But it was proved, very gently and firmly, that she had said nothing of the kind to the gentleman from Scotland Yard who had taken down her first account—in fact, to him she had declared confidently that the man had carried nothing—nothing at all; that she had seen his arms swinging up and down.

One fact—if fact it could be called—the coroner did elicit. Lizzie Cole suddenly volunteered the statement that as he had passed her window he had looked up at her. This was quite a new statement.

"He looked up at you?" repeated the coroner. "You said nothing of that in your examination."

"I said nothink because I was scared—nigh scared to death!"

"If you could really see his countenance, for we know the night was dark and foggy, will you please tell me what he was like?"

But the coroner was speaking casually, his hand straying over his desk; not a creature in that court now believed the woman's story.

"Dark!" she answered dramatically. "Dark, almost black! If you can take my meaning, with a sort of nigger look."

And then there was a titter. Even the jury smiled. And sharply the coroner bade Lizzie Cole stand down.

Far more credence was given to the evidence of the next witness. This was an older, quieter-looking woman, decently dressed in black. Being the wife of a night watchman whose work lay in a big warehouse situated about a hundred yards from the alley or passage where the crimes had taken place, she had gone out to take her husband some food he always had at one in the morning. And a man had passed her, breathing hard and walking very quickly. Her attention had been drawn to him because she very seldom met anyone at that hour, and because he had such an odd, peculiar look and manner.

Mrs. Bunting, listening attentively, realised that it was very much from what this witness had said that the official description of The Avenger had been composed—that description which had brought such comfort to her, Ellen Bunting's, soul.

This witness spoke quietly, confidently, and her account of the newspaper parcel the man was carrying was perfectly clear and positive.

"It was a neat parcel," she said, "done up with string."

She had thought it an odd thing for a respectably dressed young man to carry such a parcel—that was what had made her notice it. But when pressed, she had to admit that it had been a very foggy night—so foggy that she herself had been afraid of losing her way, though every step was familiar.

When the third woman went into the box, and with sighs and tears told of her acquaintance with one of the deceased, with Johanna Cobbett, there was a stir of sympathetic attention. But she had nothing to say throwing any light on the investigation, save that she admitted reluctantly that "Anny" would have been such a nice, respectable young woman if it hadn't been for the drink.

Her examination was shortened as much as possible; and so was that of the next witness, the husband of Johanna Cobbett. He was a very respectable-looking man, a foreman in a big business house at Croydon. He seemed to feel his position most acutely. He hadn't seen his wife for two years; he hadn't had news of her for six months. Before she took to drink she had been an admirable wife, and—and yes, mother.

Yet another painful few minutes, to anyone who had a heart, or imagination to understand, was spent when the father of the murdered woman was in the box. He had had later news of his unfortunate daughter than her husband had had, but of course he could throw no light at all on her murder or murderer.

A barman, who had served both the women with drink just before the public-house closed for the night, was handled rather roughly. He had stepped with a jaunty air into the box, and came out of it looking cast down, uneasy.

And then there took place a very dramatic, because an utterly unexpected, incident. It was one of which the evening papers made the utmost much to Mrs. Bunting's indignation. But neither coroner nor jury—and they, after all, were the people who mattered—thought a great deal of it.

There had come a pause in the proceedings. All seven witnesses had been heard, and a gentleman near Mrs. Bunting whispered, "They are now going to call Dr. Gaunt. He's been in every big murder case for the last thirty years. He's sure to have something interesting to say. It was really to hear him I came."

But before Dr. Gaunt had time even to get up from the seat with which he had been accommodated close to the coroner, there came a stir among the general public, or, rather, among those spectators who stood near the low wooden door which separated the official part of the court from the gallery.

The coroner's officer, with an apologetic air, approached the coroner, and handed him up an envelope. And again in an instant, there fell absolute silence on the court.

Looking rather annoyed, the coroner opened the envelope. He glanced down the sheet of notepaper it contained. Then he looked up.

"Mr.—" then he glanced down again. "Mr.—ah—Mr.—is it Cannot?" he said doubtfully, "may come forward."

There ran a titter though the spectators, and the coroner frowned.

A neat, jaunty-looking old gentleman, in a nice fur-lined overcoat, with a fresh, red face and white side-whiskers, was conducted from the place where he had been standing among the general public, to the witness-box.

"This is somewhat out of order, Mr.—er—Cannot," said the coroner severely. "You should have sent me this note before the proceedings began. This gentleman," he said, addressing the jury, "informs me that he has something of the utmost importance to reveal in connection with our investigation."

"I have remained silent—I have locked what I knew within my own breast"—began Mr. Cannot in a quavering voice, "because I am so afraid of the Press! I knew if I said anything, even to the police, that my house would be besieged by reporters and newspaper men.... I have a delicate wife, Mr. Coroner. Such a state of things—the state of things I imagine— might cause her death—indeed, I hope she will never read a report of these proceedings. Fortunately, she has an excellent trained nurse—"

"You will now take the oath," said the coroner sharply. He already regretted having allowed this absurd person to have his say.

Mr. Cannot took the oath with a gravity and decorum which had been lacking in most of those who had preceded him.

"I will address myself to the jury," he began.

"You will do nothing of the sort," broke in the coroner. "Now, please attend to me. You assert in your letter that you know who is the—the—"

"The Avenger," put in Mr. Cannot promptly.

"The perpetrator of these crimes. You further declare that you met him on the very night he committed the murder we are now investigating?"

"I do so declare," said Mr. Cannot confidently. "Though in the best of health myself,"—he beamed round the court, a now amused, attentive court—"it is my fate to be surrounded by sick people, to have only ailing friends. I have to trouble you with my private affairs, Mr. Coroner, in order to explain why I happened to be out at so undue an hour as one o'clock in the morning—"

Again a titter ran through the court. Even the jury broke into broad smiles.

"Yes," went on the witness solemnly, "I was with a sick friend—in fact, I may say a dying friend, for since then he has passed away. I will not reveal my exact dwelling-place; you, sir, have it on my notepaper. It is not necessary to reveal it, but you will understand me when I say that in order to come home I had to pass through a portion of the Regent's Park; and it was there—to be exact, about the middle of Prince's Terrace—when a very peculiar-looking individual stopped and accosted me."

Mrs. Bunting's hand shot up to her breast. A feeling of deadly fear took possession of her.

"I mustn't faint," she said to herself hurriedly. "I mustn't faint! Whatever's the matter with me?" She took out her bottle of smelling-salts, and gave it a good, long sniff.

"He was a grim, gaunt man, was this stranger, Mr. Coroner, with a very odd-looking face. I should say an educated man—in common parlance, a gentleman. What drew my special attention to him was that he was talking aloud to himself—in fact, he seemed to be repeating poetry. I give you my word, I had no thought of The Avenger, no thought at all. To tell you the truth, I thought this gentleman was a poor escaped lunatic, a man who'd got away from his keeper. The Regent's Park, sir, as I need hardly tell you, is a most quiet and soothing neighbourhood—"

And then a member of the general public gave a loud guffaw.

"I appeal to you; sir," the old gentleman suddenly cried out "to protect me from this unseemly levity! I have not come here with any other object than that of doing my duty as a citizen!"

"I must ask you to keep to what is strictly relevant," said the coroner stiffly. "Time is going on, and I have another important witness to call—a medical witness. Kindly tell me, as shortly as possible, what made you suppose that this stranger could possibly be—" with an effort he brought out for the first time since the proceedings began, the words, "The Avenger?"

"I am coming to that!" said Mr. Cannot hastily. "I am coming to that! Bear with me a little longer, Mr. Coroner. It was a foggy night, but not as foggy as it became later. And just when we were passing one another, I and this man, who was talking aloud to himself—he, instead of going on, stopped and turned towards me. That made me feel queer and uncomfortable, the more so that there was a very wild, mad look on his face. I said to him, as soothingly as possible, 'A very foggy night, sir.' And he said, 'Yes—yes, it is a foggy night, a night fit for the commission of dark and salutary deeds.' A very strange phrase, sir, that—'dark and salutary deeds.'" He looked at the coroner expectantly—

"Well? Well, Mr. Cannot? Was that all? Did you see this person go off in the direction of—of King's Cross, for instance?"

"No." Mr. Cannot reluctantly shook his head. "No, I must honestly say I did not. He walked along a certain way by my side, and then he crossed the road and was lost in the fog."

"That will do," said the coroner. He spoke more kindly. "I thank you, Mr. Cannot, for coming here and giving us what you evidently consider important information."

Mr. Cannot bowed, a funny, little, old-fashioned bow, and again some of those present tittered rather foolishly.

As he was stepping down from the witness-box, he turned and looked up at the coroner, opening his lips as he did so. There was a murmur of talking going on, but Mrs. Bunting, at any rate, heard quite distinctly what it was that he said: "One thing I have forgotten, sir, which may be of importance. The man carried a bag—a rather light-coloured leather bag, in his left hand. It was such a bag, sir, as might well contain a long-handled knife."

Mrs. Bunting looked at the reporters' table. She remembered suddenly that she had told Bunting about the disappearance of Mr. Sleuth's bag. And then a feeling of intense thankfulness came over her; not a single reporter at the long, ink-stained table had put down that last remark of Mr. Cannot. In fact, not one of them had heard it.

Again the last witness put up his hand to command attention. And then silence did fall on the court.

"One word more," he said in a quavering voice. "May I ask to be accommodated with a seat for the rest of the proceedings? I see there is some room left on the witnesses' bench." And, without waiting for permission, he nimbly stepped across and sat down.

Mrs. Bunting looked up, startled. Her friend, the inspector, was bending over her.

"Perhaps you'd like to come along now," he said urgently.—"I don't suppose you want to hear the medical evidence. It's always painful for a female to hear that. And there'll be an awful rush when the inquest's over. I could get you away quietly now."

She rose, and, pulling her veil down over her pale face, followed him obediently.

Down the stone staircase they went, and through the big, now empty, room downstairs.

"I'll let you out the back way," he said. "I expect you're tired, ma'am, and will like to get home to a cup o' tea."

"I don't know how to thank you!" There were tears in her eyes. She was trembling with excitement and emotion. "You have been good to me."

"Oh, that's nothing," he said a little awkwardly. "I expect you went though a pretty bad time, didn't you?"

"Will they be having that old gentleman again?" she spoke in a whisper, and looked up at him with a pleading, agonised look.

"Good Lord, no! Crazy old fool! We're troubled with a lot of those sort of people, you know, ma'am, and they often do have funny names, too. You see, that sort is busy all their lives in the City, or what not; then they retires when they gets about sixty, and they're fit to hang themselves with dullness. Why, there's hundreds of loonies of the sort to be met in London. You can't go about at night and not meet 'em. Plenty of 'em!"

"Then you don't think there was anything in what he said?" she ventured.

"In what that old gent said? Goodness—no!" he laughed good-naturedly. "But I'll tell you what I do think. If it wasn't for the time that had gone by, I should believe that the second witness had seen that crafty devil—" he lowered his voice. "But, there, Dr. Gaunt declares most positively—so did two other medical gentlemen—that the poor creatures had been dead hours when they was found. Medical gentlemen are always very positive about their evidence. They have to be—otherwise who'd believe 'em? If we'd time I could tell you of a case in which—well, 'twas all because of Dr. Gaunt that the murderer escaped. We all knew perfectly well the man we caught did it, but he was able to prove an alibi as to the time Dr. Gaunt said the poor soul was killed."

CHAPTER TWENTY

It was not late even now, for the inquest had begun very punctually, but Mrs. Bunting felt that no power on earth should force her to go to Ealing. She felt quite tired out and as if she could think of nothing.

Pacing along very slowly, as if she were an old, old woman, she began listlessly turning her steps towards home. Somehow she felt that it would do her more good to stay out in the air than take the train. Also she would thus put off the moment—the moment to which she looked forward with dread and dislike—when she would have to invent a circumstantial story as to what she had said to the doctor, and what the doctor had said to her.

Like most men and women of his class, Bunting took a great interest in other people's ailments, the more interest that he was himself so remarkably healthy. He would feel quite injured if Ellen didn't tell him everything that had happened; everything, that is, that the doctor had told her.

As she walked swiftly along, at every corner, or so it seemed to her, and outside every public-house, stood eager boys selling the latest edition of the afternoon papers to equally eager buyers. "Avenger Inquest?" they shouted exultantly. "All the latest evidence!" At one place, where there were a row of contents-bills pinned to the pavement by stones, she stopped and looked down. "Opening of the Avenger Inquest. What is he really like? Full description." On yet another ran the ironic query: "Avenger Inquest. Do you know him?"

And as that facetious question stared up at her in huge print, Mrs. Bunting turned sick—so sick and faint that she did what she had never done before in her life—she pushed her way into a public-house, and, putting two pennies down on the counter, asked for, and received, a glass of cold water.

As she walked along the now gas-lit streets, she found her mind dwelling persistently—not on the inquest at which she had been present, not even on The Avenger, but on his victims.

Shudderingly, she visualised the two cold bodies lying in the mortuary. She seemed also to see that third body, which, though cold, must yet be warmer than the other two, for at this time yesterday The Avenger's last victim had been alive, poor soul—alive and, according to a companion of hers whom the papers had already interviewed, particularly merry and bright.

Hitherto Mrs. Bunting had been spared in any real sense a vision of The Avenger's victims. Now they haunted her, and she wondered wearily if this fresh horror was to be added to the terrible fear which encompassed her night and day.

As she came within sight of home, her spirit suddenly lightened. The narrow, drab-coloured little house, flanked each side by others exactly like it in every single particular, save that their front yards were not so well kept, looked as if it could, aye, and would, keep any secret closely hidden.

For a moment, at any rate, The Avenger's victims receded from her mind. She thought of them no more. All her thoughts were concentrated on Bunting—Bunting and Mr. Sleuth. She wondered what had happened during her absence—whether the lodger had rung his bell, and, if so, how he had got on with Bunting, and Bunting with him?

She walked up the little flagged path wearily, and yet with a pleasant feeling of home-coming. And then she saw that Bunting must have been watching for her behind the now closely drawn curtains, for before she could either knock or ring he had opened the door.

"I was getting quite anxious about you," he exclaimed. "Come in, Ellen, quick! You must be fair perished a day like now—and you out so little as you are. Well? I hope you found the doctor all right?" He looked at her with affectionate anxiety.

And then there came a sudden, happy thought to Mrs. Bunting. "No," she said slowly, "Doctor Evans wasn't in. I waited, and waited, and waited, but he never came in at all. 'Twas my own fault," she added quickly. Even at such a moment as this she told herself that though she had, in a sort of way, a kind of right to lie to her husband, she had no sight to slander the doctor who had been so kind to her years ago. "I ought to have sent him a card yesterday night," she said. "Of course, I was a fool to go all that way, just on chance of finding a doctor in. It stands to reason they've got to go out to people at all times of day."

"I hope they gave you a cup of tea?" he said.

And again she hesitated, debating a point with herself: if the doctor had a decent sort of servant, of course, she, Ellen Bunting, would have been offered a cup of tea, especially if she explained she'd known him a long time.

She compromised. "I was offered some," she said, in a weak, tired voice. "But there, Bunting, I didn't feel as if I wanted it. I'd be very grateful for a cup now—if you'd just make it for me over the ring."

"'Course I will," he said eagerly. "You just come in and sit down, my dear. Don't trouble to take your things off now—wait till you've had tea."
And she obeyed him. "Where's Daisy?" she asked suddenly. "I thought the girl would be back by the time I got home."

"She ain't coming home to-day"—there was an odd, sly, smiling look on Bunting's face.

"Did she send a telegram?" asked Mrs. Bunting.

"No. Young Chandler's just come in and told me. He's been over there and,—would you believe it, Ellen?—he's managed to make friends with Margaret. Wonderful what love will do, ain't it? He went over there just to help Daisy carry her bag back, you know, and then Margaret told him that her lady had sent her some money to go to the play, and she actually asked Joe to go with them this evening—she and Daisy—to the pantomime. Did you ever hear o' such a thing?"

"Very nice for them, I'm sure," said Mrs. Bunting absently. But she was pleased—pleased to have her mind taken off herself. "Then when is that girl coming home?" she asked patiently.

"Well, it appears that Chandler's got to-morrow morning off too—this evening and to-morrow morning. He'll be on duty all night, but he proposes to go over and bring Daisy back in time for early dinner. Will that suit you, Ellen?"

"Yes. That'll be all right," she said. "I don't grudge the girl her bit of pleasure. One's only young once. By the way, did the lodger ring while I was out?"

Bunting turned round from the gas-ring, which he was watching to see the kettle boil. "No," he said. "Come to think of it, it's rather a funny thing, but the truth is, Ellen, I never gave Mr. Sleuth a thought. You see, Chandler came in and was telling me all about Margaret, laughing-like, and then something else happened while you was out, Ellen."

"Something else happened?" she said in a startled voice. Getting up from her chair she came towards her husband: "What happened? Who came?"

"Just a message for me, asking if I could go to-night to wait at a young lady's birthday party. In Hanover Terrace it is. A waiter—one of them nasty Swiss fellows as works for nothing—fell out just at the last minute and so they had to send for me."

His honest face shone with triumph. The man who had taken over his old friend's business in Baker Street had hitherto behaved very badly to Bunting, and that though Bunting had been on the books for ever so long, and had always given every satisfaction. But this new man had never employed him—no, not once.

"I hope you didn't make yourself too cheap?" said his wife jealously.

"No, that I didn't! I hum'd and haw'd a lot; and I could see the fellow was quite worried—in fact, at the end he offered me half-a-crown more. So I graciously consented!"

Husband and wife laughed more merrily than they had done for a long time.

"You won't mind being alone, here? I don't count the lodger—he's no good—" Bunting looked at her anxiously. He was only prompted to ask the question because lately Ellen had been so queer, so unlike herself. Otherwise it never would have occurred to him that she could be afraid of being alone in the house. She had often been so in the days when he got more jobs.

She stared at him, a little suspiciously. "I be afraid?" she echoed. "Certainly not. Why should I be? I've never been afraid before. What d'you exactly mean by that, Bunting?"

"Oh, nothing. I only thought you might feel funny-like, all alone on this ground floor. You was so upset yesterday when that young fool Chandler came, dressed up, to the door."

"I shouldn't have been frightened if he'd just been an ordinary stranger," she said shortly. "He said something silly to me—just in keeping with his character-like, and it upset me. Besides, I feel better now."

As she was sipping gratefully her cup of tea, there came a noise outside, the shouts of newspaper-sellers.

"I'll just run out," said Bunting apologetically, "and see what happened at that inquest to-day. Besides, they may have a clue about the horrible affair last night. Chandler was full of it—when he wasn't talking about Daisy and Margaret, that is. He's on to-night, luckily not till twelve o'clock; plenty of time to escort the two of 'em back after the play. Besides, he said he'll put them into a cab and blow the expense, if the panto' goes on too long for him to take 'em home."

"On to-night?" repeated Mrs. Bunting. "Whatever for?"

"Well, you see, The Avenger's always done 'em in couples, so to speak. They've got an idea that he'll have a try again to-night. However, even so, Joe's only on from midnight till five o'clock. Then he'll go and turn in a bit before going off to fetch Daisy. Fine thing to be young, ain't it, Ellen?"

"I can't believe that he'd go out on such a night as this!"

"What do you mean?" said Bunting, staring at her. Ellen had spoken so oddly, as if to herself, and in so fierce and passionate a tone.

"What do I mean?" she repeated—and a great fear clutched at her heart. What had she said? She had been thinking aloud.

"Why, by saying he won't go out. Of course, he has to go out. Besides, he'll have been to the play as it is. 'Twould be a pretty thing if the police didn't go out, just because it was cold!"

"I—I was thinking of The Avenger," said Mrs. Bunting. She looked at her husband fixedly. Somehow she had felt impelled to utter those true words.

"He don't take no heed of heat nor cold," said Bunting sombrely. "I take it the man's dead to all human feeling—saving, of course, revenge."

"So that's your idea about him, is it?" She looked across at her husband. Somehow this dangerous, this perilous conversation between them attracted her strangely. She felt as if she must go on with it. "D'you think he was the man that woman said she saw? That young man what passed her with a newspaper parcel?"

"Let me see," he said slowly. "I thought that 'twas from the bedroom window a woman saw him?"

"No, no. I mean the other woman, what was taking her husband's breakfast to him in the warehouse. She was far the most respectable-looking woman of the two," said Mrs. Bunting impatiently.

And then, seeing her husband's look of utter, blank astonishment, she felt a thrill of unreasoning terror. She must have gone suddenly mad to have said what she did! Hurriedly she got up from her chair. "There, now," she said; "here I am gossiping all about nothing when I ought to be seeing about the lodger's supper. It was someone in the train talked to me about that person as thinks she saw The Avenger."

Without waiting for an answer, she went into her bedroom, lit the gas, and shut the door. A moment later she heard Bunting go out to buy the paper they had both forgotten during their dangerous discussion.

As she slowly, languidly took off her nice, warm coat and shawl, Mrs. Bunting found herself shivering. It was dreadfully cold, quite unnaturally cold even for the time of year.

She looked longingly towards the fireplace. It was now concealed by the washhand-stand, but how pleasant it would be to drag that stand aside and light a bit of fire, especially as Bunting was going to be out to-night. He would have to put on his dress clothes, and she didn't like his dressing in the sitting-room. It didn't suit her ideas that he should do so. How if she did light the fire here, in their bedroom? It would be nice for her to have bit of fire to cheer her up after he had gone.

Mrs. Bunting knew only too well that she would have very little sleep the coming night. She looked over, with shuddering distaste, at her nice, soft bed. There she would lie, on that couch of little ease, listening—listening...

She went down to the kitchen. Everything was ready for Mr. Sleuth's supper, for she had made all her preparations before going out so as not to have to hurry back before it suited her to do so.

Leaning the tray for a moment on the top of the banisters, she listened. Even in that nice warm drawing-room, and with a good fire, how cold the lodger must feel sitting studying at the table! But unwonted sounds were coming through the door. Mr. Sleuth was moving restlessly about the room, not sitting reading, as was his wont at this time of the evening.

She knocked, and then waited a moment.

There came the sound of a sharp click, that of the key turning in the lock of the chiffonnier cupboard—or so Mr. Sleuth's landlady could have sworn.

There was a pause—she knocked again.

"Come in," said Mr. Sleuth loudly, and she opened the door and carried in the tray.

"You are a little earlier than usual, are you not Mrs. Bunting?" he said, with a touch of irritation in his voice.

"I don't think so, sir, but I've been out. Perhaps I lost count of the time. I thought you'd like your breakfast early, as you had dinner rather sooner than usual."

"Breakfast? Did you say breakfast, Mrs. Bunting?"

"I beg your pardon, sir, I'm sure! I meant supper." He looked at her fixedly. It seemed to Mrs. Bunting that there was a terrible questioning look in his dark, sunken eyes.

"Aren't you well?" he said slowly. "You don't look well, Mrs. Bunting."

"No, sir," she said. "I'm not well. I went over to see a doctor this afternoon, to Ealing, sir."

"I hope he did you good, Mrs. Bunting"—the lodger's voice had become softer, kinder in quality.

"It always does me good to see the doctor," said Mrs. Bunting evasively.

And then a very odd smile lit up Mr. Sleuth's face. "Doctors are a maligned body of men," he said. "I'm glad to hear you speak well of them. They do their best, Mrs. Bunting. Being human they are liable to err, but I assure you they do their best."

"That I'm sure they do, sir"—she spoke heartily, sincerely. Doctors had always treated her most kindly, and even generously.

And then, having laid the cloth, and put the lodger's one hot dish upon it, she went towards the door. "Wouldn't you like me to bring up another scuttleful of coals, sir? It's bitterly cold—getting colder every minute. A fearful night to have to go out in—" She looked at him deprecatingly.

And then Mr. Sleuth did something which startled her very much. Pushing his chair back, he jumped up and drew himself to his full height.

"What d'you mean?" he stammered. "Why did you say that, Mrs. Bunting?"

She stared at him, fascinated, affrighted. Again there came an awful questioning look over his face.

"I was thinking of Bunting, sir. He's got a job to-night. He's going to act as waiter at a young lady's birthday party. I was thinking it's a pity he has to turn out, and in his thin clothes, too"—she brought out her words jerkily.

Mr. Sleuth seemed somewhat reassured, and again he sat down. "Ah!" he said. "Dear me—I'm sorry to hear that! I hope your husband will not catch cold, Mrs. Bunting."

And then she shut the door, and went downstairs.

Without telling Bunting what she meant to do, she dragged the heavy washhand-stand away from the chimneypiece, and lighted the fire.

Then in some triumph she called Bunting in.

"Time for you to dress," she cried out cheerfully, "and I've got a little bit of fire for you to dress by."

As he exclaimed at her extravagance, "Well, 'twill be pleasant for me, too; keep me company-like while you're out; and make the room nice and warm when you come in. You'll be fair perished, even walking that short way," she said.

And then, while her husband was dressing, Mrs. Bunting went upstairs and cleared away Mr. Sleuth's supper.

The lodger said no word while she was so engaged—no word at all.

He was sitting away from the table, rather an unusual thing for him to do, and staring into the fire, his hands on his knees.

Mr. Sleuth looked lonely, very, very lonely and forlorn. Somehow, a great rush of pity, as well as of horror, came over Mrs. Bunting's heart. He was such a—a—she searched for a word in her mind, but could only find the word "gentle"—he was such a nice, gentle gentleman, was Mr. Sleuth. Lately he had again taken to leaving his money about, as he had done the first day or two, and with some concern his landlady had seen that the store had diminished a good deal. A very simple calculation had made her realise that almost the whole of that missing money had come her way, or, at any rate, had passed through her hands.

Mr. Sleuth never stinted himself as to food, or stinted them, his landlord and his landlady, as to what he had said he would pay. And Mrs. Bunting's conscience pricked her a little, for he hardly ever used that room upstairs—that room for which he had paid extra so generously. If Bunting got another job or two through that nasty man in Baker Street,—and now that the ice had been broken between them it was very probable that he would do so, for he was a very well-trained, experienced waiter—then she thought she would tell Mr. Sleuth that she no longer wanted him to pay as much as he was now doing.

She looked anxiously, deprecatingly, at his long, bent back.

"Good-night, sir," she said at last.

Mr. Sleuth turned round. His face looked sad and worn.

"I hope you'll sleep well, sir."

"Yes, I'm sure I shall sleep well. But perhaps I shall take a little turn first. Such is my way, Mrs. Bunting; after I have been studying all day I require a little exercise."

"Oh, I wouldn't go out to-night," she said deprecatingly. "'Tisn't fit for anyone to be out in the bitter cold."

"And yet—and yet"—he looked at her attentively—"there will probably be many people out in the streets to-night."

"A many more than usual, I fear, sir."

"Indeed?" said Mr. Sleuth quickly. "Is it not a strange thing, Mrs. Bunting, that people who have all day in which to amuse themselves should carry their revels far into the night?"

"Oh, I wasn't thinking of revellers, sir; I was thinking"—she hesitated, then, with a gasping effort Mrs. Bunting brought out the words, "of the police."

"The police?" He put up his right hand and stroked his chin two or three times with a nervous gesture. "But what is man—what is man's puny power or strength against that of God, or even of those over whose feet God has set a guard?"

Mr. Sleuth looked at his landlady with a kind of triumph lighting up his face, and Mrs. Bunting felt a shuddering sense of relief. Then she had not offended her lodger? She had not made him angry by that, that—was it a hint she had meant to convey to him?

"Very true, sir," she said respectfully. "But Providence means us to take care o' ourselves too." And then she closed the door behind her and went downstairs.

But Mr. Sleuth's landlady did not go on, down to the kitchen. She came into her sitting-room, and, careless of what Bunting would think the next morning, put the tray with the remains of the lodger's meal on her table. Having done that, and having turned out the gas in the passage and the sitting-room, she went into her bedroom and closed the door.

The fire was burning brightly and clearly. She told herself that she did not need any other light to undress by.

What was it made the flames of the fire shoot up, shoot down, in that queer way? But watching it for awhile, she did at last doze off a bit.

And then—and then Mrs. Bunting woke with a sudden thumping of her heart. Woke to see that the fire was almost out—woke to hear a quarter to twelve chime out—woke at last to the sound she had been listening for before she fell asleep—the sound of Mr. Sleuth, wearing his rubber-soled shoes, creeping downstairs, along the passage, and so out, very, very quietly by the front door.

But once she was in bed Mrs. Bunting turned restless. She tossed this way and that, full of discomfort and unease. Perhaps it was the unaccustomed firelight dancing on the walls, making queer shadows all round her, which kept her so wide awake.

She lay thinking and listening—listening and thinking. It even occurred to her to do the one thing that might have quieted her excited brain—to get a book, one of those detective stories of which Bunting had a slender store in the next room, and then, lighting the gas, to sit up and read.

No, Mrs. Bunting had always been told it was very wrong to read in bed, and she was not in a mood just now to begin doing anything that she had been told was wrong...

CHAPTER TWENTY ONE

It was a very cold night—so cold, so windy, so snow-laden was the atmosphere, that everyone who could do so stayed indoors.

Bunting, however, was now on his way home from what had proved a really pleasant job. A remarkable piece of luck had come his way this evening, all the more welcome because it was quite unexpected! The young lady at whose birthday party he had been present in capacity of waiter had come into a fortune that day, and she had had the gracious, the surprising thought of presenting each of the hired waiters with a sovereign!

This gift, which had been accompanied by a few kind words, had gone to Bunting's heart. It had confirmed him in his Conservative principles; only gentlefolk ever behaved in that way; quiet, old-fashioned, respectable, gentlefolk, the sort of people of whom those nasty Radicals know nothing and care less![34]

But the ex-butler was not as happy as he should have been. Slackening his footsteps, he began to think with puzzled concern of how queer his wife had seemed lately. Ellen had become so nervous, so "jumpy," that he didn't know what to make of her sometimes. She had never been really good-tempered—your capable, self-respecting woman seldom is—but she had never been like what she was now. And she didn't get better as the days went on; in fact she got worse. Of late she had been quite hysterical, and for no reason at all! Take that little practical joke of young Joe Chandler. Ellen knew quite well he often had to go about in some kind of disguise, and yet how she had gone on, quite foolish-like—not at all as one would have expected her to do.

There was another queer thing about her which disturbed him in more senses than one. During the last three weeks or so Ellen had taken to talking in her sleep. "No, no, no!" she had cried out, only the night before. "It isn't true—I won't have it said—it's a lie!" And there had been a wail of horrible fear and revolt in her usually quiet, mincing voice.

Whew! it was cold; and he had stupidly forgotten his gloves.

He put his hands in his pockets to keep them warm, and began walking more quickly.

As he tramped steadily along, the ex-butler suddenly caught sight of his lodger walking along the opposite side of the solitary street—one of those short streets leading off the broad road which encircles Regent's Park.

Well! This was a funny time o' night to be taking a stroll for pleasure, like!

Glancing across, Bunting noticed that Mr. Sleuth's tall, thin figure was rather bowed, and that his head was bent toward the ground. His left arm was thrust into his long Inverness cape, and so was quite hidden, but the other side of the cape bulged out, as if the lodger were carrying a bag or parcel in the hand which hung down straight.

Mr. Sleuth was walking rather quickly, and as he walked he talked aloud, which, as Bunting knew, is not unusual with gentlemen who live much alone. It was clear that he had not yet become aware of the proximity of his landlord.

Bunting told himself that Ellen was right. Their lodger was certainly a most eccentric, peculiar person. Strange, was it not, that that odd, luny-like gentleman should have made all the difference to his, Bunting's, and Mrs. Bunting's happiness and comfort in life?

Again glancing across at Mr. Sleuth, he reminded himself, not for the first time, of this perfect lodger's one fault—his odd dislike to meat, and to what Bunting vaguely called to himself, sensible food.

But there, you can't have everything! The more so that the lodger was not one of those crazy vegetarians who won't eat eggs and cheese. No, he was reasonable in this, as in everything else connected with his dealings with the Buntings.

As we know, Bunting saw far less of the lodger than did his wife. Indeed, he had been upstairs only three or four times since Mr. Sleuth had been with them, and when his landlord had had occasion to wait on him the lodger had remained silent. Indeed, their gentleman had made it very clear that he did not like either the husband or wife to come up to his rooms without being definitely asked to do so.

Now, surely, would be a good opportunity for a little genial conversation? Bunting felt pleased to see his lodger; it increased his general comfortable sense of satisfaction.

So it was that the butler, still an active man for his years, crossed over the road, and, stepping briskly forward, began trying to overtake Mr. Sleuth. But the more he hurried along, the more the other hastened, and that without ever turning round to see whose steps he could hear echoing behind him on the now freezing pavement.

Mr. Sleuth's own footsteps were quite inaudible—an odd circumstance, when you came to think of it—as Bunting did think of it later, lying awake by Mrs. Bunting's side in the pitch darkness. What it meant of course, was that the lodger had rubber soles on his shoes. Now Bunting had never had a pair of rubber-soled shoes sent down to him to clean. He had always supposed the lodger had only one pair of outdoor boots.

The two men—the pursued and the pursuer—at last turned into the Marylebone Road; they were now within a few hundred yards of home. Plucking up courage, Bunting called out, his voice echoing freshly on the still air: "Mr. Sleuth, sir? Mr. Sleuth!"

The lodger stopped and turned round.

He had been walking so quickly, and he was in so poor a physical condition, that the sweat was pouring down his face.

"Ah! So it's you, Mr. Bunting? I heard footsteps behind me, and I hurried on. I wish I'd known that it was you; there are so many queer characters about at night in London."

"Not on a night like this, sir. Only honest folk who have business out of doors would be out such a night as this. It is cold, sir!"

And then into Bunting's slow and honest mind there suddenly crept the query as to what on earth Mr. Sleuth's own business out could be on this bitter night.

"Cold?" the lodger repeated; he was panting a little, and his words came out sharp and quick through his thin lips. "I can't say that I find it cold, Mr. Bunting. When the snow falls, the air always becomes milder."

"Yes, sir; but to-night there's such a sharp east wind. Why, it freezes the very marrow in one's bones! Still, there's nothing like walking in cold weather to make one warm, as you seem to have found, sir."

Bunting noticed that Mr. Sleuth kept his distance in a rather strange way; he walked at the edge of the pavement, leaving the rest of it, on the wall side, to his landlord.

"I lost my way," he said abruptly. "I've been over Primrose Hill to see a friend of mine, a man with whom I studied when I was a lad, and then, coming back, I lost my way.

Now they had come right up to the little gate which opened on the shabby, paved court in front of the house—that gate which now was never locked.

Mr. Sleuth, pushing suddenly forward, began walking up the flagged path, when, with a "By your leave, sir," the ex-butler, stepping aside, slipped in front of his lodger, in order to open the front door for him.

As he passed by Mr. Sleuth, the back of Bunting's bare left hand brushed lightly against the long Inverness cape the lodger was wearing, and, to Bunting's surprise, the stretch of cloth against which his hand lay for a moment was not only damp, damp maybe from stray flakes of snow which had settled upon it, but wet—wet and gluey.

Bunting thrust his left hand into his pocket; it was with the other that he placed the key in the lock of the door.

The two men passed into the hall together.

The house seemed blackly dark in comparison with the lighted-up road outside, and as he groped forward, closely followed by the lodger, there came over Bunting a sudden, reeling sensation of mortal terror, an instinctive, assailing knowledge of frightful immediate danger.

A stuffless voice—the voice of his first wife, the long-dead girl to whom his mind so seldom reverted nowadays—uttered into his ear the words, "Take care!"

And then the lodger spoke. His voice was harsh and grating, though not loud.

"I'm afraid, Mr. Bunting, that you must have felt something dirty, foul, on my coat? It's too long a story to tell you now, but I brushed up against a dead animal, a creature to whose misery some thoughtful soul had put an end, lying across a bench on Primrose Hill."

"No, sir, no. I didn't notice nothing. I scarcely touched you, sir."

It seemed as if a power outside himself compelled Bunting to utter these lying words. "And now, sir, I'll be saying good-night to you," he said.

Stepping back he pressed with all the strength that was in him against the wall, and let the other pass him. There was a pause, and then—"Good-night," returned Mr. Sleuth, in a hollow voice. Bunting waited until the lodger had gone upstairs, and then, lighting the gas, he sat down there, in the hall. Mr. Sleuth's landlord felt very queer—queer and sick.

He did not draw his left hand out of his pocket till he heard Mr. Sleuth shut the bedroom door upstairs. Then he held up his left hand and looked at it curiously; it was flecked, streaked with pale reddish blood.

Taking off his boots, he crept into the room where his wife lay asleep. Stealthily he walked across to the wash-hand-stand, and dipped a hand into the water-jug.

"Whatever are you doing? What on earth are you doing?" came a voice from the bed, and Bunting started guiltily.

"I'm just washing my hands."

"Indeed, you're doing nothing of the sort! I never heard of such a thing—putting your hand into the water in which I was going to wash my face to-morrow morning!"

"I'm very sorry, Ellen," he said meekly; "I meant to throw it away. You don't suppose I would have let you wash in dirty water, do you?"

She said no more, but, as he began undressing himself, Mrs. Bunting lay staring at him in a way that made her husband feel even more uncomfortable than he was already.

At last he got into bed. He wanted to break the oppressive silence by telling Ellen about the sovereign the young lady had given him, but that sovereign now seemed to Bunting of no more account than if it had been a farthing he had picked up in the road outside.

Once more his wife spoke, and he gave so great a start that it shook the bed.

"I suppose that you don't know that you've left the light burning in the hall, wasting our good money?" she observed tartly.

He got up painfully and opened the door into the passage. It was as she had said; the gas was flaring away, wasting their good money—or, rather, Mr. Sleuth's good money. Since he had come to be their lodger they had not had to touch their rent money.

Bunting turned out the light and groped his way back to the room, and so to bed. Without speaking again to each other, both husband and wife lay awake till dawn.

The next morning Mr. Sleuth's landlord awoke with a start; he felt curiously heavy about the limbs, and tired about the eyes.

Drawing his watch from under his pillow, he saw that it was seven o'clock. Without waking his wife, he got out of bed and pulled the blind a little to one side. It was snowing heavily, and, as is the way when it snows, even in London, everything was strangely, curiously still. After he had dressed he went out into the passage. As he had at once dreaded and hoped, their newspaper was already lying on the mat. It was probably the sound of its being pushed through the letter-box which had waked him from his unrestful sleep.

He picked the paper up and went into the sitting-room then, shutting the door behind him carefully, he spread the newspaper wide open on the table, and bent over it.

As Bunting at last looked up and straightened himself, an expression of intense relief shone upon his stolid face. The item of news he had felt certain would be printed in big type on the middle sheet was not there.

CHAPTER TWENTY TWO

Feeling amazingly light-hearted, almost light-headed, Bunting lit the gas-ring to make his wife her morning cup of tea.

While he was doing it, he suddenly heard her call out: "Bunting!" she cried weakly. "Bunting!" Quickly he hurried in response to her call.

"Yes," he said. "What is it, my dear? I won't be a minute with your tea." And he smiled broadly, rather foolishly.

She sat up and looked at him, a dazed expression on her face.

"What are you grinning at?" she asked suspiciously.

"I've had a wonderful piece of luck," he explained. "But you was so cross last night that I simply didn't dare tell you about it."

"Well, tell me now," she said in a low voice.

"I had a sovereign given me by the young lady. You see, it was her birthday party, Ellen, and she'd come into a nice bit of money, and she gave each of us waiters a sovereign."

Mrs. Bunting made no comment. Instead, she lay back and closed her eyes.

"What time d'you expect Daisy?" she asked languidly. "You didn't say what time Joe was going to fetch her, when we was talking about it yesterday."

"Didn't I? Well, I expect they'll be in to dinner."

"I wonder, how long that old aunt of hers expects us to keep her?" said Mrs. Bunting thoughtfully. All the cheer died out of Bunting's round face. He became sullen and angry. It would be a pretty thing if he couldn't have his own daughter for a bit—especially now that they were doing so well!

"Daisy'll stay here just as long as she can," he said shortly. "It's too bad of you, Ellen, to talk like that! She helps you all she can; and she brisks us both up ever so much. Besides, 'twould be cruel—cruel to take the girl away just now, just as she and that young chap are making friends-like. One would suppose that even you would see the justice o' that!"

But Mrs. Bunting made no answer.

Bunting went off, back into the sitting-room. The water was boiling now, so he made the tea; and then, as he brought the little tray in, his heart softened. Ellen did look really ill—ill and wizened. He wondered if she had a pain about which she wasn't saying anything. She had never been one to grouse about herself.

"The lodger and me came in together last night," he observed genially. "He's certainly a funny kind of gentleman. It wasn't the sort of night one would have chosen to go out for a walk, now was it? And yet he must 'a been out a long time if what he said was true."

"I don't wonder a quiet gentleman like Mr. Sleuth hates the crowded streets," she said slowly. "They gets worse every day—that they do! But go along now; I want to get up."

He went back into their sitting-room, and, having laid the fire and put a match to it, he sat down comfortably with his newspaper.

Deep down in his heart Bunting looked back to this last night with a feeling of shame and self-rebuke. Whatever had made such horrible thoughts and suspicions as had possessed him suddenly come into his head? And just because of a trifling thing like that blood. No doubt Mr. Sleuth's nose had bled—that was what had happened; though, come to think of it, he had mentioned brushing up against a dead animal.

Perhaps Ellen was right after all. It didn't do for one to be always thinking of dreadful subjects, of murders and such-like. It made one go dotty—that's what it did.

And just as he was telling himself that, there came to the door a loud knock, the peculiar rat-tat-tat of a telegraph boy. But before he had time to get across the room, let alone to the front door, Ellen had rushed through the room, clad only in a petticoat and shawl.

"I'll go," she cried breathlessly. "I'll go, Bunting; don't you trouble."

He stared at her, surprised, and followed her into the hall.

She put out a hand, and hiding herself behind the door, took the telegram from the invisible boy. "You needn't wait," she said. "If there's an answer we'll send it out ourselves." Then she tore the envelope open— "Oh!" she said with a gasp of relief. "It's only from Joe Chandler, to say he can't go over to fetch Daisy this morning. Then you'll have to go."

She walked back into their sitting-room. "There!" she said. "There it is, Bunting. You just read it."

"Am on duty this morning. Cannot fetch Miss Daisy as arranged.—Chandler."

"I wonder why he's on duty?" said Bunting slowly, uncomfortably. "I thought Joe's hours was as regular as clockwork—that nothing could make any difference to them. However, there it is. I suppose it'll do all right if I start about eleven o'clock? It may have left off snowing by then. I don't feel like going out again just now. I'm pretty tired this morning."

"You start about twelve," said his wife quickly. "That'll give plenty of time."

The morning went on quietly, uneventfully. Bunting received a letter from Old Aunt saying Daisy must come back next Monday, a little under a week from now. Mr. Sleuth slept soundly, or, at any rate, he made no sign of being awake; and though Mrs. Bunting often stopped to listen, while she was doing her room, there came no sounds at all from overhead.

Scarcely aware that it was so, both Bunting and his wife felt more cheerful than they had done for a long time. They had quite a pleasant little chat when Mrs. Bunting came and sat down for a bit, before going down to prepare Mr. Sleuth's breakfast.

"Daisy will be surprised to see you—not to say disappointed!" she observed, and she could not help laughing a little to herself at the thought. And when, at eleven, Bunting got up to go, she made him stay on a little longer. "There's no such great hurry as that," she said good-temperedly. "It'll do quite well if you're there by half-past twelve. I'll get dinner ready myself. Daisy needn't help with that. I expect Margaret has worked her pretty hard."

But at last there came the moment when Bunting had to start, and his wife went with him to the front door. It was still snowing, less heavily, but still snowing. There were very few people coming and going, and only just a few cabs and carts dragging cautiously along through the slush.

Mrs. Bunting was still in the kitchen when there came a ring and a knock at the door—a now very familiar ring and knock. "Joe thinks Daisy's home again by now!" she said, smiling to herself.

Before the door was well open, she heard Chandler's voice. "Don't be scared this time, Mrs. Bunting!" But though not exactly scared, she did give a gasp of surprise. For there stood Joe, made up to represent a public-house loafer; and he looked the part to perfection, with his hair combed down raggedly over his forehead, his seedy-looking, ill-fitting, dirty clothes, and greenish-black pot hat.

"I haven't a minute," he said a little breathlessly. "But I thought I'd just run in to know if Miss Daisy was safe home again. You got my telegram all right? I couldn't send no other kind of message."

"She's not back yet. Her father hasn't been gone long after her." Then, struck by a look in his eyes, "Joe, what's the matter?" she asked quickly.

There came a thrill of suspense in her voice, her face grew drawn, while what little colour there was in it receded, leaving it very pale.

"Well," he said. "Well, Mrs. Bunting, I've no business to say anything about it—but I will tell you!"

He walked in and shut the door of the sitting-room carefully behind him. "There's been another of 'em!" he whispered. "But this time no one is to know anything about it—not for the present, I mean," he corrected himself hastily. "The Yard thinks we've got a clue—and a good clue, too, this time."

"But where—and how?" faltered Mrs. Bunting.

"Well, 'twas just a bit of luck being able to keep it dark for the present"—he still spoke in that stifled, hoarse whisper. "The poor soul was found dead on a bench on Primrose Hill. And just by chance 'twas one of our fellows saw the body first. He was on his way home, over Hampstead way. He knew where he'd be able to get an ambulance quick, and he made a very clever, secret job of it. I 'spect he'll get promotion for that!"

"What about the clue?" asked Mrs. Bunting, with dry lips. "You said there was a clue?"

"Well, I don't rightly understand about the clue myself. All I knows is it's got something to do with a public-house, 'The Hammer and Tongs,' which isn't far off there. They feels sure The Avenger was in the bar just on closing-time."

And then Mrs. Bunting sat down. She felt better now. It was natural the police should suspect a public-house loafer. "Then that's why you wasn't able to go and fetch Daisy, I suppose?"

He nodded. "Mum's the word, Mrs. Bunting! It'll all be in the last editions of the evening newspapers—it can't be kep' out. There'd be too much of a row if 'twas!"

"Are you going off to that public-house now?" she asked.

"Yes, I am. I've got a awk'ard job—to try and worm something out of the barmaid."

"Something out of the barmaid?" repeated Mrs. Bunting nervously. "Why, whatever for?"

He came and stood close to her. "They think 'twas a gentleman," he whispered.

"A gentleman?"

Mrs. Bunting stared at Chandler with a scared expression. "Whatever makes them think such a silly thing as that?"

"Well, just before closing-time a very peculiar-looking gent, with a leather bag in his hand, went into the bar and asked for a glass of milk. And what d'you think he did? Paid for it with a sovereign! He wouldn't take no change—just made the girl a present of it! That's why the young woman what served him seems quite unwilling to give him away. She won't tell now what he was like. She doesn't know what he's wanted for, and we don't want her to know just yet. That's one reason why nothing's being said public about it. But there! I really must be going now. My time'll be up at three o'clock. I thought of coming in on the way back, and asking you for a cup o' tea, Mrs. Bunting."

"Do," she said. "Do, Joe. You'll be welcome," but there was no welcome in her tired voice.

She let him go alone to the door, and then she went down to her kitchen, and began cooking Mr. Sleuth's breakfast.

The lodger would be sure to ring soon; and then any minute Bunting and Daisy might be home, and they'd want something, too. Margaret always had breakfast even when "the family" were away, unnaturally early.

As she bustled about Mrs. Bunting tried to empty her mind of all thought. But it is very difficult to do that when one is in a state of torturing uncertainty. She had not dared to ask Chandler what they supposed that man who had gone into the public-house was really like. It was fortunate, indeed, that the lodger and that inquisitive young chap had never met face to face.

At last Mr. Sleuth's bell rang—a quiet little tinkle. But when she went up with his breakfast the lodger was not in his sitting-room.

Supposing him to be still in his bedroom, Mrs. Bunting put the cloth on the table, and then she heard the sound of his footsteps coming down the stairs, and her quick ears detected the slight whirring sound which showed that the gas-stove was alight. Mr. Sleuth had already lit the stove; that meant that he would carry out some elaborate experiment this afternoon.

"Still snowing?" he said doubtfully. "How very, very quiet and still London is when under snow, Mrs. Bunting. I have never known it quite as quiet as this morning. Not a sound, outside or in. A very pleasant change from the shouting which sometimes goes on in the Marylebone Road."

"Yes," she said dully. "It's awful quiet to-day—too quiet to my thinking. 'Tain't natural-like."

The outside gate swung to, making a noisy clatter in the still air.

"Is that someone coming in here?" asked Mr. Sleuth, drawing a quick, hissing breath. "Perhaps you will oblige me by going to the window and telling me who it is, Mrs. Bunting?"

And his landlady obeyed him.

"It's only Bunting, sir—Bunting and his daughter."

"Oh! Is that all?"

Mr. Sleuth hurried after her, and she shrank back a little. She had never been quite so near to the lodger before, save on that first day when she had been showing him her rooms.

Side by side they stood, looking out of the window. And, as if aware that someone was standing there, Daisy turned her bright face up towards the window and smiled at her stepmother, and at the lodger, whose face she could only dimly discern.

"A very sweet-looking young girl," said Mr. Sleuth thoughtfully.

And then he quoted a little bit of poetry, and this took Mrs. Bunting very much aback.

"Wordsworth," he murmured dreamily.[35] "A poet too little read nowadays, Mrs. Bunting; but one with a beautiful feeling for nature, for youth, for innocence."

"Indeed, sir?" Mrs. Bunting stepped back a little. "Your breakfast will be getting cold, sir, if you don't have it now."

He went back to the table, obediently, and sat down as a child rebuked might have done.

And then his landlady left him.

"Well?" said Bunting cheerily. "Everything went off quite all right. And Daisy's a lucky girl—that she is! Her Aunt Margaret gave her five shillings."

But Daisy did not look as pleased as her father thought she ought to do.

"I hope nothing's happened to Mr. Chandler," she said a little disconsolately. "The very last words he said to me last night was that he'd be there at ten o'clock. I got quite fidgety as the time went on and he didn't come."

"He's been here," said Mrs. Bunting slowly.

"Been here?" cried her husband. "Then why on earth didn't he go and fetch Daisy, if he'd time to come here?"

"He was on the way to his job," his wife answered. "You run along, child, downstairs. Now that you are here you can make yourself useful."

And Daisy reluctantly obeyed. She wondered what it was her stepmother didn't want her to hear.

"I've something to tell you, Bunting."

"Yes?" He looked across uneasily. "Yes, Ellen?"

"There's been another o' those murders. But the police don't want anyone to know about it—not yet. That's why Joe couldn't go over and fetch Daisy. They're all on duty again."

Bunting put out his hand and clutched hold of the edge of the mantelpiece. He had gone very red, but his wife was far too much concerned with her own feelings and sensations to notice it.

There was a long silence between them. Then he spoke, making a great effort to appear unconcerned.

"And where did it happen?" he asked. "Close to the other one?"

She hesitated, then: "I don't know. He didn't say. But hush!" she added quickly. "Here's Daisy! Don't let's talk of that horror in front of her-like. Besides, I promised Chandler I'd be mum."

And he acquiesced.

"You can be laying the cloth, child, while I go up and clear away the lodger's breakfast." Without waiting for an answer, she hurried upstairs.

Mr. Sleuth had left the greater part of the nice lemon sole untouched. "I don't feel well to-day," he said fretfully. "And, Mrs. Bunting? I should be much obliged if your husband would lend me that paper I saw in his hand. I do not often care to look at the public prints, but I should like to do so now."

She flew downstairs. "Bunting," she said a little breathlessly, "the lodger would like you just to lend him the *Sun*."

Bunting handed it over to her. "I've read it through," he observed. "You can tell him that I don't want it back again."

On her way up she glanced down at the pink sheet. Occupying a third of the space was an irregular drawing, and under it was written, in rather large characters:

"We are glad to be able to present our readers with an authentic reproduction of the footprint of the half-worn rubber sole which was almost certainly worn by The Avenger when he committed his double murder ten days ago."

She went into the sitting-room. To her relief it was empty.

"Kindly put the paper down on the table," came Mr. Sleuth's muffled voice from the upper landing.

She did so. "Yes, sir. And Bunting don't want the paper back again, sir. He says he's read it." And then she hurried out of the room.

CHAPTER TWENTY THREE

All afternoon it went on snowing; and the three of them sat there, listening and waiting—Bunting and his wife hardly knew for what; Daisy for the knock which would herald Joe Chandler.

And about four there came the now familiar sound.

Mrs. Bunting hurried out into the passage, and as she opened the front door she whispered, "We haven't said anything to Daisy yet. Young girls can't keep secrets."

Chandler nodded comprehendingly. He now looked the low character he had assumed to the life, for he was blue with cold, disheartened, and tired out.

Daisy gave a little cry of shocked surprise, of amusement, of welcome, when she saw how cleverly he was disguised.

"I never!" she exclaimed. "What a difference it do make, to be sure! Why, you looks quite horrid, Mr. Chandler."

And, somehow, that little speech of hers amused her father so much that he quite cheered up. Bunting had been very dull and quiet all that afternoon.

"It won't take me ten minutes to make myself respectable again," said the young man rather ruefully.

His host and hostess, looking at him eagerly, furtively, both came to the conclusion that he had been unsuccessful—that he had failed, that is, in getting any information worth having. And though, in a sense, they all had a pleasant tea together, there was an air of constraint, even of discomfort, over the little party.

Bunting felt it hard that he couldn't ask the questions that were trembling on his lips; he would have felt it hard any time during the last month to refrain from knowing anything Joe could tell him, but now it seemed almost intolerable to be in this queer kind of half suspense. There was one important fact he longed to know, and at last came his opportunity of doing so, for Joe Chandler rose to leave, and this time it was Bunting who followed him out into the hall.

"Where did it happen?" he whispered. "Just tell me that, Joe?"

"Primrose Hill," said the other briefly. "You'll know all about it in a minute or two, for it'll be all in the last editions of the evening papers. That's what's been arranged."

"No arrest I suppose?"

Chandler shook his head despondently. "No," he said, "I'm inclined to think the Yard was on a wrong tack altogether this time. But one can only do one's best. I don't know if Mrs. Bunting told you I'd got to question a barmaid about a man who was in her place just before closing-time. Well, she's said all she knew, and it's as clear as daylight to me that the eccentric old gent she talks about was only a harmless luny. He gave her a sovereign just because she told him she was a teetotaller!" He laughed ruefully.

Even Bunting was diverted at the notion. "Well, that's a queer thing for a barmaid to be!" he exclaimed. "She's niece to the people what keeps the public," explained Chandler; and then he went out of the front door with a cheerful "So long!"

When Bunting went back into the sitting-room Daisy had disappeared. She had gone downstairs with the tray. "Where's my girl?" he said irritably.

"She's just taken the tray downstairs."

He went out to the top of the kitchen stairs, and called out sharply, "Daisy! Daisy, child! Are you down there?"

"Yes, father," came her eager, happy voice.

"Better come up out of that cold kitchen."

He turned and came back to his wife. "Ellen, is the lodger in? I haven't heard him moving about. Now mind what I says, please! I don't want Daisy to be mixed up with him."

"Mr. Sleuth don't seem very well to-day," answered Mrs. Bunting quietly. "'Tain't likely I should let Daisy have anything to do with him. Why, she's never even seen him. 'Tain't likely I should allow her to begin waiting on him now."

But though she was surprised and a little irritated by the tone in which Bunting had spoken, no glimmer of the truth illumined her mind. So accustomed had she become to bearing alone the burden of her awful secret, that it would have required far more than a cross word or two, far more than the fact that Bunting looked ill and tired, for her to have come to suspect that her secret was now shared by another, and that other her husband.

Again and again the poor soul had agonised and trembled at the thought of her house being invaded by the police, but that was only because she had always credited the police with supernatural powers of detection. That they should come to know the awful fact she kept hidden in her breast would have seemed to her, on the whole, a natural thing, but that Bunting should even dimly suspect it appeared beyond the range of possibility.

And yet even Daisy noticed a change in her father. He sat cowering over the fire—saying nothing, doing nothing.

"Why, father, ain't you well?" the girl asked more than once.

And, looking up, he would answer, "Yes, I'm well enough, my girl, but I feels cold. It's awful cold. I never did feel anything like the cold we've got just now."

At eight the now familiar shouts and cries began again outside.

"The Avenger again!" "Another horrible crime!" "Extra speshul edition!"—such were the shouts, the exultant yells, hurled through the clear, cold air. They fell like bombs into the quiet room.

Both Bunting and his wife remained silent, but Daisy's cheeks grew pink with excitement, and her eye sparkled.

"Hark, father! Hark, Ellen! D'you hear that?" she exclaimed childishly, and even clapped her hands. "I do wish Mr. Chandler had been here. He would 'a been startled!"

"Don't, Daisy!" and Bunting frowned.

Then, getting up, he stretched himself. "It's fair getting on my mind," he said, "these horrible things happening. I'd like to get right away from London, just as far as I could—that I would!"

"Up to John-o'-Groat's?"[36] said Daisy, laughing. And then, "Why, father, ain't you going out to get a paper?"

"Yes, I suppose I must."

Slowly he went out of the room, and, lingering a moment in the hall, he put on his greatcoat and hat. Then he opened the front door, and walked down the flagged path. Opening the iron gate, he stepped out on the pavement, then crossed the road to where the newspaper-boys now stood.

The boy nearest to him only had the *Sun*—a late edition of the paper he had already read. It annoyed Bunting to give a penny for a ha'penny rag of which he already knew the main contents. But there was nothing else to do.

Standing under a lamp-post, he opened out the newspaper. It was bitingly cold; that, perhaps, was why his hand shook as he looked down at the big headlines. For Bunting had been very unfair to the enterprise of the editor of his favourite evening paper. This special edition was full of new matter—new matter concerning The Avenger.

First, in huge type right across the page, was the brief statement that The Avenger had now committed his ninth crime, and that he had chosen quite a new locality, namely, the lonely stretch of rising ground known to Londoners as Primrose Hill.

"The police," so Bunting read, "are very reserved as to the circumstances which led to the finding of the body of The Avenger's latest victim. But we have reason to believe that they possess several really important clues, and that one of them is concerned with the half-worn rubber sole of which we are the first to reproduce an outline to-day. (See over page.)"

And Bunting, turning the sheet round about, saw the irregular outline he had already seen in the early edition of the *Sun*, that purporting to be a facsimile of the imprint left by The Avenger's rubber sole.

He stared down at the rough outline which took up so much of the space which should have been devoted to reading matter with a queer, sinking feeling of terrified alarm. Again and again criminals had been tracked by the marks their boots or shoes had made at or near the scenes of their misdoings.

Practically the only job Bunting did in his own house of a menial kind was the cleaning of the boots and shoes. He had already visualised early this very afternoon the little row with which he dealt each morning—first came his wife's strong, serviceable boots, then his own two pairs, a good deal patched and mended, and next to his own Mr. Sleuth's strong, hardly worn, and expensive buttoned boots. Of late a dear little coquettish high-heeled pair of outdoor shoes with thin, paperlike soles, bought by Daisy for her trip to London, had ended the row. The girl had worn these thin shoes persistently, in defiance of Ellen's reproof and advice, and he, Bunting, had only once had to clean her more sensible country pair, and that only because the others had become wet though the day he and she had accompanied young Chandler to Scotland Yard.

Slowly he returned across the road. Somehow the thought of going in again, of hearing his wife's sarcastic comments, of parrying Daisy's eager questions, had become intolerable. So he walked slowly, trying to put off the evil moment when he would have to tell them what was in his paper.

The lamp under which he had stood reading was not exactly opposite the house. It was rather to the right of it. And when, having crossed over the roadway, he walked along the pavement towards his own gate, he heard odd, shuffling sounds coming from the inner side of the low wall which shut off his little courtyard from the pavement.

Now, under ordinary circumstances Bunting would have rushed forward to drive out whoever was there. He and his wife had often had trouble, before the cold weather began, with vagrants seeking shelter there.

But to-night he stayed outside, listening intently, sick with suspense and fear.

Was it possible that their place was being watched—already? He thought it only too likely. Bunting, like Mrs. Bunting, credited the police with almost supernatural powers, especially since he had paid that visit to Scotland Yard.

But to Bunting's amazement, and, yes, relief, it was his lodger who suddenly loomed up in the dim light.

Mr. Sleuth must have been stooping down, for his tall, lank form had been quite concealed till he stepped forward from behind the low wall on to the flagged path leading to the front door.

The lodger was carrying a brown paper parcel, and, as he walked along, the new boots he was wearing creaked, and the tap-tap of hard nail-studded heels rang out on the flat-stones of the narrow path.

Bunting, still standing outside the gate, suddenly knew what it was his lodger had been doing on the other side of the low wall. Mr. Sleuth had evidently been out to buy himself another pair of new boots, and then he had gone inside the gate and had put them on, placing his old footgear in the paper in which the new pair had been wrapped.

The ex-butler waited—waited quite a long time, not only until Mr. Sleuth had let himself into the house, but till the lodger had had time to get well away, upstairs.

Then he also walked up the flagged pathway, and put his latchkey in the door. He lingered as long over the job of hanging his hat and coat up in the hall as he dared, in fact till his wife called out to him. Then he went in, and throwing the paper down on the table, he said sullenly: "There it is! You can see it all for yourself—not that there's very much to see," and groped his way to the fire.

His wife looked at him in sharp alarm. "Whatever have you done to yourself?" she exclaimed. "You're ill—that's what it is, Bunting. You got a chill last night!"

"I told you I'd got a chill," he muttered. "'Twasn't last night, though; 'twas going out this morning, coming back in the bus. Margaret keeps that housekeeper's room o' hers like a hothouse—that's what she does. 'Twas going out from there into the biting wind, that's what did for me. It must be awful to stand about in such weather; 'tis a wonder to me how that young fellow, Joe Chandler, can stand the life—being out in all weathers like he is."

Bunting spoke at random, his one anxiety being to get away from what was in the paper, which now lay, neglected, on the table.

"Those that keep out o' doors all day never do come to no harm," said his wife testily. "But if you felt so bad, whatever was you out so long for, Bunting? I thought you'd gone away somewhere! D'you mean you only went to get the paper?"

"I just stopped for a second to look at it under the lamp," he muttered apologetically.

"That was a silly thing to do!"

"Perhaps it was," he admitted meekly.

Daisy had taken up the paper. "Well, they don't say much," she said disappointedly. "Hardly anything at all! But perhaps Mr. Chandler'll be in soon again. If so, he'll tell us more about it."

"A young girl like you oughtn't to want to know anything about murders," said her stepmother severely. "Joe won't think any the better of you for your inquisitiveness about such things. If I was you, Daisy, I shouldn't say nothing about it if he does come in—which I fair tell you I hope he won't. I've seen enough of that young chap to-day."

"He didn't come in for long—not to-day," said Daisy, her lip trembling.

"I can tell you one thing that'll surprise you, my dear"—Mrs. Bunting looked significantly at her stepdaughter. She also wanted to get away from that dread news—which yet was no news.

"Yes?" said Daisy, rather defiantly. "What is it, Ellen?"

"Maybe you'll be surprised to hear that Joe did come in this morning. He knew all about that affair then, but he particular asked that you shouldn't be told anything about it."

"Never!" cried Daisy, much mortified.

"Yes," went on her stepmother ruthlessly. "You just ask your father over there if it isn't true."

"'Tain't a healthy thing to speak overmuch about such happenings," said Bunting heavily.

"If I was Joe," went on Mrs. Bunting, quickly pursuing her advantage, "I shouldn't want to talk about such horrid things when I comes in to have a quiet chat with friends. But the minute he comes in that poor young chap is set upon—mostly, I admit, by your father," she looked at her husband severely. "But you does your share, too, Daisy! You asks him this, you asks him that—he's fair puzzled sometimes. It don't do to be so inquisitive."

And perhaps because of this little sermon on Mrs. Bunting's part when young Chandler did come in again that evening, very little was said of the new Avenger murder.

Bunting made no reference to it at all, and though Daisy said a word, it was but a word. And Joe Chandler thought he had never spent a pleasanter evening in his life—for it was he and Daisy who talked all the time, their elders remaining for the most part silent.

Daisy told of all that she had done with Aunt Margaret. She described the long, dull hours and the queer jobs her aunt set her to do—the washing up of all the fine drawing-room china in a big basin lined with flannel, and how terrified she (Daisy) had been lest there should come even one teeny little chip to any of it. Then she went on to relate some of the funny things Aunt Margaret had told her about "the family."

There came a really comic tale, which hugely interested and delighted Chandler. This was of how Aunt Margaret's lady had been taken in by an impostor—an impostor who had come up, just as she was stepping out of her carriage, and pretended to have a fit on the doorstep. Aunt Margaret's lady, being a soft one, had insisted on the man coming into the hall, where he had been given all kinds of restoratives. When the man had at last gone off, it was found that he had "wolfed" young master's best walking-stick, one with a fine tortoise-shell top to it. Thus had Aunt Margaret proved to her lady that the man had been shamming, and her lady had been very angry—near had a fit herself!

"There's a lot of that about," said Chandler, laughing. "Incorrigible rogues and vagabonds—that's what those sort of people are!"

And then he, in his turn, told an elaborate tale of an exceptionally clever swindler whom he himself had brought to book. He was very proud of that job, it had formed a white stone in his career as a detective. And even Mrs. Bunting was quite interested to hear about it.

Chandler was still sitting there when Mr. Sleuth's bell rang. For awhile no one stirred; then Bunting looked questioningly at his wife.

"Did you hear that?" he said. "I think, Ellen, that was the lodger's bell."

She got up, without alacrity, and went upstairs.

"I rang," said Mr. Sleuth weakly, "to tell you I don't require any supper to-night, Mrs. Bunting. Only a glass of milk, with a lump of sugar in it. That is all I require—nothing more. I feel very very far from well"—and he had a hunted, plaintive expression on his face. "And then I thought your husband would like his paper back again, Mrs. Bunting."

Mrs. Bunting, looking at him fixedly, with a sad intensity of gaze of which she was quite unconscious, answered, "Oh, no, sir! Bunting don't require that paper now. He read it all through." Something impelled her to add, ruthlessly, "He's got another paper by now, sir. You may have heard them come shouting outside. Would you like me to bring you up that other paper, sir?"

And Mr. Sleuth shook his head. "No," he said querulously. "I much regret now having asked for the one paper I did read, for it disturbed me, Mrs. Bunting. There was nothing of any value in it—there never is in any public print. I gave up reading newspapers years ago, and I much regret that I broke though my rule to-day."

As if to indicate to her that he did not wish for any more conversation, the lodger then did what he had never done before in his landlady's presence. He went over to the fireplace and deliberately turned his back on her.

She went down and brought up the glass of milk and the lump of sugar he had asked for.

Now he was in his usual place, sitting at the table, studying the Book.

When Mrs. Bunting went back to the others they were chatting merrily. She did not notice that the merriment was confined to the two young people.

"Well?" said Daisy pertly. "How about the lodger, Ellen? Is he all right?"

"Yes," she said stiffly. "Of course he is!"

"He must feel pretty dull sitting up there all by himself—awful lonely-like, I call it," said the girl.

But her, stepmother remained silent.

"Whatever does he do with himself all day?" persisted Daisy.

"Just now he's reading the Bible," Mrs. Bunting answered, shortly and dryly.

"Well, I never! That's a funny thing for a gentleman to do!"

And Joe, alone of her three listeners, laughed—a long hearty peal of amusement.

"There's nothing to laugh at," said Mrs. Bunting sharply. "I should feel ashamed of being caught laughing at anything connected with the Bible."

And poor Joe became suddenly quite serious. This was the first time that Mrs. Bunting had ever spoken really nastily to him, and he answered very humbly, "I beg pardon. I know I oughtn't to have laughed at anything to do with the Bible, but you see, Miss Daisy said it so funny-like, and, by all accounts, your lodger must be a queer card, Mrs. Bunting."

"He's no queerer than many people I could mention," she said quickly; and with these enigmatic words she got up, and left the room.

CHAPTER TWENTY FOUR

Each hour of the days that followed held for Bunting its full meed of aching fear and suspense.

The unhappy man was ever debating within himself what course he should pursue, and, according to his mood and to the state of his mind at any particular moment, he would waver between various widely-differing lines of action.

He told himself again and again, and with fretful unease, that the most awful thing about it all was that he wasn't sure. If only he could have been sure, he might have made up his mind exactly what it was he ought to do.

But when telling himself this he was deceiving himself, and he was vaguely conscious of the fact; for, from Bunting's point of view, almost any alternative would have been preferable to that which to some, nay, perhaps to most, householders would have seemed the only thing to do, namely, to go to the police. But Londoners of Bunting's class have an uneasy fear of the law. To his mind it would be ruin for him and for his Ellen to be mixed up publicly in such a terrible affair. No one concerned in the business would give them and their future a thought, but it would track them to their dying day, and, above all, it would make it quite impossible for them ever to get again into a good joint situation. It was that for which Bunting, in his secret soul, now longed with all his heart.

No, some other way than going to the police must be found—and he racked his slow brain to find it.

The worst of it was that every hour that went by made his future course more difficult and more delicate, and increased the awful weight on his conscience.

If only he really knew! If only he could feel quite sure! And then he would tell himself that, after all, he had very little to go upon; only suspicion—suspicion, and a secret, horrible certainty that his suspicion was justified.

And so at last Bunting began to long for a solution which he knew to be indefensible from every point of view; he began to hope, that is, in the depths of his heart, that the lodger would again go out one evening on his horrible business and be caught—red-handed.

But far from going out on any business, horrible or other, Mr. Sleuth now never went out at all. He kept upstairs, and often spent quite a considerable part of his day in bed. He still felt, so he assured Mrs. Bunting, very far from well. He had never thrown off the chill he had caught on that bitter night he and his landlord had met on their several ways home.

Joe Chandler, too, had become a terrible complication to Daisy's father. The detective spent every waking hour that he was not on duty with the Buntings; and Bunting, who at one time had liked him so well and so cordially, now became mortally afraid of him.

But though the young man talked of little else than The Avenger, and though on one evening he described at immense length the eccentric-looking gent who had given the barmaid a sovereign, picturing Mr. Sleuth with such awful accuracy that both Bunting and Mrs. Bunting secretly and separately turned sick when they listened to him, he never showed the slightest interest in their lodger.

At last there came a morning when Bunting and Chandler held a strange conversation about The Avenger. The young fellow had come in earlier than usual, and just as he arrived Mrs. Bunting and Daisy were starting out to do some shopping. The girl would fain have stopped behind, but her stepmother had given her a very peculiar, disagreeable look, daring her, so to speak, to be so forward, and Daisy had gone on with a flushed, angry look on her pretty face.

And then, as young Chandler stepped through into the sitting-room, it suddenly struck Bunting that the young man looked unlike himself—indeed, to the ex-butler's apprehension there was something almost threatening in Chandler's attitude.

"I want a word with you, Mr. Bunting," he began abruptly, falteringly. "And I'm glad to have the chance now that Mrs. Bunting and Miss Daisy are out."

Bunting braced himself to hear the awful words—the accusation of having sheltered a murderer, the monster whom all the world was seeking, under his roof. And then he remembered a phrase, a horrible legal phrase—"Accessory after the fact." Yes, he had been that, there wasn't any doubt about it!

"Yes?" he said. "What is it, Joe?" and then the unfortunate man sat down in his chair. "Yes?" he said again uncertainly; for young Chandler had now advanced to the table, he was looking at Bunting fixedly—the other thought threateningly. "Well, out with it, Joe! Don't keep me in suspense."

And then a slight smile broke over the young man's face. "I don't think what I've got to say can take you by surprise, Mr. Bunting."

And Bunting wagged his head in a way that might mean anything—yes or no, as the case might be.

The two men looked at one another for what seemed a very, very long time to the elder of them. And then, making a great effort, Joe Chandler brought out the words, "Well, I suppose you know what it is I want to talk about. I'm sure Mrs. Bunting would, from a look or two she's lately cast on me. It's your daughter—it's Miss Daisy."

And then Bunting gave a kind of cry, 'twixt a sob and a laugh. "My girl?" he cried. "Good Lord, Joe! Is that all you wants to talk about? Why, you fair frightened me—that you did!"

And, indeed, the relief was so great that the room swam round as he stared across it at his daughter's lover, that lover who was also the embodiment of that now awful thing to him, the law. He smiled, rather foolishly, at his visitor; and Chandler felt a sharp wave of irritation, of impatience sweep over his good-natured soul. Daisy's father was an old stupid—that's what he was.

And then Bunting grew serious. The room ceased to go round. "As far as I'm concerned," he said, with a good deal of solemnity, even a little dignity, "you have my blessing, Joe. You're a very likely young chap, and I had a true respect for your father."

"Yes," said Chandler, "that's very kind of you, Mr. Bunting. But how about her—her herself?"

Bunting stared at him. It pleased him to think that Daisy hadn't given herself away, as Ellen was always hinting the girl was doing.

"I can't answer for Daisy," he said heavily. "You'll have to ask her yourself—that's not a job any other man can do for you, my lad."

"I never gets a chance. I never sees her, not by our two selves," said Chandler, with some heat. "You don't seem to understand, Mr. Bunting, that I never do see Miss Daisy alone," he repeated. "I hear now that she's going away Monday, and I've only once had the chance of a walk with her. Mrs. Bunting's very particular, not to say pernickety in her ideas, Mr. Bunting—"

"That's a fault on the right side, that is—with a young girl," said Bunting thoughtfully.

And Chandler nodded. He quite agreed that as regarded other young chaps Mrs. Bunting could not be too particular.

"She's been brought up like a lady, my Daisy has," went on Bunting, with some pride. "That Old Aunt of hers hardly lets her out of her sight."

"I was coming to the old aunt," said Chandler heavily. "Mrs. Bunting she talks as if your daughter was going to stay with that old woman the whole of her natural life—now is that right? That's what I wants to ask you, Mr. Bunting,—is that right?"

"I'll say a word to Ellen, don't you fear," said Bunting abstractedly.

His mind had wandered off, away from Daisy and this nice young chap, to his now constant anxious preoccupation. "You come along to-morrow," he said, "and I'll see you gets your walk with Daisy. It's only right you and she should have a chance of seeing one another without old folk being by; else how's the girl to tell whether she likes you or not! For the matter of that, you hardly knows her, Joe—" He looked at the young man consideringly.

Chandler shook his head impatiently. "I knows her quite as well as I wants to know her," he said. "I made up my mind the very first time I see'd her, Mr. Bunting."

"No! Did you really?" said Bunting. "Well, come to think of it, I did so with her mother; aye, and years after, with Ellen, too. But I hope you'll never want no second, Chandler."

"God forbid!" said the young man under his breath. And then he asked, rather longingly, "D'you think they'll be out long now, Mr. Bunting?"

And Bunting woke up to a due sense of hospitality. "Sit down, sit down; do!" he said hastily. "I don't believe they'll be very long. They've only got a little bit of shopping to do."

And then, in a changed, in a ringing, nervous tone, he asked, "And how about your job, Joe? Nothing new, I take it? I suppose you're all just waiting for the next time?"

"Aye—that's about the figure of it." Chandler's voice had also changed; it was now sombre, menacing. "We're fair tired of it—beginning to wonder when it'll end, that we are!"

"Do you ever try and make to yourself a picture of what the master's like?" asked Bunting. Somehow, he felt he must ask that.

"Yes," said Joe slowly. "I've a sort of notion—a savage, fierce-looking devil, the chap must be. It's that description that was circulated put us wrong. I don't believe it was the man that knocked up against that woman in the fog—no, not one bit I don't. But I wavers, I can't quite make up my mind. Sometimes I think it's a sailor—the foreigner they talks about, that goes away for eight or nine days in between, to Holland maybe, or to France. Then, again, I says to myself that it's a butcher, a man from the Central Market. Whoever it is, it's someone used to killing, that's flat."

"Then it don't seem to you possible—?" (Bunting got up and walked over to the window.) "You don't take any stock, I suppose, in that idea some of the papers put out, that the man is"—then he hesitated and brought out, with a gasp—"a gentleman?"

Chandler looked at him, surprised. "No," he said deliberately. "I've made up my mind that's quite a wrong tack, though I knows that some of our fellows—big pots, too—are quite sure that the fellow what gave the girl the sovereign is the man we're looking for. You see, Mr. Bunting, if that's the fact—well, it stands to reason the fellow's an escaped lunatic; and if he's an escaped lunatic he's got a keeper, and they'd be raising a hue and cry after him; now, wouldn't they?"[37]

"You don't think," went on Bunting, lowering his voice, "that he could be just staying somewhere, lodging like?"

"D'you mean that The Avenger may be a toff, staying in some West-end hotel, Mr. Bunting? Well, things almost as funny as that 'ud be have come to pass." He smiled as if the notion was a funny one.

"Yes, something o' that sort," muttered Bunting.

"Well, if your idea's correct, Mr. Bunting—"

"I never said 'twas my idea," said Bunting, all in a hurry.

"Well, if that idea's correct then, 'twill make our task more difficult than ever. Why, 'twould be looking for a needle in a field of hay, Mr. Bunting! But there! I don't think it's anything quite so unlikely as that—not myself I don't." He hesitated. "There's some of us"—he lowered his voice—"that hopes he'll betake himself off—The Avenger, I mean—to another big city, to Manchester or to Edinburgh. There'd be plenty of work for him to do there," and Chandler chuckled at his own grim joke.

And then, to both men's secret relief, for Bunting was now mortally afraid of this discussion concerning The Avenger and his doings, they heard Mrs. Bunting's key in the lock.

Daisy blushed rosy-red with pleasure when she saw that young Chandler was still there. She had feared that when they got home he would be gone, the more so that Ellen, just as if she was doing it on purpose, had lingered aggravatingly long over each small purchase.

"Here's Joe come to ask if he can take Daisy out for a walk," blurted out Bunting.

"My mother says as how she'd like you to come to tea, over at Richmond," said Chandler awkwardly, "I just come in to see whether we could fix it up, Miss Daisy." And Daisy looked imploringly at her stepmother.

"D'you mean now—this minute?" asked Mrs. Bunting tartly.

"No, o' course not"—Bunting broke in hastily. "How you do go on, Ellen!"

"What day did your mother mention would be convenient to her?" asked Mrs. Bunting, looking at the young man satirically.

Chandler hesitated. His mother had not mentioned any special day—in fact, his mother had shown a surprising lack of anxiety to see Daisy at all. But he had talked her round.

"How about Saturday?" suggested Bunting. "That's Daisy's birthday. 'Twould be a birthday treat for her to go to Richmond, and she's going back to Old Aunt on Monday."

"I can't go Saturday," said Chandler disconsolately. "I'm on duty Saturday."

"Well, then, let it be Sunday," said Bunting firmly. And his wife looked at him surprised; he seldom asserted himself so much in her presence.

"What do you say, Miss Daisy?" said Chandler.

"Sunday would be very nice," said Daisy demurely. And then, as the young man took up his hat, and as her stepmother did not stir, Daisy ventured to go out into the hall with him for a minute.

Chandler shut the door behind them, and so was spared the hearing of Mrs. Bunting's whispered remark: "When I was a young woman folk didn't gallivant about on Sunday; those who was courting used to go to church together, decent-like—"

CHAPTER TWENTY FIVE

Daisy's eighteenth birthday dawned uneventfully. Her father gave her what he had always promised she should have on her eighteenth birthday—a watch. It was a pretty little silver watch, which Bunting had bought secondhand on the last day he had been happy—it seemed a long, long time ago now.

Mrs. Bunting thought a silver watch a very extravagant present but she was far too wretched, far too absorbed in her own thoughts, to trouble much about it. Besides, in such matters she had generally had the good sense not to interfere between her husband and his child.

In the middle of the birthday morning Bunting went out to buy himself some more tobacco. He had never smoked so much as in the last four days, excepting, perhaps, the week that had followed on his leaving service. Smoking a pipe had then held all the exquisite pleasure which we are told attaches itself to the eating of forbidden fruit.

His tobacco had now become his only relaxation; it acted on his nerves as an opiate, soothing his fears and helping him to think. But he had been overdoing it, and it was that which now made him feel so "jumpy," so he assured himself, when he found himself starting at any casual sound outside, or even when his wife spoke to him suddenly.

Just now Ellen and Daisy were down in the kitchen, and Bunting didn't quite like the sensation of knowing that there was only one pair of stairs between Mr. Sleuth and himself. So he quietly slipped out of the house without telling Ellen that he was going out.

In the last four days Bunting had avoided his usual haunts; above all, he had avoided even passing the time of day to his acquaintances and neighbours. He feared, with a great fear, that they would talk to him of a subject which, because it filled his mind to the exclusion of all else, might make him betray the knowledge—no, not knowledge, rather the—the suspicion—that dwelt within him.

But to-day the unfortunate man had a curious, instinctive longing for human companionship—companionship, that is, other than that of his wife and of his daughter.

This longing for a change of company finally led him into a small, populous thoroughfare hard by the Edgware Road. There were more people there than usual just now, for the housewives of the neighbourhood were doing their Saturday marketing for Sunday. The ex-butler turned into a small old-fashioned shop where he generally bought his tobacco.

Bunting passed the time of day with the tobacconist, and the two fell into desultory talk, but to his customer's relief and surprise the man made no allusion to the subject of which all the neighbourhood must still be talking.

And then, quite suddenly, while still standing by the counter, and before he had paid for the packet of tobacco he held in his hand, Bunting, through the open door, saw with horrified surprise that Ellen, his wife, was standing, alone, outside a greengrocer's shop just opposite.

Muttering a word of apology, he rushed out of the shop and across the road.

"Ellen!" he gasped hoarsely, "you've never gone and left my little girl alone in the house with the lodger?"

Mrs. Bunting's face went yellow with fear. "I thought you was indoors," she cried. "You *was* indoors! Whatever made you come out for, without first making sure I'd stay in?"

Bunting made no answer; but, as they stared at each other in exasperated silence, each now knew that the other knew.

They turned and scurried down the crowded street. "Don't run," he said suddenly; "we shall get there just as quickly if we walk fast. People are noticing you, Ellen. Don't run."

He spoke breathlessly, but it was breathlessness induced by fear and by excitement, not by the quick pace at which they were walking.

At last they reached their own gate, and Bunting pushed past in front of his wife.

After all, Daisy was his child; Ellen couldn't know how he was feeling.

He seemed to take the path in one leap, then fumbled for a moment with his latchkey.

Opening wide the door, "Daisy!" he called out, in a wailing voice, "Daisy, my dear! where are you?"

"Here I am, father. What is it?"

"She's all right." Bunting turned a grey face to his wife. "She's all right, Ellen."

He waited a moment, leaning against the wall of the passage. "It did give me a turn," he said, and then, warningly, "Don't frighten the girl, Ellen."

Daisy was standing before the fire in their sitting room, admiring herself in the glass.

"Oh, father," she exclaimed, without turning round, "I've seen the lodger! He's quite a nice gentleman, though, to be sure, he does look a

cure. He rang his bell, but I didn't like to go up; and so he came down to
ask Ellen for something. We had quite a nice little chat—that we had. I
told him it was my birthday, and he asked me and Ellen to go to Madame
Tussaud's with him this afternoon." She laughed, a little self-consciously.
"Of course, I could see he was 'centric, and then at first he spoke so
funnily. 'And who be you?' he says, threatening-like. And I says to him,
'I'm Mr. Bunting's daughter, sir.' 'Then you're a very fortunate girl'—
that's what he says, Ellen—'to 'ave such a nice stepmother as you've got.
That's why,' he says, 'you look such a good, innocent girl.' And then he
quoted a bit of the Prayer Book. 'Keep innocency,' he says, wagging his
head at me. Lor'! It made me feel as if I was with Old Aunt again."

"I won't have you going out with the lodger—that's flat."

Bunting spoke in a muffled, angry tone. He was wiping his forehead
with one hand, while with the other he mechanically squeezed the little
packet of tobacco, for which, as he now remembered, he had forgotten to
pay.

Daisy pouted. "Oh, father, I think you might let me have a treat on my
birthday! I told him that Saturday wasn't a very good day—at least, so I'd
heard—for Madame Tussaud's. Then he said we could go early, while the
fine folk are still having their dinners." She turned to her stepmother, then
giggled happily. "He particularly said you was to come, too. The lodger
has a wonderful fancy for you, Ellen; if I was father, I'd feel quite
jealous!"

Her last words were cut across by a tap-tap on the door.

Bunting and his wife looked at each other apprehensively. Was it
possible that, in their agitation, they had left the front door open, and that
someone, some merciless myrmidon of the law, had crept in behind them?

Both felt a curious thrill of satisfaction when they saw that it was only
Mr. Sleuth—Mr. Sleuth dressed for going out; the tall hat he had worn
when he had first come to them was in his hand, but he was wearing a coat
instead of his Inverness cape.

"I heard you come in"—he addressed Mrs. Bunting in his high,
whistling, hesitating voice—"and so I've come down to ask you if you and
Miss Bunting will come to Madame Tussaud's now. I have never seen
those famous waxworks, though I've heard of the place all my life."

As Bunting forced himself to look fixedly at his lodger, a sudden doubt
bringing with it a sense of immeasurable relief, came to Mr. Sleuth's
landlord.

Surely it was inconceivable that this gentle, mild-mannered gentleman
could be the monster of cruelty and cunning that Bunting had now for the
terrible space of four days believed him to be!

He tried to catch his wife's eye, but Mrs. Bunting was looking away, staring into vacancy. She still, of course, wore the bonnet and cloak in which she had just been out to do her marketing. Daisy was already putting on her hat and coat.

"Well?" said Mr. Sleuth. Then Mrs. Bunting turned, and it seemed to his landlady that he was looking at her threateningly. "Well?"

"Yes, sir. We'll come in a minute," she said dully.

CHAPTER TWENTY SIX

Madame Tussaud's had hitherto held pleasant memories for Mrs. Bunting. In the days when she and Bunting were courting they often spent there part of their afternoon-out.

The butler had an acquaintance, a man named Hopkins, who was one of the waxworks staff, and this man had sometimes given him passes for "self and lady." But this was the first time Mrs. Bunting had been inside the place since she had come to live almost next door, as it were, to the big building.

They walked in silence to the familiar entrance, and then, after the ill-assorted trio had gone up the great staircase and into the first gallery, Mr. Sleuth suddenly stopped short. The presence of those curious, still, waxen figures which suggest so strangely death in life, seemed to surprise and affright him.

Daisy took quick advantage of the lodger's hesitation and unease.

"Oh, Ellen," she cried, "do let us begin by going into the Chamber of Horrors! I've never been in there. Old Aunt made father promise he wouldn't take me the only time I've ever been here. But now that I'm eighteen I can do just as I like; besides, Old Aunt will never know."

Mr. Sleuth looked down at her, and a smile passed for a moment over his worn, gaunt face.

"Yes," he said, "let us go into the Chamber of Horrors; that's a good idea, Miss Bunting. I've always wanted to see the Chamber of Horrors."

They turned into the great room in which the Napoleonic relics were then kept, and which led into the curious, vault-like chamber where waxen effigies of dead criminals stand grouped in wooden docks.

Mrs. Bunting was at once disturbed and relieved to see her husband's old acquaintance, Mr. Hopkins, in charge of the turnstile admitting the public to the Chamber of Horrors.

"Well, you are a stranger," the man observed genially. "I do believe that this is the very first time I've seen you in here, Mrs. Bunting, since you was married!"

"Yes," she said, "that is so. And this is my husband's daughter, Daisy; I expect you've heard of her, Mr. Hopkins. And this"—she hesitated a moment—"is our lodger, Mr. Sleuth."

But Mr. Sleuth frowned and shuffled away. Daisy, leaving her stepmother's side, joined him.

Two, as all the world knows, is company, three is none. Mrs. Bunting put down three sixpences.

"Wait a minute," said Hopkins; "you can't go into the Chamber of Horrors just yet. But you won't have to wait more than four or five minutes, Mrs. Bunting. It's this way, you see; our boss is in there, showing a party round." He lowered his voice. "It's Sir John Burney—I suppose you know who Sir John Burney is?"

"No," she answered indifferently, "I don't know that I ever heard of him."

She felt slightly—oh, very slightly—uneasy about Daisy. She would have liked her stepdaughter to keep well within sight and sound, but Mr. Sleuth was now taking the girl down to the other end of the room.

"Well, I hope you never will know him—not in any personal sense, Mrs. Bunting." The man chuckled. "He's the Commissioner of Police—the new one—that's what Sir John Burney is. One of the gentlemen he's showing round our place is the Paris Police boss—whose job is on all fours, so to speak, with Sir John's. The Frenchy has brought his daughter with him, and there are several other ladies. Ladies always likes horrors, Mrs. Bunting; that's our experience here. 'Oh, take me to the Chamber of Horrors'—that's what they say the minute they gets into this here building!"

Mrs. Bunting looked at him thoughtfully. It occurred to Mr. Hopkins that she was very wan and tired; she used to look better in the old days, when she was still in service, before Bunting married her.

"Yes," she said; "that's just what my stepdaughter said just now. 'Oh, take me to the Chamber of Horrors'—that's exactly what she did say when we got upstairs."

A group of people, all talking and laughing together; were advancing, from within the wooden barrier, toward the turnstile.

Mrs. Bunting stared at them nervously. She wondered which of them was the gentleman with whom Mr. Hopkins had hoped she would never be brought into personal contact; she thought she could pick him out among the others. He was a tall, powerful, handsome gentleman, with a military appearance.

Just now he was smiling down into the face of a young lady. "Monsieur Barberoux is quite right," he was saying in a loud, cheerful voice, "our English law is too kind to the criminal, especially to the murderer. If we conducted our trials in the French fashion, the place we have just left would be very much fuller than it is to-day. A man of whose guilt we are absolutely assured is oftener than not acquitted, and then the public taunt us with 'another undiscovered crime!'"

"D'you mean, Sir John, that murderers sometimes escape scot-free? Take the man who has been committing all these awful murders this last month? I suppose there's no doubt he'll be hanged—if he's ever caught, that is!"

Her girlish voice rang out, and Mrs. Bunting could hear every word that was said.

The whole party gathered round, listening eagerly. "Well, no." He spoke very deliberately. "I doubt if that particular murderer ever will be hanged."

"You mean that you'll never catch him?" the girl spoke with a touch of airy impertinence in her clear voice.

"I think we shall end by catching him—because"—he waited a moment, then added in a lower voice—"now don't give me away to a newspaper fellow, Miss Rose—because now I think we do know who the murderer in question is—"

Several of those standing near by uttered expressions of surprise and incredulity.

"Then why don't you catch him?" cried the girl indignantly.

"I didn't say we knew where he was; I only said we knew who he was, or, rather, perhaps I ought to say that I personally have a very strong suspicion of his identity."

Sir John's French colleague looked up quickly. "De Leipsic and Liverpool man?" he said interrogatively.

The other nodded. "Yes, I suppose you've had the case turned up?"

Then, speaking very quickly, as if he wished to dismiss the subject from his own mind, and from that of his auditors, he went on: "Four murders of the kind were committed eight years ago—two in Leipsic, the others, just afterwards, in Liverpool,—and there were certain peculiarities connected with the crimes which made it clear they were committed by the same hand. The perpetrator was caught, fortunately for us, red-handed, just as he was leaving the house of his last victim, for in Liverpool the murder was committed in a house. I myself saw the unhappy man—I say unhappy, for there is no doubt at all that he was mad"—he hesitated, and added in a lower tone—"suffering from an acute form of religious mania. I myself saw him, as I say, at some length. But now comes the really interesting point. I have just been informed that a month ago this criminal lunatic, as we must of course regard him, made his escape from the asylum where he was confined. He arranged the whole thing with extraordinary cunning and intelligence, and we should probably have caught him long ago, were it not that he managed, when on his way out of the place, to annex a considerable sum of money in gold, with which the wages of the asylum staff were about to be paid. It is owing to that fact that his escape was, very wrongly, concealed—"

He stopped abruptly, as if sorry he had said so much, and a moment later the party were walking in Indian file through the turnstile, Sir John Burney leading the way.

Mrs. Bunting looked straight before her. She felt—so she expressed it to her husband later—as if she had been turned to stone.

Even had she wished to do so, she had neither the time nor the power to warn her lodger of his danger, for Daisy and her companion were now coming down the room, bearing straight for the Commissioner of Police. In another moment Mrs. Bunting's lodger and Sir John Burney were face to face.

Mr. Sleuth swerved to one side; there came a terrible change over his pale, narrow face; it became discomposed, livid with rage and terror.

But, to Mrs. Bunting's relief—yes, to her inexpressible relief—Sir John Burney and his friends swept on. They passed Mr. Sleuth and the girl by his side, unaware, or so it seemed to her, that there was anyone else in the room but themselves.

"Hurry up, Mrs. Bunting," said the turnstile-keeper; "you and your friends will have the place all to yourselves for a bit." From an official he had become a man, and it was the man in Mr. Hopkins that gallantly addressed pretty Daisy Bunting: "It seems strange that a young lady like you should want to go in and see all those 'orrible frights," he said jestingly.

"Mrs. Bunting, may I trouble you to come over here for a moment?"

The words were hissed rather than spoken by Mr. Sleuth's lips.

His landlady took a doubtful step towards him.

"A last word with you, Mrs. Bunting." The lodger's face was still distorted with fear and passion. "Do not think to escape the consequences of your hideous treachery. I trusted you, Mrs. Bunting, and you betrayed me! But I am protected by a higher power, for I still have much to do." Then, his voice sinking to a whisper, he hissed out "Your end will be bitter as wormwood and sharp as a two-edged sword. Your feet shall go down to death, and your steps take hold on hell."[38]

Even while Mr. Sleuth was muttering these strange, dreadful words, he was looking round, glancing this way and that, seeking a way of escape.

At last his eyes became fixed on a small placard placed above a curtain. "Emergency Exit" was written there. Mrs. Bunting thought he was going to make a dash for the place; but Mr. Sleuth did something very different. Leaving his landlady's side, he walked over to the turnstile, he fumbled in his pocket for a moment, and then touched the man on the arm. "I feel ill," he said, speaking very rapidly; "very ill indeed! It is the atmosphere of this place. I want you to let me out by the quickest way. It would be a pity for me to faint here—especially with ladies about."

His left hand shot out and placed what he had been fumbling for in his pocket on the other's bare palm. "I see there's an emergency exit over there. Would it be possible for me to get out that way?"

"Well, yes, sir; I think so."

The man hesitated; he felt a slight, a very sight, feeling of misgiving. He looked at Daisy, flushed and smiling, happy and unconcerned, and then at Mrs. Bunting. She was very pale; but surely her lodger's sudden seizure was enough to make her feel worried. Hopkins felt the half-sovereign pleasantly tickling his palm. The Paris Prefect of Police had given him only half-a-crown—mean, shabby foreigner!

"Yes, sir; I can let you out that way," he said at last, "and p'raps when you're standing out in the air, on the iron balcony, you'll feel better. But then, you know, sir, you'll have to come round to the front if you wants to come in again, for those emergency doors only open outward."

"Yes, yes," said Mr. Sleuth hurriedly. "I quite understand! If I feel better I'll come in by the front way, and pay another shilling—that's only fair."

"You needn't do that if you'll just explain what happened here."

The man went and pulled the curtain aside, and put his shoulder against the door. It burst open, and the light, for a moment, blinded Mr. Sleuth.

He passed his hand over his eyes. "Thank you," he muttered, "thank you. I shall get all right out there."

An iron stairway led down into a small stable yard, of which the door opened into a side street.

Mr. Sleuth looked round once more; he really did feel very ill—ill and dazed. How pleasant it would be to take a flying leap over the balcony railing and find rest, eternal rest, below.

But no—he thrust the thought, the temptation, from him. Again a convulsive look of rage came over his face. He had remembered his landlady. How could the woman whom he had treated so generously have betrayed him to his arch-enemy?—to the official, that is, who had entered into a conspiracy years ago to have him confined—him, an absolutely sane man with a great avenging work to do in the world—in a lunatic asylum.

He stepped out into the open air, and the curtain, falling-to behind him, blotted out the tall, thin figure from the little group of people who had watched him disappear.

Even Daisy felt a little scared. "He did look bad, didn't he, now?" she turned appealingly to Mr. Hopkins.

"Yes, that he did, poor gentleman—your lodger, too?" he looked sympathetically at Mrs. Bunting.

She moistened her lips with her tongue. "Yes," she repeated dully, "my lodger."

CHAPTER TWENTY SEVEN

In vain Mr. Hopkins invited Mrs. Bunting and her pretty stepdaughter to step through into the Chamber of Horrors. "I think we ought to go straight home," said Mr. Sleuth's landlady decidedly. And Daisy meekly assented. Somehow the girl felt confused, a little scared by the lodger's sudden disappearance. Perhaps this unwonted feeling of hers was induced by the look of stunned surprise and, yes, pain, on her stepmother's face.

Slowly they made their way out of the building, and when they got home it was Daisy who described the strange way Mr. Sleuth had been taken.

"I don't suppose he'll be long before he comes home," said Bunting heavily, and he cast an anxious, furtive look at his wife. She looked as if stricken in a vital part; he saw from her face that there was something wrong—very wrong indeed.

The hours dragged on. All three felt moody and ill at ease. Daisy knew there was no chance that young Chandler would come in to-day.

About six o'clock Mrs. Bunting went upstairs. She lit the gas in Mr. Sleuth's sitting-room and looked about her with a fearful glance. Somehow everything seemed to speak to her of the lodger, there lay her Bible and his Concordance, side by side on the table, exactly as he had left them, when he had come downstairs and suggested that ill-starred expedition to his landlord's daughter. She took a few steps forward, listening the while anxiously for the familiar sound of the click in the door which would tell her that the lodger had come back, and then she went over to the window and looked out.

What a cold night for a man to be wandering about, homeless, friendless, and, as she suspected with a pang, with but very little money on him!

Turning abruptly, she went into the lodger's bedroom and opened the drawer of the looking-glass.

Yes, there lay the much-diminished heap of sovereigns. If only he had taken his money out with him! She wondered painfully whether he had enough on his person to secure a good night's lodging, and then suddenly she remembered that which brought relief to her mind. The lodger had given something to that Hopkins fellow—either a sovereign or half a sovereign, she wasn't sure which.

The memory of Mr. Sleuth's cruel words to her, of his threat, did not disturb her overmuch. It had been a mistake—all a mistake. Far from betraying Mr. Sleuth, she had sheltered him—kept his awful secret as she could not have kept it had she known, or even dimly suspected, the horrible fact with which Sir John Burney's words had made her acquainted; namely, that Mr. Sleuth was victim of no temporary aberration, but that he was, and had been for years, a madman, a homicidal maniac.

In her ears there still rang the Frenchman's half careless yet confident question, "De Leipsic and Liverpool man?"

Following a sudden impulse, she went back into the sitting-room, and taking a black-headed pin out of her bodice stuck it amid the leaves of the Bible. Then she opened the Book, and looked at the page the pin had marked:— "My tabernacle is spoiled and all my cords are broken ... There is none to stretch forth my tent any more and to set up my curtains."[39]

At last leaving the Bible open, Mrs. Bunting went downstairs, and as she opened the door of her sitting-room Daisy came towards her stepmother.

"I'll go down and start getting the lodger's supper ready for you," said the girl good-naturedly. "He's certain to come in when he gets hungry. But he did look upset, didn't he, Ellen? Right down bad—that he did!"

Mrs. Bunting made no answer; she simply stepped aside to allow Daisy to go down.

"Mr. Sleuth won't never come back no more," she said sombrely, and then she felt both glad and angry at the extraordinary change which came over her husband's face. Yet, perversely, that look of relief, of right-down joy, chiefly angered her, and tempted her to add, "That's to say, I don't suppose he will."

And Bunting's face altered again; the old, anxious, depressed look, the look it had worn the last few days, returned.

"What makes you think he mayn't come back?" he muttered.

"Too long to tell you now," she said. "Wait till the child's gone to bed."

And Bunting had to restrain his curiosity.

And then, when at last Daisy had gone off to the back room where she now slept with her stepmother, Mrs. Bunting beckoned to her husband to follow her upstairs.

Before doing so he went down the passage and put the chain on the door. And about this they had a few sharp whispered words.

"You're never going to shut him out?" she expostulated angrily, beneath her breath.

"I'm not going to leave Daisy down here with that man perhaps walking in any minute."

"Mr. Sleuth won't hurt Daisy, bless you! Much more likely to hurt me," and she gave a half sob.

Bunting stared at her. "What do you mean?" he said roughly. "Come upstairs and tell me what you mean."

And then, in what had been the lodger's sitting-room, Mrs. Bunting told her husband exactly what it was that had happened.

He listened in heavy silence.

"So you see," she said at last, "you see, Bunting, that 'twas me that was right after all. The lodger was never responsible for his actions. I never thought he was, for my part."

And Bunting stared at her ruminatingly. "Depends on what you call responsible—" he began argumentatively.

But she would have none of that. "I heard the gentleman say myself that he was a lunatic," she said fiercely. And then, dropping her voice, "A religious maniac—that's what he called him."

"Well, he never seemed so to me," said Bunting stoutly. "He simply seemed to me 'centric—that's all he did. Not a bit madder than many I could tell you of." He was walking round the room restlessly, but he stopped short at last. "And what d'you think we ought to do now?"

Mrs. Bunting shook her head impatiently. "I don't think we ought to do nothing," she said. "Why should we?"

And then again he began walking round the room in an aimless fashion that irritated her.

"If only I could put out a bit of supper for him somewhere where he would get it! And his money, too? I hate to feel it's in there."

"Don't you make any mistake—he'll come back for that," said Bunting, with decision.

But Mrs. Bunting shook her head. She knew better. "Now," she said, "you go off up to bed. It's no use us sitting up any longer."

And Bunting acquiesced.

She ran down and got him a bedroom candle—there was no gas in the little back bedroom upstairs. And then she watched him go slowly up.

Suddenly he turned and came down again. "Ellen," he said, in an urgent whisper, "if I was you I'd take the chain off the door, and I'd lock myself in—that's what I'm going to do. Then he can sneak in and take his dirty money away."

Mrs. Bunting neither nodded nor shook her head. Slowly she went downstairs, and there she carried out half of Bunting's advice. She took, that is, the chain off the front door. But she did not go to bed, neither did she lock herself in. She sat up all night, waiting. At half-past seven she made herself a cup of tea, and then she went into her bedroom.

Daisy opened her eyes.

"Why, Ellen," she said, "I suppose I was that tired, and slept so sound, that I never heard you come to bed or get up—funny, wasn't it?"

"Young people don't sleep as light as do old folks," Mrs. Bunting said sententiously.

"Did the lodger come in after all? I suppose he's upstairs now?"

Mrs. Bunting shook her head. "It looks as if 'twould be a fine day for you down at Richmond," she observed in a kindly tone.

And Daisy smiled, a very happy, confident little smile.

That evening Mrs. Bunting forced herself to tell young Chandler that their lodger had, so to speak, disappeared. She and Bunting had thought carefully over what they would say, and so well did they carry out their programme, or, what is more likely, so full was young Chandler of the long happy day he and Daisy had spent together, that he took their news very calmly.

"Gone away, has he?" he observed casually. "Well, I hope he paid up all right?"

"Oh, yes, yes," said Mrs. Bunting hastily. "No trouble of that sort."

And Bunting said shamefacedly, "Aye, aye, the lodger was quite an honest gentleman, Joe. But I feel worried, about him. He was such a poor, gentle chap—not the sort o' man one likes to think of as wandering about by himself."

"You always said he was 'centric," said Joe thoughtfully.

"Yes, he was that," said Bunting slowly. "Regular right-down queer. Leetle touched, you know, under the thatch," and, as he tapped his head significantly, both young people burst out laughing.

"Would you like a description of him circulated?" asked Joe good-naturedly.

Mr. and Mrs. Bunting looked at one another.

"No, I don't think so. Not yet awhile at any rate. 'Twould upset him awfully, you see."

And Joe acquiesced. "You'd be surprised at the number o' people who disappears and are never heard of again," he said cheerfully. And then he got up, very reluctantly.

Daisy, making no bones about it this time, followed him out into the passage, and shut the sitting-room door behind her.

When she came back she walked over to where her father was sitting in his easy chair, and standing behind him she put her arms round his neck.

Then she bent down her head. "Father," she said, "I've a bit of news for you!"

"Yes, my dear?"

"Father, I'm engaged! Aren't you surprised?"

"Well, what do you think?" said Bunting fondly. Then he turned round and, catching hold of her head, gave her a good, hearty kiss.

"What'll Old Aunt say, I wonder?" he whispered.

"Don't you worry about Old Aunt," exclaimed his wife suddenly. "I'll manage Old Aunt! I'll go down and see her. She and I have always got on pretty comfortable together, as you knows well, Daisy."

"Yes," said Daisy a little wonderingly. "I know you have, Ellen."

Mr. Sleuth never came back, and at last after many days and many nights had gone by, Mrs. Bunting left off listening for the click of the lock which she at once hoped and feared would herald her lodger's return.

As suddenly and as mysteriously as they had begun the "Avenger" murders stopped, but there came a morning in the early spring when a gardener, working in the Regent's Park, found a newspaper in which was wrapped, together with a half-worn pair of rubber-soled shoes, a long, peculiarly shaped knife. The fact, though of considerable interest to the police, was not chronicled in any newspaper, but about the same time a picturesque little paragraph went the round of the press concerning a small boxful of sovereigns which had been anonymously forwarded to the Governors of the Foundling Hospital.

Meanwhile Mrs. Bunting had been as good as her word about "Old Aunt," and that lady had received the wonderful news concerning Daisy in a more philosophical spirit than her great-niece had expected her to do. She only observed that it was odd to reflect that if gentlefolks leave a house in charge of the police a burglary is pretty sure to follow—a remark which Daisy resented much more than did her Joe.

Mr. Bunting and his Ellen are now in the service of an old lady, by whom they are feared as well as respected, and whom they make very comfortable.

NOTES

¹ A police officer named Joseph Chandler was the first official on the scene at Annie Chapman's murder.

[1] A police officer named Joseph Chandler was the first official on the scene at Annie Chapman's murder.

[2] Very roughly, one late-19th century pound is equal to 70 modern pounds in terms of buying power (Michael Nisbet, "Inflation and Contemporary Equivalents to Victorian Money," *Victorian Web,* accessed April 1, 2015, http://www.victorianweb.org/economics/inflation.html). 30 shillings is one and a half pounds, equivalent to just over 100 modern pounds.

[3] A reference to engraver Charles Heath's popular women's periodical *Heath's Book of Beauty* (1833-1847, continued as *Book of Beauty* to 1848). The centerpiece of each issue was a series of engravings of fashionable women.

[4] A pay-on-demand service for gas delivery common in lodging houses and low-income neighbourhoods.

[5] 25 shillings is a typical rent for an arrangement of this sort. Mr. Sleuth offers double the amount Mrs. Bunting requests, a relatively extravagant amount. The "two pounds, or two guineas" he suggests is equivalent to approximately 150 modern pounds.

[6] Bible quotation: Psalm 107:30.

[7] Edwin Henry Landseer (1802-1873): fashionable British painter and sculptor now best known for his four bronze lions in Trafalgar Square.

[8] Bible quotation: Proverbs 7:27.

[9] Captain Thomas Coram opened a series of 'Foundling Hospitals,' the first in 1741, to care for the children of the poverty-stricken women of London's underclasses. These hospitals were essentially orphanages which also provided training in various trades to prevent their wards from returning to the streets.

[10] Definitions of vegetarianism often included any diet lacking red meat.

[11] Similarly, conspiracy theorists have posited police involvement in the Ripper murders since the early days of the case.

[12] Tonics for symptoms of anxiety and nervous distress were readily available from chemists in the late Victorian era. They were largely unregulated, but contained potent and addictive ingredients such as cocaine, morphine, and opium.

[13] With the advent of modern antibiotics, scarlet fever has become a rare and treatable illness. In the nineteenth century, however, it was one of the most dreaded diseases of childhood: often fatal, and highly contagious.

[14] Lowndes is referencing the so-called "double event" of the Ripper case: the murders of Elizabeth Stride and Catherine Eddowes in the early hours of September 30, 1888.

[15] Lowndes specifies that the Avenger murders take place in the West End of London, removing them from the Ripper's East End, with its reputation for criminality and squalor.

[16] The Black Museum, or the Crime Museum of Scotland Yard, was established in 1874 for the purpose of housing crime memorabilia and assisting investigators with their study of criminality. It still exists, and has never been open to the public.

[17] The Balham mystery is a reference to the Charles Bravo murder case of 1876, which Lowndes fictionalized in her 1926 novel *What Really Happened*.

[18] The use of fingerprints in the detection of crime was nascent at the time *The Lodger* is set; Scotland Yard opened its Fingerprint Bureau in 1901—a slight anachronism in the text.

[19] Jack Ketch (died 1686): executioner in the court of Charles II. Infamous for the cruelty of his executions.

[20] Charles Peace (1832-1879): burglar and murderer whose sensational crime sprees shocked and titillated Victorian England.

[21] A probable reference to Mary Pearcey (born 1866, executed 1890), who murdered her paramour Frank Hogg's wife and baby. Perhaps due to the brutality of her crimes, she is sometimes posited as a Ripper suspect. Her likeness did indeed grace Madame Tussaud's Wax Museum, and the noose used to hang her is on display in Scotland Yard's Black Museum.

[22] Madame Tussaud's is a famous and longstanding London waxwork museum.

[23] A series of taunting letters supposedly written by the killer was an important element of the media coverage of the Ripper case. Attribution of the letters has never been confirmed.

[24] This association of the victims' blood as ink is an allusion to the "Dear Boss" letter of 25 September, 1888, ostensibly sent by the Ripper, and widely reprinted in the press. The letter reads, in part, "I saved some of the proper red stuff in a ginger beer bottle over the last job to write with but it went thick like glue and I cant use it. Red ink is fit enough I hope ha. ha [sic]." (See "Ripper Letters," *Casebook*, accessed April 1, 2015, http://www.casebook.org/ripper_letters).

[25] Similar criticisms of police and the Home Office arose during the Ripper crisis.

[26] Emile Gaboriau (1832-1873): French detective fiction pioneer whose character Monsieur Lecoq (based on real life criminal-turned-detective Eugène François Vidocq), predated Sherlock Holmes by decades.

[27] As virtually all London newspapers reported, bloodhounds were considered by Ripper investigators on several occasions in early October 1888, and tests occurred on October 9 and 10, although they were never actually used.

[28] Again, Lowndes emphasizes that the Avenger is firmly based in the West of London, in contrast to the Ripper's East End location.

[29] Bible quotation: Proverbs 9:18.

[30] Bible quotation: Ecclesiastes 7:25.

[31] The play is Shakespeare's *Macbeth*; this line is uttered by Lady Macbeth during her famed sleepwalking scene in the final act.

[32] Similarly, Sir Charles Warren (1840-1927) bowed to public criticism and resigned as Commissioner of Police just before the Ripper's final murder of Mary Jane Kelly.

[33] In cases of suspicious or unexpected death, a coroner's inquest would be held in order to determine the probable cause of death. If the jury returned a verdict of murder, the case was forwarded to a grand jury for prosecution.

[34] Victorian radicals advocated on behalf of the working classes for legislative reform and other social parity measures.

[35] Romantic poet William Wordsworth (1770-1850).

[36] Northeasternmost village in Scotland; often called "the start of Great Britain."

[37] All of these theories as to the identity of the killer also circulated during the Ripper crisis: the killer was said to be a sailor, a butcher, an escaped lunatic, and many other possibilities including a doctor, a woman, a Jew, an American, and a royal personage. (For a comprehensive list of suspects, see "Suspects," *Casebook*, accessed April 1, 2015, http://www.casebook.org/suspects.)

[38] Bible quotation: Proverbs 5:4.

[39] Bible quotation: Jeremiah 10:20.